❧LICHGATES

BOOK ONE OF THE GRIMOIRE SAGA

A NOVEL BY S.M. BOYCE

Ourea awaits.

[signature]

— Jan 2015 —

(sorry... my head's still
in 2014...)

THE GRIMOIRE SAGA

Lichgates (#1)
Treason (#2)
Heritage (#3)
Illusion (#4)

THE OUREAN CHRONICLES

The Misanthrope: Stone's Story (#1) *Fall 2015*
The First Vagabond: Cedric's Story (#2) *Fall 2015*
The Demon: Deidre's Story (#3) *Fall 2015*

DEDICATIONS

I wrote this book for you.
Stay awesome.

TO MY BETA READERS:

Dad, Syl, Aly, Chaney, Adrienne, Dustin,
Mom, and my dearest Geoff

Thank you. Without you, everyone in Ourea would have slightly
stranger names and would probably still be twiddling their
thumbs, stuck in that typo-riddled dream called "draft one."

TABLE OF CONTENTS

❧CHAPTER ONE
THE HUMAN

Kara Magari pushed her way down an unkempt trail in the Rocky Mountains, its trees hunching and swaying overhead as she crunched her way along the rotting foliage that served as a carpet. The canopy grew steadily thicker and swallowed the setting sunlight, casting a murky green glow over her pale skin as she hiked. Her hiker's build made her look a year or two younger than she really was—a curse at twenty—but she knew she would be grateful for it someday.

She ran a hand through her blond hair as she examined the forest. This was a new path, one she found on the way back to her car after an early dinner at the visitor center. She bit her lip and scanned the empty forest. Even though there hadn't been any empty beer cans or syringes littering the way, solo hiking on an unfamiliar trail was never safe. It would be dark in just a few hours.

She patted the side pocket of her backpack. The edges of her stun gun pushed against the cloth. Kara smirked—she would be fine.

Two minutes later, the footpath ended at a simple gazebo built from unpainted wood. Low-hanging branches hid half of its paneled roof, and a tree trunk on either side blocked the way around. Waist-high wooden railings surrounded most of the structure, but left a break in the fencing just wide enough to walk through. A path stretched from this opening across the gazebo to the other side, where yet another gap in the rails would let her through to the blinding daylight. Benches lined the miniature lane through the shelter.

The landscape on the other side was blurred and bright: a stark contrast to the heavy green glow of the forest, where only freckled rays of sunlight could break through the leaves. She narrowed her eyes as she got closer to the gazebo, but couldn't distinguish anything through the sun's sharp glare.

A plank of wood framed with odd carvings had been nailed to the space above the entrance, and she squinted in an effort to read the dull cuts and make out the word:

Lichgate.

She shrugged and stepped up onto the wooden aisle. As soon as she set foot inside, her stomach lurched. Her cheeks flushed, and she covered her mouth to suppress bile.

A blue light flared out of the corner of her eye. It had come from the edge of the lichgate, but as she leaned over to inspect the space by her head, she couldn't find anything reflective or even blue.

She took a deep breath before tossing her pack on one bench and lounging on the other until her stomach settled. Maybe she should have checked the sell-by date on the chicken salad she'd eaten at the visitor center.

Kara closed her eyes and listened to the wind rustling through the leaves, her body relishing the cool air as it coursed along her neck. She breathed deeply again, and her gut relaxed.

She leaned back against the bench and sighed. Since her dad had first strapped her to his back twenty years ago and trudged down the East Inlet to Adams Falls, she'd spent every summer of her life vacationing in the Rockies. Her family had hiked almost every trail, but this one was not on her worn and ripped map.

Memories of past hiking trips slipped into her mind: her dad laughing as he tripped over a root; Kara discovering an antique diamond earring caught under a rock in a stream; her mom rattling off tips about hiking as she pointed out wildlife.

Kara's shoulders tensed. Her breath caught. She wasn't supposed to let herself think about her mom.

Her heart sank as the pain rushed in anyway. Six months. She'd been forced to live without her mom—her best friend—for six whole months.

Hollow echoes of sirens and shrieking tires tugged at her mind, but she pushed them away. Even on a secluded path hidden from the world, she couldn't give into thoughts like those. She would lose it and start crying. After that, there would be no telling when she would get it together enough to drive back to the rental house.

Her dad couldn't be doing too great, either. He was probably at the rental, eyes out of focus as he stared at the same page of a crime novel for hours.

Neither of them handled grief well.

Kara promised herself she would hug him when she got back—a

good old Magari bear hug. Maybe mimicking one of his painful cuddles would get a little laugh out of him.

Early this morning, Kara had tiptoed by his bedroom before he even woke up. She'd wanted to wait around and check on him before she left, but she'd written him a note instead. She couldn't stay in the house. The first thought to hit her that morning had been: *Mom died exactly six months ago. You'll never get her back.*

Not a happy wake up call.

Kara cleared her throat and tried to focus on cheerful things. She had to distract herself, or she really would lose what little control she had.

Tony. Last summer, Kara's stomach tied in knots every time she walked into the trail café because she knew she would see *him*—the gorgeous cashier with green eyes and dark hair. According to the white plastic square on his shirt, his name was Tony. She and her mom always giggled over how Kara would turn red as a tomato when he made eye contact, and her mom even dared Kara to ask him out, once. He always smiled when they walked in, as if he liked that he could make Kara blush without even speaking, but she could never quite muster the courage to actually follow through on her mother's dare.

But she'd changed. Life had lost its flavor since her mom died.

When Kara had gone to the café on her first day back this summer, she saw Tony through the window. She'd waited for that familiar surge of adrenaline and desire, but it never came. She didn't even blush when Tony smiled from his place at the front. She'd forced a smile in return, but it must have come out as a grimace. The boy had faltered and looked quickly away. He had avoided her eye since then.

She didn't mind the isolation, though. Not really. In a strange way, she kind of liked it. She often saw family friends on the paths, and they never just let her enjoy the peace that came from a silent hike. She'd already been trapped in a chat with her dad's previous tennis partner once today. And on her way back to the car, her mother's old yoga buddy had appeared around a bend. If Kara hadn't doubled back and slipped onto the first trail she'd seen—the one that led her to the gazebo—the woman might have made eye contact, which meant an inevitable hour-long conversation. Kara just didn't have the energy.

Kara wanted to enjoy talking to people, but she just didn't. She could only think about how to get away from the discomfort of inevitably having to answer questions about her mother, whom nearly everyone had loved.

Since the funeral, Kara's only escape came while hiking. The Montana Rockies were her haven. And when she hiked, she did so alone.

Kara spent a lot of time alone, lately. Probably too much, but she liked the reprieve. When she hiked, she could finally clear her mind. She could forget. A bit of her fear and anger dissolved away with every breeze that rustled the canopy. She simply walked, and nature entertained her. The woods were her home away from home. They were safe. They didn't pity her or offer tissues or send her to therapy.

She would feel alive again someday, even though the grief made that difficult. For now, she would just hike.

But in the darkest pit of her mind—the one she most ignored—she knew solitude wasn't the answer. Kara's hikes only helped her avoid the real problem: that, deep down, she blamed herself for her mother's death. She had no idea what to do about that guilt.

A tear built up in Kara's eye, but she used the heel of her palm to wipe it away. She cleared her throat and pushed herself to her feet.

No more thinking.

She glanced around to get her bearings, a ball already forming in her throat. She needed to distract herself, and focusing on happy things had just led to more terrible memories. She instead focused on trying to figure out where she was.

Now that she was sitting in the gazebo—or lichgate, whatever—she could see the view previously blocked by the low-hanging branches. The structure hugged the edge of a cliff and overlooked a valley surrounded on all sides by a mountain range. A river flowed into a broad lake about a half mile into the distance. This wasn't Lone Pine Lake, since there wasn't a waterfall nearby. She craned her neck and stood, leaning against the frame for a better view. It didn't look like Bluebird Lake, or Mills Lake, either. The wind picked up and carried the stale musk of dried leaves and grass.

Where am I?

She pulled her compass from her bag and checked it before glancing up at a pack of clouds that partially hid the sun. The path hadn't turned south, and she knew her fair share of the Montana trails by heart. This had to be a new valley, one she'd somehow never explored. Her mom would've loved this!

Kara sighed. Her hand reached to the locket around her neck, but she stopped. Hikes were for letting go, not remembering.

She stepped off the other side of the gazebo. Again, there was a kick in her gut and a flash of blue light. Her stomach tightened, and she leaned against a tree for support. Bark caught in her fingernails.

No more chicken salad!

A strong breeze scaled the cliff and ruffled her hair. It was more of a rocky hill than a cliff, really, and the mossy slope wasn't all that steep. It leveled out about forty feet down after a curvy trail.

She pulled out her phone to check the time. Another minute ticked forward, but she had about an hour before her dad sent out any rescue parties. She grinned and looked back at her pack, but left it. This wouldn't take long, and she didn't want the extra weight.

Kara used the tree as leverage to hop onto the sturdy path below. Step by step, she inched down the trail. Occasionally, she needed to wedge her tennis shoe into a cranny to slide down to the next section, but other than that, she could take it slow and steady.

After only a few minutes, she reached the valley and squinted back up to where the gazebo's roof peeked through the trees. Not bad. With her finger in the air, she traced the way she'd taken, starting at the lichgate and going over each step in her head. But when she examined the base of the hill, her finger hovered and came to a stop.

Built into the rock was a marble door shrouded with overhanging roots and dangling moss that clung to its frame like bangs. The gray stone was the exact color of the cliff rock, so she would have missed it if she hadn't been looking closely.

She brushed her hand along the door's smooth stone. It was simple, like the lichgate, and had a round stone knob. A small emblem carved into the rock at eye level looked like a four-leaf clover made of crescent moons.

Her fingers itched on the handle. The temptation to explore something ancient pulled her toward the door.

C'mon, Kara. Think this through. There's a door in the mountain and you're going to open it? You have no idea what's behind—

The ground trembled with a sudden force that knocked her against the cliff. The wind stopped, dissolving with a *hiss* into the hot summer sky. She scanned the valley. Several somethings cracked in the ground under her feet.

A sinkhole broke into the turf about fifteen feet away, swallowing the grass and dirt. A man's voice roared through the fissure and echoed across the lake. When his cry died on the still air, there was silence.

Kara remembered to breathe, and sudden relief washed through her chest as she did. She shifted her weight to leave and even made it a few feet up the path, but she paused as a chorus of men shouted through the hole in a language she didn't understand. Smoke pitched from the small crater.

Thunder rumbled overhead. A dark cloud churned in the sky, and her heart fell into her stomach; there hadn't even been a single fluffy cloud up there ten minutes ago. That didn't make sense at all—how could the weather shift so suddenly?

She glanced to the door and then back up the trail, hesitating, but her decision was soon made for her.

A blinding bolt of moss-colored lightning flashed, striking something in the sinkhole. The hairs on her arms stood on end. Heat coursed through her calves, and she caught her breath. Her ears rang.

Wait. That lightning was definitely *green*.

The cliff trembled as a deafening boom shattered the air. A drizzle of rain began, but it quickly melted into heavy drops that pelted her skin and clung to her hair. Another rumble coursed along the far edge of the valley. Kara needed shelter, and the last place she would go in a lightning storm was up a hill.

She turned back and twisted the door's handle, sighing with relief as it opened—unlocked—and swung inward. Still, as wet as it was outside and as much as she wanted a safe place to wait out the rain, she lingered on the threshold to examine the room.

Mud covered everything from the floor to the ceiling, and since there weren't any supports to hold the roof, she couldn't figure out how the ten-by-ten dirt shelter hadn't caved in yet. The air within was heavy, moist with the rot of dead leaves, and her only guiding light streamed in from behind her. Roots dangled from the ceiling like stalactites reaching for the floor. The wind picked up, howling as it pelted rain against her back.

She tested the ground with her sneaker. The dirt floor supported her weight, so she tip-toed into the room and left the door open. Rain fell in lingering drops on the threshold before disappearing into the growing pools of mud. She stuck her hands in her pockets and watched the raging storm outside.

A flash of dark brown blurred past her.

She jumped. A tan flicker snaked along the roof, and clumps of soil fell in sheets. She glared at the ceiling, holding her breath as the settling dust rained onto her shoes.

It had almost looked like a root moving, but—no, that was crazy.

Another streak of motion raced down the opposite wall. It passed through a shaft of light, and Kara saw its pointed, wooden tip. Tiny veins sprouted from it like hairs, digging into the dirt so that it could travel.

It *was* a root moving.

She bolted for the door, but she never made it.

A second spiny vine shot up from the floor and wrapped around her leg. It pulled. She tripped, falling into the first root as it snaked along the far wall. Dirt poured over her head, blinding her. She coughed on bits of decaying bark. The root tugged again and yanked her onto her hands and knees. It dragged her toward the center of the room. She reached for the knife strapped to her free ankle, the one her mom had—

No. She couldn't think of Mom. Not now.

A third root wrapped around her waist. Yet another grabbed her hand as she reached for the blade. The roots flipped her onto her back. With a bang, the door snapped shut. Her stomach churned. The floor disappeared. She fell, and the roots let go.

⚜

Kara tumbled through the darkness. Whenever she tried to scream, dirt filled her mouth and nose. She eventually just held her breath, closed her eyes, and waited to be crushed in the landing.

Two roots broke her fall and bent with her, slowing her momentum but bruising her ribs in the process. Her hands slid off the grubs and mud as she grappled for something to stop her fall. Her cheeks flushed, and her stomach floated into her throat, heaving and twisting with her body.

She took a deep breath and thudded against something solid. She covered her head with her arms. Light poured around her as she held her position, waiting to fall deeper into whatever she'd gotten herself into *this* time. Her shoulder throbbed from the landing. Ringing hummed in her ear, but this was a new, silent place. She peeked through two fingers.

Dirt clung to her now-ripped jeans, and red smudges covered the exposed skin on her arms. Her shoes were caked in mud. Blood seeped through a rip in her sleeve, and a purple bruise had already begun to spread over her kneecap. She searched her arms and shins to feel for breaks, but nothing stung. That was good, but her phone had disappeared and her pack was still in the gazebo.

She leaned against the something solid that had broken her fall, which turned out to be a stone desk. Blood from her arm smudged the side where she landed, its red streak a vivid contrast to the desk's white polish. A matching stone chair sat a foot or so from the desk, as if whoever had last sat in it had only just left.

Her hair was a mess of tangles and soil, and the streaks of mud on her cheeks smelled like a combination of carrots and crusty leaves. She brushed away as much of it as she could, rubbing the last of the dirt out of her eyes and wiping her face with the least-filthy bit of her shirt. The edges of her vision blurred, but the room slowly came into focus.

Stone shelves canvassed every wall from the floor to the twelve-foot ceiling. Every inch of every shelf was covered in books, each bound in colorful leather and labeled with gold symbols she couldn't read. There were no doors in the walls of bookshelves, and the only light came from a pane of glass in the roof. Crimson sunlight leaked into what could only be a submerged library.

Kara eyed the skylight before pulling herself onto the desk and reaching for the window, but it was at least six feet away. Without any rope, she would never be able to escape through it.

She peeked over her shoulder, trying to figure out how she'd gotten into the room in the first place, but the only evidence of her fall was the pile of dirt where she'd been sitting. It was as if she'd appeared from thin air.

I'm trapped.

Kara sat on the desk and wiped the sweat from her palms onto her jeans. Her breaths became more and more shallow as adrenaline spiked in unison with her pulse. The ringing became a scream in her ear.

"Chill. Out," she said rhythmically.

She closed her eyes and took a few deep breaths to distract herself from the panic. Her chest rose and fell until the rush of her heartbeat faded from her head. When she could control her breathing again, she stared at the floor and debated her very limited options.

Something glittered from a gap in a desk drawer, so she hopped to the floor with a soft *thud* and knelt to get a good look. There was no handle on the drawer, but she was able to slip her fingers through the opening and drag it out of the desk. The rock groaned from the effort. As it finally slid open, a sunbeam skirted around her and cast her shadow onto the book hidden inside. It was wrapped in thin silver chains, but had no padlock.

The air in the small room stalled as it had before the storm: stagnant and suddenly heavy. The muscles between her shoulders tightened, and her neck tensed.

Hidden deeper within the drawer was a thick sheet of parchment paper. Kara set this aside, covered as it was in an illegible, spidery script. The book's faded red leather was porous and soft, its title written in gold lettering that had long ago begun to chip so that now, only spotted lines comprised the runic letters.

The chains wrapped around the cover like metal vines, and instead of a padlock, they had all been fused together in the book's center. In this mess of iron was a small silver pendant, hung from a short chain and set into the fused metal like a key in a lock. It was the same symbol that had appeared on the door: a crude four-leaf clover comprised of thin crescent moons. A brilliant diamond glittered from its center.

Her hands inched along the pages trapped beneath the odd lock and brushed the silver vines in the process. The metal burned her fingertips. She dropped the book, which thumped on the desk. Pain shot through her arm.

Someone whispered in her ear.

She whipped her head around and held her breath, but the library was empty and quiet once more. Her shoulders tensed, and her body told her to run, *run!* But there was nowhere to run to. The library had no door and only one inaccessible window.

Maybe she wasn't *supposed* to open the book. The thought alone made her want to open it even more.

She sat in the chair, tore off a bit of her sleeve, wrapped it around her hand, and dug her thumbnail beneath the pendant. It shifted. The cold vines stung her thumb through the fabric, but she gritted her teeth and jiggled the pendant again. The necklace moved above her finger and finally popped. Something else clicked.

The sound of metal slithering over fabric made her freeze. The iron vines unwound themselves and fell from the book, and for the second time that day, she suppressed a scream as inanimate things moved. The metal twisted away, clattering to the floor.

The air thickened again, weighing on her neck. A shiver raced down her back. Her hips pressed into the chair, as if someone was pushing hard on her shoulders. Another whisper chorused in her ear. Even though her breath caught in her throat, she didn't try to find the source. She doubted anything would be there if she looked.

She slid her thumb under the now-unlocked cover, pausing for only a second before she flipped it open.

A gale blew through the room from nowhere, ruffling pages and tearing books from their shelves. It ripped around her, whipping her hair so that her face and neck stung. The pendant's diamond glowed blue.

The blood in her veins seemed to boil, scorching her from within. Pins and needles ravaged every inch of her body. Sweat dripped down her back and chilled in the gusting wind. The ripped shreds of her shirt stuck to her bruises. She opened her mouth, but the air was gone. She couldn't scream.

All at once, everything settled. The library was silent, the pain in her body dissolved, and all she could hear was that incessant ringing.

"Holy—!" She couldn't even finish her thought. She wiped her face, her mouth, her neck. Something scratched her skin.

The little clover pendant glittered in her hand. She stared at it, gaping. Something started clicking. It was a steady noise: *flick, flick, flick.*

She gasped.

The *flick* sound came from the book, which was—well, it was—its pages were turning. The room was motionless, the air heavy and still again, but the pages flipped on their own, one after the other. After a minute or two, they finally stopped when a page drifted slowly to rest on its brothers.

"Holy..." she whispered. She sat on the edge of the immobile stone chair and peered at the open book while keeping as far a distance from it as she could.

A drawing covered both pages. The loose sketch showed a cliff overlooking a lake, a river, and a valley, and on top of the cliff was a lush forest. She squinted at a familiar sloping path up the cliff face and saw, hidden in the overhanging branches of the trees, the lichgate's roof. And there, at the base of the path, was the marble door. Beside it, a man draped in a blue cloak lounged against the rock.

He peered up at her from beneath his hood, his face draped in shadow. One of his hands pointed to something off the page. She looked to where he was pointing and found the little note she'd brushed aside earlier. It still lay on the desk, somehow unaffected by the gale which had ripped books off their shelves.

She flipped to the next page, but before she could read more than a few words, the page shook itself free of her grip and settled once more on the landscape and the man.

She grumbled and turned the page again, but it once more wrenched itself free and turned back to the drawing of the cloaked man who pointed to the letter. She huffed and moved the book so that he was pointing at a bookshelf.

His arm moved against the motion of the book so that he still pointed to the letter.

Kara gasped and grabbed the loose parchment from the desk, taking the hint and leaning as far back into the chair as she could.

The letter had been gibberish before, but she caught a word she knew as she scanned the page. Then another. And another. Her hand covered her mouth as she read, horrified.

From the moment you read these words, you will be hunted. If you wish to survive what will come, you must pay attention.

Because you have found this Grimoire, you will come to know my world: Ourea. It's a beautiful place, but its creatures are unforgiving and brutal. Ourea is a hidden pocket of the earth and has always been locked away, accessible only through the lichgates. Since you found this book, you have already discovered one of these portals. You can never return to the life you knew once you step through a lichgate.

Thousands of magical and non-magical species live here, but three are notable above all others: drenowith, isen, and yakona. Be wary of them all.

Drenowith are known in human lore as muses; they change form freely and don't age. Isen are mostly evil, as their kind harvest souls to remain immortal and can don their prey's appearance at will. But I believe that my people, the yakona, are far worse. We as a race have mastered magic, but we are divided and live in secluded, warring kingdoms. They will be the death of me, though all I ever wanted was peace.

To learn more, ask your Grimoire. It will always answer if you ask the right question.

You must be cautious. When you opened this Grimoire, you became its next master, and you will be known as the Vagabond. Only you can read these pages, and the vast knowledge held here is a coveted thing. I trust to you its secrets, its stories, and its fearful power. A daunting world awaits you, but I hope you discover the beauty hidden in even the most vile of things.

Tread carefully, Vagabond. Guard the Grimoire as you would your life because everything you hold dear will one day depend upon what it tells you.

The lines in Kara's forehead deepened. She reread the short letter, holding her breath the whole time. A thought pulled on her mind, but her pulse raced too quickly for her to pay much attention to it at all.

CHAPTER TWO
THE YAKONA

Braeden Drakonin ran his thick hands over a cavern wall he'd found deep in the tunnels of some unknown mountain in Ourea. The yakona's short black hair stuck to his olive skin, which was covered in sweat from the four days he had spent on this hunt. He was close.

He held up his hand and a gray fire erupted in the air above his palm, fueled by the magic that coursed through his body. The blaze flickered in the dark cave, casting its light across the glossy wall to give him a better view. Its white stone blocks were perfectly aligned without a single crack in the ancient mortar, and the fortification stretched across the cavern in an unnatural line that blocked off half of the cave. Its edges met the curved slope of the organic cave walls, the design bending to fill every possible gap in the rock with a white brick. Engraved into the center of the wall with thin, silver lines was a large symbol: a four-leaf clover the size of his head, made of four crescent moons that looped through each other.

This was it.

Finally, after twelve years of dead leads and the dying hope that it even still existed, he had found the Grimoire. It waited, somewhere behind this wall, for its new master. It waited for *him*.

He'd grown up listening to the legends of the Vagabond, as had every yakona child for the last thousand years. Most children daydreamed of finding the priceless treasures hidden in the Vagabond's abandoned village; Braeden, however, had only ever dreamed of becoming a vagabond himself to escape having been raised to kill. He was a prince and Heir to the Stele: an evil kingdom filled with vile yakona that preferred torture to diplomatic negotiation. Becoming a vagabond was the only escape from that life. Though he'd escaped the Stele as a child twelve years ago—living another life while his kingdom thought he was dead—his luck wouldn't last much longer. He needed to find the Grimoire before his father learned the truth.

Braeden stepped back, examining the cavern as he looked for a door. A sunken tower had fallen across two of the four entrances to the cave, but the worn stone blocks scattered on the floor were all that remained of it. Aside from the collapsed spire, the cavern was completely bare. The solid white wall didn't have a trace of a hinge or a handle. His stomach twisted into a knot as a slow realization washed over him.

There *was* no door.

Dread shot through him. "No. There has to be a way in. There has to be *something*."

He ran his hands along the Grimoire's clover symbol, hunting for a clue, but his search turned up nothing.

"No." His voice shook as he smacked the wall with his palms. The stacked bricks shuddered, and the gray fire in his hand fizzled out. The room plunged into darkness once more. He pulled on his hair and repeated the word over and over, his voice growing louder as panic bubbled in his gut.

He finally lost all sense of self-control.

"No!"

Braeden's fingers cracked as he lifted a nearby boulder that was easily half his size. He dug his hands deeper into its crevices to secure a solid grip and hurled the giant rock into the wall.

The boulder smashed over the symbol and crumbled into powder from the force. The wall trembled, and the shock of the blow sent a roar up the mountainside that split the ceiling. Sharp sunlight dissolved the cave's gloom with thin rays that beamed down from this new skylight above. He threw himself against the wall for support and took a deep, shaky breath, but it only made the loathing race faster through his veins. He dug his hand into a crack in the wall, using it as a brace to steady himself.

Pebbles drizzled from his palm and sprinkled onto the floor before he realized that he had crushed the rock in his bitter, absentminded rage. His chest heaved. His knees shook. He clenched his teeth and glared at the smooth, polished wall he had tried to smash open.

There wasn't even a scratch on it. The Grimoire symbol's silver lines glinted in the meager sunlight, taunting him.

Heat crawled beneath his skin like a swarm of beetles, spiking from where it smoldered in his gut before it slithered into his chest. His fingers twitched. He curled his hand into a fist and let the hatred take him.

He punched the rough bricks, bones cracking as he broke his hands across the wall.

The skin on his knuckles ruptured, spraying his black blood over the clover symbol in a thin shower. He cursed and spat on the floor, but the skin on his hands knit itself back together in quick stitches, repairing the broken veins and shattered bones almost as quickly as he broke them. His fist healed in a matter of seconds, but that was one of the few benefits of being a yakona prince: only those with a royal bloodline could heal so quickly.

He glared at the wall and punched it once more, throwing everything he had into the attack. Layers of black, bloody splatters covered the white stone and the symbol that proved the Grimoire was so, so close.

The searing sting in his hand forced him to his knees until he could heal again. He leaned his head against the wall and forced himself to take sharp, deep breaths that hurt his lungs, but at least the momentary calm cleared his mind. He turned and sank to the floor. Light blinded him from the new ceiling he had ripped into the roof, forcing him to squint into the shadows as he tried to think.

The slow, hollow echo of someone clapping broke across the cavern. He glanced up, searching the darkness.

A woman materialized from the gloom and finished her final clap as she came into view, her skin glowing with the warm tint of honey in the hazy light. Gentle brown curls nuzzled the soft arch of her neck, and the glint of a sword shone from around her waist. She let loose a disappointed sigh as she looked him over: a noise that reminded him to breathe. Her perfume clung to the air now that she was closer.

When he smelled a rosy combination of lilac and pine, he jumped to his feet. That meant she was an isen—a soul thief. She could steal his magic and trap his soul for centuries with a single prick from the barb hidden in her right palm.

"How did you find this place?" he demanded, drawing his sword.

His mind tensed. The familiar heat that fueled his magic raced through his body as he focused. Black flames erupted in the spaces between the fingers of his free hand.

"What with all the yelling and rocks smashing it wasn't that hard to just follow you." She spoke slowly, as if tasting every syllable before it was released from her pink lips.

The isen shifted her weight, examining her nails, and the golden glint of a cross around her neck caught his eye. Her white shirt billowed over her shoulders but clung to her waist, accentuating the curves of her body.

Sunlight reflected off of his blade, pulling his mind back into focus. This was an isen. This was the enemy.

"Well, I feel like killing something, so this is convenient," he said.

She chuckled. "You're more adorable than I thought you'd be, but I didn't come for banter. I'm here to take you home. Your father wants to talk to you, especially since you let him think you were dead for twelve years. I'm fairly certain sons aren't supposed to do that to their fathers."

"I have no idea who you are or how Carden found me, but I will never go back."

A hazy, distant memory of a square made from black thorns flitted through his mind. It was the Stele kingdom's coat of arms, painted onto the side of the carriage that had smuggled him out of the castle and out of his father's control. The isen's voice drew him back to the present.

"Carden figured you'd say that."

Braeden spun the sword in his hand. "That life is behind me."

"I think I can make you change your mind. If not, though, I hear these gentlemen are very convincing."

She gestured into the darkness and at her command, dozens of figures materialized from the shadows. Each uniformed soldier had dark gray skin and a wide face with eyes that had no whites to them. Smoke billowed from the pores on their arms and necks, snaking around the silver and black tunics of Carden's army as they approached in a thickly knit formation. Braeden's mouth went dry, and he backed against the wall. There were easily sixty of them. He was outnumbered.

"Steady, boys. Don't touch him unless I tell you to." She shot a look to them over her shoulder.

"Do they know you're an isen?" His grip on his sword tightened with the hope that they did not.

"Of course they know, peanut. That's what makes us all such great friends."

"How could Carden trust you? Has he gone insane?"

"Probably. Your father has become a little, well, *eccentric* since you left. Now come along. I'd hate to have to hurt you."

She grinned. The smirk cast dark lines across her beautiful face and suggested that she would actually enjoy following through on her threat. He dug his heel against a small shelf in the floor. If this was his last fight, then he was ready. He had nothing left.

The isen just laughed. "You can huff and puff all you want, boy. It's useless. Carden already told me about the one thing that scares you."

She lifted a set of steel wrist cuffs from the pack on her belt and dangled them from her index finger. Thin spikes, just long enough to cut into the skin, bore inward on the shackles. Their tips glimmered with the green poison that could subdue even the strongest king and make him a compliant pawn.

Braeden's heart skipped a beat out of habitual fear. He took a deep breath to fight the growing panic as he tried—and failed—to smother the sparking embers of childhood memories: a dark dungeon, rank with rotting bodies; the piercing agony of the cuffs; Carden's laughter as Braeden, eleven, screamed and was forced to endure pain for refusing to torture a prisoner. He had to learn the ways of ruling a nation, Carden had said, and their nation excelled at punishing others.

With a deep breath, he snapped back to the present. Dust stung his nose, and his heart slowed as the memories vanished. He needed to concentrate. Killing isen was what he did best.

He settled into his stance and, with an unseen twist of his hand, shot six dark bolts of smoke from his palm. Each was aimed for the woman who had again glanced down to her fingernails, but she ducked out of the way without looking up, her gold cross glinting as she traveled.

The smoky curse landed instead on the unfortunate guards who had flanked her when she first appeared. It took root in their pores. Black vines sprouted from the smoke and raced up their necks. It choked them, spreading over their skin like a virus that forced itself into their mouths and came out their ears. They fell to the cave's floor, thrashing as they tried to scream.

The isen sidestepped a fallen guard and drew her sword. Braeden swung. She parried. Her elbow cracked on his face.

Agony splintered across his cheek and forehead, but the skin began to stitch itself back together as soon as the pain spread. The stinging thawed. He grabbed and twisted her arm, forcing her to her knees. His hand shot for her now-vulnerable throat, but she wriggled free and his fingers slipped through her cold, soft curls instead. Guards ran toward their fight, but the isen held up her hand and glared at them.

"He's mine!" she snapped.

Braeden grinned. She was arrogant. Good.

The isen turned back to him. "This is far more entertaining than I expected, little prince!"

She shot her fist into the cavity below his throat too quickly for him to block. He couldn't breathe. He lunged for her neck to return the favor. She ducked out of his reach, and he snatched the gold cross instead. Breath returned to him. She backed away, and her gold chain broke as she disappeared into the darkness with a wink.

He threw the cross to the ground and scanned the shadows as he searched for her. The world returned around him in a sudden wave of screams. As he'd fought the isen, more of the guards had fallen prey to the curse. At least half of them writhed on the floor, wrapped in black vines that pulsed with their every movement.

A rush of gray in the corner of Braeden's eye captured his attention. A soldier stumbled into the far wall, glaring as black vines climbed up his arm. Black smoke billowed from the soldier's ears and mouth. He yelled and ran for Braeden.

Thunder rumbled through the tear in the roof. Braeden looked upward and caught sight of a dark cloud brewing in the sky. He reached for it, focusing his mind on the storm outside, and churned the cloud from afar with the heat that raced through his body.

The thundercloud swirled and darkened until the ceiling's edges caved and dirt fell to the floor without a wind to push it. A boom shook the cavern. He grunted and pulled harder on the cloud with his mind. A bead of sweat ran down his nose.

The cloud gave in.

Brilliant green lightning flashed and filled the room, freezing the chaos in a blinding flare of grass-colored light. Thunder rattled the cave again. The air hummed. Everything froze in the blast until, like a sudden breath, the soldier slumped on the floor.

Sunlight glinted off the Grimoire's clover symbol on the wall. Braeden's stomach twisted one last time. For a second, he forgot the murderous din and the death all around him.

A flicker of movement sped by in his peripheral vision, and he turned in time to catch the shadow of long, curly hair running along one of the side tunnels. He bolted toward it and into a dark tunnel, which was lit only by the thin wisps of light that poured from occasional adjacent passageways.

His footsteps reverberated down the hall, mingling with the fading screams of the chaos he'd left behind. He paused, sniffing the air for pine or lilac. All he smelled was dust.

A low chuckle rumbled past him, surrounding him. It came from ahead and from behind, from above and below, but he was somehow still alone in the passage.

Something shifted its weight in the shadows of a dark side tunnel to his left. He narrowed his eyes and pressed himself against the jagged cave wall, his lungs pausing in the suspense. Heat coursed through him. He took a deep breath and peered around the corner into the vacant darkness.

The cold metal hilt of a sword struck his jaw. His jawbone cracked. Skin split, and blood rushed down his neck. He fell to his knees. Breath came in ragged gasps. He gagged. His vision blurred. Numbing warmth pooled on the broken bits of his bone as the skin, once again, began to heal.

His arms were pulled behind his back, and a new agony bit into his wrists. He stifled a yell. Bile and stomach acid bubbled along the back of his teeth, but he kept it at bay. An icy torment throbbed in his veins and pooled in his chest, stopping his body from healing. Blood trickled in hot rivers down his neck.

The isen squatted beside him, but he couldn't lift his head to see her face.

She sniggered and pinched his nose as if he was a child. "These cuffs are *extra* potent, in case you get any ideas."

She hoisted him to his feet, and a fresh wave of searing pain shot through his body. His chest ached. Blood dripped from the spikes in his wrists and fell in thick drops to the floor.

"Who *are* you?" he asked through gasping breaths.

"My name is Deidre, darling"—she brushed some dust off of his shoulder—"and I always win."

❧CHAPTER THREE
THE GRIMOIRE

Kara rubbed her temples and leaned on the submerged library's stone desk, her eyes unfocused as she stared at the letter she could now magically read. She didn't try to tell herself to calm down, to chill out, or to breathe. Her only thought was of how royally she'd screwed herself over by walking through that gazebo or lichgate or whatever it was.

She had walked through a door in a mountain. A ten-by-ten dirt closet had swallowed her phone. Her pack and stun gun had probably already been eaten by a bear. She had heard whispers while alone in a massive, underground library and opened a secret book called the Grimoire, which was apparently pretty important. She'd discovered a hidden pocket of Earth called Ourea.

In an effort to stay calm, she took deep breaths. It didn't work. Each breath became a panicked gasp as she tried to figure out what was going on. Only, she *couldn't* figure out what was going on. That's why she was panicking.

It was a vicious cycle.

The *flick, flick, flick* of the Grimoire's turning pages stole her focus. The last page lingered in the air as it fell to reveal a small block of red text on the otherwise empty beige paper.

> I wish I could have caused no pain or fear, but such isn't a reality of life. A treasure has been awoken within you— you are now a vagabond of Ourea.

She groaned. "Yeah, thanks, I gathered that much. So what happens now?"

The pages flipped to another image of the hooded figure, but this time he wore a thick leather band wrapped around his wrist. Spidery red text adorned the paper beside him. Something was off about the drawing, and she leaned in for a closer look. It took her a second to realize the clover pendant in her hand was also drawn into his wrist guard.

The last blood-red rays of the day poured through the skylight. She sighed. Her dad's search party would head out any minute, scanning the ditches for her body. Oh, he was going to *love* this story.

She resigned herself to the impending lecture and leaned in to read the red text besides the drawing.

> This is the Vagabond as he was in life. He wrote the observations of his travels here, creating me over his lifetime. The trials he faced were treacherous, and you will fare the same. The life of a vagabond isn't an easy one.
>
> I was made to open only for the gifted and the strong. Be patient in the times to come and trust yourself, for you are worthy of the power here.
>
> Though it may sometimes seem as if life is decided for us, remember that in all actions before this, you made the choices which brought you here. You alone decide where to go next. There is always choice.

"Freaking awesome." She rubbed her eyes. Apparently, it was *her* fault she'd been dragged by a root down a dirt closet.

She fiddled with her locket and looked down once again at the tiny clover amulet. Its diamond wasn't blue anymore, though it did shimmer. She slid it over her head with a quiet sigh, and the clover dangled just above her collarbone.

"Look, I just want to get home. How do I get out of here?"

The pages flipped toward the back, where a sketch of the library consumed the page and more spidery red text described how to open a secret door in one of the shelves. She lifted the book and carried it with her as she looked for the way out. At least using the Grimoire was easy enough. That had to be some small compensation for the unrestrained hell it had already brought upon her.

Kara scanned the shelves for a few minutes, browsing through titles like *The History of Isen Guilds, Earaks are Evil,* and even *All Anyone Will Ever Need to Know about Beer* before she finally found *The Ways of Peace,* the green cover mentioned in the Grimoire's instructions. It was the last on its shelf to survive the gale from earlier, as the rest of its neighbors littered the floor. She took care not to step on them as she reached for the green book and pulled, rolling it back on a hinge. The crack of splitting rock broke across the room.

A rumble quaked through the library. More books fell. Two shelves pulled inward on the opposite wall, opening like doors and missing the edges of the desk by inches. Beyond the confines of her book-lined prison was a dark cavern, its roof riddled with holes that leaked in the twilight and dripping lines of rainwater. The broken remnants of a white castle tower lay against the side of the cave, most of its bricks crushed to dust.

But Kara had a visitor.

A brunette looked up from where she knelt on the floor. The fading light caught the glint of a golden cross in her hand as flowing curls coursed over her loose white tunic. The stranger paused, watching the library with narrow eyes, but quickly stood and sneered.

Kara forced herself to swallow the rising sting of fear in her throat. She should've just stayed in the stupid library.

❧CHAPTER FOUR
CAGED

Kara's pulse raced. Her body couldn't take this kind of stress for much longer. The brunette standing in the cave laughed and slid the gold cross into her pocket.

"It really is my lucky day!" the woman said. "So the Vagabond's back, now? And it only took a thousand years. We were beginning to think you would never show up."

Her arsenal of snappy comebacks exhausted, Kara shrugged. The brunette meandered closer, her loose curls sliding over her neck as she gloated. She stopped only when she could graze the Grimoire with her long, pale fingers.

The old leather book imploded at the woman's touch, scattering its dust in the air. Kara gasped, and the clover pendant's diamond glowed blue from where it hung around her neck.

"Bring it back!" the woman demanded.

Kara stuttered, unsure of what to say.

"I said bring it back!"

"I don't know how!"

"Don't lie to me." The brunette grabbed Kara's collar and lifted her to her toes.

She seized the woman's freckled wrists without thinking. Heat flooded through her hands, just as it had when she pulled the clover pendant out of the lock, and something sparked in her palm. Blue light exploded from her fingers.

The woman sailed backward and crashed against a bookshelf, but Kara fell lightly back on her feet and examined her hands. All of the freckles and wrinkles of her palm were in the right place. There was no sign at all that lightning had just exploded from her fingers.

Books tumbled off the shelves, burying the brunette in parchment and crinkled leather that fell away just as quickly when the woman stood a second later. Her shoulders hunched as she glared, but she didn't come closer. As much as Kara wanted to run, her feet would not listen.

"How long have you been the Vagabond?"

"Um—"

"You can't even control what you are, can you?"

"Well—"

A white streak blazed across her vision, and the woman was gone. Something grabbed her shoulder and shoved her into the nearest bookshelf, pulling one of her hands behind her. An itchy material scratched her wrists. Before Kara could take another breath, the woman spun her around. Kara's hands were now bound in front of her with thick rope.

"Hey! You can't—"

The woman laughed. "I already did. My name is Deidre. I want you to remember that, because this was too easy. You'll want a rematch someday, and I'll be more than happy to oblige."

Deidre dug her nails into Kara's arm and pulled her away from the study. The rope wriggled like a worm as Kara struggled. Its fibers dug deeper into her wrists, stinging her fingertips with pins and needles as it cut off circulation to her hands. She stopped resisting, and the rope, in turn, was still.

They turned down a dark tunnel. Kara couldn't see, and the only sensation besides the moldy damp of the cave was Deidre's nails as they bruised her skin. They walked for a few minutes, slowing only when they neared the entrance to another passage. Light splashed from it, illuminating gray rocks that cast shadows into the hallway. They walked through, and the glare blinded Kara until her eyes adjusted to the rows of pale gray flame emanating from dozens of torches.

A massive cavern stretched into the expanses above, dissolving beyond the light's edge into solid darkness. The torchlight illuminated a swarm of ash-gray creatures. The pores on their arms hissed, releasing streams of hot mist that hovered above them. She stopped to gape, but the brunette shoved her forward. Several of the gray monsters snickered or leered at the rips in her clothes.

Something roared nearby. Kara jumped. To her left, two lumbering monsters leaned on their forearms like apes. They loomed over her, their bodies clunky blocks of rock that sent pebbles falling to the earth with each movement. Each had a pair of gaping holes served as a nose.

Their lipless mouths cracked and tore as they roared, revealing three rows of stubby teeth.

"What—?"

"Trolls," Deidre interrupted. "Don't get too close. We want you in one piece, at least for now."

The brunette tightened her grip on Kara's shoulder and turned her toward the trolls. The beasts snorted and shuffled in place, revealing glimpses of a wheeled metal cage that was attached to them with thick leather straps.

One troll lowered its head, leaning closer when Kara passed, and its brown iris shrank as it focused on her with a look of uneasy curiosity. When she was close enough to touch it, the creature lunged, twisting its head to snap at her neck.

Deidre swatted its nose, and it recoiled, screaming. Kara's knees shook, but her captor continued walking as if nothing had happened, dragging her around to the back of the cage where two gray-skinned soldiers had already opened its gates. Another prisoner sat in the corner of the jail, his hands bound behind his back.

"I didn't do anything wrong!" Kara said, finding her voice.

Deidre threw her into the cage. "Everybody's done something, darling."

The gates slammed closed with a rattle. Kara swallowed hard and pushed herself into an empty corner of her prison. One of the soldiers peered through the bars, eyeing her over the brim of a crooked nose that looked as if it had been broken and left untended more than once in his life. He was easily seven feet tall, and everything about his build was stocky and squared: his jaw, his head, even his shoulders. He muttered something, his words rolling together too quickly for her to understand, and then he shouted in a foreign language to a group of soldiers nearby. They all looked over to where she sat in the mobile jail and laughed.

She draped her tied hands around her knees and tried to calm down, but she was thrown off balance when the crack of a whip sent the trolls and their cage lurching forward. Her cellmate stifled a groan and leaned against the bars, his dark hair sticking to the edges of his olive face.

He was at most a few years older than her but in much better shape, with broad shoulders and toned arms. Though his clothes were torn, there weren't any scratches or cuts on his skin. He caught her eye and cocked an eyebrow, and it was then that she realized her uncontrollable breath came in quick, shallow bursts. She was hyperventilating.

"Hey," he muttered. "Calm down. You'll be fine."

"Like hell!" She stared out at the throngs of soldiers marching, steam oozing from their pores. "We're going to die, aren't we?"

"Relax. We might not. Look at me."

She glared at him, fitful butterflies dancing a tarantella in her gut.

"Good. Tell me your name."

"Kara. Yours?"

"Braeden. I don't mean to be rude, Miss Kara, but what are you even doing here?"

"I was hiking! And then there was this door, and these roots—"

"Wait," he interrupted, his eyes flitting once over her. "You're not a yakona? What are you?"

"I'm human! And you're what, an elf? Are *you* a yakona?"

He chuckled, but the laugh didn't make it past the thin wrinkle at the corner of his mouth. He shifted his weight without answering and brushed her leg with his boot.

"Sleep. You'll need your energy."

"I couldn't possibly—" She yawned and rubbed her face.

A sudden rush of exhaustion swept from her toe to her head, as if his touch had summoned it. She leaned into the bars. Her breathing slowed, and she heard him mutter something as she pressed her cheek into the iron. She slept.

※

A beam of light broke through the corner of Kara's eye. Her skin prickled with cold, and bits of ice stuck to the ends of her eyelashes. She shivered, and her body swayed, but the cold metal of a rod against her face kept her from falling over in her half-asleep stupor. It was almost like she was still in that cage.

She jolted awake.

A snowcapped dirt road faded into trees behind her, visible through the thick bars of the jail. A white blanket coated the forest to her right as the hot wisps of her breath froze on the air. She shivered.

Her cellmate remained curled in his corner. Behind him, the road dropped off in a sheer cliff shrouded by the fog of a low cloud. The gorge was hundreds of feet deep, its floor masked by a black mist that convulsed and spun. Giant shadows with no shape sped through the haze, churning it.

Braeden stirred, shifting his weight in his sleep. Dark smudges lined his jaw and neck, and he wore a green tunic with dark pants. His clothes definitely weren't something Kara could find at the mall.

The cage rocked and thudded. The wheels clattered over cobblestone. They passed a tall gate, and its broad doors shut behind them. More gray-skinned men walked along a battlement above the gate, shouting to each other.

Crowded black buildings dotted the edges of the new road, each a dozen stories tall and squished beside its neighbors. Frost sprawled across every window.

Braeden shifted away from her so that, for the first time, she could see his hands. Thick metal shackles dug into his bruised wrists. Trails of a black liquid coursed over the handcuffs, dripping from his fingers onto the wooden floor of their prison.

Something rustled in the far corner. She spun around, but instead of a gray soldier or the brunette woman, she saw only a small white fox. The little creature leaned against the bars and cocked its head, eyeing her as its giant ears flicked around to absorb the trolls' hulking movements.

The fox trotted over and sniffed the torn hem of her jeans before looking up with its striking blue eyes. She reached out with her bound hands and gently scratched its chin. It hummed with pleasure. Kara grinned.

"At least not everything here is scary," she said.

The little fox popped its eyes open and stared at her for a moment before it changed shape. Its fur melted away into the wet scales of a red lizard with a single black stripe running down its spine. Kara yelped as the fox-now-lizard creature scurried over the wood and out of sight. She covered her face with her hands and cursed beneath her breath.

She stifled a sob. "I want to go home."

"Ourea isn't the sort of place you can leave. It always drags you back," Braeden mumbled, awake now.

"More comforting words of wisdom?" she asked, peering through her fingers to catch his bruised and battered gaze.

"No. You hardly seemed fond of that." He stretched his fingers out behind him, and drops of the black liquid fell faster from around the cuffs as he moved.

"What's wrong with your hands?"

"These shackles have poisoned spikes."

She whistled. "Wow. Can I do anything to help?"

"No, but thank you."

"Is that black stuff the poison?"

"I guess you could say that."

"Is that a yes?"

Braeden frowned. "It's my blood."

"Wait, your blood is black?"

Well, it wasn't the weirdest thing she'd seen in the last twenty four hours. She had yet to recover from those stupid roots and the book that turned its own pages.

"You know, blood is kind of important, Braeden. It's not usually a poisonous thing."

"It's a long story."

She gestured at the cage. "I'm not exactly going anywhere."

"I think everything will become painfully obvious if we are headed for the same place, which I hope we aren't." His expression darkened, his eyebrows casting a shadow over his eyes. He looked up at her, and a chill crept down her neck.

"Wow. It's been a pleasure talking to you, too. To think, I was going to take those cuffs off you." She leaned against the cell wall as they took another bend in the road.

"As kind an offer as that is, only the person who put them on can take them off. And I meant only that you will not want to go where I'm being taken."

"Oh," she said. "Sorry."

He shrugged and stared at the floorboards. "I've been running from Carden for a long time. I always wondered when he'd catch up to me."

"Who's Carden?"

He glanced past her. "I think you're about to find out."

Deidre appeared at the end of the cage. "All right, kiddies, we're home."

The prison skidded to a stop. Its back doors swung open on their own, slamming against the metal bars with a bang. Several gray guards climbed in and grabbed her arms and waist with sweaty hands, pulling her to her feet before she even had a chance to stand. Her cellmate stifled several sharp cries of pain from behind her as other soldiers shoved him forward as well.

The guards steered her out of the cage and toward a flight of steps that led to the main doors of a castle. Black spires and spiked battlements soared on either side of the palace, stabbing the overcast sky while mountains and a dark forest crowded the horizon.

The soldiers cleared a path so that Deidre could lead the procession into the castle. Guards hurried Braeden through after the brunette, but he didn't resist. He watched the floor, furrowed creases distorting the skin around his eyes.

A guard's grip tightened around Kara's arm, and his breath tickled her neck, making her shudder. He laughed and forced her through the doorway into a throne room teeming with hooded figures and gray faces.

Black marble layered the walls and floor. Thick, evenly-spaced columns dotted the vast hall and supported a giant stained glass dome above, which cast red and gray light across the throngs of monsters below.

The crowd had been jeering and laughing when the doors opened, but the room hushed when they saw Braeden. Bodies parted to give him a clear path through to the end of the hall, and Kara caught her breath. Hundreds of tall, gray-skinned men and women filled the room, their faces twisted in snarls, but they were outnumbered by creatures that were even more frightening. Centaurs reared to better vantage points, kicking others in the head as they did. Several hairy minotaurs snorted, snot dripping from their noses as they gazed at the procession without blinking. Wolves howled from some unseen place.

Three black marble thrones sat on a raised platform at the end of the room, growing ever-nearer as Kara's silent convoy walked closer. Another gray-skinned man sat in the center throne but stood as the crowd parted. He was even taller than the soldier who had examined her back in the cave, his skin a deeper charcoal color than the rest. He sneered.

When they were close enough, the soldier's grip on her arm tightened. He kicked the back of her knee, forcing her to the tile floor. She winced and glared at the man by the thrones, but he was smirking at Braeden and apparently uninterested in her pain.

"It has been too long, son," he said, beginning down the platform's steps.

Kara couldn't place his accent. He drew out his vowels and overly enunciated his consonants, as if pausing to adore the sound of his own voice.

She looked at the gray man and turned back to Braeden. Their jaws were both square, their hair dark, but Braeden's olive skin tone contrasted starkly from his father's ashen complexion.

"Now look. The human is confused." The man turned to Kara, and the edge to his voice made her skin crawl.

"Stop, Carden," Braeden said, gritting his teeth. Something clicked in her mind, and she thought back to their short conversation in the mobile prison: Braeden had been running from his own father.

Carden crossed his arms. "Why are you not in your natural form, boy? You look hideous."

"No." Braeden shook his head. "Never again. Not willingly."

"Unwillingly, then."

Carden grabbed the crown of his son's head. A gray light rippled across Braeden's skin, and his body convulsed, the skin fading from its olive tone to the same charcoal gray color as his father's. The green shirt tightened as he grew taller, and smoke poured from the rips in his clothes. Kara gasped.

Carden laughed and released his son's head, allowing Braeden's skin to fade back to the olive hue she recognized. Braeden caught her eye with a sharp glare before shaking his head and returning his gaze to the floor.

"Welcome home, boy!" Carden's voice boomed.

"I don't want this!" Braeden's voice echoed over his father's and commanded the hall's attention. "All I want is to be left alone. I won't get in your way. I never have."

"You haven't yet, no. But when I couldn't produce another Heir with the bloodline, I realized you weren't dead. You have a duty to your people to help me turn the tides of this world. Our banishment will end in my lifetime, and I must have an Heir to follow me. You don't have a choice."

Kara glanced from the king to the prince chained at his feet before she turned to look at the plethora of monsters in the towering throne room. Not only was he a prince, but he could change shape to look like the gray-skinned creatures all around her. She shook her head and shivered. She was in deep.

"Why is the human here, isen?" Carden asked.

Icy panic raced through Kara's chest, but was made worse when she realized exactly what Carden had said. He'd called Deidre an isen, so—according to the letter Kara read back in the library—Deidre could steal souls. She could've stolen *Kara's* soul, but had instead brought her here. Why?

"She's a present." Deidre grinned and pulled Kara to her feet.

Carden frowned. "She is too thin."

The isen chuckled. "Not that sort of present. This is the Vagabond."

Carden paused, but burst into laughter shortly thereafter. He wiped a gleeful tear from his eye. Kara twisted her arm in the brunette's grip, but the movement stung the bruises already there from her fall in the dirt room.

The king studied her, and his smile faded. "What is that around her neck?"

She followed his gaze, and a pang of regret made her swallow hard. The completely visible clover pendant hung next to her locket, its diamond still glowing blue.

Without moving from his place on the steps, the king reached for the necklace. The pendant hovered in the air and floated in front of her eyes.

He grinned. "I stand corrected. This is remarkable."

Carden walked down the final steps by his throne to stand in front of her, and she craned her neck to see his face. He seized the pendant in his thick fingers, but her hands rose to meet his in reflex.

A wave of heat coursed through her at his touch, much like it had when Deidre grabbed her in the library. It shot through her veins, making her fingertips pulse. A spark cracked in the air between them, and Carden flew backward into his chair on the platform.

The hall was silent. Her eyes widened. She couldn't breathe. After all, throwing an evil king across the room had to be one of the easiest ways to die. A familiar thought tugged at her mind, but she pushed it away again to focus on the moment. The heat still circulated in her veins, though it was quickly dissolving once more into panic.

Carden snickered, his laughter ringing in a higher pitch than before. The bellow coursed through the crowd of monsters as they followed suit.

"Brilliant! A human who can use magic! She is the Vagabond after all. Have a seat, my dear," he said, gesturing to the throne at his left. "I am afraid that it has been largely unused by the Queen for some time."

He shot a look to Braeden, who glared back.

"That's really nice and everything," she said, her heart pounding too loudly for her to hear her own voice. "But I just want to go home."

"To your family?"

"Yes."

"I would rather they join us here, if that is your only reason for leaving. We are quite entertaining. Deidre will even find them for you. Simply tell her where they are."

The isen smirked. Kara wasn't getting out of this.

"Now, sit," Carden commanded.

Kara tried to devise a more eloquent argument, but Deidre grabbed her arm. Before she could resist, or speak, or even look over, the isen dragged her to the throne and flung her into the stone seat. Kara's back was tender from the impact, a massive bruise no doubt already forming on the space between her shoulder blades.

A quick glance around the room confirmed her fears: each of the monsters in the hall watched her. Everyone knew, now, what she was, despite how the letter had warned her to be careful. Even Braeden studied her with a calculating expression. He glared at her, his stare intense and unbroken until his father commanded his attention again. She took a shaky breath and saw the red lizard from earlier dart through a few soldiers' legs. It crawled along the floor, squirming and slithering closer to her seat.

She finally let herself listen to the nagging thought which had been floating around the back of her mind since she'd opened the Grimoire: She wasn't going to survive this.

❧CHAPTER FIVE
THE STELE

Braeden eyed Kara as she sat in his mother's old throne, but he winced and looked away when the spikes jostled in his wrists. The poison circulating through his blood had already scarred every vein. Even when he did get the cuffs off, he would not be able to think straight until he healed.

His knees ached from the chilly marble, so he shifted his weight to ease the searing pain. A spike dug deeper and tapped his bone. He bit his cheek to keep from screaming and hunched his shoulders. In the floor's reflection, Carden flourished his hands and lectured about duty and obligation, but Braeden tuned him out.

A red lizard darted toward Kara. The new Vagabond stared at the crowded hall, her grip tight on the stone and her knuckles white. She didn't move. He couldn't even tell if she was breathing.

Another flash of color captured his waning attention span as a second, green lizard scuttled behind Carden's throne. It slithered around the other side and paused, its beady eyes glistening as it looked out over the room.

"It's time for you to embrace what you really are!" Carden said, loud enough now to catch Braeden's attention. "Our kind was *eternally* banished for a failed coup thousands and thousands of years ago. We are still hunted by the other kingdoms, forbidden to travel through Ourea as they do, out of punishment for an act we did not commit! Did your twelve years with the enemy make you forget your own heritage?"

Braeden could only shake his head.

"*I* taught you what it means to rule, boy. *I* built the foundation that made you what you are today. I taught you how to do what must be done to protect your people."

Braeden glared up at the king. "Is that why you killed Mother?"

"None betray me, not even those I love," Carden said, so quietly that Braeden had to strain to hear him.

"You—!"

"You have a rare opportunity," Carden interrupted. "Because you were just a child when she stole you away from me, I will give you a second chance. Don't repeat your mother's mistake."

The king returned to his throne and bellowed his next words so that they reverberated off the walls of the cavernous hall.

"Stand and accept what you were born to be, my son."

"Never."

"Like I said, it's not a choice."

Carden reached toward him and clenched his hand into a fist. Braeden's stomach tightened, as if his father had reached into his gut and squeezed. He curled over himself, stifling the agonizing yell in his throat.

The king twisted his hand and opened his palm, where sparks snapped and fizzled. Braeden's muscles tore at the movement. Popping noises surged along his biceps and neck. His veins chilled and slowed. He unconsciously stood at a twitch of Carden's finger. Braeden's grip on his form was slipping. Smoke escaped his pores. Organs shifted. He screamed in pain until a heavy weight fell on his chest and closed his throat.

"Screams are for the weak," Carden said.

The weight eased off Braeden's lungs, letting him sink back to the floor as the internal tearing and popping stopped. The staggering numbness returned. His cuffs twisted as he moved, and searing fire coursed through his veins. Tremors pulsed through him.

Carden scowled from his chair, and the green lizard from earlier peered from the shadows beside the throne. Its outline blurred for a moment, but returned to normal so quickly that Braeden questioned what he'd seen.

It flickered again, more prominently this time.

Dark lines melted around its face. It grew taller, its skin stretching and pouring into the space around it. In a matter of seconds, the lizard filled the massive hall as it transformed into a dragon.

Braeden's mouth went dry.

The dragon reared its head above the stunned hall and roared. The creature's tail landed squarely on Carden's chest, sending him flying into a support column by the main entry. The pillar crumbled on top of the king, burying him, and the dome it supported shattered. The dragon thrashed its wings against the walls by the thrones. Chunks of black marble pummeled downward, cracking the polished floor. Glass rained down on the cloaked subjects. A stampede began for the door.

A new, shriller roar echoed through the great hall, shooting chills through Braeden's body. A red dragon with a long black stripe down its spine stood over Kara, baring its thick teeth. One dragon was bad enough, but two would be unstoppable. He tried to stand, to run, to possibly escape and at minimum find cover, but one of the spikes shifted and lodged into his bone. The pain buckled his knees.

Another patch in the ceiling crumbled. Pebbles and thick shards of painted glass showered to the floor. What yakona remained fled. Braeden grit his teeth, forced himself to his feet, and staggered to the edge of the hall.

Two thick claws engulfed him, pulling him into the air and pressing the spikes deeper into his hands with a single, deft motion. He cried out as the throbbing agony pulsed through his arms. Shimmering green scales blotted out the sky. The red dragon appeared in the air beside them, Kara tucked away in its claws.

The familiar weight of his father's control returned on Braeden's chest. Hatred coursed through his mind like a fever. He turned to the floor. Carden lay trapped beneath the rubble, a shredded look of fury consuming his gray face, and Braeden lost himself to the final ounces of his father's remaining energy.

Kill the dragon, he was told. *Rip it apart. Return.*

He writhed, consumed by his father's commands, but the green dragon clutched him tighter until the pain of the poisoned cuffs outweighed even his father's will. He dangled in the dragon's claws and watched the Stele recede from sight.

For at least twenty minutes, the dragons soared over the Stele's black, snowcapped forests. The trees disobeyed the wind, bending instead to follow Braeden as he passed them. Carden's monsters sped through the forests below, sinister shadows that traced his every move.

Whispers of his father's orders echoed on the air. Braeden scanned the sky behind them, but nothing followed. A mountain range loomed in the distance, and his heart pounded with excitement. This was the edge of the Stele's domain.

The dragons reeled upward, flying over the summit. Frigid gusts of wind bit his face as they peaked and circled to a meadow on the other side, which was far enough down the slope that the snow had dissolved into slush and cold mud. The grass was brown, and only the pine trees flourished, but he still wished for solid ground much sooner than it came.

The red dragon set Kara down in the meadow; Braeden, however, was dropped with less care. When the claws released him into the air a few feet above the sparse grass, the spikes jostled in his skin. He thudded to the ground and did not try to stand.

Nearby, a huff of air shot past Braeden like a breath from a bull's nose. The red dragon glared at him. It sprinted toward him so fast that he did not have time to react. It grabbed him with one claw, kicking the air from his body as they shot through the meadow. The dragon flickered and changed shape again, melting into her human form as they hurled toward the mountain. Her copper-colored skin and pale hair shimmered in the dying sunlight before she shoved him against a cliff with one hand on his chest.

Rocks broke against his spine and tore through his tunic. The cuffs ripped open the skin they touched, sending bolts of crippling pain through his arms and back. He cursed, but choked on the pebbles and dust that rained over them. The shape-shifter threw her free arm to the side, as if pointing off into the forest, and a thin white blade slid into her palm from the depths of the air around her. She held it to his neck.

"Stop!" Kara yelled.

Braeden squinted back to where he'd sat only seconds before. The green dragon flickered and shifted into a man. He unbound Kara's hands but grabbed her shoulder to stop her from running over. She fought with him, murmuring inaudibly, but he shook his head and whispered something Braeden couldn't hear.

The woman's grip tightened. "Braeden Drakonin, listen closely to me. I am not fond of your father. Had you not defied him in his own court, we would have left you. But mark me, yakona. If you betray our trust, death will become a mercy before I am done with you."

"I get that a lot. But yes, I understand."

She released him. Her blade disappeared in a puff of purple smoke. She grimaced at him as if she smelled something foul, but snapped her fingers. His shackles fell to the ground.

He grabbed his wrists and sank to the mossy grass in relief, too exhausted to thank her or to wonder how she'd done it. The black pools of his wounds knit themselves together, but the process was slow. They congealed and bubbled, the poison resisting his body as it mended itself. His half-healed jaw grafted, but the internal sting of broken veins persisted. Muscles wove themselves back together. Bones popped as they finally slid back into place. The poison continued to circulate as his body tried to heal around it, and it would be hours before no scars remained. Even then, the internal tremors would continue.

He examined the shifter-woman. Her pale blond hair fell to her waist, where it rolled out in small curls. Patches of copper in her tan skin glistened in the sun. Her piercing blue eyes crinkled in an expression of annoyance.

"You two are drenowith. Muses," he said.

"Yes."

"I thought you were just myths."

"As we prefer. I'm Adele, and this is Garrett."

She gestured toward the other muse. He had rusty hair, the color of embers in a fire, but his skin was the same coppery shade as Adele's.

Garrett released his grip on Kara's shoulder. She ran to Braeden and knelt beside him.

"Are you okay?" she asked.

"Fine," he said. "Thank you."

Kara turned to Adele. "How did you undo his shackles? I thought only the person who put them on could take them off."

"We are above yakona laws, young Vagabond."

"Well, thank you for saving us, then."

"The first Vagabond was our friend, to whom we owed a debt. It's now paid. What is your name?"

"Kara. So you're muses, huh? All the letter said about you is that you're shape-shifters. Can you become anything?"

"Anything we imagine," Garret said.

Braeden tried to avoid looking at the muse he'd been ordered to kill.

Kara shook her head. "This is insane. So, you knew the Vagabond and you obviously don't age. Are you immortal?"

"Not immortal," Adele corrected. "While we don't grow old, we can die. Everything is mortal, even Earth."

"It's hard to believe that a human found the Grimoire," Garrett interrupted.

"I agree," Adele said. "The first Vagabond lost faith in his kind not long before he disappeared, so I suspected his successor wouldn't be a yakona. Still, I never thought it possible that his protégé could be a human."

"I'm starting to redefine my idea of possible," Kara said with a laugh.

"I am curious, Kara," Garrett said as he leaned against a tree. "What language do you believe you're speaking?"

"What kind of a question is that?"

"Please, humor me."

"English."

Braeden's heart skipped a beat. She'd said it with such conviction that he wanted to believe her.

"We aren't speaking English," Braeden said. "You're speaking our common language."

"What—?" She laughed. "I don't even know what that is!"

Garrett chimed in before Kara could continue. "I know this is confusing, my girl, but listen closely. The first Vagabond often created new vagabonds, and when he did, he would inherently pass on some of his gifts to them. However, it seems that he passed on everything he ever achieved to you because you have his Grimoire. Among other things, you now possess an intuitive understanding of the languages he knew."

She paused, seeming to grapple with the concept. "That doesn't even make sense. I mean, why does it sound like English to me? And wouldn't language evolve over a thousand years?"

"You do have a strange accent." Braeden chuckled.

Kara glared at him, so he cleared his throat and tried to forget his poorly-timed joke.

"No, nothing much changes here," he added.

Garrett crossed his arms. "Please entertain me with an experiment. I will need your cooperation, young prince. It will not hurt you, at least not in body."

How comforting.

Kara shuddered. "This is freaking me out."

"If you do possess this gift, it will help you to protect yourself," Garrett said.

She sighed and nodded, so the muse continued.

"The vagabonds were famous for their ability to search another's mind. If the gift lives on, you will be able to see the moment which has most defined our young prince's life to this day. It's rarely a pleasant encounter"—Garrett glanced to Braeden—"but this gift might save your life. Give me your hand."

She obeyed by shoving her hand at him, which Garrett then pressed against Braeden's forehead. Her touch tickled his skin, and he noticed for the first time that her eyes were gray.

A spark shocked the space beneath her finger. Ice pooled on his forehead, and his breath chilled in his lungs. All color and light dissolved into a black haze. The muses disappeared into the darkness, as did the forest and the mountain. Kara was the last to dissolve from view, and all was dark.

White and gold wisps wove upward from the ground, twisting and shimmering until they formed the figure of the woman he so sorely missed.

Mother's ghost appeared before him, glowing and smiling from where she sat opposite him in a carriage. She was draped in the gleaming gold outline of a long fur coat, her black hair cascading in rich curls around her perfect face. Her hands, her smile, her mouth: everything was suspended in this memory, every gesture blurring as the world moved a second too slowly. Her eyes were as dark as her hair, but they glittered as she grinned at him. He had forgotten how beautiful she was.

"The Villing Caves are just a few hours away. Are you excited? There are frozen dragons there!" Her voice bounced and echoed, forcing him to relive the same words many times. She laughed and leaned in, pinching his nose. The touch left frost on his skin.

The carriage stopped suddenly, throwing her back into her seat. A scream echoed in the darkness. His mother's frantic eyes caught his.

"Stay hidden," she ordered. "Don't come out, no matter what you see."

She brushed his cheek with her icy fingers and closed a panel in the carriage, sealing him inside the secret compartment. He peered through a hole in the wood in time to see her lean through a window, her head disappearing into the shadows outside. She screamed, but it was interrupted by a choking sound.

A frail hand reached into the carriage and pulled on her neck, lifting her from her seat. She grabbed the window frame with her hands, nails breaking as she fought to pull herself back in. A squishing noise resonated through the small carriage, the wet sound of something sharp slicing flesh, and his mother fell limp against the window. The hand released her and stretched its fingers. A silver barb retracted from the palm.

"Leave the boy and the woman," a voice called from outside. "Blood Carden is coming for them."

The darkness faded. The meadow grass returned blade by blade as Braeden returned to reality. He rubbed his eyes as the memory ended, his head pounding and his arms soaked with cold sweat. Garrett and Adele stood by and watched in silence. Kara sat across from him, her lips parted as she tried to form words, but all she could do was stare.

"The gift survived, then," Garrett said.

Kara's wide eyes were wet, and she tugged at the locket on her neck. "Braeden, was that your mom?"

He bit his cheek and avoided saying anything until he could lift his head long enough to speak. "Yes."

"Braeden, I—"

"They're coming! We need to hide." Adele glanced into the calm forest behind her.

"What?" Kara asked. "Can't you just do the dragon thing again and get us out of here?"

"They're watching the skies," Garrett said as he shook his head.

Kara stood and offered Braeden a hand. He snorted at the idea that such a scrawny girl could lift him, but accepted her offer anyway because the poison still stung his veins and made movement a chore. The muses walked past him toward the base of the mountain.

Adele placed her hand on the sheer rock, which heaved like water at her touch and dripped slowly away to reveal a hidden cavern. Air leaked from this new chamber all at once, a heavy sigh that blew over them long enough to dry most of the lingering sweat on Braeden's neck. The stone hummed as Adele turned and beckoned.

"Hurry. We have no time left to wait."

❦CHAPTER SIX
HORDES

Drops of liquid rock slid along the edges of the cave entrance that had been a solid wall a moment ago. Braeden cocked an eyebrow and tried to hide his surprise. He'd never seen *that* before.

Garrett ushered him into the cave after Kara. Inside, a thin waterfall trickled and splashed over a few small boulders in a corner. The forest was visible through the rock wall, although an opaque gleam drained the world of all color except for muted browns and tans. Adele was the last to enter the cave, and more rock drizzled over the entrance once she was safely through. The droplets fell from above in a gushing shower, drawing thin lines of stone over the air. Soon, the strings of the hardening mountain solidified into a seamless wall, sealing the four of them inside.

Braeden brushed his hand along the newly-formed cliff face. The cool stone pushed against his palm: smooth, hard, and impassible. Kara grinned nearby and shook her head.

"What was that?" she asked.

"There is no name for the conversations muses have with the earth," Adele replied.

"Does that mean you don't know?"

Garrett chuckled and Adele smirked, but neither answered.

"The two of you wait here while we decided what to do next," Garrett said. He led Adele into the depths of the cave, and more rock drizzled away as they walked, giving them endless room to pace and debate.

Kara sighed and rubbed her neck. "I don't see why we couldn't keep going. I mean, there's nothing out there. It's so calm."

Braeden turned back to the forest. Distant trees bent against the wind and crashed out of sight, trampled by the horde that, from the way the trees curved, was at least a hundred strong. If she couldn't see that, this girl apparently had no idea what she'd gotten herself into.

Even armed with the Grimoire, she didn't seem to stand much of a chance.

"What are you thinking about?" she asked.

"Nothing." He glanced back to her and forced a thin smile.

She scoffed. "*That* was convincing."

Kara sat beside the waterfall and leaned her head against the wall, looking off into the murky forest and avoiding his gaze as if she'd read his mind. The rough wall pushed against his back as he sat beside her and toyed with what to say, but he lost his train of thought in the silence. The waterfall gurgled over its small boulders, and with each echoing splash, his internal healing tremors grew softer. It wouldn't be much longer before he was completely healed and able to bury yet another terrible memory of the Stele.

"So people don't really trust you, huh?" Kara's voice snapped him from his thoughts.

He laughed. "What gave it away?"

"Something about being thrown against a cliff by a dragon."

"All things considered, that was one of the warmer receptions I've had in my life."

"That's terrible," she said with a chuckle.

He shrugged. "I'm a Stelian. My people are dangerous."

"What has Carden done to make people so angry?"

"It's not just Carden. The Stele has a history of killing and enslaving other yakona as retribution for our banishment. *That* is why Stelians are killed on sight, no matter what Carden may prefer to think. We are feared because he murders and plunders."

"Why? Just to do it?"

"Well, you heard his tirade. We were banished millennia ago because a distant ancestor supposedly discovered a way to steal the bloodline from other yakona royal families. They say that's why the city of Ethos fell. No one could trust each other anymore. No one has for a long time."

"What's Ethos?"

"All the kingdoms were united once, way back, and lived together in a massive city called Ethos. That's where Deidre threw you into the prison with me."

"Oh, all right. But stealing bloodlines? What did he do, drain their blood?"

Braeden paused. This was the Vagabond, master of the Grimoire and Ourea's history. "How do you not know any of this, Kara?"

"Well, *excuse* me. I haven't exactly had a chance to read the manual."

He laughed. "All right, then. Bloodlines are sacred to yakona. Every kingdom is ruled by a Blood and an Heir. The Blood is the king—or queen, since we have female Bloods, too. They're born with the royal bloodline, which lets them control their people."

"Like Carden controlled you?" She blushed as soon as she spoke, but it was too late. "I'm sorry, Braeden. That was rude."

"No, I don't mind," he lied. "But yes, that is a good example. The Heir also has the bloodline, but can't control any subjects until the Blood dies and the Heir takes the throne. The bloodline is unique and sometimes hard to discover, but the easiest way to tell if a yakona is a royal is in how quickly he or she heals. Royals heal almost instantly."

"Like you did when those spikes came off?"

"Yes, exactly."

She shuddered, but remained silent. Braeden ran his thumb over where the scars from the spikes should have been. They'd healed faster than he thought they would.

"Carden is different," he continued. "He's worse than anyone before him because he does more than just kill. He *destroys*. Death becomes a mercy, one he does not always allow. For instance—"

His jaw tensed and the words stopped as he once again recalled the memory she'd dragged from him in the meadow. The waterfall's gurgling took over the room. There was the occasional shuffle of her shoe on the floor, or the rustle of her shirt catching on the rock wall as she shifted her weight, but the conversation came to an abrupt end.

He was content to never continue, to let the silence last until the army had come and gone, but he heard his own voice before he realized he was speaking.

"When I was a boy, Carden made me torture a prisoner. The way she screamed"—his voice broke—"I'd never heard anything so terrible."

"I'm sorry," Kara whispered.

"He made me burn her, break her bones, split her skin open. It went on forever. I had no idea who she was, then, but I found out later that she was a Blood: Aislynn of the Ayavel kingdom, which happens to be the only other race that can shift form like Stelians. The rest— Hillside, Losse, Kirelm—they think that gift is just a myth. I never wanted to correct them.

"Torturing Aislynn was the first time I felt guilt. She begged me to stop, to just kill her, but I could never help her while Carden watched—and he was always watching. I think Mother did love him, once, but she realized then what he was and what he wanted me to be. She dragged me out of bed that night and hid me in one of the carriages. Aislynn was already there. You saw the rest."

"But what happened next?" she asked. "I mean, the isen in your memory said Carden was coming for you. He knew where you were."

"An isen hunter named Richard found us before Carden could. He's Hillsidian, so I shifted form." Braeden gestured to his body. "Hillside is one of the yakona kingdoms, and I guess you could say they look like humans."

"I take it the others don't?"

"Not even close. You saw Carden." He shook his head and sighed. *And you saw me, the real me.* He glared at the floor and continued, not wanting to pause long enough to let her remember.

"Aislynn lied to Richard for whatever reason—out of gratitude to Mother, maybe. She told him that I was a Hillsidian orphan she'd rescued, and so far as I know, she has never said anything to the contrary. Richard brought me to Hillside, where I discovered that his wife was none other than the Hillsidian Blood. They adopted me, though I still can't figure out why."

"I'm going to go off topic here," Kara muttered, "but you said that Stelians and, what, I guess they're called Ayavels?"

"Ayavelians."

She rolled her eyes. "Okay, Ayavelians. I was close. You said you all can change form. Can you become a dragon, like the muses?"

Braeden laughed before he could stop himself. It was a real laugh, a full one, and he hadn't laughed like that in years. It faded to a chuckle when Kara's eyebrows bent and she blushed, but he enjoyed it. She punched his shoulder.

"Don't laugh at me! I don't know these things yet!"

"I apologize." He bit his cheek to quell his laughter. "No. I can change form to look like a member of any one of the other kingdoms, but that was after years of practice. Only muses can become anything."

"See? That wasn't so hard to answer," she said, grumbling.

"You know, you're the only person who has ever heard my story."

"Well thanks, I guess. My friends say I'm a good listener. Dad still thinks that I should become a therapist, but in my experience they're not much help." She rubbed her face. "But you probably don't even know what a therapist is."

He shrugged. "I go into the human world all the time. I know quite a few things about your kind."

"Of course you do."

"So what is this experience you have with therapists?"

"Ah," she muttered, suddenly very interested in the dirt under her fingernails. "I don't know. My Mom died a few months ago. I have a private session each week, but we haven't really gotten anywhere."

"Maybe you're so good at listening that you have no idea when to speak."

"Let's not talk about me."

"But—"

A tree shuddered and snapped, falling to the ground only a few dozen yards away. Braeden stood and braced himself, forgetting in his moment of sudden focus that he'd been about to point out her hypocrisy. A shadow raced through the trees along the front edge of the meadow: big and fast and blurry. The light echo of its paws reverberated through the ground so that he could barely distinguish it from his own heartbeat.

His breath caught in his throat as he waited for the creature to crash into the meadow, but he still wasn't ready when it did. The beast tore up clumps of grass as it ran and suddenly paused, glaring at the mountain. Braeden stopped breathing. Kara gasped.

"What the *hell* is that?" she asked.

It was an earak, standing still as a statue except for its heaving chest. Its ear twitched toward them when Kara spoke. This one was five times Braeden's size and by far the largest that he had ever seen. Hundreds of crooked teeth hung far beyond its lips like rusty knives in its flat, boxy head. A hump in its back rocked as it shifted weight across its six massive paws. It smelled the air. Earaks were trackers and had the best sense of smell on Earth. It would find them.

After two more giant whiffs of the late morning breeze, the monster scratched the ground and slung its nose into the dirt, leaving gray strings of saliva on the tufts of grass. Each sniff brought it a giant paw print closer to the mountain. The trees picked up a fitful wind and danced behind the creature.

Finally, it brought its nose to the base of the cliff wall and pressed itself against the rock, its snot catching on crags and loose boulders. It peered through, eyes unfocused, and in a fleeting glance caught Braeden's eye. He forced his mouth shut with a hard swallow. His lungs hurt from not breathing, but he did not dare to fill them.

The beast howled into the mountain, the noise a jarring scream in the calm morning. Dust showered from the roof. Braeden reached for his sword, and the familiar dark gray flame lit itself in his free palm.

The earak reached a paw up to its eye level and slowly dragged its claws against the rock. The shrill screech echoed through the cave. Braeden shuddered. The claw left a long scar that distorted his view of the forest.

Another, distant howl broke across the air. The earak leaned in the direction of the noise, ears pinned to its head as it decided what to do. Then, as swiftly as it had bounded into the clearing, it was gone, racing for its fellow monster.

Braeden cursed and sucked in air. He threw his sword back in its scabbard, and the gray flame in his hand flickered out as relief washed over him.

Kara sat and pushed herself against the rock, cradling her head in her hands. "What *was* that?!"

He knelt in front of her to see if she was all right. Her face was pale, and the skin around her eyes wrinkled with fear. As he opened his mouth to answer her, she froze. Her gaze shifted around him, so he turned. The army that had pummeled through the trees from afar was just now crashing into the clearing.

The horde trampled the meadow grasses as they shoved past each other. A centaur bolted into sight, its hairy skin rippling as it ran. A pack of wolves followed closely behind, biting and snarling at anything that came too close. A hundred gray-skinned Stelians filled in the gaps of the odd company, their pores steaming as they yelled to one another.

A minotaur bellowed something unintelligible and raced after the earak, breaking through a group of yakona and shoving them to the ground on its way. The army hollered and sprinted after it.

"We need to go," Braeden said.

Adele appeared suddenly, making him jump, but she ignored him and eyed the scratch in the mountain. Garrett knelt to help Kara to her feet.

"I just want to go home," Kara grumbled.

"But Vagabond," Adele said. "Ourea is your home now."

"No way. This place is nuts. You all can keep it."

"The Grimoire brought you here," Adele insisted. "Whether you like it or not, you can never go back to the life you had. Creatures like that will hunt you anywhere you go, even if you leave Ourea."

"This is who you are." Garrett looked down at her over the brim of his nose. "You are the Vagabond. I think you better understand what that means, now."

The remaining color in Kara's cheeks faded. Even her pink lips flushed white. She stared into the now-empty meadow, and Braeden wished he could help her somehow.

Garrett sighed. "The fact of the matter is you are the only one powerful enough to read the Grimoire. Yakona and isen alike are willing to kill to control the magic in that book, so any shred of the normal life you had is gone. Leaders from every race will hunt you for wealth and for power, and anyone who helps you risks dying because of it. That means if you returned to your human life, you would be found and your family and friends would become leverage against you."

"That's why Carden wanted you to invite your family to the Stele," Braeden added. "In case you hadn't figured that one out already."

"Won't they find out where Dad is anyway?" Kara rubbed her temples and took deep, useless breaths. "Shouldn't I warn him about all of this?"

Adele set a hand on the girl's shoulder. "If you returned to even say goodbye, Kara, they would follow you. They have your scent and they will find you, wherever you go. Carden wants that book. He wants you and he wants Braeden. If you stay away from your family, they will be safe."

"I have to at least tell Dad that I'm okay. If I just disappeared—and so soon after Mom—" She slunk against the cave wall, cradling her head in her hands. Her eyes glistened, but she bit her lip and winced from the effort.

Adele cradled Kara's chin and wiped away a tear. There was a thin cracking sound, like ice breaking, and the water crystallized on the muse's fingertips until it glistened like a diamond. Adele wove her spidery fingers around it and, in a matter of seconds, created a small silver pendant that looped twice over itself. The glimmering tear-diamond shone from its center.

"This pendant will tell me if you are in trouble," she said. "I can't replace your father, Kara, but this stone will help me keep you safe."

The muse draped the circular pendant around her own neck. Kara examined her over the brim of her nose, eyes narrowed and confused.

"Why are you all helping me?"

"You remind me of someone I lost." Adele took a deep, steadying breath. "I failed him. I will not fail you."

Kara looked at the floor. "Thank you, but I'm sorry. I just can't leave Dad. Not now."

"You should never say that you can't do something. There are always choices, even in a situation like this: you can go home and lead Ourea's demons to his door; you can run away from the responsibilities you took upon yourself by opening the Grimoire; or you can embrace this world and conquer the challenges the Vagabond left for you. Someday, you will see your father again. I promise."

"Abandon my dad or get him killed? Adele, that's not a choice."

Kara ran her hands through her hair, pulling on the roots. Braeden leaned against the wall and suppressed a sigh. This would take some time, then.

"I guess I would rather he think I disappeared than get him killed. I just—" Her voice cracked and the rest came out a whisper. "I just hope he forgives me."

Garrett set a hand on her shoulder. "You should focus more on what lies ahead. You're lucky to have the Grimoire to help you. Do you know what its clover symbol means?"

She shook her head, but wouldn't look up.

"The Vagabond told me once that it represents the four primary roads you can take in life: happiness, hatred, success, and failure. They are balanced choices, always intertwined with each other, and whichever of the four paths you take will lead you down another. The stone in its center is experience, a Mecca of wisdom bred from the lessons learned and mistakes made. Keep that with you and you will never be lost.

"And prince"—Garrett turned to Braeden with a scowl—"whether or not it's wise to do so, I trust your intentions are good. We need you to take Kara to Hillside. She will feel the most welcome there, I think, and you know the way. Will you do this?"

"Of course."

Braeden wanted to tell himself he was helping her because it was the good and selfless thing to do, but that was a lie and he knew it. He hadn't been able to find the Grimoire, true, but its keeper had found him instead. It was possible he could still use the book.

Adele whistled, and a shadow trotted through the wall. Braeden jumped. Its blurred edges made it almost impossible to see, but when he did find the angle at which it became visible, he couldn't help but grin.

It was a flaer: the only creature in Ourea that could walk through walls. Its narrow face and sleek body made it look like an oversized dog, except that it was as tall as a horse. Its long fur coat glistened, and its tail rocked from side to side like a pendulum.

Adele introduced the flaer as Rowthe and explained what it could do, but Braeden's mind was busy phrasing how he would ask Kara for help. She seemed to be naïve, so a straightforward approach might work. The longer he waited, though, the more she would learn and the more careful he would have to be with his request. Then again, if he—

"It's Ourea," Kara muttered. Her voice pulled him from his thoughts and back into the cold little cave with the long scratch on its wall. "There are dragons and monsters. Of course this thing can take us through *walls*." Her voice was so low that neither muse acknowledged she'd said anything at all.

Braeden grinned. At least this new vagabond was fun.

"If you ever need Rowthe, simply whistle for him. He will come to you," Adele said.

The flaer crept up to Kara and lowered its nose into her hand. She was calm, breathing steadily once more, and scratched its ears in a withdrawn welcome. Rowthe stood still as she used a boulder to climb onto its back, but it pranced and pinned its ears against its head when Braeden tried to do the same.

"Be kind, Rowthe," Adele muttered.

The flaer flicked an ear toward her as she spoke and rooted itself in place at her command. It craned its neck toward Braeden as he walked around to hoist himself onto its back. It stomped as he mounted.

"Go directly to Hillside and don't stop," Adele commanded. "Once my trust is broken, prince, you will never get it back."

He nodded from his perch behind Kara, avoiding eye contact to quell the rising tide of sarcastic rebuttal. He turned to wish Adele the best, despite their cold welcome, but she and Garrett were gone. The cave was quiet, empty and still, and Kara nudged his side.

"Which way, Braeden?"

He paused. She was still pale, her eyes downcast and conflicted. Adele had told him not to break the muses' trust, but he didn't care about them. If he wanted anyone's loyalty, it was Kara's.

"Do you want to see your father?" he asked.

She twisted around and scanned his face. "Are you testing me right now?"

"You made me relive losing Mother. I would give anything to have spoken to her once more, to tell her that I would find my own way. You have that chance."

"I don't want to get him killed, Braeden."

"Then we need to hurry. We can take him with us to Hillside before anyone finds him. He will be safe there. You, however, need to be prepared with a quick explanation of what's going on so that he comes with us. We will not have much time to explain."

Her hands tightened into fists as she weighed the consequences of this new option. Her gaze flitted around the room, no doubt waiting for the muses to appear again, but it was calm.

"My Camry is in a parking lot on Salish Mountain in the Montana Rockies," she said.

Rowthe's ears pricked backward, as their destination must have flashed across Kara's mind. The creature took a few short steps and bolted through the wall. A sharp kick twitched in Braeden's stomach as they passed through the rock, and before he could blink, they were racing through an underground cavern somewhere in the mountain's depths. Their sprint left him no choice but to wrap his arms around Kara in an attempt to grab the beast's mane, but she hardly seemed to care that he'd touched her. Her eyes shifted out of focus.

Doubt panged in his gut. He hoped this wasn't a mistake.

CHAPTER SEVEN
HOME

Kara could barely see in the dark tunnels and caverns through which Rowthe ran. The walls blurred by, passing too quickly to appreciate. Guilt and panic wrestled in her stomach when she thought about seeing her father. But, despite the nerves, the adrenaline keeping her awake began to fade. The sleep in the lumbering cage was, apparently, not enough to sustain the constant rush of excitement Ourea offered. Her eyelids drooped, only snapping open with each kick to her stomach that came from passing through yet another wall.

Eventually, her eyes glazed over and the deep exhaustion won. Her last thought as she fell into a deep sleep involved the hope that Braeden would keep her from falling.

Kara awoke to a sudden, cold breeze. They were in a parking lot staring at her borrowed multi-colored Camry as the calm night chirped around them. Leaves rustled in the wind. A sprinkling of stars dotted the dark blue sky above. Braeden dismounted, and she slid off as well. She didn't notice he'd offered her a hand until she landed on her feet.

She studied the night sky. "Wasn't there daylight when we left Ourea? How long was I out?"

He shrugged. "Lichgates take you to a pocket of the earth, so that was a different place, in a different—well, I guess you could call it time zone. I would say only about six hours have passed since Deidre threw you in that cage with me."

She walked toward the car and shook her head, restraining a sarcastic comment about where Ourea could stick its time zones and monsters.

The Camry wasn't *actually* hers. She rented it from a local couple each summer for next to nothing. It was their extra car, rusty and dented, which she assumed had long ago been paid-off and kept only out of convenience. It had only one headlight. Though mostly green, it did have a blue hood and a yellow passenger's side door. Oh, it was a thing of *beauty*. It was also the only car in the lot. It wouldn't jump alive any second. It might not start, but that had nothing to do with magic. It was just old.

She shoved her hands into her jean pockets and looked out over the poorly lit gravel lot. The hikers who came here every day had normal lives that came and went. They didn't know a thing about Ourea or the lichgate on the secret trail.

Maybe it was all a dream. Maybe she was about to wake up in the gazebo, or even better, in her car, never to see Ourea again. Then, she could get back to her life.

"Kara?"

Her eyes sprang back into focus. She was leaning on the car, looking out over the parking lot. Braeden stood by the passenger's side door, one hand resting on the hilt of his broadsword. She laughed and simultaneously stifled the urge to cry.

"Are you all right?"

She nodded and reached for her keys, the metal rattling as she pulled them out of her pocket. A dawning realization made her pause with one hand on the door handle.

"Of all the—my keys survived those roots, but my seven *hundred* dollar phone didn't? Are you kidding me?"

"What about roots, now?"

"Nothing." She sighed and unlocked her door.

She had to fiddle with the cracked handle until it opened, and when it finally did, she slipped into the driver's seat. The cloth chair rubbed her bruised back through the tears in her shirt. She reached across the passenger seat to unlock the other door, but paused halfway. She could probably leave Braeden. Nothing was stopping her from driving off and pretending that this had never happened. Her fingers hovered on the handle, but she ultimately reached across the final inch of space and opened the door with another sigh. He unbuckled his scabbard and held it as he climbed in.

Kara glanced through the rear-view mirror as Rowthe slunk into the forest with a swish of his shadowy tail. She said a little prayer to the engine, held her breath, turned the key, and breathed again only once the car started. Braeden's sword hilt rattled against the window, and the prince in her passenger's seat fidgeted with his seatbelt.

"That doesn't work. Just hold it if we pass a cop."

He laughed. "Fantastic. I can survive isen, but I'm not certain I could survive a crash in this archaic box."

"Something tells me you can't exactly be a car guru."

"I told you that I travel out to the human world all of the time, remember? I usually find my way out here on isen hunts. I spent half of my adult life out here."

Kara took a deep breath and gripped the wheel tighter.

Just go with it.

"Right. So how do you find the isen?" she asked.

She shifted gears, toying with the fantasy of driving her borrowed car along the old, hidden trail and straight into the lichgate. In her daydream, the gazebo exploded in what she considered to be just revenge. Lots of fire was involved.

"We get reports of missing yakona, usually," he said, answering the question she'd already forgotten she'd asked. "Whenever there are rumors of even one isen, I have to investigate. When Richard taught me to hunt them, it was the only thing I could do better than anyone else. Since Hillside is the closest thing I have to a home, this is how I repay them."

"I can't tell which you hate more, isen or Carden."

He scowled and looked out the window as she turned onto the main road. She should've kept her stupid mouth shut.

"Isen enslave souls. It's hard not to hate something like that," he said.

It took roughly fifteen minutes to get to the rental house, which had light streaming from every window. The car bounced as it pulled into the driveway and sputtered as she threw it into park. She unbuckled her seatbelt and took a deep breath before she could bring herself to slide out of the car.

"Stay here, Braeden."

"Do you think he'll like it if he sees me when he looks out the window? I should come in."

She leaned on the Camry and examined the prince. His smudged green tunic and black pants matched the thick broadsword resting against the window. Its silver hilt peeked from the green leather scabbard and glinted in the street light. She cocked an eyebrow.

"You look like something out of a trashy romance novel."

"I promise it'll be worse if I stay out here."

"You don't know my—whatever. Suit yourself."

She slammed the door and headed inside, avoiding the cracks in the sidewalk on her way. A row of bushes lined the path and Molly, her father's limestone gargoyle, peered out from under one of them. Molly was about the size of a cat and bared its stone teeth from behind the sharp leaves, serving its purpose as the guardian of spare keys.

Kara twisted the front doorknob without trying the lock, and the door opened with a loud creak. The tiny hallway was warmer than the cool summer night outside, but she left the door ajar for the yakona behind her. She doubted her dad would care about the electric bill much longer.

There were several doorways along the hall, each leading to the various rooms of the first floor. Stairs hugged the wall to the right, and a china cabinet filled with photos rested against the wall across from them. Her dad had packed every photo they owned this year and set them up in their rental home as soon as they'd walked in. That way, he'd reasoned, her mom could be there with them on this lonely summer trip.

Kara swallowed the uncomfortable tightness in her throat and looked over the shelves. Her well-documented childhood sat on the wooden planks in frames and poorly made macaroni art.

A sharp thud and a muffled curse came from behind her. She turned to see Braeden rubbing his head, and on his second try, he took much better care to duck through the entry. He loomed in the hallway once he was through, the hardwood floors creaking as he walked, and his loud bang was answered by a flush upstairs.

"Lovely, Dad," Kara muttered.

"Your mother was a beautiful woman," Braeden said, nodding to a family portrait framed in the cabinet.

She wanted to say, 'so was yours,' but she never got the chance.

Bathroom light flooded the upstairs hallway. Her dad barreled around the corner and down the stairs, only stopping when he saw her standing in the foyer. He crumpled his newspaper and took the last four steps in a single leap before he wrapped his arms around her and pulled her into the tightest hug of her life.

"Are you okay? Who is that? Where were you? Why didn't you—"

"Dad, I'm fine, but we don't have much time. You need to sit."

She pushed him into the dining room and into one of its antique chairs, but she didn't know what to say once he sat down. Her dad's eyes flitted between her and Braeden, no doubt trying to figure out what was going on using the few clues he had.

"You'll never guess what I found today, Dad."

"You are in so much trouble, kid. I don't care if you're 'just taking a break' from college. If you live in my house you need to be in touch with me! I was scared out of my mind, Kara! Your phone went to voicemail, you—"

"I know, Dad. I know. I'm sorry. Some roots ate my phone. Well, no, that's part of the story. I should start at the beginning."

"Look at those scratches! Your shirt—did you fall again? Are you okay?" He reached out to check her arms for bruises.

"What? No. Well, kind of. But Dad, just listen!"

Kara took off the clover pendant and set it in front of him. He glanced at the necklace, but quickly glared at her again.

"Girl, you have two seconds to give me answers."

"I found a secret path while I was on Salish. It took me to this gorgeous overlook with a little gazebo. Well, it wasn't a gazebo. It was a lichgate—no, I'll explain that part in a minute—I walked through it and I took this second little trail down a cliff. There was this door—no, Dad, listen!—a door in the mountain. I'm serious!" She cut off his very reasonable argument that people don't build doors in mountains.

"It started raining so I opened the door and it kind of, well, roots grabbed me and ate my phone and I left my pack in the lichgate. I fell into this library and found a book and there was whispering, and then—" She groaned. "This isn't working."

She rubbed her face in frustration as Braeden desperately tried to stifle his laughter behind one of his massive hands. Her dad pointed a firm finger at him.

"You rufied my daughter, didn't you?"

"No, sir."

"I'm getting my shotgun"—he pointed again to the prince—"you better be gone when I come back. And young lady, you'd better not move."

He glared at Kara and thundered from the room.

"Dad!"

Braeden shrugged. "You tried, Kara. I'll grab him and we can explain later."

She tapped the necklace. "Grimoire, what do I have to do to make you come back? Book, come on!"

Her dad returned with his shotgun in time to see glittering specks of dust jump and spark out of the necklace. They gleamed and congealed until they formed the glimmering blue outline of a book. As they all watched in the heavy silence, the Grimoire solidified. The stone in the pendant was clear once more.

The Grimoire's thick red cover and aged pages were as heavy and real as they had been in the library. Kara sighed with relief and rubbed the binding.

Her dad sat down and stared at the book, the gun forgotten in his hand. He reached out to touch the leather as if it would bite him and flinched when his fingers grazed the spine. He jumped up from the table, rubbed his neck until it was red, and looked back at Kara. He didn't even blink.

"What was *that*?"

"That's called magic, old man," a woman said from the doorway. "And tonight, your baby girl became one of the most coveted magical artifacts on the planet."

Kara recognized that voice. Panic raced through her body. She slipped the clover necklace over her neck and pushed her chair back, its wooden legs scraping against the hardwood floor. A familiar brunette strode into the dining room.

Braeden drew his sword, and her dad did a double-take at the outdated weapon when he raised his shotgun.

Deidre clicked her tongue at the Stelian prince and grinned. "Haven't you learned your lesson, boy? I always win."

He wrung his hands on the sword hilt. "Not this time. Kara, you need to go."

"Hold on there, Prince Charming. I just want to have a little chat. Girls only." Deidre said. She looked at her reflection in a mirror on the wall and patted her hair as she spoke.

"Kara, why can't you have any *normal* friends?" Her dad ran his hand over his receding hairline and licked his lips. His hand shook as he hovered over the trigger, his eyes shifting from the isen to the yakona without knowing what either of them truly was. He pointed the shotgun at Deidre.

"Oh, how scary." She snickered.

"That's enough! You and the boy need to get out of here. Now!"

Deidre glanced toward the Grimoire sitting on the table and walked toward it. Kara grabbed it and held it to her chest, backing away without knowing what else to do. Deidre shifted her gaze and walked with her, matching her pace.

"You can't run from me, little one," she said.

Kara held her breath and wished that the Grimoire was hidden like it had been before. She thought over the library, trying to figure out how she'd made it disappear the first time.

The book glowed in her hands as if it had read her thoughts, casting blue light on everyone in the room. It imploded, leaving a cluster of dust suspended in the air. Kara coughed. The stone in the pendant glowed blue. Deidre continued forward, only a dozen feet away, now, but Kara stopped when her back hit the wall.

Braeden ducked between her and Deidre, his sword raised to the isen's neck. The demon laughed but stopped moving, throwing her hands up in mock surrender. Her dad took a step closer, his shotgun still trained on Deidre, but he grunted.

"Kara, why do I get the feeling that this gun is useless right now?"

"I'm sorry, Dad."

"Get to the car, both of you!" Braeden ordered.

"I wouldn't do that," Deidre said. "All of Ourea is looking for the two of you. Some were only a few miles behind me. I promise that I'm your least painful option. Just come on over here, Kara dear, and I'll make all this nastiness go away."

"Kara, get out of here!" Braeden yelled again.

He raised his free hand and every vase in the room floated at the command. He flicked them toward Deidre with a sudden twitch of his fingers. Glass and porcelain hurled toward her. The isen shifted her gaze to Braeden and winked; when she did, all but one of the vases shattered. Flowers and potpourri rained onto the floor. Water splattered and rushed along the hardwood. Deidre smirked, lifting a freckled hand toward the last airborne vase and making a fist. It exploded in mid-air.

Kara froze, back to the wall, as shards of glass flew into her hair. Her dad grabbed her wrist and ran for the back door, clenching his shotgun so tightly that his knuckles bleached from the effort. She ran with him but turned her head in time to see Deidre lunge. The isen's outstretched hands reached for Kara's neck. A thin, silver barb extended from her right palm like a cat's claw.

Braeden dove faster, though, and grabbed the isen's outstretched arm, spinning her around so that she flew onto the table with a hard crash. The wood shattered beneath her weight, shooting splinters into the air. Something outside wailed. The lights flickered. Window panes shook, and her dad stopped short at the back door. He peered through the glass and shivered at whatever he saw. Kara turned back to the fight.

Deidre pushed herself to her feet and swung at Braeden. He ducked, his fist erupting into black flame. She slid behind him and kicked out his knee, sending him to the floor long enough for her to wrap her arm around his neck. His face went purple from the lack of air. She spun him onto his back and kicked him in the gut with the heel of her boot. He sputtered and curled around the blow, but Deidre grabbed his collar and hurled him through the dining room wall with a single, crushing blow.

He barreled into the night as the cool summer darkness leaked through the ripped wallpaper and splintered wood of the shattered wall. The power flickered and popped as it went out completely.

Moonlight shone a spotlight on the now-dark room, icing Deidre's cold face as she stood and cracked her neck. The isen snarled and charged Kara again, fingers once more outstretched.

Kara lifted her hands in defense. Her veins smoldered. The familiar heat from the library raced through her, making her pulse ricochet through her ears. Time slowed. Every ringlet on Deidre's head rippled behind her like a slow wave in the air. Warmth pooled in Kara's palm, ready to spring, just waiting for a command.

Something threw its weight against her shoulder, tossing her off-balance. She toppled. The floor loomed closer, and the moment sped up once more. She looked back as Deidre wrapped her hand around her dad's neck. The isen scowled, but couldn't stop. The silver barb dug into his spine. His body tensed. His breath stopped. Deidre's eyes glazed over. In seconds, he choked and fell with a thud to the ground.

Kara screamed. Her heart pushed against her ribcage as her father's corpse stared back at her with wide eyes.

Deidre's skin stretched and cracked. Bits broke away and fell to the ground to reveal the familiar nose and bushy eyebrows of her dad's face beneath the demon's. His features overwhelmed hers until he stood next to his own limp body.

Kara screamed again as he looked down at her and blinked.

"Take care of yourself. I love you, Bear," he said. His voice was calm.

He bent down and kissed her forehead, but she couldn't speak. His face started to ripple, the skin peeling and cracking once more as he spoke.

"You need to look in the bottom of the photo cabinet. I'm starting to think you'll need what I found before we left Tallahassee."

His face melted. Drops of skin rolled along his cheeks like wax and pooled in the growing cracks on his face. His brow wrinkled and peeled, revealing Deidre's flawless face underneath. Kara froze in horror as the isen took over once more, unable to move until the dark brunette curls finally popped from his head and her dad was gone.

"No! Dad!"

Kara grabbed the shotgun out of his corpse's lifeless hand and set the barrel against the isen's forehead. Deidre's eyes were still unfocused. She stared ahead, unseeing, as the thick barrel made a dent in her smooth skin.

Kara pulled the trigger.

It clicked.

He hadn't loaded the gun.

Kara grabbed the shotgun by the barrel and whacked Deidre in the face with the butt of the gun, sending her to the floor. She jumped over the demon without waiting to see where she fell and bolted to the hallway, fighting for her breath as she tore open the drawers of the photo cabinet. She found a small, antiquated chest in the bottom drawer. It had a worn brass lock and no key hole.

"There are only a few things in this world that you should never do," Deidre said from behind her. "Pissing me off is one of them."

The isen seized her arm, spun her around, and shoved her into the cabinet. Glass shattered. Cloth ripped. Kara's arms and neck stung. Deidre sneered and pressed her deeper into the glass and memories. Picture frames crashed to the floor. Thick shards of the broken shelves sliced Kara's arms, cutting through her already stained shirt.

"I'll kill you!" Kara reached for the isen's face and ran her nails along the icy eyes, drawing blood from one eyelid. Deidre screamed and threw her against another wall. She landed with a hard, heavy thud.

Kara's head spun. Her vision blurred. The right side of her body was numb. The floor became the wall and the roof disappeared as the world tilted around her. A hazy figure loomed on the ceiling—or was it the floor? The shadow had dark, wavy hair. Five of its fingers reached for her neck.

Another hazy figure materialized behind the first one. They both dissolved into darkness as the throbbing pain in Kara's head forced her into unconsciousness.

CHAPTER EIGHT
THE KINGDOM OF HILLSIDE

Cozy warmth engulfed Kara in a comfortable blend of just right and perfect. A hot towel lay on her forehead, and as she brushed the warm cotton, a bead of water fell down the crevices in her fingers. Orange light poured through her eyelids. Her head ached. She would have given anything to never have to open her eyes or think or feel or hurt again, but an urgent worry tugged on her mind and she couldn't ignore it. She ran her hands over the space beside her, savoring the chill of a satin sheet and the soft indents of a mattress. A cold draft of air blew across her cheek.

All at once, she remembered.

She screamed and bolted upright, her vision still blurred from the throbbing ache that wracked her skull. Every muscle burned. Her ear and eyebrow stung.

Green figures loomed everywhere, each with no face and no outline. Brown columns and gold pools surrounded her. The figures leaned in. A dozen hands pushed and pulled her backward, back into the pillows and sheets. She fought them. Murmuring buzzed through the room. She shot a kick toward the nearest figure and caught him in the chest.

"Ow! Kara, relax!"

It was Braeden's voice. She stopped.

The hands released her, and she rubbed her eyes until her vision cleared. The brown columns were bedposts on a canopy bed. The sheer gold curtains that surrounded the bed frame had been pulled back and draped over the posts in thick folds. A green comforter wound around her, tangled in her legs and arms, and a full-length mirror in the corner reflected a forest through the window. The hands belonged to several gaping women, each wrapped in a long, green dress. Some held towels and water while others balanced piles of white gauze in their hands, but every one of them wore an identical, confused expression.

"Ladies"—Braeden's voice came from her right—"may we have a minute?"

He sat in an ornate wooden chair beside the bed, his hair a tangled mess. Deep bags puffed under his eyes, and black smudges streaked along his chin and neck. Red patches stained his clothes. *Blood*. Kara shivered.

The ladies hurried out of the room, setting the gauze and other equipment on a table at the foot of the bed. Most avoided her gaze, but the last to leave smiled warmly through the crack in the door before it clicked shut behind her.

The smile was probably meant to be reassuring, but the woman's brunette curls and the freckles on her nose just reminded Kara of the way Deidre had sneered when she'd shoved her into the glass photo cabinet.

Vomit tickled her throat. Her cheeks flushed again. She occupied herself with analyzing the stitching in the comforter, counting the threads to avoid thinking or remembering. She didn't notice Braeden speaking until he lifted her chin.

He shifted to sit on the blanket and studied her, stretching his arm as far as it could go. His callused hands rubbed against her jaw line as he tilted her head.

"What are you doing?" she asked, pulling away from him.

"You hit that glass cabinet head first. I wanted to make sure that the wounds were healing. They are, but you're still in shock. How are you feeling physically? Is there any pain?"

Oh, there was pain.

She returned to the gold thread, but even counting the curves in the lining couldn't stop the coming flood of tears. She hid her face in her knees and gripped her legs closer, trying and failing to stifle the sobs. Her dad's face haunted her.

"I got him killed, Braeden. I led Deidre right to him, even after Adele—" Her voice broke, and she cried into her torn and bloody jeans. Braeden patted her once on the back and cleared his throat several times.

"He, uh, he's not—" Braeden sighed and shifted closer. "Look. This is my fault. I let you go when I was supposed to just bring you here. Hey, look at me."

He gently pushed her shoulders back so that she had to lift her head, but she chose instead to stare out the window. The green canopy of a forest reflected hot sunshine, and a mountain ridge broke across the close horizon and the otherwise clear sky.

"Where are we?" she asked.

"Hillside."

"Where's Rowthe?"

"Rowthe returned to the muses after we arrived here," he answered, eyes shifting to the floor. "Kara, stop changing the subject. This was too close a call. I can't forgive myself for what I let you do."

She pushed her cheek against her purple and black knee, which was exposed through the large rip in her jeans that she'd gotten from the dirt closet. The sting from pushing against the bruise cleared her head.

"I can't blame you for my choices," she said. "I knew it wasn't safe."

A gust of wind shoved against the outside wall with a sudden blow that rattled the window. Braeden kept quiet, thankfully. Kara didn't want him to speak. She used the silence to stare and think, and this time, she let her memories take over.

She was five. She stood on her dad's sneakers as he stomped around the kitchen, swinging her hands around with his. Her mom walked in and started laughing at the awkward dance. They were waltzing, her dad informed her, and she shouldn't interrupt masters while they practiced.

Kara meant to laugh, but it came out as a whimper.

Her fingers ached, but when she stretched them to alleviate the soreness, she flinched as a sharp and searing pain raced through her entire arm. Every inch of her torso was covered in either her bloody shirt or strips of green cloth that were stained with dark red splotches. Another bandage on her neck tightened as she stretched her back, and the base of her skull stung as if she'd set it against a hot burner. She glanced over to Braeden, whose emerald tunic was ripped up to his elbows.

"We barely escaped," he said. "So I only had enough time to heal your larger wounds. The longer you wait to heal an injury, the more energy and effort it takes, so your less severe scratches will just have to heal naturally."

She sighed. "Well, thank you."

He glared at her, eyes narrowing in confusion. "How are you not trying to kill me?"

She cocked an eyebrow. "Well, *I'm* sorry. Hand me your sword."

"I just don't understand how you can be so calm."

Her throat caught on another wave of sobs, but she swallowed hard and managed to quell them. "It's what my mom would have wanted. She always said to be smart and be nice because what we do affects more people than we think. I can't blame you for something I agreed to do, even if I don't want to admit it's my fault."

He scoffed, but it evolved quickly into a laugh. "You are stronger than I gave you credit for, Vagabond."

"Thanks, I think."

"All of Ourea knows about you now," he said. "Deidre was trying to attack *you*, not your father. I hope you know that. She was trying to steal your soul to gain control over the Grimoire. If your father hadn't stepped in, you would have become her slave."

"Slave?"

"I'm guessing she was a few hundred years old, but an isen isn't naturally immortal," he explained. "They have to steal a soul every decade or so to keep their youth. But when they steal a soul, they also steal its physical appearance, skills, and even its magic. We yakona fear them because they trap your soul for as long as they live. Deidre was definitely aiming for you, not your father."

Kara cradled her head in her hands and remembered the barb in the isen's palm. Her heart skipped a few beats at the thought of what it could possibly be like to be trapped in another body, unable to control anything.

"Oh Dad," she whispered. "I'm so sorry."

She had a fuzzy view of the room through her fingers, but she noticed something flit across the mirror. A crane burst through the window, landing on the floor and flapping its wings to steady itself in the gale that followed it in. Braeden stood and drew his sword. The crane flickered and grew taller, until its feathers dissolved into coppery skin. Adele now stood before them.

The muse wore the same clothes from when she and Garrett had rescued them, but this time she was armed with a murderous glare. She didn't even blink as the wind from the open window rustled her hair, churning the pale curls in the same way it toyed with the tree canopy beyond the window.

"How could you be so foolish?" she asked, her gaze fixed on Kara.

"I—"

Adele lifted the circular pendant around her neck. The diamond which had once been one of Kara's tears reflected green and blue specks of light.

"This becomes warm to the touch when you are in trouble, Vagabond, and did so less than an hour after I left you alone. I know which choice you made. You are young, but I still thought you were wiser than that!"

"I can explain—" Braeden started.

"I was speaking to our Council about the two of you, no less," she said, ignoring him. "But one does not leave the Council for anything on this earth. I had to wait to be released when I knew that you were in danger and I could do nothing about it. I can't help you if you do such reckless things!"

Adele took a deep breath and glared out the window.

"However, I can't be harsh. You made a choice and you will forever suffer the consequences. Hopefully, you will make future decisions more carefully."

Kara whimpered as the guilt settled deeper into her gut. Every time she closed her eyes, she relived the distorted way his mouth opened when Deidre stabbed his spine with the barb in her palm.

She buried her head in her knees and wrapped her arms under her legs so tightly she could hardly breathe. The lemon scent of her dad's fabric softener clung to her jeans, mixed with the rotten stench of dried blood and sweat. The mattress shifted under the weight of another body, but she didn't look up.

"Forgive yourself, but learn from this," Adele said, her voice close and quiet. "Forgive but never forget."

Kara sighed. Numbness seeped into her aching arms and neck until the energy, guilt, and hatred evaporated and all that remained was exhaustion. Her skin lost its feeling and its warmth. The world faded until the only thought she could sustain without the urge to cry involved taking a shower.

"I think she needs to be alone, Adele," Braeden said.

"Call someone to draw her a bath, then. There is more that she and I must discuss."

"She needs to rest," he said, grumbling. A second later, his warm hand rubbed Kara's shoulder. "I'll be back after you've had some time to yourself, if you would like my company."

She set her chin on her knees and forced a smile, but the only thing she wanted at that moment was the bath. He walked out of the room and shut the door without looking back. Adele continued speaking as if he'd never been there in the first place.

"Has the Blood requested your presence?"

"Come on, Adele, I just woke up."

"She will want to speak with you soon, regardless. Yakona royals aren't sympathetic. You must be careful, Kara. You will not have many allies here, and I will not always be able to help you. I am not supposed to be here, even now."

"I'll try."

Her voice softened to barely a whisper. "Garrett trusts Braeden, though I can't bring myself to do so. I concede that he alone saved you from Deidre. It's clear that he will protect you, but what worries me is that I don't know *why* he wants you safe. I fear that it's only because he hasn't figured out how to control you, but Garrett disagrees.

"Because of Garrett's trust, I must urge you not to speak of Braeden's past. If he were to be discovered, they would kill him without a second thought for his many years of service, and you would be without a guardian. Ourea is a vicious world. Though the two of you are unlikely friends, you must protect each other."

"I won't say anything."

"Good. Be cautious."

Adele shifted in her seat and changed form. Her copper skin shrank into tawny feathers, her body rippling until she was a tiny sparrow. She chirped once, pecked at Kara's shoe, and shot through the still-open window.

Kara stared at the flapping shutters and ran her fingers through her hair. She threw herself backward into her pillow, dirty and sweaty and finally alone. A blue light glowed from under her chin, and when she touched her neck, her fingers fumbled across the cold clover pendant. The rays of the stone's blue light danced as she moved her fingers over it.

In an effort to figure out how she'd summoned it before, she imagined the Grimoire in her hands. The memory of its soft leather cover filled her palms and prickled her fingertips.

Dust sprang from the pendant. The blue light in the gem faded to nothing as the funnel of shimmering ash pooled in her lap and congealed into the familiar and very solid red cover of the Grimoire.

Without waiting for her to ask a question, the book flipped open to a picture of the hooded Vagabond. He leaned against a dead tree, its naked branches marking the foreground of the image while a dark forest consumed the landscape behind him. There was no text. She picked at the corner of the page with her fingers.

"You didn't tell me it would be this bad."

The Vagabond's lips twitched into a smile. Her heart jumped. She shifted the page for better light, but the smile was gone when she looked again. Shivers raced up her back, but she took a deep breath. It could have been a play of the light, or even her eyes shifting from her exhaustion. She was hardly at her best.

"So what do I do now?"

The pages flipped again with their own fitful intensity and finally settled on a page that had only one line of neat, handwritten red text.

> Find the Vagabond's village. The secrets there will make you stronger.

"How do I find it?"

A single page turned.

> There is a map which will lead you there, but it was broken into four pieces to keep the village's location safe. Each piece is hidden in one of the four kingdoms the Vagabond visited. Once assembled, this map is your key into the village. Find all four and you will find your way.

"Man," she grumbled, rubbing her neck. She didn't want to find a village. She didn't want to keep this book. She *wanted* to go home, to go back in time, to forget all of this.

The pages flipped again and settled on a thick chunk of text.

A VAGABOND'S PURPOSE
JOURNAL ENTRY #537

> When I became the Vagabond, I sought to restore the peace treasured by the lost city of Ethos before its great collapse, when it crumbled from within. Ethos was a mighty city where all of the yakona kingdoms lived as one, but even in my day it's an ancient legend. Now, war is endless and hopeless.

I am feared because I have no blood loyalty to my Hillsidian king. For a yakona, loyalty isn't a choice. The Blood can control his subjects at any moment and, if powerful enough, from afar. It's a dangerous and frequently abused gift. My freedom is therefore both envied and loathed.

I am an orphan and was raised in Hillside, but left the city to travel and learn. I discovered Ourea's wonders and its failures, writing of them in the journal I later adapted to become this Grimoire. This book has a life of its own, can think for itself, and has no limit to the number of its pages. To sort through my entries, merely ask the right question. Its pages will find the answer.

Above all else, I learned this: in all things, there must be balance. I sought to teach this to the world, to remind all yakona of the greatness with which we once ruled Ourea, but my teachings were misconstrued. Those who listened heard only that I had no loyalty. I was allowed to travel to every kingdom except for the Stele, but only because I was seen as a novelty. A curiosity. I was tolerated.

There were a select few who I came across in my journeys who wished to be free from the loyalty which enslaved them, and I gave them that freedom. They became vagabonds, though they never had Grimoires of their own. Some stayed to help me in my journeys, while others continued on with their own lives; either way, they were free to do as they pleased. You, too, will someday learn to create vagabonds as I once did.

The Bloods misinterpreted my intentions when I made some of their people vagabonds. They thought of me as a threat, however fervently I insisted otherwise. I wanted peace, but all they could understand was war. I was forced into hiding because of my actions, but I don't regret what I did. I never will, as freedom so often comes with a price.

Rumors spread that my book could dominate entire kingdoms, which I thought to be ridiculous—at first. I had simply not yet asked the right question. Once I did, I realized my studies had, indeed, found the weakness in each of the kingdoms except for the one which I was never permitted to visit: the Stele. My quest for knowledge had brought forth a weapon that could destroy all but the most savage way of life.

If you are to take my place, you must trust no one who has a blood loyalty. The time will come when you will doubt everything you stand for, but you must push forward and never stop. Don't let others speak for you, or you will lose your voice forever.

Kara leaned back against the headboard but didn't lift her eyes from the pages. They began to flip again, one after another, until the book turned to the back cover. A single sentence was carved into the hard binding, written in a crooked and hasty script.

You are the last of us.

❦CHAPTER NINE
QUESTIONS

"You didn't hear a thing I just said, did you?"

Kara jumped at the voice and pulled the Grimoire to her chest in her surprise. She had tuned out everything else in her room at Hillside as she read, and it took her a moment to get her bearings.

A slender girl in a simple green gown with no sleeves stood at the foot of the bed, hands making dents in the soft blanket as she leaned on the comforter. The Hillsidian girl had rich black hair, brown skin, and a wide smile that covered most of her face. She laughed.

"I apologize if I scared you! My name's Twin. I've actually been here for a good five minutes, just talking away. I thought you heard me come in. I brought you clothes."

Twin held up the dress in her hands.

"Oh, thank you!"—Kara paused—"I hope this isn't rude, but may I please have some pants?"

The girl laughed as if it had been a moderately interesting joke and draped the dress over the mirror, blocking the view of the forest. Kara closed the Grimoire and settled into the bed as Twin closed the window.

"Braeden asked me to help you while you stay with us in Hillside, so if you need anything, just let me know." Twin glanced over a shoulder. "What book are you reading?"

Kara cleared her throat. "It's nothing."

"That sounds exciting." Twin giggled and walked into an adjoining room behind the mirror, which Kara hadn't noticed before. The rush of water filling a tub resonated across the room's tile.

Kara rubbed the small diamond in her pendant and wished the Grimoire away. The red leather glowed and broke into dust that spiraled into her pendant. The diamond gleamed, blue once more.

She stood, wincing as she put weight on her feet. The throbbing in her muscles worsened. Standing was painful, but she hobbled to the window in a stubborn effort to look out onto the forest. Beyond even the most distant line of trees were towering, snowcapped mountains, where clouds scraped the summits and reflected sunlight from the noon sky.

"Well, that should be ready for you," Twin announced as she came back into the room. "I will let you control the heat as you please, of course."

"Is there a temperature gauge or something?"

"What?" Twin paused, rubbing her hands together and waiting for the punch-line.

"You know, a knob. A handle, or—"

"You can use whatever method of water-warming you prefer, but I have never heard of this knob technique."

"What? Oh—" Kara laughed. "I'm human. I don't know magic, or at least, I'm not very good at it. So unless there's a knob in there, I can't really do anything."

"You—You're human?" Twin's cheeks flushed green.

"Oh. Um..." Kara bit her lip. Was that supposed to be a secret? *Oops.*

Twin gaped, unable to move, and Kara sighed deeply. That had been stupid. There were gentler ways of introducing herself.

"Look, I'm sorry. I didn't think it would matter," Kara said, brushing Twin gently on her bare shoulder to reinforce the apology.

The light in the room drained, dissolving into the same darkness that had preceded Braeden's memory. Gold and white wisps sprang from the floor and circled around her, streaking across the black horizon in thick strokes as they painted the tree line of a forest. Other wisps carved out a path and created a tall woman with a small nose. She was muscled, with a thick sword at her waist, and she wore a tunic with loose pants. She snapped her head to the side and pulled out her sword, glaring into the forest as the wisps of light finished drawing her.

This memory was a year old, though Kara wasn't sure how she knew that or why it was important. The trees' delayed movement streaked through the air with slow trails of golden light that shuddered and disappeared on an imagined wind. The world slowed to an unnatural crawl. Her limbs moved for her, forcing her to walk forward.

The woman spun and shoved Kara into a bush.

The rough branches scratched her cheeks as she fell, but she was completely hidden when, seconds later, a man charged into the clearing. He was built from gray veins of light that burned and dissolved around him like smoke. His black eyes had no whites to them and their lifeless glint made her shudder, even in this half-lit world of memories. He lunged at the woman with the sword.

Kara couldn't move from her hiding place, even when every inch of her body screamed to jump up and help. The woman swung as he attacked. She missed his neck by an inch. He ducked and drew his own sword, swinging at her with quick, sharp jabs. She parried. He pulled a dagger from his boot and aimed for her throat, but she punched his jaw and knocked him backward.

He rolled, recovered, and shot toward her, hiding the dagger in his hand. Even though the woman saw the threat and tried to duck out of his way, she couldn't move fast enough. The small knife dug into her chest, and she fell to her knees. The man backhanded her into the grass.

Her chest heaved in a desperate attempt to breathe while her nails dug into the skin around the wound. A new color bled into the dream world as a thin trail of green poured over the golden wisps that comprised the woman's fingers. The strange man grinned and knelt, tearing off a key that dangled from a chain around the woman's neck.

Panic ate into Kara's mind when she saw the necklace, corroding all sense of self-preservation. That key was important. It involved all of Hillside's safety.

Her legs bolted forward on their own while her fingers reached for the dagger in her own belt. She jumped on the man and stabbed his eye before he even saw her move. He screamed and dropped the key, staggering and falling to the ground more than once as he retreated into the shimmering forest. She could still hear his howls of pain long after he had disappeared into the trees.

She crawled over to the woman and grabbed the hand now stained with green light. More of this new color smeared across Kara's fingers as she lifted the cold hand to her mouth and kissed it over and over. She didn't know what else to do.

The woman squeezed Kara's hand and looked around with unfocused eyes. Trails of hot breath hung in the air as her chest rose and fell in irregular bursts. She watched the sky until her breathing shuddered and stopped completely.

Kara was left alone in the field, the only proof of what had happened smeared across her palms in dark green streaks.

Light returned in a sudden, intense stream as Kara pulled free from Twin's memory and returned to the bedroom in Hillside. Twin was on the ground, tears streaming down her cheeks, so Kara bent down to help her up. The girl screamed and scooted back against the wall.

"What are you?!"

"Look, Twin, I'm sorry—"

"How—*why* did you make me relive that?"

"What did I just see?"

Twin's wide eyes quivered until she threw an arm over her face to hide the tears. She pushed herself to her feet and used the wall to regain her balance before she bolted from the room, tripping over her own legs in the process. She ran out and left the door open.

"Twin! Wait!"

Kara's body still ached, but she hurried for the door and stared out into the empty hallway. Thick red carpet with gold detail covered the floor. Red and gold wallpaper lined the walls, and countless wooden doors filled the corridor. Framed portraits of regal men and women in furs and silks hung in the space between each door, and two open staircases with thick railings descended from either end of the hallway. At the far end was a larger door, with green filigree etched into its frame. The air outside her room was still and undisturbed, without even a soul on the stairway. Twin was gone.

"I need to learn to control that," Kara said to herself.

She slapped the doorframe in her frustration, but the thick wood swallowed the noise. She shut the door and headed for the bathroom, grabbing the dress as she walked by the mirror. A sash fell onto a pair of boots, so she grabbed whatever clothing she could find and threw it all in a pile in the restroom before she closed that door as well.

White tile covered the floor and walls of the bathroom, which held a tub, a wooden dresser with several drawers, and a sink. The bathtub was nestled into a corner of the room, its edges lined with perfumes and soaps. There was no faucet—no way to add water at all, actually— and yet it was somehow filled to the brim. She combed her fingers through the clear water and grimaced. It was lukewarm, just barely hot enough for a bath, but the dried blood on her arms and neck cracked with her every movement. The simple fact was that she smelled like old sweat and this bath was not just for her own benefit.

The topmost dresser drawer sat slightly open and contained two white towels, so she pulled them out and sat on the edge of the tub. She braced herself and began removing her bandages, the linen pulling at her healing cuts as she unwound each one. Tattered cloth after tattered cloth piled beneath her until all of her scabbed-over wounds were exposed. She unzipped her jeans, yanked off what remained of her shirt, and slipped into the water.

The lukewarm bath soothed the hot skin around her scrapes and cuts, even if it did make her want to shudder in discomfort. She leaned back and stared at the ceiling, reliving the murder that Twin had witnessed.

Kara had an unconscious guess that the woman had been Twin's sister, though she didn't know quite how she could tell. She had sensed a similar bond between Braeden and the woman in his memory; the jarring panic at their deaths gave the familial relationship away.

The man in Twin's memory, however, remained a mystery. His skin had smoked, which suggested that he was a Stelian, but there was no way to know for sure unless Twin confirmed it, and that wasn't likely to happen. Kara blew bubbles beneath the water to distract herself from the guilt.

Water lapped over her nose as she soaked. The currents flowing over her skin grew colder, until she finally couldn't stomach it any longer and pulled herself out of the bathtub.

Droplets of water splattered on the white tile as she wrapped one towel around her body and rubbed her hair with the other in an effort to dry it as much as possible. She slipped into the green dress and tied the sash, doing her best to keep it from flopping, but each try made the tails more uneven. She gave up, took a deep breath, and opened the bathroom door.

Twin sat alone on the bed, her head hung, but blinked away her deep, heartbroken meditation as Kara walked into the room.

"What are you?" Twin repeated.

"I'm the Vagabond."

The girl nodded and glanced Kara over. "I heard rumors about your return, but I never thought you would be a woman. The Vagabond is supposed to be a heroic warrior, and you, well—"

Kara scoffed and folded her arms. "Don't flatter me or anything."

Twin shrugged. "You forced me to relive the most horrifying memory I have, so I'm not altogether fond of you at the moment."

"I can't control it yet. I'm sorry."

"I forgive you." Twin examined Kara's dress and forced a laugh. "You look ridiculous."

Kara curtseyed. "Thank you."

The Hillsidian smiled and walked over. She set her hands on Kara's temples. A rush of heat flew from her fingers, and the excess water in Kara's hair evaporated with a hiss. Twin turned her around to adjust the hopeless sash.

"Thank you," Kara said again, but she meant it this time. She ran her hands through her clean, dry hair.

"You're welcome."

"So, uh, is this a bad time to ask for pants?"

"I think it's unbecoming for a woman to wear pants, but you are an exception, I suppose. Give me the chance to look for something. Few women wear pants here, so a pair that fits you won't be easy to find."

"Thanks, Twin."

Kara looked over her shoulder to find the girl staring at the floor, her eyes out of focus while her hands tied the bow with practiced ease.

"That woman in my memory was my older sister," she confessed in a soft voice. "My real name is Moranna, but everyone calls me Twin because I look just like her. Everyone loved her, since she was fierce and powerful, but she and I were always complete opposites. One of the Queen's generals had promoted her days before she was killed."

Kara swallowed her questions and let Twin speak. A year of silence weighed on the girl's face, straining her voice and creating frustrated wrinkles on her otherwise smooth skin.

"We were walking along some trails beyond Hillside because she wanted to teach me not to fear the woods. Out of nowhere, she stopped talking and suddenly froze. I asked her what was wrong, but she shoved me into the bushes. And, well—"

"—and I saw the rest," Kara finished.

"I haven't left Hillside since."

"Have you ever told anyone else about this?"

"Only the Queen and her generals. I was forbidden to say anything more out of fear that it would induce panic. I'm supposed to say she died on a mission."

"I'm sorry." Kara pulled the girl into a hug. Twin flinched, but when the memory didn't return, she wrapped her arms around Kara and hugged back.

Tears sprung into Twin's eyes again. "He murdered her for a key to the kingdom. That's what scares me most."

"Is that what that key on her neck was?"

Twin pushed away and slapped her hands over her mouth. Her eyes widened, and she gasped.

"I shouldn't have told you that!"

"Does everyone have a key?"

"I—oh, *Bloods*," she cursed and sat on the bed. "No. Only a select few are ever allowed the freedom to leave without Blood approval. If you want to explore the world outside, you have to have a guide with a key. Some people never leave Hillside in their entire lives."

"Then I hope this place is bigger than it looks."

"It is. I have to ask, though, why was I forced to relive that memory in particular?"

"I can't control it, remember? I just see the moment that most defines who you are now. It just happens."

"You should buy gloves, then."

"I'll keep that in mind."

"Well, it's only fair that you tell me your memory."

"That's not going to happen." Kara laughed, but her smile faded. She couldn't have told anyone her memory if she'd wanted to. She didn't know it.

Someone knocked on the door and opened it before either of them could answer. Braeden looked in and paused, eyeing Kara as she stood by the window. He had a patch of gauze on his cheek. A bit of green bled through its center.

"Dresses become you," he said.

"Well look at that." Twin poked Kara's rib and smiled. "Apparently, even girls who never wear dresses look good in them."

With Braeden's arrival, the dark lines on Twin's face dissolved, and she laughed like she had when she first brought in the dress. Kara leaned back and caught her breath at how easily the girl had slipped back into her old self. The smile was forced, though, and her shoulders still slouched as she curtseyed and hurried through the door.

Kara pointed to the gauze on Braeden's jaw. "What happened to your face?"

"Ah, right. Well, brothers fight a lot."

"Why were you fighting, and why is it stained green?"

"We were sparring, and Hillsidian blood is green."

She nodded at his subtle hint and kept silent. He must have gotten cut while they were sparring and used someone else's blood to line the gauze after he healed too quickly. She wondered how he'd gotten the green blood.

"Would you be interested in a tour of the city, Kara?"

"Anything to get out of this room."

She walked into the hallway, and he led her toward the large door at the end of the passage.

"Braeden, Twin knows about me."

"How?"

"That weird memory thing I do."

"*Bloods*. Please try not to touch anyone else, will you? That sort of knowledge over someone's deepest thoughts could make people fear you. Touch only clothing. We might need to get you gloves."

"Man, you too?"

He grumbled something she couldn't hear and opened the door with the green filigree. She shielded her eyes at the sudden sunlight, waiting for her vision to adjust to the bright day outside. A platform extended a few feet from the threshold, and from there, a bridge crossed into the open air. The bridge's ropes had been nailed to the trunk and glued with a rosy, gleaming substance.

The rope bridge ended in a massive tree, which rose into the sky across from her and was so wide that its edges were cut off as she stared at it through the doorway. Dozens of bridges crossed to it from various places above and below, swinging gently as Hillsidians walked along them. She glanced down to the ground at least sixty feet below, but when she glanced upward, the tree's branches didn't even begin for a hundred feet. Its leaves rustled in a massive canopy hundreds of feet above that.

"That must be the biggest tree in the world!"

"That's the smallest of the five trees that make up the castle. We are standing in the largest one."

"The castle is made of five trees this big? This is amazing!" She stared at the ground and giggled.

He laughed. "I like it, too."

She raced out onto the bridge without testing it and stopped only when she was halfway across. The bridge swayed in small strokes beneath her, but it was the view that made her stomach churn with a rush of adrenaline and joy.

Two dozen roads stretched out from the castle like the rays of a sun, their edges lined with massive trees. Each tree was dozens of stories tall and as thick and round as a house, with windows that circled the trunk every ten feet or so to mark each new floor. Their branches pushed against their neighbors, creating a canopy that stretched in a perfect line along a bustling road that went on for miles.

The crisp, sweet air rushed along her face and nipped her neck. Hillsidians on the bridges waved to each other and shouted greetings before they slipped through the dozens of doors along the bark-covered castle walls.

"The Blood asked to speak with you, but the meeting isn't supposed to start for another hour," Braeden said, stopping beside her. "Let me show you a bit of my home."

Ten minutes later, after more bridges and a maze of hallways, Kara followed Braeden out into the large cobblestone courtyard from which the city's roads began. Each of the wide roads went on for a mile or more and ended in a tall golden gate in the distance. The courtyard itself, however, was massive and wide enough to encompass the main doors of two of the castle's five trees. These two trees stood in front of the other three, so that the castle was a close-knit clump of bark and branches tied together with rope bridges.

Hundreds of Hillsidians walked through the courtyard, and thousands more strolled along its neighboring streets. Children ran through the crowds, ducking lightly around the throngs of people, while the shoppers meandered by the stores on each avenue and enjoyed the afternoon heat. The crowds were ablaze with gossip. Men and women alike grinned and sniggered as they chattered about everything and nothing all at once.

Everyone was dressed in brilliant greens, beiges, and browns. Some men wore simple pants and tunics, their sleeves rolled up to reveal thick arms, while most ladies in the crowds wore long gowns that grazed the spotless cobblestone. A few of these women even wore thin gold tiaras that glittered in the radiating afternoon light, and they walked in pairs with their chins held high as they chatted. More than one of these clusters giggled as Braeden strode by.

One young woman wiped away invisible dust from her gown and smiled to him, brushing her honey-colored hair over her shoulder to reveal a slender neck. He, however, ignored her completely and continued down the road. The girl scowled after Kara, fanning her face as she turned and hustled away.

"She was flirting with you, Braeden. Did you miss that?"

"That wasn't flirting," he said.

"You're oblivious."

"No, just cautious. I try to avoid involvement."

She forced a humorless smile and glanced down at the stones in the road, pausing long enough in the shock of what she saw that he walked a good distance ahead.

The stones were changing shape.

They shifted and molded around each other, congealing to match the contours of the feet that walked over them. One of the stones even took on the shape of her face while she stared at it. It stuck out its tongue, the small heap of rock gliding out with the grate of stone scraping brick, and the stony face blew an inaudible raspberry. She laughed.

"Hillside is quirky," Braeden said, suddenly at her side once more. "It's good to see you smile after everything you've been through."

"I can't even think about anything bad right now. I needed this."

"Sorry to mention this, then, but I need to ask something of you," he said, lowering his voice so that it came out as a barely audible hiss. "You can't tell anyone that I was with you in the Stele."

"Then how did we meet?"

"The muses needed a guide to bring you here, so they found me while I was on my way back from my isen hunt. Tell them that. Drenowith are legendary here and no one knows just what they are capable of doing. They will believe it."

"Okay."

Several of the shops had tables set up on the roadside. Trays lined these tables, each filled with something different. Some had jewels that glittered as she passed, while others brimmed with fish or vegetables. Vendors laughed and chatted with their patrons, exchanging thin gold coins for their wares.

Any human alive would have been lost in the Hillside crowd. Hillsidians with every skin tone passed by, and blondes walked hand-in-hand with brunettes. Everyone looked different and no one seemed to care.

"Here we are," Braeden said.

He stopped at a shop with a particularly gnarled trunk and rifled through the small tables outside. She laughed when she realized that he had found a few trays of gloves.

The shopkeeper trotted out to them and welcomed them with a broad smile. His face was as wrinkled as his shop, and the silver hair that dangled around his ears framed his brown eyes. When Braeden insisted that they didn't need help, he flitted away to another customer.

The prince rummaged through several boxes before he handed Kara a pair for approval. A thin woven braid along the edges of each finger accented the dark brown leather gloves. Small pieces of opal had been sewn into each cuff.

"Do you like those?" he asked.

"They're beautiful, but are you seriously that afraid of me touching people?"

He grinned. "Yes."

A breathless young boy ran up to them from the crowd. He bent over his knees, huffing. "Master Braeden, the Queen would like to start the meeting early."

"Thank you." Braeden slid a coin in the boy's hand. "And that's because I know you've forgotten to get your mother's birthday present, Thomas."

Thomas blushed and bowed. "Thank you, Master Braeden. I did."

Braeden ruffled the boy's hair and ducked into the shop to pay the merchant, leaving Kara to pull on her new gloves. She tested them by wiggling her fingers as Thomas bowed again and rushed back into the crowded street.

"Are you ready?" Braeden asked when he returned.

"I have no idea."

"You'll be fine."

They walked back to the castle, which loomed overhead, and it became rapidly evident that they hadn't walked as far as she'd initially imagined. After just a few minutes, they stood at the main doors of the castle's second tree, which opened out onto the stone courtyard. These doors were propped open, and a dozen soldiers lined the edges of the stairs which led to them. Each guard stared straight ahead, unmoving.

Braeden jogged up the steps two at a time while Kara hurried to keep pace, following him through the entryway and toward a second set of broad doors that were easily twice her height.

He leaned on one of the doors, which creaked open beneath his weight to reveal a massive throne room. Two dozen white marble pillars supported the ceiling above, which was lined with thick windows that let in the summer light. Sheer green tapestries hung from the space between each pillar and rippled as the door opened. The walls and floors were covered with the same white marble as the pillars.

At the far end of the room was a raised platform shaped like a crescent moon, and on it sat three marble thrones, two of which were draped in more of the sheer, emerald green fabric that hung between the pillars. The largest chair was centered against the wall, while the two smaller thrones had been set on either side of it in a layout that reminded Kara of Carden's throne room.

A woman wearing a gold gown stood beside the middle seat, her auburn hair pulled into a bun. A shimmering golden crown inset with emeralds adorned her head.

"Oh." Braeden stopped at the door and didn't enter.

"What?"

"It seems like the Queen wants to speak with you beforehand," he said, nodding toward the woman as he nudged Kara through the door.

Kara's stomach twisted into a knot. "I have to go in there alone?"

"You'll be fine," he repeated. "So you know, her name is Lorraine, but you need to address her either as the Queen or the Blood. Nothing else."

"Why?"

A shadow passed over his face and he grimaced, his eyes trailing out of focus. He shook his head. "Just trust me."

"You're not exactly instilling me with confidence, here."

"Don't keep her waiting."

He patted Kara's shoulder and disappeared back into the hallway, letting the giant doors swing closed behind him. She turned back to the woman standing at the other end of the huge room and tried to smile, but the corners of her mouth twitched and she couldn't hold it. She coughed through the nerves in her stomach and began the considerable walk to the thrones.

The Queen nodded in welcome and cradled her hands in front of her with a delicate twist in her slender wrists. Her gown's tall collar framed her thin face. Kara suppressed the urge to simultaneously curtsey and bow, and luckily found herself speechless instead.

"Welcome, Miss Catherine Magari," the Blood said. Her voice echoed and danced along the walls.

Kara's eyebrow twitched at hearing her full name, but she swallowed the urge to correct it. "Thanks. It's a pleasure to meet you."

"I pray that your time in Ourea has not been altogether horrible."

"It's been...interesting."

The Queen tightened her grasp on her own fingers as she looked Kara over and sighed. Kara's gut twisted. She'd already disappointed the Queen and she'd barely said anything yet.

"Before I introduce you to my generals, Vagabond, I must prepare you for what is to come. For now, I trust who you are based on Braeden's word alone, but you must prove yourself when we are in the war room. Are you prepared to do so? They will need to see the Grimoire as proof."

"I can do that." Kara nodded. Sweat licked her palms and neck.

The Queen eyed Kara's empty hands as if expecting something more, but continued when nothing else was said.

"Come, then."

The Blood retreated to the wall behind her thrones and rapped her knuckles on the stone. A hidden door opened to reveal a torch-lit hallway, but she turned and waited instead of immediately walking through.

Kara shuffled up the steps and passed the thrones, running her fingers against the cool silk fabric that lined the central chair. The touch sent a sharp chill through her bones and into her heart.

She stifled a yelp and cradled her hand. Ice crystals clung to the skin that had touched the fabric, stinging her with their cold fire. The Queen watched her, one eyebrow furrowed in barely contained annoyance. The regal woman stood with her arms behind her back and her chin raised, piercing Kara with cold eyes.

"The Drapes of Hillside are one of our many defenses. Should anyone without the Hillsidian bloodline touch the fabric for very long, they will turn to ice. If I recall the legends correctly, the Vagabond himself dealt with them. I should have hoped that he would write to warn his own Heir to avoid them."

Kara decided against saying anything and instead locked eyes with the Queen. She did not break eye contact until the Blood turned and led the way down the dark and endless hall.

"You must be wary of the world around you, Vagabond," the Queen added over her shoulder.

Kara shook her head and followed, cradling her hand as she crossed into the hidden passageway. Once she was through, the door hummed and swung closed. She took a deep breath and continued behind the woman in the trailing gown.

The Blood made a dozen turns, passing doors and hallways and dozens of identical sconces. She maneuvered the halls with practiced mastery, stopping in front of a closed door after Kara was certain she would never find her way out again without a guide.

The Queen rested her hand on the knob, but paused and tilted her head just enough to look at Kara over her shoulder.

"My kingdom is built upon fearlessness, Vagabond. We value strength and cunning above all else. Still, I know the tides are changing. Our ways aren't long for this world, and I often fear that we will destroy ourselves. Millions will look to you to fill the growing gaps in our armor, but I just can't imagine how you were chosen for this. You are a child, not a warrior."

Kara's cheeks burned. *You're welcome.* She wanted to scream. She furrowed her eyebrows and opened her mouth to speak, but before she could respond, the Queen shook her head. Her once-steely eyes trembled, and she clutched the handle for support.

"I desperately hope you prove me wrong," she said.

The Blood twisted the knob and a flood of daylight broke into the dark hall. The woman dissolved into the room, leaving Kara standing just beyond the hazy midday rays even as she heard her name from within.

The Queen could be right. This could all be a mistake. Kara didn't know what she was doing. She was twenty. She'd found this war-torn pocket of the earth yesterday. It didn't make sense for her to care about its problems. If Ourea didn't want her, she had no reason to try to save it. She hadn't chosen this.

The clover pendant hummed, warming the skin on her neck, and the little blue stone glimmered up at her. According to the Grimoire, she *did* choose this. She had, after all, pulled the clover from the book. It wouldn't have opened for her unless it believed that she was strong enough.

She sighed. If this world didn't want her, she would try to save it anyway: for her dad, for her mom, and because being the Vagabond was all she had left. Maybe she still had a purpose, even if it didn't involve the only world she'd thought was real. She rolled up her sleeves and walked into the room, her back arched so much that it ached.

Two of the room's walls were made of solid windows, which shed blinding light onto a long wooden table in the room's center. The Queen sat at the head of the table, while men filled the rest of the seats. Some turned to each other and murmured. Others strained to look behind her, certain that she wasn't the end of the convoy. Braeden managed a thin smile from his place near the Queen and gave her the smallest of waves.

The Queen took a deep breath. "Miss Catherine, these are my generals and advisors. This is my husband, Richard, and my son, Gavin. You have, of course, already met my son Braeden."

She gestured as she spoke, pointing first to Richard, who sat to her left and looked to be about fifty. His tunic betrayed a muscled build, and he wore a thick golden crown on his neatly-trimmed brown hair. He nodded to Kara and smiled broadly in welcome.

The Queen had then gestured to Gavin, a young man on her right who watched Kara from the seat next to Braeden. Gavin peered over his hand, which he had placed over his mouth at the introduction. He was built like his father, but blond, and she couldn't read his expression.

"My friends, this is the Vagabond," the Queen announced.

The room hushed. Leaves scraped across the glass as the wind rustled through the world outside. A chair creaked, but otherwise, everyone was still.

❧CHAPTER TEN
COUNCIL

Braeden gauged the room's reaction as the Queen revealed that Kara was the Vagabond. She stood by the entry as the door swung closed behind her, her eyes scanning the reserved faces at the table. Most of the yakona frowned. They seemed to be waiting for the Queen to laugh, as if Kara was an uninteresting joke.

Richard, however, couldn't contain his excitement, and there was no doubt in Braeden's mind that the king was debating which question to ask first. It seemed as if the man had forgotten to breathe.

When Braeden was a boy, Richard had recited the Vagabond's legends from memory before bed each night. The stories had sparked his hope that someday, he could be a vagabond, too: that someday, he could be free.

The Queen's generals leaned back in their chairs and shook their heads, grumbling when they once again found their voices.

Braeden turned to look at his adoptive brother Gavin, who watched Kara without blinking as she took the only available seat across the table. Her lips formed a thin line as the room hummed. Gavin's face was smooth, but his eyes were ravenous. His gaze flickered over to Braeden, and he shifted in his seat when they made eye contact, but the hunger in his expression couldn't be hidden. Braeden sighed, annoyed. That look meant the wheels in Gavin's mind were churning out ways in which this could benefit him.

"Welcome, Vagabond," Richard finally said. The grumbles and mutterings hushed. "How did you come across the Grimoire?"

"Yes, we are most curious," someone else said. It was General Mino, who looked Kara over and shook his head. He towered in the seat next to her, almost twice her size.

"That's a long story." Kara chuckled, but the room didn't laugh with her. She cleared her throat. "I was hiking and found a lichgate, but I didn't know what it really was at the time."

She described the door in the mountain and how the roots inside had dragged her into a sunken library. She'd opened the Grimoire and read about the Vagabond.

Here, Richard leaned in closer. Braeden suppressed a smile.

Kara continued and, when she explained how Deidre had found her in Ethos, she told the invented story that Braeden had given her in the market. He released a quiet sigh and relaxed his shoulders. She'd been alone in the cage, she lied, and had been alone when she went to the Stele.

"Do you know how to find your way back?" Gavin interrupted, leaning his elbows onto the massive wooden war table.

"Sorry, I have no idea."

Gavin grumbled under his breath and leaned back once more, hiding his mouth with his hand as Kara continued with the altered tale of how the muses had helped her escape. The room gasped at their mention. Everyone leaned in closer, now, finally interested in the tale. If the muses had helped her, their faces said, the tides had just changed considerably.

The Queen, however, did not react to anything Kara said. The woman's face was as solid and smooth as Gavin's, untouched by the thoughts Braeden knew to be racing through her overactive mind. Once, a year ago, he'd asked her what she was thinking when they'd been in a similar war room because a fleet of soldiers from another kingdom had ventured too close to the Hillsidian border. She'd shared her strategy with him and assembled ten times as many soldiers as she'd needed, reasoning that these foreign yakona were likely scouts sent to find Hillside and its villages. She'd led the attack herself and killed twenty soldiers within fifteen minutes. No one threatened her kingdom and survived.

Braeden had never again asked what the Queen was thinking.

He shifted his gaze around the table. General Mino, with his coal-black skin contrasting the gold trim of his tunic, leaned his massive, muscular form as far away from Kara as possible. He scowled when he caught Braeden looking at him.

Braeden broke eye contact and watched Kara. As she spoke, no one interrupted. No one questioned her story. They didn't even clear their throats. Everyone simply waited, unwavering and still, as she spoke and often averted her gaze from Gavin's particularly intense stare.

In all fairness, Braeden had tried to prepare Gavin during their impromptu sparring match after Adele had ordered him out of Kara's room, but the Hillsidian prince had a habit of not listening.

"...and then I was knocked unconscious."

Kara stopped speaking. Braeden blinked his way out of his thoughts and back into the war room. Chairs squeaked as the Queen's council turned to face him, and he realized that Kara had already described as much as she knew before she awoke in Hillside.

The truth was he'd run into the house seconds before Deidre had shoved Kara into the glass cabinet. Fear coursed through him when he saw the thick trails of blood surging over the shards of glass. He'd worried, then, that the Vagabond—his one chance at freedom—was going to die.

He'd lost control.

Kara, lying almost unconscious on the floor, hadn't known what exactly came to her rescue. She hadn't known that he let the smoldering darkness within consume him, but he didn't think he could have won without its help.

His hand twitched beneath the table from its place on his knee. He forced a soft, steady breath in an effort to keep calm.

"Well," Kara said. "I don't know how we got out of there."

"I knocked Deidre unconscious," he lied, forcing a smile as he mimed jabbing an invisible head in front of him. His face was calm, hiding the nerves fluttering in his gut. More than a decade of lying had its advantages.

"And you didn't kill her?" General Mino slammed his fist into the table. "The isen, especially Deidre, are some of the greatest threats the kingdoms face!"

"That's enough, General." The Queen dismissed his outburst with a wave of her thin hand. Mino crossed his arms and sat back in his seat.

"I doubted she was far from waking up," Braeden lied again. "Since Kara was hurt, we needed to get out of there."

He'd actually fought Deidre for at least another ten minutes, breaking through walls and windows before the sirens had started. The isen tried desperately to run for Kara at every chance, but he threw her across the room or through a sink each time she turned away from him. Once the sirens began, she paused, watching him long enough to accept that she would lose if she stayed. She retreated.

"You knocked her out cold, huh? Impressive!" Gavin patted him on the shoulder. Braeden forced himself to smile at the compliment, but Gavin was already watching Kara again.

The Queen nodded once. "You did well, Braeden. Miss Catherine, thank you for sharing your story. You are welcome here anytime and for as long as you please. We of course wish for you to make Hillside your home, as it once was for the first Vagabond. Whatever your quest becomes, we will guard you and guide you through it.

"That said, the other kingdoms will want you to visit them as well. You obviously understand by now that the weight of your presence in our world again means more than just welcome. The thick tensions that have grown between our kingdoms for eons will only ignite further if you are hoarded here, and we can't risk an unnecessary war. You aren't ruled by anyone, but I ask that you go. Otherwise, the Bloods will think that I have kept you here as a weapon."

"Mother, the other kingdoms don't have to know that she's real. We could explain away the rumors," Gavin said gently, smiling to Kara as he spoke. His tone made Braeden want to punch him in the mouth, but he shook his head instead and tried to guess at the half-formed plot boiling in his brother's mind.

The Queen sighed and massaged her temples. "Gavin, they already know. One day you will see that the world has much keener eyes than you. Don't be foolish."

"I simply believe that we shouldn't throw her back into the fray so soon. She should be allowed to rest."

"By no means would we do such a thing. If you choose to leave, Vagabond, we will supply you with everything you need. The other kingdoms will meet us in a safe location, where our men will be forced to wait while they take you to their Blood."

"No one trusts each other here, do they?" Kara peered around the table and even caught Braeden's eye for a second.

"It has always been so," the Queen said, shaking her head. "Only two yakona have ever seen all of the kingdoms beside the Stele: The first Vagabond and our era's Blood Aislynn of Ayavel. Even Aislynn is blindfolded when she's brought into the city. She has been granted this right in recent years only because of her, shall we say, *unrelenting* quest for peace. But ours is a deep and bitter hatred. Your Grimoire will know."

"Yes, Kara," Richard said. "May we see it?"

"Of course."

Kara rubbed her pendant with her thumb and held her breath. A funnel of gleaming blue ash spun from the necklace and assembled on the table in the shape of a large book. The glow dissolved, congealing into a dark red leather cover. Even though he'd already seen it once before, Braeden caught his breath as the thousand-year-old book became solid on the table.

This was it. The answer to his decade-long search sat in front of him, just waiting for the right question. For *his* question.

He forced himself to lean back and blink the lust from his eyes. He took a deep, quiet breath, but his heart wouldn't stop racing. General Mino had seen his reaction—that much was clear from the way Mino's scowl deepened—but it was too late to do anything about that. Braeden busied himself with looking at Kara and pretending nothing had happened.

She grinned and ran her fingers over the cover, apparently oblivious to how silent the room had become. No one breathed as she toyed with the great book's corners, tracing its edges.

"What have you learned thus far?" the Queen asked.

Braeden's intuition flared. Something was amiss with the question.

"I can see someone's most influential memory," Kara answered. "I figured that you wouldn't want me to demonstrate it, though, since it's such an invasive thing for me to see."

Richard raised his hand. "I would be honored, actually."

Braeden laughed and the flash of worry thawed in his gut.

"I would rather see the Vagabond's gift for myself," the Queen interjected. "But in private. Kara, would you grant me a moment once the gentlemen have left?"

"Oh, well, of course." Kara raised her eyebrows.

Braeden did not envy whatever she was going to see.

"We must first discuss Deidre," the Queen continued. "If she is working for Blood Carden, then Ourea is a darker world than I thought."

"I suspect that she serves only as a double-agent to Niccoli." Mino grunted in annoyance. "She would learn intimate details of the Stele in that manner. I don't see their alliance as a threat to us."

"Wait. Who's Niccoli?" Kara asked.

Mino huffed impatiently. "The oldest known isen. He leads what is rumored to be the largest isen guild in existence. He is incredibly powerful."

Richard stretched himself in his seat and looked out a window as he recounted one of the first history lessons Braeden had ever learned. "It was Agneon who was truly fierce, though. He was first seen about two hundred years ago and lived a short life as far as isen are concerned. He was far more powerful than Niccoli, but because the guild leader was his master, Agneon had to do as he was told. Hillsidians as recent as my father fought against him. It's believed that the drenowith finally killed him, and for good reason, because he hunted more drenowith than any other creature. They were his favorites."

"Good riddance, then," Kara said.

"Niccoli's guild has not been as powerful since Agneon was killed," the Queen added. "They have returned to squabbling with other isen and have mostly left us alone, except for a few who break ranks now and again. But for that, we have Braeden." She smiled, and he nodded to her in gratitude for the compliment.

"There's more than one isen guild?" Kara leaned onto the table, eyes wide and curious. "Where are they?"

"I wish we knew," Braeden said. "There are guilds throughout Ourea and even some in the human world, but all we have to go on are rumors, since no one has ever found a guild and lived long enough to talk about it. We've never actually seen more than a few isen together, but they always report back to their master. They have to."

Someone knocked at the door. The Queen waved her hand, and the door swung open to reveal an empty hallway. A small card flittered through the doorframe, floating as if on a breeze, and fell to the table in front of her. A small orchid bloomed from the card as it landed, and the Queen smiled.

"Braeden, you have a guest waiting for you in the throne room. You are dismissed."

He didn't *want* to be dismissed. He didn't want to let the Grimoire out of his sight. His mouth opened out of turn, and every face looked at him when he did not bow and leave. As surreal as it was, he spoke.

"If I may, my Queen, I would like to go as Kara's guide when she leaves. I know Ourea well, since I travel between the lichgates so often. Since Deidre is after the Grimoire, there's no telling what other isen will be hunting the Vagabond, too. I can help."

The Queen smiled, the cold lines of her grin seeping into her eyes. She obviously recognized something in his words that he did not quite understand himself.

"I apologize, Braeden, but the answer is no," she said. "I need you elsewhere. I was going to speak of this later, but there are reports of an isen threatening one of our villages. You must help them. My people can't live in constant fear of their own forests."

"I'd actually like his help, if you don't mind," Kara interjected. "I can wait until he gets back. After all, you did say you would send people to help me. I would feel better going with someone I know."

Gavin shifted his weight and glared at the floor from behind his hand, barely suppressing a grumble at her words. Braeden resisted the urge to grin.

The Queen glared at them both, acknowledging their exchange with an annoyed sigh before she answered Kara.

"Even if you did wait, Vagabond, he could never join you in the other kingdoms and would be forced to wait while you went on. You are alone in this. Braeden, retire to your guest. All but Richard and the Vagabond must also leave."

The dismissed council members stood. Braeden nodded to the Queen and left, frustrated, but the hair on his neck stood on end when he passed through the door. He turned in time to see Kara watch him leave, her eyebrows pinched with concern as the door slowly shut in his face.

Gavin leaned against a wall in the hallway, smirking and examining Braeden as the door closed. They waited in silence for the generals and advisors to disappear into the labyrinth of doors and hallways.

"You failed to mention the Vagabond's a girl," Gavin said when they were alone.

"I tried during our match, but you talk too much."

"It changes everything."

"It changes nothing!"

Gavin cocked an eyebrow and his grin widened. "You seem fond of this one, brother. Did I cross some line?"

"I just want to protect the Vagabond."

"Of course." Gavin laughed, turning down the corridor that would take him to the armory. He shook his head and chuckled quietly to himself.

Braeden wanted to hit his head against the wall at his own stupidity. Gavin thought this was a game, now. That was all anyone in the world was to him: a pawn or a puzzle piece. The women of Hillside had a habit of swooning when they saw the Hillsidian prince, and Gavin would no doubt expect the same from Kara. Braeden turned down a different passage, heading toward the throne room and whoever waited for him.

That's how he plans to control the Grimoire, then. He expects Kara to giggle and fan herself when he walks by. She might not be the warrior everyone expected, but she's no idiot.

Braeden forced himself to take a few slow breaths as he maneuvered the labyrinth, snickering to himself as he envisioned all the ways Kara would reject the prince's advances. If this was a game, it would be fun to see Gavin lose.

❧CHAPTER ELEVEN
BLOOD

Braeden rapped on the labyrinth door to the throne room. It opened long enough for him walk onto the moon-shaped platform before it slid closed behind him, invisible in the wall once more. The emerald draperies hanging from between the pillars billowed as he entered.

A tall woman with pale blond hair stood at the foot of the stairs and, when the drapes moved, she turned her head to face him. When recognition set in, he laughed and hurried down the steps.

"Aislynn!"

"It's good to see you, Braeden."

She smiled and pulled him into a hug, her opaque skin reflecting blue and green specks of light as sunlight hit her through the windows. She pulled away with a smile and patted his back, catching his gaze.

Ayavelians were unique: each of Aislynn's eyes had three pupils, and when she twisted her eyebrows just right, each of them betrayed a different emotion.

She looked at him with curiosity and glee, but her innermost eye tried to hide her fear, as it had since the day they met. His smile wavered. She would always be afraid of him, and there was nothing he could do about it. Aislynn could never forgive him for what she'd endured when he was a boy—at least, not completely—and he never once blamed her for it. He cleared his throat in the silence.

"How long will you be here this time, Aislynn?"

"I leave in the morning, but Evelyn will keep Hillside company for a few weeks yet whilst I go about my travels."

He grimaced and looked around to see if Evie, the younger, spitting image of her Aunt Aislynn, was nearby. Sure enough, she watched him from behind one of the draperies with a disdainful glare that made him grateful she didn't know his true nature.

"It's a pleasure to see you again," Evie said in a dry tone, turning to examine her nails as she spoke. She nodded to him without a smile, her obligatory welcome apparently fulfilled, and pushed through the doorway into the hall.

"For her attitude, you'd think she was actually an Heir," he muttered.

Aislynn jabbed his side and clicked her tongue at him, but smiled nonetheless at his joke. "I promised my sister when she died that I would care for Evelyn, and since I am childless, she is all I have. My advisors may have actually found a way to give her the bloodline, though they are still evaluating the risks. I have faith that she will rule one day, so you must be kind to her."

"Sorry." He scratched the gauze on his cheek. The itchy cotton irritated his skin and he longed to take it off.

Aislynn's eyes shifted to the gauze. She pinched his jaw and rubbed the green stain before slipping her arm through his and leading him from the throne room.

"I thought you were legendary for never allowing yourself to be wounded in a match," she chided.

"I made a mistake."

"You recovered nicely."

"I was careless. It won't happen again."

"Good. Shall we speak in the orchard? I have much to tell you."

They meandered through the halls while he made a conscious effort to match Aislynn's slow pace. Portraits of long-dead Hillsidian Bloods and their families lined the halls. She looked at each one, absorbed yet again in the same paintings which had hung in the hall the last hundred times they'd taken this route to the orchard.

They eventually walked through the set of massive doors leading to the apple trees that surrounded Hillside Lake. The air baked his face as they stepped from the overhanging shadows of the castle, and crimson specks of light danced off of Aislynn's skin as they walked into the sun. Two Hillsidian girls carrying towels stopped as the light glided across Aislynn's arms, and their lips parted in fascination.

Braeden snapped his fingers at them to shatter their gaping awe. They bowed, blushing, and ran inside as he and Aislynn continued their silent parade. He was quiet until they passed the first row of trees lined with early summer apple blossoms, where it was least likely that someone would be listening.

"Aislynn, why don't you ever change form to avoid the stares?"

"You will not like my answer, my friend."

"I want to know."

She shot him a fleeting glance. "I have two reasons, then. First of all, I like to keep that gift a secret to protect those I care about. Secondly, I will not hide. I am a Blood of my people and I visit the other kingdoms to promote tolerance, so I present myself with that in mind."

The unspoken truth in her words stung. She had never been forced to hide who and what she was, while lying was all Braeden had ever known. For half his life, he hadn't even slept in his natural form. He could never let his guard down.

Aislynn changed the subject as they walked deeper into the rows of trees. "I wish to meet the Vagabond, but I doubt I'll have a moment to speak with her alone. I therefore wish for you to give her something for me, if you don't mind."

Aislynn reached into a crease in her flowing gown and pulled out a small, blue square. Two ends of the stone were jagged and uneven, as if it was a corner that had been snapped off of something greater. It was only an inch or so thick, with flecks of gold shimmering in the dark blue stone. Lines, mostly meaningless, had been engraved along its face, but in one corner was the Grimoire's clover symbol. She set it in his palm.

"What is this?"

"I don't know. It was discovered centuries ago in our gardens, hidden in one of the walls. I think it was meant to be found by the next Vagabond. Thus, I wish for young Miss Catherine to have it."

"I'll give it to her," he said, shaking the urge to correct Kara's name.

Aislynn smiled as she picked an apple from one of the trees and set the red fruit in his free hand. He shoved the small blue stone into his pocket as she looked around. She eyed the trees, no doubt making sure they were alone. Braeden listened for footsteps, but heard only the wind as it blew through the orchard.

She lowered her voice. "Now that we've taken care of that, I must speak to you about another matter. Blood Carden's men are patrolling a wider border. I question his intentions. There are rumors that he has been trying to conceive another child, but that none are born with the bloodline. I fear he knows that you are still alive."

Braeden just laughed.

Her eyes flared with annoyance and surprise, but the unwavering fear remained. His laughter faded as he sat on the grass beneath a tree, but he waited to speak until she tucked her dress beneath her knees and sat beside him.

"I'm sorry," he whispered. "But I found Kara because we were both captured and taken to the Stele. Carden spiked me and made me kneel at his feet. He knows full well that I'm alive."

"How did you escape? Did he control you?"

"Of course he did. That's what he does. If I'm near him, I have no control. Two muses saved us."

"Drenowith *helped* you?"

"Why do you sound so surprised?"

"I have met a few in my lifetime. Braeden, they aren't kind creatures."

"What makes you say that? They saved us. They couldn't have orchestrated our separate captures to fake a rescue."

"Braeden, drenowith orchestrate whatever they wish. We are fragile toys in their immortal lives. Never forget that." She breathed deeply and tapped her cheek.

He squeezed the apple in his palm and replayed the rescue in his mind. He'd never questioned his luck, but their timing had indeed been too perfect. The apple cracked beneath the pressure from his hand.

"They aren't immortal," he corrected, remembering Adele's comment in the meadow.

"What?"

"One of the muses said that. They can die, they just don't age."

Aislynn narrowed her eyes, each of her six pupils flickering with deep and heavy thought. Whatever she was thinking about had dissolved even her fear of him.

"They can die?" she asked.

"They said it was possible." His heart skipped a beat at her sudden focus. He wished he hadn't said anything.

"Should you meet these muses again, I urge you to not trust them," she said, still very much lost in her thought. "These creatures don't care for our wars or our ways. Their only care is for the earth."

"If that was true, then they wouldn't have saved us," he reasoned.

"They must have some greater use for you. Drenowith are dangerous things that never act without the authority of their Council. If they interfere, they do so slowly and very often falsely. I must meet with the Queen now, but Braeden, you must not trust them if you see them again. Promise me."

"I will be careful."

She smiled and cupped his chin in farewell, her skin cold to the touch. His mind flashed to the memory Kara had dragged from him, remembering the way his mother's hand had left frost on his nose when she touched him. He lost himself to the wispy contours of the memory and didn't notice Aislynn walk toward the castle.

When he finally blinked himself out of his thoughts, he was alone in the orchard. He pushed himself to his feet and brushed the dirt from his pant legs before walking toward the lake. Once he found it, he sat on the shore and gazed out to where the water met the sheer wall of the mountain side. There were said to be caves beneath the surface, but no one dared explore them because of the countless rumored merfolk sightings. Those creatures enjoyed filleting trespassers.

It was for that superstitious reason alone that he decided against hurling rocks into the pool, as much as he wanted to throw something to vent his frustration. Instead, he plucked a few stray blades of grass from the shore and sat on a half-submerged boulder, shredding them bit by bit and letting the shards pile on the rock beneath him.

"That brother of yours sure talks a lot."

Instinct sent his hand flying for his sword, but when he saw Kara on the grass beside him, he sighed and slid the blade back into his scabbard. She cocked an eyebrow. She wore pants and a loose tunic, now, and she'd pulled her hair into a bun. A few stray curls framed her face.

"You shouldn't sneak up on me," he scolded.

"Apparently not. Sorry."

"You changed clothes?"

She modeled the tunic, looking over the loose sleeves tied at her wrists. He frowned. The cotton dress had flattered her curves, but the loose pants and tunic dwarfed her.

"It's still not jeans and a T-shirt, but it works," she said.

He turned back to the water and continued to rip apart the grass. A breeze whispered across the apple trees and shed blossoms onto the wind so that they landed in heaps on the lake's surface. The mountain's reflection rippled and broke across the water.

"How was your meeting with the Queen?" he finally asked, trying to fill the silence.

There was no answer, so he looked over his shoulder to see if she was still there. She was, but she examined her gloved hands with unfocused eyes.

"I don't want to talk about it, but I have to say that only an idiot would ever make that woman angry."

"Welcome to the real Hillside."

They sat in silence.

"I'm in over my head, Braeden."

"You're smart. You'll figure it out," he said with a grin.

She smiled back. "Thanks."

"So did you just finish speaking with the Queen?"

"No, I was with Gavin. He found me afterward."

Of course he did. Braeden shook his head.

"He showed me the dining area and we just talked for a while. He seems nice."

Braeden brushed his shredded grass into the water. "You can't trust him."

"What? His family adopted you. He's your brother. How could you say that?"

"He's my brother, which means I know him better than you do. He only wants to use you, Kara."

"I think you're being hard on him. He was nothing but nice," she said.

He shifted his weight on the rock, and the small blue stone Aislynn gave him jabbed his side. It sent a wave of pain shooting up his back, and he grumbled. The stone was warm when he pulled it from his pocket. He stood and moved to sit beside her, slipping the small blue square into her hands as he did.

"What's this?" Kara asked.

"I have no idea," he admitted. "Aislynn asked that I give it to you. She said her ancestors found it a few centuries ago in their gardens, but since it has the Grimoire symbol on it, she wanted you to have it."

Kara studied it, lips pursed. It was clear that she had no idea what it was, either, so he stretched out on the grassy lakeshore. She cleared her throat several times, as though she was about to say something, but always swallowed her words at the last minute.

She slipped the stone into her pocket. "What's eating you? Since that meeting you've seemed off. Different."

"I'm perfectly fine," he lied.

"For someone who hides who he really is, you're a terrible liar."

He glared through his half-closed eyelids, and she blushed.

Whispering about Carden to Aislynn was risky enough when they'd spoken in hushed voices, but Kara hadn't even tried to be quiet.

"Never say that out loud, even as a joke, or when alone," he said. "This is all I have, Kara. I can't risk losing it."

"Is that why you're so upset? You feel like you're lying to these people?"

"You need to stop."

She ripped out a few blades of grass, leaned over to him, and sprinkled them over his head. He leaned forward and brushed off the pieces that caught in his ear.

"What—?"

"Look, Mr. Tall, Dark, and Dangerous, I'm already in as deep as a stranger can go. I've met royalty—sorry, *Bloods*—and I was chased by an army. I saw dragons. There's a vicious isen thing trying to kill me. My dad—" She stopped short, her breath hitching.

"Basically, you don't scare me," she went on. "You've got a troubled past, well so do I. Most people do. We do things we're not proud of, things we wish we could take back, but what's done is done and all you can do is try to redeem yourself in the present. So cut the crap. I'm just trying to help you out."

She marched back through the orchard and disappeared behind a wave of apple blossoms that shook free on a breeze. He grinned and watched her disappear. When she was gone, he resumed his stare into the lake.

Ripples on the still surface caught his eye. A large white head peeped above the water, its hair highlighted with every shade of blue. The mermaid had no color in its solid white eyes, which scrutinized him for a moment before it slid back beneath the water. He brushed the last of the grass from his hair.

Mr. Tall, Dark, and Dangerous, huh? He laughed. Where had she even come up with that?

❦CHAPTER TWELVE
SECRETS

Kara walked down the only path she could find in the orchard and wondered if the Grimoire would be able to tell her why Braeden was so frustrating.

After about ten minutes, the trees along the trail grew thicker, which meant she had somehow transitioned from the orchard to the forest. She set her hands on her head and examined the woods, biting her lip in defeat. She'd wanted to go to her room, not take a hike. The leaf-covered trail behind her was as wide and flat as a road and easy to navigate, but she wasn't ready to face Braeden yet.

The summer sun beat on her neck through breaks in the trees, and she could smell the warm salt of her sweat. The air was clear, cleaner than even her favorite routes through the Rockies. The crystal sky blistered through the gaps in the leaves above as the canopy rustled with small furry creatures that scurried from limb to limb, too fast to see. Leaves fell to the ground as they ran, marking the creatures' route as they coursed through the branches.

She took a deep breath and couldn't suppress the smile that spread across her lips. Hikes were for letting go, so that was exactly what she would do. Her boots crunched on fallen sticks as she turned away from Hillside and began her impromptu trek.

The air was cool, but not cold, and breezes snaked through the neck of her loose tunic, drying the sweat on her back. The wind pulled the scents of bark and copper from the pines, which tickled her throat. She reached in instinct for the water bottle she didn't have and laughed at herself when it wasn't there.

A woodland chorus of chattering leaves drowned out any nearby streams, so she continued along the trail. She rubbed her pendant and listened to nature until the gurgle of a brook hissed from around a bend in the narrowing road.

The stream's high banks dwarfed its shallow water as it twisted through the forest, hidden as it was behind a row of thick oak trees. Patches of sandy ground lined the edges of the creek, just wide enough to stand on, and the roots of a gnarled old willow dug uneven stairs into one of these narrow embankments. Kara took the makeshift steps one by one until she reached the riverbed and stepped out onto the few feet of space which separated the mud wall from the current.

She knelt to take a sip. The water was sweet, with what she could have sworn was a subtle note of apple, and she drank until her mind buzzed and all she wanted to do was sit and watch the water. Cold dirt pressed against the back of her head as she leaned against the river wall, but it was a soothing contrast to the warm beams of sunlight that fell through the treetops and heated her cheeks. She closed her eyes and savored the day.

A weight pressed against her lap and when she looked down, the Grimoire's faded crimson binding rested on her outstretched legs. She hadn't meant to summon it, but she shrugged. She might as well ask it something while she was alone.

"Can you teach me something about magic?"

The cover flipped open, but none of the pages flicked forward. The hair on her neck prickled.

A flash of heat poured over her shoulders and down her arms. The freckling light dissolved around her and left an inverted imprint on her vision. Though the sound of the stream bubbled by, she could no longer see it.

A thin ball of light appeared a few feet away. It stretched and unwound into thin wisps that whirled and popped as they took on the shape of a figure. They formed the outline of a cape, and then a hood, and then the pointed tip of a nose. They continued spinning and curving until a man stood before her, made of the same stuff through which she'd seen Twin's and Braeden's memories. He raised his head to look at her.

A *crack* snapped in her ear. She flinched. Shades of green and patches of brown flooded her vision, and the rush of the stream became a deafening roar. The air was sweeter, though, and she found an unknown smell, like honey, sifting through the wind as it passed her. Even though the darkness had receded, the wispy figure before her had not. He stood still, silent, and watchful, and she could see the creek through him, bustling about on its way.

"Vagabond?" she whispered, as if he would dissolve if she spoke any louder.

He nodded.

"How? Where did you—?"

"You called." His cloak shifted to reveal a wispy hand, which pointed to the open Grimoire in her arms.

"Well, technically—"

"Excellent!" The hood shifted so that his nose pointed to her pocket. She wished she could see his face.

"You already have one of the four map pieces," he continued. "I'm impressed!"

"I—what?"

"The stone in your pocket."

She pulled out the square Braeden had given her. The dark blue stone reflected glinting streaks of sunlight, and its flecks of gold twinkled like stars. It was vaguely familiar, but she didn't know why.

"That is one of the four map pieces," the transparent Vagabond said. "When you find the other three, it will become the key that will open the door to my village. It's imperative that you find them soon."

"Why?"

"The village is hidden and safe. I left many unfinished projects there, and I hope you will finish them."

"What projects?"

He laughed. "At least you aren't afraid to ask questions. That is essential to surviving as a vagabond."

"You didn't answer me, though."

"I will, someday. The secrets there can't be told. You must see them to understand. Oh, it's good to speak again!" He laughed. "For a thousand years, I had little company."

Nice change in subject. "So what are you? A ghost?"

"I suppose so. My soul is tied to the Grimoire, like a soul living in another's body."

"Oh, so it's really you answering when I ask it a question."

"No. The Grimoire is its own entity, filled with all of my observations from life. When you ask a question, it takes you to the journal entry that will answer you. I, however, am a real spirit. I was a man once. The Grimoire has never known life the way I have, so it has been rather dull company. I sat alone, waiting for someone to pick up where I left off."

"I'm in way over my head," she said again, not intending to do so out loud.

"Have faith in yourself. You would have been killed by now if you weren't strong enough to survive Ourea. The Grimoire would have found a new master if that was the case. Yet, here you are."

"As comforting as *that* is, I still have no idea what I'm doing."

"Few do. That's why you must find my village—well, your village, I suppose. It will help you."

"Right, the map," she mused. She rubbed the blue stone and put it back in her pocket. "So where are the other pieces?"

"There is one piece in Hillside, Ayavel, Kirelm, and Losse. Where are we now?"

"We're in Hillside, but Braeden says this was from Aislynn. She's the Ayavelian Blood."

"Who is this Braeden?"

"I think that's a conversation for another time," she answered, glancing around. If she couldn't speak to Braeden about his past by the lake, there wasn't much chance that a forest with lots of hiding places was much safer.

"Very well," he muttered. "Four of my vagabonds each hid a map piece in the various kingdoms' gardens, so it is best for you to look there first. I wish I could tell you where they are, but not even I know, since...well, I died before they could tell me. It worries me that the Ayavelian Blood found one. That means they were not hidden well enough. I hope you are still able to find the rest."

"Wow. That's reassuring," she said, but she cleared her throat. "Sorry if that was rude. I guess I should cut back on the sarcasm."

"I am unfamiliar with that term, but I will try to remember it. Now, why did you bring me forward?"

"I wanted to learn something about magic."

"The first technique I learned was flame manipulation. Do you know it?"

She shook her head. *I don't know anything.*

"We will start with that, then. You must first stretch out your palm," he said. He raised his sheer hand until it was just in front of him and bent his elbow. His hand relaxed, and he twisted his palm until it faced the sky. She copied the movement.

He tapped her arm. "Your elbow is too stiff. Relax your body. Tense your mind."

She took a deep breath and sank into her stance. The sweet air tickled the space between her eyes, so she focused on the sensation.

"Good," he said. "Think of the wood around you. Smell it. Imagine the rough grain of the bark on your skin."

She remembered running her hands over tree bark as she climbed up the stiff slopes of the Rockies. The curves and dips in the wood always reminded her of small rivers or old scars. The coppery bite of pine needles clung to her nose.

"Now," he continued, "feel the breeze sweep over you and grab it. Pull it into your hand."

The wind combed through her hair. She wasn't sure how she could grab something like air, but she listened to the rustle of leaves scraping against each other and to the way the breeze whistled past her ear. Her wrists and cheeks tingled. She closed her eyes.

"Now all you need is a *spark*."

Her fingers twitched.

The movement was soft, but it was enough to jerk her from the sweet mountain memories. Her veins smoldered. Her muscles numbed. The icy race of adrenaline throughout her body dissolved the warm tingle and cleared her mind of all thought. The sensation shook her knees, and she lurched forward as if someone had pushed her. Her eyes snapped open.

A ball of lavender fire sparked in her palm, flickering in the same breeze she'd used to create it.

Kara laughed so hard her cheeks hurt. The purple flame crackled, but as the memories and her control over her meditation faded, so did the flame. When all that remained was a thin trail of violet smoke, she laughed again and remembered to breathe.

"I did it!" She looked up to thank the Vagabond, but he was gone. Her smile dissolved, but the thrill didn't.

She pushed herself to her feet in time to see a tall figure race barefoot into the curve of the path. It took her a second to recognize Twin's twisted and tear-stained face, but the Hillsidian girl didn't see her at all as she disappeared deeper into the forest.

Kara pulled herself over the tall bank and climbed onto the path, getting a few streaks of mud on her shirt in the process. She began after the pattering feet, but a pang of guilt ran through her. Twin was likely running from the memory she'd seen this morning. Of everyone in Hillside, Kara was probably the last person Twin would want to talk to about it. She might not want to see *anyone*.

After all, Kara had wanted to be alone when mourning Mom. She hadn't answered the texts or emails from her friends, who were only trying to show their support. She'd pushed her dad to leave Florida on an early summer trip to escape the house calls. She'd pushed *everyone* away. But all she'd really wanted was for someone to force her to let them listen.

She took a deep breath and raced down the path toward Twin.

The trail followed the creek, and Kara lost track of how long she ran. Twigs snapped beneath her boots until the growing sting in her throat forced her to pause and breathe.

In the silence between breaths, she heard someone singing. It was a sweet and heartbreaking sound that made her want to laugh and cry and sleep all at once, and it chorused through the wood with an ever-growing vibrato. The sound rose and fell without purpose in a song that she'd never heard before.

She followed the melody, and as it grew louder, she found a spring and a small clearing. The small pool was surrounded with reeds, which grew along the bank where the spring dribbled away into a stream. The song was loudest here, and even though Kara could see Twin standing in the water, she couldn't believe that the beautiful sound could come from any mortal creature.

The knee-high hem of the girl's dress floated in the pool around her, and her eyes were closed so tightly that her brow creased from the strain. She poured her heart into the song, so that even the reeds on the bank tilted toward her as she sang. Kara knelt behind a tree and listened. Though she wanted to leave the girl in peace, she couldn't walk away from that *sound.*

The water beneath the floating skirt began to churn. At first, there were only ripples, but as the power in Twin's voice grew, so did the water's reaction. The ripples became bubbles that broke and heaved, hiccupping across the girl's skin and leaving beads of spring water along her arms. A blob of water rose from the churning pool, dripping as it stood. Excess liquid drained and splashed away until a figure made of churning spring water stood in front of Twin. It cupped her cheek with a wet hand, but she did not open her eyes or stop singing.

Reeds pulled themselves through the blob's feet, climbing upward and coating the water in a muscular layer of weeds until the figure developed a thin waist and curved hips. Thinner, darker reeds sprung from its head to imitate hair, and rich, chocolate-colored skin bubbled through to give the creature a face.

It was Twin's sister, born again from water and weeds. Kara gaped, her breath gone.

The dead Hillsidian's face broke into a warm smile. She beamed down at her little sister with thick brown eyes and lifted the girl's chin, and only then did the song break away with a sob. Twin cried and pulled the water woman into a hug.

The figure shattered as Twin touched it. Spring water shot in every direction from under Twin's grasp, leaving her soaked in the water that had brought her sister back for a single, tragic moment. She grabbed for the reeds as they fell and she screamed in frustration, falling back into the spring with them. The pool came to her waist now that she was on her knees, and it lapped and crested over her until she screamed again and threw the weeds away. She shook and sobbed until Kara couldn't tell water from tears.

Kara bit her lip. It would only make matters worse to let Twin know that she'd seen everything, but a single, selfish thought kept her rooted in place: Twin had brought her sister back. If Kara could create lavender fire in her palm on the first try, there was nothing stopping her from learning how to do this too, even if it took time. There was nothing stopping her from bringing her mom back.

Twin reeled around, glaring into the woods and wiping her face with wet hands. "Who's there?"

Kara looked at the snapped twig below her foot. In her envy, she hadn't even heard the sound of wood breaking. She couldn't escape without Twin seeing her, so she took a deep breath, walked out from her hiding place, and leaned against the tree.

Twin groaned and pulled herself out of the spring. "You again."

"I'm sorry. I just wanted to help you. I thought you would want someone to talk to."

Kara meant to stop there, but her mouth continued without giving her a chance to think first.

"Twin, that was your sister, wasn't it?"

"You don't understand."

"I know that was her."

"It wasn't, not really."

"Teach me how to do it. Please, Twin."

"Absolutely not! This is an addiction, Kara. I can't stop."

"I don't care what you think it is! I have to see Mom and Dad again. I'd give anything for that."

Twin shook her head. "No."

"Please!"

"No! Your parents are *dead*!"

Kara gasped as she studied the hatred in Twin's face. The forest weighed on the silence that followed. Kara narrowed her eyes, scowling to suppress the urge to cry.

"My last memory of my mom involves blood and a body cast, Twin! Sometimes, I can't even remember her face. And my dad died even though I was just trying to keep him safe. Please. I need to see them one more time. Just once." Kara covered her mouth as the tears started. Guilt ate into her and stung every inch of her body.

"No."

Kara shoved the girl's shoulder, and Twin buckled under the blow. "You brought your sister back! You have to teach me how to do it!"

"It's not real, Kara!"

"I don't care!"

"That—that *thing* was not my sister! That was nothing but an empty memory, and I become weaker every time I see it. I lose that much more of my resolve to keep going. It kills me every time I watch her face become nothing but reeds, and yet I am completely lost and alone until I see her again! She was everything I had left!

"I'm not strong, Kara," Twin continued, her voice softening. "No one expects anything from me. I'm a jester, a joke, a bubble that floats around and makes people laugh. No one has ever taken a moment to find out if I'm all right. I'm not. I'm weak. But vagabonds lead hard lives, and an addiction like this will destroy you. Everyone expects you to be the hero, so act like one!"

Kara leaned back against the tree, bile shooting into her mouth. Memories flooded her mind: the blood on Mom's seat; the beads of broken glass on the dash; the expression of terror frozen on her dad's face. Kara's knees shook. Rage and hatred and anger and guilt all festered within her.

"If you're weak, Twin, it's because you won't help someone who needs it!"

Kara raced back through the trees and left Twin in the clearing before the girl could respond.

There was no path to follow anymore. The trees were only a few feet apart, and the low branches pulled Kara's hair as she bolted through them. She didn't stop, not even when her throat stung and she gasped for air.

With every footfall, she tried to remember the shape of her mom's nose or the way her eyebrow twisted when she was angry, but there was a void where the memories should have been. When she thought of her dad, she couldn't shake the image of his eyes as they slipped out of focus for the last time.

She tripped over a root and dove into the ground, skidding on a slick layer of dead leaves. Her knees shook, and she couldn't push herself to her feet. Instead, she scooted over to the nearest tree to catch her breath, unsure of where she was or how long she'd been running. The trees all looked the same: tall and naked for the first dozen feet before their branches stretched upward. A blood-red sun broke through the canopy.

Her heart rate slowed until the pounding in her head became manageable. She could hear the wind again, as well as the leaves that crunched beneath her whenever she shifted her weight. A waterfall roared behind a patch of trees somewhere to the left.

She stood without debating her choice and followed the noise to a cliff, where the waterfall rushed into a dark blue pool below. Her mind cleared bit by bit as she watched the sun glitter against the surging water. A thin trail led toward the waterfall and out onto a ledge behind the cascading sheet of water, where the shadowed hints of a cave appeared through breaks in the steady stream. She headed closer to see for herself.

Moss and slime layered the trail when the dirt ended and the slippery rock began. Her boot slipped more than once as she inched her way across it, but she relished the distraction and slid into a shallow cave after a few minutes of heavy focus and tip-toeing.

The air in the cave was ten degrees colder, and a refreshing chill spilled over her as she stepped inside. The humid air smelled like rain-drenched grass after a thunderstorm, and moisture condensed on her nose as she looked around. The ceiling was eight or so feet tall, so she could easily stand, but it wasn't very deep; even the dusk's fading evening light was enough to illuminate every nook and cranny. Loose hair stuck to her neck in the humidity, but at least the small boulders in the cave were dry enough for her to sit on them. She found a stone that had a smooth curve to it like a chair, as if someone had sat there a million times before her.

When she was as comfortable as one can be when leaning against a rock, she rubbed the pendant and summoned the Grimoire into her lap. The sunlight wouldn't last much longer, so she massaged her eyes and accepted that she would spend the night outside.

"Can I bring back the dead?" she asked the book.

The pages flipped in answer.

It's possible.

Her heart leapt. "How? How do I do it?"

The pages flipped again.

The Vagabond forbade his followers from bringing back the dead.

"Just tell me how to do it!"

The page turned.

Strength comes from learning lessons that are difficult to bear, and death is one of the hardest to embrace. There is a world which follows this one and once it's seen, we aren't meant to return. This is one of the balances which can't be distorted. That sort of disharmony throws whole worlds into disarray.

To keep the dead in this life is selfish. You must believe that they are in a better place, no matter how soon they were called there. Those who are strong will live with the memory of their loved ones until they too may join them some distant day.

Death is part of the ultimate balance. It's to be left to nature's command. Remember that grief is a necessary pain. It's your only way to heal. To starve it will destroy you.

Kara finished the last sentence as the final rays of sunlight set behind the forest. Dusk settled into the cave as she closed the Grimoire and held it to her chest. She couldn't debate with it if she couldn't read its answers.

The waterfall's delicate curtain swayed on a breeze. The twilight soothed her. Crickets chirped to the heartbeat of the gushing water. She closed her eyes and listened to the lullaby, but the crunch of rocks beneath feet disrupted the song.

She jolted forward and listened again, trying to sift through the ensemble of water and wind. Sure enough, there was another snap and a shuffle. Someone—or something—had begun along the path to her waterfall.

Kara scooted against the wall closest to the noises and pressed her body on the rock. The sharp crags of the cave pulled against her tunic. Her mind raced. She didn't know if she was even in Hillside anymore. It could be a yakona or even a wild animal, just coming home after a hunt to find a dirty little human armed with a big red book.

There was only one way in and out; she was trapped. She could trip whoever it was and send them over the waterfall, which would give her enough time to scoot out along the edge and escape. It was a short enough fall that they probably wouldn't be hurt.

The crunching stopped, and she heard a deep breath. She held hers. A head appeared around the corner, its short black mess of hair framing a handsome olive face.

"Hey there," Braeden muttered.

"I was about to whack you with the Grimoire," Kara said, setting the book on the floor with a relieved sigh.

He laughed. "I'd be honored to receive such a beating, but I apologize if I startled you."

"It's fine." She sat back against the smooth boulder and Braeden sat across from her, grinning as she settled against it. Her eyes stung.

"You know, of all the places in Hillside, I was pretty surprised that you came here," he said.

"Why?"

"This is where I used to come to be alone. I doubt that anyone knows about it, not even Gavin. I always find the noise comforting."

The coursing water rushed over them, its echo reverberating through the rock as if to prove his point.

He cleared his throat. "I also apologize if I was curt with you down at the lake. I had a lot on my mind."

She sighed. "It didn't help that I was trying to pry into your life. It's not my business, so I guess I'm sorry, too. We're even."

"That works for me."

"So how did you find me?"

"I track things for a living."

"Ah, right."

The rush of the waterfall overtook the small cavity. In the hush, Kara's mind shifted everywhere: the cave and its dank honeydew smell; Twin, sopping wet and screaming that there was no bringing the dead back; her mother's hand releasing its grip seconds before the hospital heart monitor flat lined. Kara's cheeks flushed more with each passing image, so she grasped desperately for the next available memory: her conversation with the Vagabond.

There were three more pieces to that map, and finding the old ghost's village was as good a distraction from the pain as any. It was purpose and a sense of direction. If the other kingdoms wanted her to visit anyway, it was the perfect chance to find the map corners without letting anyone know what she was doing.

At some point while she was lost in thought, Braeden had closed his eyes. A thin smile played on his lips as the water roared over them. He might not be able to go to the kingdoms with her, but at the very least, he might have some advice.

She opened her mouth to tell him about the map, but her words fell flat. Her gut twisted at the thought telling anyone about the village. The hair on her neck tingled, just as it had when she'd found the Grimoire.

She held her tongue.

"You okay?" he asked, eyes still closed.

"Not really."

"Do you want to talk about it?"

"Not really," she repeated.

"Would you rather be alone?"

"No. Sort of." She sighed. "Yes."

"I'll leave you, then."

He shuffled out of the cave, the retreating crunch of his footsteps adding to Kara's lullaby of rushing water and crickets and wind.

The Grimoire shook from its place on the floor. Its cover parted when she glanced over to it, as if something was wedged beneath its pages, so she flipped it open. A wrinkled handkerchief lay on a blank page, a plain "V" stitched into its corner.

"Thanks," she said. The knot in her throat tightened as she picked it up, and memories flooded back to her without warning.

Her mother had already looked like a corpse in the ICU, with all of those hoses and tubes keeping her alive. Kara's hand ached from her mom's unconscious grip, but that wasn't the punishment. The real torture came when she woke up and tried desperately to speak, even though her mouth was always too dry. When she looked around, she'd seen everything and recognized nothing.

Kara didn't know which of her parents' deaths hurt her more. Her dad's face had contorted in unimaginable pain when Deidre stole his soul. The expression hadn't faded, even when he was a corpse on the living room carpet. She didn't know how, but he'd somehow controlled the isen long enough to tell her he loved her.

That, she had *not* deserved.

Twin asked me what my most influential memory was, but I have no idea. It has to be Mom or Dad dying, but how could I possibly pick one?

She leaned back against the rock wall and closed her eyes, rubbing her temples. Maybe it wasn't something she could choose for herself.

Sleep came without much of a warning, circling her mind until she pressed her cheek deep into the smooth boulder she'd so unknowingly borrowed from Braeden. Her last fleeting thought before she slept wasn't about Twin or her mom or even her dad. As she let the exhaustion take her, she realized she'd forgotten to ask the Vagabond for his real name.

❧CHAPTER THIRTEEN
THE WATERFALL

When Kara woke still in the cave behind the waterfall, she covered her eyes with a hand to shield them from the blinding sun. She lay on the floor, the handkerchief stained and stretched over the Grimoire as if it was a pillow. The waterfall diluted the sun into a haze as she looked out on the brilliant morning. She shoved the handkerchief into her pocket and rubbed the clover pendant to wish the Grimoire back into the stone.

The day was even brighter when she ducked out onto the path and hiked back to the cliff. Empty forests loomed on all sides, and as she looked around, she started to wonder if Braeden really had left. That was, at least, until she found him asleep on a boulder the size of a car.

He sat up and rubbed his eye. "You might not want to walk much farther. I always set quite a few traps before I sleep on a rock."

"Do you often sleep on rocks?"

"Sadly, yes." He laughed and offered her a seat beside him.

"I hope I didn't worry anyone," she said, pulling herself up onto the boulder.

"Of course you worried people. You're the Vagabond. You're priceless. Richard almost rallied the army. The Queen had to assure everyone that you were safe as long as I found you."

Exhaustion stung the skin around her eyes, so she didn't respond. She was flattered and insulted all at once at being considered "priceless." She wanted to say something, anything, but every time she looked up, the sun made her eyes sting and water. Relief pooled in her temples whenever she closed her eyes. He set a warm hand on her back.

"Did something happen yesterday, Kara?"

She wanted to rest her head on his arm and just go back to sleep, but she leaned back on her palms instead. When she didn't answer, Braeden brushed her shoulder with his. She glanced over and shook her head.

He nodded and slid off the boulder without another word, offering her a hand once he was on the ground. She took it and slid off as well, but he motioned for her to wait as he took a few steps toward the forest. The woods were quiet. Besides the rushing waterfall, there weren't any sounds. The birds didn't sing, and even the wind had disappeared overnight.

He lifted a hand to the forest and bowed his head. Sharp hisses sprang from the underbrush in response, and the bushes rustled. Gray light snaked through the trees. The silence broke all at once. Birds chirped, and leaves scraped each other as if on cue.

"What was that?" she asked.

"Those were the traps I mentioned. I needed to release them, so that no one would run across them later on accident."

"What happens if someone gets caught in one of them?"

"That isn't something you want to know," he said. He forced a smile and led the way back to Hillside.

✗

No one in the castle acknowledged that Kara had disappeared for a night without telling anyone why. No one asked what made her run off, or even mentioned that she'd left at all. Braeden assured her this was out of respect for her privacy, but when she went to the dining hall, the averted glances of the soldiers suggested something more. The conversation lulled when she passed, and more than one Hillsidian stretched across two places, making their half-filled tables seem full. So, in the week after that first breakfast back at the castle, she brought her meals to the waterfall and spent her time training by Braeden's boulder.

Each morning, the sun would break through her open curtains and illuminate the small gift that always appeared overnight: a small satchel filled with fruits, cheeses, and a water flask. She never questioned it and hoped it came from Twin, who had vanished. No one else appeared to replace her.

A week dragged by. Kara pried more secrets from the Grimoire while in her solitude, using the isolation to master the flame. She then graduated to fireballs and an intense technique she called sparklers, which set the ends of her hair on fire the first time she tried it.

The waterfall served as her backdrop as she meditated, read, and practiced; with each new technique, her panic at what Ourea expected of her as its last vagabond ebbed ever-so-slightly. The Grimoire seemed to prefer lectures to lessons, unfortunately, and in her studies, she read more magical theories than she had time to practice. Still, it was valuable.

Magic had nothing to do with spells and structured law, but was more a mastery of focusing her mind on a certain task and bending energy to control it. It was tiresome. She often walked back to the castle before the sun set just so that she could sleep, always slipping through the halls to avoid any communication on the way back to her room.

On her eighth day of the solitary lessons, Braeden caught her attention as she walked through the door by the orchard on her way to the waterfall. She sighed. She still didn't want any company, even his.

"Can I join you?" he asked, grabbing her satchel from her arm without waiting for her answer. He snatched a roll from its depths and took a bite.

"I—hey, don't eat my food! And no offense, but I'd rather be alone."

"Be nice." He nudged her and grinned. "If you let me come, I'll show you a magic trick."

"Which one?"

"Come on." He winked, but didn't answer her question as he jogged along the trail toward the waterfall with her food and water, leaving her little option but to follow.

He slowed to a walk as she came up beside him, but they didn't talk for a fair bit of the way. Birds chirped in the twittering forest, hidden in the canopy, and now and again one would dive into the underbrush beside the trail. The woods were sprightly today, the trees doing their lively dance with the wind. Little rodents with bushy tails as long as their brown bodies raced across branches, but she stopped herself from assuming that they were squirrels. Considering the other creatures she'd already met in Ourea, the little squirrel-things could probably breathe fire or something. She kept away from them.

"Why have you kept to yourself this week?" Braeden asked. The breeze rustled his hair. He kept one hand in his pocket and wrapped the satchel's strap around the other as he moved closer to her.

"I like being alone," she said.

"Something tells me that isn't true."

She shrugged. The distant roar of the waterfall started as they turned a corner in the trail.

"I hope this doesn't seem rude, but you should remember that you're the Vagabond," he said. "Most of the kingdom hasn't even seen you. You're supposed to be shaking hands and—well, what's the phrase? You should be out kissing babies."

"I don't like kids."

He laughed. "That's not quite what I meant."

"I know."

They took a bend in the trail and the waterfall loomed in front of them, its mist rising as the day warmed. Braeden set her satchel on the boulder, but she picked it up and slung the bag over her shoulder. She missed her hiking pack; it was a thing of comfort to have some weight on her back.

"So, what's this magic trick you said you were going to show me?" she asked. She rolled up her sleeves as the sun climbed higher and toasted her skin.

"It's called blades. Have you learned it? You make an arrow from the air around you."

"Nope. Will you show me?"

"Gladly."

He faced the woods and pressed his fingers together, settling his hands close to his chest. The breeze picked up as if in response to his movement and blew harder when he turned his fingers away from his body. His hands shook for a second, as if he was trying to steady them in an earthquake. A ripple of air shot from his fingers with a sharp hiss. It broke through a limb on a tree and sent the branch crashing to the ground.

"That's so cool!" She laughed, clapping before she set her hands in front of her to mimic him.

"Whoa! Hey, now." He shuffled out of her way before she realized that she'd been aiming at him.

He stepped behind her, wrapping his fingers around her wrists so that he could angle her toward the forest. Her heart skipped a beat. She held her breath and tried to tell herself that she was just nervous about performing magic in front of someone.

"Keep your arms relaxed and focus on your fingers. Pull the air toward you," he said, his voice low.

Water misted on the backs of her arms, carried by a strong gust that flew along the falls and tangled her hair. The wind poured over her hands and ducked through her palms. Her muscles tensed.

"Don't be frustrated if—"

Braeden's words were cut off by a dull thump in a nearby tree trunk. Kara jogged over to take a look.

The top layer of bark had been stripped away, leaving a small nick in the tree. The clean sliver of wooden skin lay on the grass, and the wind picked it up and carried it deeper into the forest.

"Darn." She sighed and used the trunk to push herself to her feet. "That wasn't nearly as good as yours."

"I—" He pouted in a stunned silence before he laughed.

"What's wrong?"

"It took me two months to do what you just achieved on your first try. That's just not fair, Kara."

"Oh. Sorry?"

He shrugged. "No, it's a good thing. This one can help you out of almost any situation, and it might even impress the Kirelm Blood. He's not easy to win over."

"Have you met him?"

"No, but I have heard stories, and none of them are very flattering. Mind, few of them are actually from his people, but the Kirelm Blood isn't very fond of women in positions of power. I'm curious to see what he thinks of you."

"I caught that little compliment." She poked his side. "You can't get on my good side that easily."

He grinned. "You watch. I'll win you over."

"So, are we supposed to go to Kirelm first?" she asked. It took an awkward, silent second before she remembered that he wasn't going with her.

"Yes, *you* will be going to Kirelm first," he answered. "I will be hunting isen in the nearby villages."

"I forgot," she said. "When are you supposed to leave?"

"Yesterday. There was a delay in my travel plans."

"What was the delay?"

He just smiled. "Try again."

"I, um—do you want me to rephrase the question?"

He laughed. "No, try the technique again."

"So you're not going to answer me?"

"No."

She laughed along with him. "All right, then."

Kara turned to face the trunk, locking her fingers and pointing them toward the tree. He took a step closer, looming in her peripheral vision.

"Try relaxing your fingers more this time," he said, brushing his hand along hers to demonstrate. "Curve them, instead of locking them out like that. Focus your mind on your fingertips and pull the air itself into your palms. If you relax, you will be able to harness the energy in the elements instead of using your own. That way, you can fight longer. Just pull in the air and direct where you want it to go."

Kara settled into her stance and set all of her weight on her heels. The wind whistled by her ear and shifted through her loose hair, tickling her neck as she took a deep breath and cleared her mind. A pulse blinked in her fingertips, but it wasn't hers. It beat at a much slower pace.

She closed her eyes. The rhythm grew stronger, so she reached out to it with her mind and tried to breathe in a deep, steady pattern. Her veins boiled, and a shock raced through her body. The zing reminded her of the spark which had blown Deidre across the library. A hot breeze blew again over her shoulders, along her hands, and down through her palms.

Another thin ripple broke from her fingers and cut through the air, but it was much more prominent this time. Wood split with a sudden whack, like an axe hitting a tree. A white slice broke across the bark, visible even from where she stood a dozen feet away. She hadn't cut anything in half, but Braeden's expression would have suggested otherwise. She threw her hands in the air in victory.

"That is entirely unfair," he muttered. "How can you improve so quickly?"

"I didn't do it right, though," she pointed out. "I didn't cut anything in half."

"I couldn't even make the tiniest blade for ages," he said, crossing his arms. "What else can you do?"

"I've been working on a few fire techniques," she said, shrugging. "And I think I found another one that can let me control roots."

"I guess I shouldn't doubt anything about the Grimoire and its keeper."

He ran a hand through his hair and leaned against the boulder. After a minute, he stood and began pacing, his black hair slightly brown in the sunlight as he looked out over the waterfall and its river below. He bit his cheek as he walked, but otherwise, his carefree face was smooth. There was no way of telling from a glance just how much of his life was a lie. She sighed.

"Braeden, I've been pretty selfish."

"What? How?"

"You—" She stopped, uncertain of how to word what she wanted to say. "You've done so much to keep me safe, and I appreciate that. I figure that you must have plenty of questions for the Grimoire. I just want you to know that I'd be happy to ask it anything you wanted. It's my way of saying thank you for everything."

"Thank you, Kara. I admit that I do have a question for it, but it's not safe to ask while in Hillside." A shadow crossed his face, but he rubbed his neck and looked away before she could figure out what it meant.

"Oh," she mused, glancing around the forest's empty morning. "I thought this would be a safe place, though, if Gavin doesn't even know about it."

"We're still in Hillside," Braeden said. "You're almost never alone, even when you're certain no one else could be around."

"Sure, but—"

"There you are, Vagabond!" a woman shouted from beyond a curve in the trail.

Kara jumped and turned to see Adele's coppery skin as the muse walked along the trail toward them. Garrett was close behind, but while Adele walked with a smooth and carefree gait, his eyes flitted across the forest. His gaze would linger on a bush or in the canopy, his jaw clenched as he watched, before his eyes shifted again to examine the rest of the underbrush. He finally looked at Kara, settling his intense scrutiny on her. She curbed the impulse to shudder.

Adele smiled. "We have convinced the drenowith Council to meet with you. It was not an easy task, so we must take you there now, before minds change."

"Where is it?" Braeden stopped pacing, his hand suddenly resting on the hilt of his sword. He was calm, but his smile was gone, and he rubbed his thumb on the handle. Kara balked. Where had the sudden tension come from?

"We have discussed your joining us, prince," Garrett answered. "And you may. However, you may not come into the Council."

"But—"

"There is no debating this," Garrett interrupted. "It's not your world, Braeden, and you aren't welcome there. It took us this long to even convince them to see Kara. Verum would never allow you as well."

"Is Verum really someone's name?" Kara interjected. She stepped between the men and nudged Braeden's shoulder in what she hoped was a subtle warning for him to relax.

"It's more his purpose than his name," Adele answered, glaring at Garrett. "There are three sides to every story: yours, your foe's, and the truth. Verum always knows the truth. The Council wants to see your intentions before they will make any further decisions regarding you."

"What decision do they have to make? I don't matter to them."

"The Grimoire matters to everyone, Kara, as does its keeper," Adele corrected. "Even those as old as the dirt have something to learn."

"We will take you, but we must blindfold you both." Garrett cupped one hand and reached into it the other one, like a magician pulling cards out of his sleeves. Instead of cards, though, he pulled two red silk scarves from the air.

"Braeden, you must stay hidden once we arrive," Adele said. "The Council can never know that you were there."

"I may not know much about drenowith, but I'd imagine it's a crime to lie to your Council," Braeden said. "Why should I hide?"

"Sometimes one must disobey in order to protect those who simply don't yet understand," Garrett retorted, glaring at the prince whose hand wound ever-tighter around his sword. Kara wondered who would win if they fought, though she was fairly certain Braeden would lose in a matter of minutes.

"Come," Adele said. She turned up the trail, her hair billowing behind her, but Garrett stood motionless.

Kara finally set her hand on Braeden's arm. He snapped his head toward her, his eyes even darker than before, but his gaze melted ever-so-slightly when he saw her expression. Garrett turned without another word and began up the trail after Adele.

"What is *wrong* with you?" she asked.

She made to follow Garrett without waiting for an answer, but Braeden wrapped his fingers around her arm and pulled her back. He moved in between her and the drenowith and leaned in to whisper.

"Kara, how did they know to come to the rescue? The Stele isn't a place to be infiltrated, not even by muses. The timing was too perfect."

She huffed, but stumbled over a response when she couldn't think of any reasonable explanation. Her heart beat a little faster at the realization.

"We shouldn't go," he said, his voice urgent. "And you definitely shouldn't go into their Council alone."

"Look, you have a point, but there is such a thing as coincidence. We were lucky, Braeden, and we should be grateful. Some things you just can't explain. I mean *look* at this place!" She gestured around to the waterfall and to the glowing blue clover pendant on her neck.

"It's foreign to you, but not to me. I fully understand this world," he said.

She spoke quietly, so that only he could hear. "You understand *your* world. Not theirs. They may live in Ourea, but you don't really know anything about them. There is no possible way for them to have coordinated us both being kidnapped like that. So, since it's more likely that they were just passing through when they saw us, the fact remains that they didn't have to save us. You could still be there, locked in shackles or already dead. Who knows what would have happened to me. If we can't trust them, we can't trust anyone."

"If those are our choices, then we can't trust anyone."

"Well I trust them, Braeden. You're wrong."

"I hope so," he mused.

"Are you with me or not? I can't make you go."

"Of course I'll go," he said, grumbling.

"That was the least encouraging 'yes' I have ever heard." She turned and walked toward the muses.

The red silk scarf Garrett had summoned from thin air was cool when Adele wrapped it around Kara's face. The fabric pressed on her eyelids, so she kept them closed and just listened. She heard Braeden groan as a breeze scurried by, thick with lavender and maple. The waterfall still thundered nearby. Twigs cracked as the muses finished tying the blindfolds.

The air to Kara's left shuddered. A sleek limb slid underneath her, lifting her feet off of the ground. It rose and she slid downward along it until it leveled out into what she assumed was the base of a neck. She grabbed it in instinct, and the thin crevices of delicate scales were as soft as a cotton shirt. Her stomach rocked and wind gushed in a cold gust over her face. The steady beating of wings flapped beside her.

She leaned into the neck and took a deep breath, hoping with all her heart that Braeden was, in fact, wrong.

❦CHAPTER FOURTEEN
THE DRENOWITH

Wind pummeled Kara's face as she soared, blindfolded, on the back of whatever creature Adele—or was it Garrett?—chose to become this time. Her hair whipped and stung her neck. The current of air swarmed past her ears with such ferocity that after a few minutes all she could hear was an incessant ringing. The frigid wind numbed her cheeks and the tips of her ears, and it wasn't long before she couldn't feel her skin at all. The loss of feeling did, however, distract her from the biting cold that raced up her sleeves, along her back, and out her collar, and for that she could only be grateful.

Her stomach lurched again and the wind blowing over her face slowed, signaling a drop in altitude. She clenched her eyes tighter behind the blindfold and wrapped her arms around her mount's scaly neck. The air warmed, but her skin still tingled. The momentum stopped with a sudden, soft thud. The cotton-soft scales moved out from underneath her so that she was once more on her feet.

Garrett's voice broke the ringing in her ear. "You may remove your blindfold, Kara."

A lazy wind teased the curls on her neck, tickling her. She pulled off the red sash and blinked until the world came back into focus.

They'd landed on a level platform cut into a mountain that looked out over the treetops of a forest. Vertigo shook her center of balance. She threw herself against the mountain wall to stable herself, but the dizziness stuck. Every nerve in her body prickled. The sheer cliff face stretched above her, blocking out half of the sky.

There was a small cave in the wall of the mountain, only a few feet taller than Kara herself and not much wider. It was dark inside. The smell of moss and the echo of water dripping through the rock made the crevice an unwanted mystery. A streak of blue slithered in her peripheral vision.

Garrett stood nearby, but Adele had not shifted back into her human form; she was a small blue dragon, about the size of a horse and completely different from the red one that had rescued Kara from the Stele. Its scales were softer, and its thin head was long, probably three feet at least, with two spiraling horns jutting from the top of its head. Adele's rich blue eyes distracted Kara—for a moment, at least—from the fact that Braeden was not with them.

"Where is—?"

"Safe," Garrett interrupted. He shook his head once in a slow, subtle motion that implied they couldn't discuss this further.

Her stomach churned again, but this time it wasn't from the vertigo or the drop in altitude. She looked him over and took a deep breath, wishing that she knew where Braeden was.

Adele the blue dragon stretched her wings and crawled onto the cliff face, digging her sharp claws into the rock so that she could hang on the side of the mountain. Pebbles cascaded past her, bouncing off of each other as she ripped them from the stone. She paused and watched Kara as the wind picked up around them.

"You must go alone," Garrett said, nodding to the crevice.

"Why aren't you guys coming?"

"We have already made our arguments in your favor. This trial is yours alone."

"Wait, this is a trial now?"

"They're deciding whether you're worthy of drenowith intervention, Kara. They will judge you."

Garrett's form flickered and popped. He shifted into a blue dragon that was larger but otherwise identical to Adele's new form and raced up the mountainside without pausing to say another word. Dust and small rocks tumbled past in his haste. Adele, however, waited. She made a soft noise, like a dove cooing, and then tore up the mountain after him.

Kara took another deep breath and peered into the cave. It was dark after the first couple of feet, so her first instinct was to listen. Steady dripping echoed from its recesses and the sharp zing of moss and slime caught in her nose. She ran her hands along the cave wall as a guide and inched her way through the darkness.

Her eyes didn't adjust, even after five minutes of shuffling through the pitch black cave, and the nerves in her stomach twisted with a vengeance that broke her focus each time she tried to start a fire in her palm. She wanted to call out, to see if someone was nearby or if the cave would end soon, but her lungs deflated and her voice caught in her throat.

Light winked into view ahead on the left. It was close. She headed for it. The glow brightened, and shapes bled into view: boulders and the recesses of a massive cavern. When she reached the entry, she paused and examined this new cave.

The ceiling was a hundred feet high, and small breaks in the rock above let in daylight that illuminated the white birds soaring overhead such that they glowed. The birds ducked and rolled, swerving around the thick stalactites which hung from the ceiling. A towering waterfall in the distant corner of the cavern tumbled into a pool, which broke away in creeks through deep channels carved into the rock. One of these streams passed in front of her and disappeared into a break in the wall. The echoes of water rapids gushed from its depths.

The walls were lined with a green and blue fog that hummed with a life of its own. Kara brushed her fingers through the mist, which wrapped itself around her hand at her touch. The fog shifted over her skin, leaving a tingling itch everywhere it passed. She shook it off.

Across the stream, about thirty feet away, a clump of stalagmites rose from the floor. Each was a dozen or so feet tall and as clear as glass, but they glinted in the light and distorted the world behind them.

A small man sat in a throne carved into the center of the cluster. He wore a simple, tan robe and hunched over himself on his perch, his hands folded in his lap. The wrinkles on his face cascaded over each other, hiding his eyes and rippling to his chin. Two wiry gray eyebrows clung to his forehead and told her where to find his eyes if he did ever manage to open them.

"Welcome, Vagabond," he said. The cavern's acoustics amplified his voice until it was a bellow. A few birds resting on the top of his massive throne flew off at the sound.

"I am Verum," he continued. "I see that which you don't see in yourself and that which you wish to hide. Be still and don't be afraid."

Figures appeared from behind the throne, and as she saw each new face, her fear became more difficult to suppress. A colossal, red serpent with yellow stripes slithered around the throne on the last few feet of its tail, most of its body raised as it sniffed the air with its tongue. Human figures in green satin robes joined the snake, but Adele and Garrett were not among them. A minotaur walked around the throne and glared with cold black eyes that made her heart skip a beat.

He was several feet taller than her and thick wool covered his entire body. His bull's head finished with thick, sharpened horns, and as she looked him over, she recalled the minotaur that huffed its way past the hidden cave after she'd escaped the Stele. She forced herself to swallow hard, since this couldn't be the same beast, but the racing panic would not dissolve.

The minotaur cleared his throat. "Child, drenowith don't lightly intervene. It's not our purpose and not our way. But considering that fate brought you to meet not one, but two of our kind, we are considering whether you are truly worthy to keep them near. They have chosen to stay by you, should the Council permit, though the rest of us can't understand why."

Kara didn't know what to say, so she glanced back to Verum. His eyebrows were higher on his forehead, now, and two green eyes watched her from behind his wrinkles.

"Did you know that the first Vagabond learned most of his gifts here, in this hall?" Verum asked. "All those years ago, Adele took the young man as her pupil."

"I had no idea. Adele never told me."

Kara's mind raced back to the small cave with the scar in the wall, when the muses had told her she could never go home. "*You remind me of someone I lost,*" Adele had said. "*I failed him. I will not fail you.*" Had she failed the Vagabond, then?

"Do you understand why we are hesitant to help you?" Verum asked.

"I have a guess."

"What is that guess?"

"You don't know if yakona are worth saving."

"Life is always worth saving."

"Why, then?"

He hunched farther in his chair and coughed before scooting to the edge of his seat. He gripped the throne's arm with his thin fingers, their wrinkles visible even from where she stood by the entrance. She walked closer so that he wouldn't have to strain his voice, crossing the stream to close the gap between them as he spoke.

"It was Adele that once taught the Vagabond to break a yakona's bloodline loyalty, but we never imagined the consequences such a gift would bring against him. To us, it was knowledge learned for its own sake, but it changed him from a prophet to a threat. His knowledge drove greater fissures through the tensions of his people. It was his power and vast understanding of magic that ultimately destroyed him.

"We prefer to be myths, Vagabond, for when we interfere as we did then, we so very often destroy. Yet here you are, a human who knows little of this world, and you do need our help. Ourea is a fascinating and deadly place."

He sighed. "I am therefore torn. The Grimoire is a powerful tool, one you alone can wield. Should your intentions in its use be flawed, I will not permit any drenowith near you. There are few of us left in this age. We must protect each other. I will search your mind, now, to discover these truths."

"I hope this doesn't sound rude," she interjected. "But I don't even *have* intentions yet. I'm still learning."

He frowned. "You don't need to speak for this. Your mind will tell me all I need to know."

Well *that* was comforting.

Verum closed his eyes and leaned back in his seat. Fingers brushed Kara's arm. She turned, but there was only the rock wall behind her. The unseen hands crept along her neck to her temples. Her body froze. She couldn't move. The base of her neck began to throb. Her bones suddenly ached. The dull pain pounded in her head until it clouded her ears. Her eyes twitched.

Verum's frown deepened. His wrinkles grew longer.

"Why does your mind insist that you killed your own mother?"

Kara stopped breathing. The raging gust of the waterfall faded. All she could hear was a ringing noise, like she'd heard on the flight over. Her words stuck in her throat, and she watched the old man with a barely beating heart. He was going to make her relive everything, but all she'd ever wanted was to forget.

"Your heart vies for redemption and yet also longs for peace," he continued. "These two forces are destroying you from within."

Memories sprang, unbidden, from the depths of her mind. She pushed against them, but they shrugged off the chains with which she'd tried to subdue them and consumed her once again.

It's a hot and humid Tallahassee night. Rain licks the windshield. Miles of wet road shift beneath the headlights. Spanish moss hangs from the low tree canopy along the road.

"Stop," she whispered. The invisible hands dug into the base of her neck.

Mom is sitting in the passenger's seat, clutching her stomach from the stabbing pain. It has lasted all evening and it's so bad that she said she can barely see. Her face flushes green and she holds her hand to her mouth, suppressing the bile. The hospital is just three miles away. Miccosukee Road is the fastest route.

The tires skid once, but Kara recovers.

"We shouldn't have gone this way." Her mother's voice echoed in Kara's mind, drowning out even the ringing.

"Please," Kara begged.

She tried to look up at the old man in his throne, but her eyes were blurry. She couldn't see past the tears. She was somehow kneeling. Her knees ached. She must have fallen hard on them. The memory pulled her back.

"You know I don't like this road, Kara. Too dangerous at night."

They veer around a curve. Mom heaves again. The vomit splashes down the seat and hits the floor mat in chunks. Another curve. The stench burns the air in the cabin. The car races over a hill.

Kara stuttered, her cheeks hot and flushed. She sobbed. Her temples and her throat and her knees all stung. She pushed against the memory, fighting to stay in the cavern and not relapse into reliving that night again. Not again.

"Please, God, not again," she sobbed.

But the memory recoiled and pushed harder as she battled it. She was losing.

A ditch passes beneath the headlights. The car skids, but recovers one last time. The curves are sharper on this stretch of the road.

"Kara, for God's sake! Slow down—"

Mom rolls her window down. She misses. More vomit spills on the seat. The sweat on her brow makes her hair stick to her face like glue.

"Slow down." The words repeated in Kara's head until they no longer made sense, until they were just a meaningless echo in her mind.

They were the last words Mom ever said.

The road snaps to the left. The yellow reflector is there, hidden by a low-hanging tree, but it isn't visible in time. The car hydroplanes. They scream and slide. The ditch looms suddenly into view and is gone just as quickly. The tires squeal and screech. Metal crunches. Glass shatters. A scream is cut short.

Mom is in the passenger seat. She's staring out the front of the car, eyes out of focus. There's a deep gash from her temple to her jaw. It's bleeding and bubbling. It's really deep.

"STOP!" Kara screamed.

She tried to yell again and swear at the old man, but she was sobbing too hard to do anything. Her shoulders ached and shook. Her knees trembled, even though she was curled on the floor. Breath came in shaky bursts because of the thick, choking tears.

It took a moment of wiping away the hot trails from her face, but she did look up at the old man through the sobs. She could see him, but the rest of the Council members were just blurred figures in her peripheral vision. He glared down at her with his beady little green eyes.

The tension in her forehead dissolved. The memories abated and, for a moment, she could breathe again. Relief flooded her lungs. She buried her face in the dust on the floor and covered her head.

"You are damaged, Vagabond. You can't expect to heal a broken world until you yourself are whole."

"I don't want this," she said.

"In your world, you were not found guilty of murder, unintentional or otherwise," Verum continued, ignoring her. "Yet the guilt eats away at you. You are a murderer, but only in your own mind."

Her cheeks burned. She tightened her hands into fists and her knuckles bleached white. Her stomach twisted. Numbness ate at her from the inside out. She wanted to scream, to run, to defend herself, but the painful truth had been finally dragged from her.

The hall was still except for the race of the waterfall. The wet-soil smell of mold suddenly pricked her nose. She tried to speak, but her voice was a crackled whisper with no meaning. Her head was too heavy to lift. She couldn't meet anyone's eye.

Her heart slowed after a few steady breaths so that she couldn't hear her pulse anymore, which was a start. She pushed herself to her knees, plucked up what remained of her pride, and finally looked back at Verum. The sage wrapped his fingers one over the other, slowly.

"Why, if you were not found guilty, does this death eat away at you?" he asked.

She just shook her head in response.

"Do you consider yourself above the law?" he continued. "Have you defied it?"

"No, sir." She tasted the lie on her tongue as she spoke. When Verum opened his mouth to continue, to catch her in her dishonesty, she held up her hand to stop him.

"I'm not above *your* laws."

"But of course you consider yourself above our laws. You have the gifts of the Vagabond, the coveted knowledge of his Grimoire, and you would use your new powers to conquer death. I see it in the way you carry yourself, in the way you speak, more so than in your mind. Your parents were both lost because of something you did. Family means more to you than anything else, yet you are an orphan. At your own doing, no less."

She bit her tongue and looked at the floor, swallowing the growing knot in her throat as she tried to answer him.

"Death isn't your law," she finally said.

"No, but the earth is our law. Balance is our order. We guard Her ways because without a world in which to live, there is no life. Death is a part of this balance and you will never overcome Him. Remember that above all else, because your attempts to do so will be your undoing."

His eyes shifted from green to black. She shuddered.

"Human, you aren't fit to protect Ourea. Not yet, at least. Return to me when you have healed yourself and we may once more breach this question."

"Are you saying—?"

"You may not have drenowith guides until we speak again. You will leave now."

With that, he closed his eyes. She became aware of the room once more. They were alone, she and Verum. The other drenowith were long gone, and the ancient man was now as still as the crystal throne in which he sat.

A hand grazed her back. She snapped her head around, certain that the old man was searching for more memories, searching for more ways to torture her.

But it was only Garrett. He rested a hand on her shoulder and tried to smile, but the grin dissolved with a few twitches of his lips as he turned her back toward the cave through which she'd entered. The walk was silent and quick, and soon the sun broke around a bend in the tunnel. Adele waited on the platform outside, still a blue dragon. She nudged Kara's shoulder and knelt so that she could hop on. Kara obeyed.

Adele jumped off of the platform, gliding down on a draft to the forest below, but Kara barely registered the movement. Her head began to ache again. Groggy thoughts and memories resurfaced, spliced together in blood-soaked fragments.

"Kara?"

The voice was familiar, deep and concerned, but she didn't want to look up. She didn't acknowledge that she'd heard anything.

"What did you people do to her?!"

"She will be fine, prince."

"Kara, look at me." The voice grew louder. Hands brushed her face. They were warm and covered most of her cheek. She leaned into one and closed her eyes. The hands pulled her in and her ear brushed the soft fabric of a shirt. A heartbeat thudded against her eardrum, slow and steady, like a clock.

"Have her sit," Adele's muffled voice said. She'd shifted back to human form, then. Kara didn't open her eyes or look around. The heartbeat faded and her face was cold as the shirt pulled away. She was ushered onto a rough log and hands rubbed her arms, warming her with the friction.

"What was the verdict, Adele? Garrett?"

Silence.

There was a frustrated sigh. "Kara, drink this."

A flask pressed against her lips and she drank without thinking. A hot liquid burned her tongue and throat. She coughed and sputtered. Her mind snapped awake. The burning trailed down her throat and into her stomach.

She gasped. "What *is* that?"

"Whiskey. Magical stuff," Braeden answered with a grin.

She coughed again and looked around. They were in a forest. Trees arched above them, their green branches interwoven with one another such that they looked like supports in an attic. She sat on a log at the edge of a small clearing, and Braeden sat beside her. Garrett leaned against a tree with his back turned, but Adele was close, her arms wrapped around her torso as if she was somehow cold despite the hot day. She hunched her shoulders, and her eyebrows twisted in remorse.

"Hang the Council," Garrett said.

Adele shook her head. "No, my love."

"They're wrong."

"Verum has never been wrong."

"There's a first time for everything. Kara can be strong enough to succeed, but she needs help to get to that point. If we leave—"

"If they discover us, we will be killed for treason!" Adele said, her voice the barest whisper.

"*You* promised to never fail her, not me, yet even I know it's wrong to abandon her now," he snapped.

Adele whipped her head back as if he'd hit her.

"Guys, I'm right here," Kara said, standing. "I don't want anyone to die. I'll just figure this out on my own."

Adele sighed. "No, Garrett is right. The pendant I made for you when we met is a promise, one that would shame me should I ever break it. I was just so certain that they would understand," she said, looking down to the forest floor and fingering the round necklace with Kara's tear-diamond in its center.

"We must be careful," Garrett said, voice gentle once more. "Kara, when we return you to Hillside, you should leave immediately for the other kingdoms so that you don't stay in one place for very long. We have devised a way for Braeden to join you, if the prince is so inclined."

Braeden nodded. "Of course I will, though I have an idea of what you want me to do."

Adele pulled out a small pouch from her pocket and emptied the contents onto her palm. In it were two objects: a small blue orb and a triangle carved from marble the color of a mushroom. Roses were etched in fine detail into the triangle's corners. Adele left it alone, picking up the blue orb instead. A hazy green swirl snaked through it in the sunlight.

"These are the keys to both Losse and Kirelm. The only way for Braeden to join you is to pose as a member of their kingdom, as he has in Hillside. These keys will convince them of his loyalties to their crown."

"He just shows them a key and he's in?" Kara asked. "Great security."

Braeden grimaced. "No, not quite. Remember? Each kingdom's people look different, Kara."

"Ah, right. So you're going to change form? Like you did at the Stele?"

"That's our hope," Garrett said. "You will not be safe if you go alone to either Kirelm or Losse. Even while you were in Hillside, we worried."

Adele returned the keys to their pouch and threw it to Braeden before she reached behind the log, pulled out a brown backpack, and threw that to him as well.

"What is this?" he asked, catching it.

"Clothes for each of the kingdoms, as well as a sword from Ayavel. You need to be armed, prince, but a Hillsidian sword will raise suspicion. Aislynn is neutral to all of them, so she sends tribute and frequently trades. They will not question this blade."

Braeden knelt and rifled through the bag before he stood and shook his head.

"The Queen ordered me to kill an isen in the Eastern Hillside villages. She let me stay longer only to—um—" He stopped himself, his eyes flickering over to Kara and then to the grassy forest floor. He cleared his throat.

"I'll take care of the isen and give you the credit," Garrett said. "It's ideal cover to throw Hillside off your scent while you are with the Vagabond."

Braeden nodded. "That works."

"She will need to see you now so that she can recognize you later," Garrett pointed out.

"Right."

Braeden stood and dragged the pack into the nearby bushes. He took off his shirt, and Kara blushed, though she couldn't quite bring herself to look away. He had thick arms and a muscular torso with a single, thick scar down the right side of his chest. A thorny tattoo with sharp barbs and spikes spiraled down his arm, starting at his left shoulder and ending at his elbow. He glanced to her and shrugged when he caught her eye.

"What? I don't want to rip my clothes."

Kara didn't mind.

He closed his eyes and took a deep breath as the air around him shimmered and hummed. His skin faded to a dull shade of blue, and he grew a good two feet taller, but thinner at the same time. His ears inched backward, moving farther up his head, and his straight black hair grew out until it touched his shoulders. His eyes moved closer together and tripled in size, the black irises stretching until the whites were gone like they had been in his Stelian form. Kara shuddered at the memory, but was sure to smile when he looked over.

"That's awesome." She laughed. Braeden chuckled along with her and seemed to relax his shoulders.

"That is his Lossian form," Adele explained, unimpressed. "You will likely visit Losse second, since Kirelm is closer."

Braeden took that as his cue. The air hummed again. His now-blue skin dulled until it was tan once more, and continued to fade until it became as silver as a suit of armor without its shine. His shoulders broadened. He grew even taller. Large, black wings sprouted from his shoulder blades as Adele glanced nervously into the forest over her shoulder.

"Could you pick him out of a crowd, Kara?" Garrett asked.

"Maybe out of a lineup in Hillside," she quipped. Kara could remember that tattoo, provided that wasn't a commonality as well. She wondered if the other kingdoms mandated shirts. She hoped not and suppressed the urge to laugh at her own little joke.

"He should wear this, then." Garrett pulled a white shell necklace from his pocket. "It's an Ayavelian piece, just like the sword, so the other kingdoms will not think anything of it."

Kara nodded. "The necklace will help."

Braeden slipped the shell necklace over his head and returned to his Hillsidian self. Kara blushed at his bare chest again and tried not to stare. She'd done enough of that already. She turned and walked toward the edge of the clearing, searching for something to occupy her in an attempt to avoid creating awkward tension before what seemed like it would be a long trip.

"Vagabond, hold your foot!" Adele shouted.

Kara froze mid-stride and hoped that was what 'holding one's foot' meant.

Adele rushed to her and knelt, lifting a small blue egg from underneath her raised boot. Kara backed away and found the broken remnants of a nest that had fallen from a tree. Twigs and pine needles were strewn across the grass, the bulk of the nest flattened from its fall. Only the egg had survived. Blue egg shells littered the wreckage, implying that other eggs had either hatched already or hadn't been so lucky.

"What kind of bird is that?"

Adele smiled and held out the beautiful little blue orb without answering. It was polished and smooth, about the same size as a robin's egg, and had hundreds of tiny facets in it. The smooth dents made the egg gleam like a sapphire. Kara reached for it and rubbed the shell. It was as hard and cool as marble, and a faint orange glow radiated from its center. Adele grinned and shook her head, the tension of her argument with Garrett apparently already forgotten.

"Guard this egg," she commanded. "Don't worry, as it obviously doesn't break easily. Rub it often between your palms to keep it warm."

"What is it?" Kara asked again.

"A wonderful sign. You will see," Adele answered, but her grin faded. She held Kara's jaw with her gentle fingers, so soft to the touch that Kara almost didn't believe they were there.

"You have been through so much already, my girl, but the true hardships have not even yet been asked of you. I will help you as best I can, but I am afraid that I can't promise much."

Braeden yelled in agony, as if someone had run him through with a sword. Kara looked over, their moment broken. He cursed, the scream laced with pain so vicious and deep that it sent birds flying, startled, from a nearby tree. He grabbed his hand. His face twisted in pain as he fell onto the grass.

"What is it? What happened?" Garrett grabbed the prince's arms and helped him onto a fallen log.

Braeden's face flushed, his eyebrows distorted. He closed his eyes and white streaks grazed his temple.

Adele sat beside him and rested her hand on his back, setting her palm between his shoulders. Her entire body glowed white. The light ran down her arm and into his back, and at its touch, his breath slowed. His face relaxed.

"I felt this—a ripping sensation in my wrist," he said, his voice thin. "It was the worst pain I have ever felt in my life. Something terrible is happening. I think it involves Carden."

"Do you know where?" Adele asked.

He gazed off, his eyes out of focus. He watched the grasses twitch in the breeze as if they could speak to him.

"Hillside," he muttered.

❧CHAPTER FIFTEEN
AMBUSH

At the same moment Kara was led from the drenowith cavern, Blood Lorraine of Hillside patrolled her favorite path in all her kingdom, listening as her forest danced in the sunlight. There was nothing like a Hillsidian summer. She savored the aromatic blast of lavender and the heavy scent of clover on the breeze. Somewhere in the canopy, birds twittered.

The sunlight warmed her neck, which was left bare in this particular gown. She'd opted for a green dress without the collar today, to better enjoy the wind and to make her walk more pleasant. Woven leather trimmings hemmed the dress's seams, and her sleeves flared out over her deceptively tiny hands. Opponents underestimated her because she appeared so frail, but that was what she'd always wanted. However fragile she looked, she'd spent decades training in the very armory where Gavin now reigned.

The world grew more beautiful every day: more precious, as if it would fade away at any moment. Bit by bit, she relinquished her kingdom to her son without him even realizing. She'd even left her Sartori blade for him today, to examine while she walked.

She sighed. The legendary Sartori was her favorite weapon, one of only six in existence; only one had been made for each kingdom, too long ago to remember, and only a kingdom's royal bloodline could wield its blade. It was laced with an almost incurable poison and could become anything from a sword to a walking stick, shifting into whatever its master needed. It—

A soft shock froze her body. Blue light flickered in her peripheral vision. She became suddenly aware of the hidden lichgate through which she'd passed. An unknown meadow stretched before her, its tall orange grasses a carpet for the small hill a short ways off. Trees behind her lined the edge of the meadow.

Only the wind kept her company. The trees swayed, but no wildlife ran by. Her stomach clenched at a blend of smoke and sulfur and something else she couldn't place. The strange clawed its way into her lungs.

The breeze died, but the rotten stench grew stronger, until she could smell its subtle oak undertones. It was warm and unknown, with hints of musk and almond blurring its way through the acidic rot, but the meadow was calm and empty. She caught her breath and edged back toward the forest from which she'd come.

A Hillsidian with olive-colored skin and black hair ducked through the tree line to her left. The tall man grinned as he sauntered closer.

Why does he look so familiar?

"Braeden?" she called.

"Not quite," the man said. He took steady paces toward her, and she could see brow-lines etched into his forehead; wrinkles around his eyes; large pores along his nose and cheeks that gave his skin a worn, leather-like appearance. No, he was older than Braeden.

Blood Lorraine held her ground, even though her every instinct was to bolt through the lichgate and back to safety. Shame twisted in her stomach. She'd killed hundreds in her lifetime, and yet her instinct was to *run?* His stench clogged her nose, rooting her in place. Something about him was simply wrong.

"Who are you?" she demanded.

"I can see why the boy likes this form, though," he said, ignoring her question. "It's very easy to blend in when one is Hillsidian. Everyone around here is so trusting."

He pulled a thick blade from a scabbard on his back. Though Blood Lorraine did not recognize the man, she'd long studied his sword. He wielded the Stele's Sartori, a great black blade with silver poison that glistened on its edges as he lowered its point to the grass. He sneered.

She caught her breath in that frightful second of discovery. This was Blood Carden: master of the Stele—and Braeden's father.

Carden lunged. The blade lifted, aimed for her throat. Lorraine rolled out of the way and slid along the grass. She plunged her hands deep into the dirt as she moved, kicking up a trail of grass and small rocks that were buried in the soil. A green mist enveloped her as she skidded.

Horror and dread stabbed at her from within and fueled her as she summoned the only weapon that stood a chance against the Stele's Sartori. The weight bled into her hands, familiar and heavy and comforting. With a sharp cry, she summoned her own Sartori from the dirt.

Gavin could look at it later.

Back in Hillside, Gavin settled deeper into his mother's chair and admired her Sartori blade. It was beautiful, especially in its sword form. It had thick green steel and ornate silver designs etched into the blade itself. The hilt was heavier than he'd ever imagined her capable of wielding.

He tested it in one hand and then the other before he looked around her study. Ancient and invaluable books passed down for thousands of generations littered her shelves and her desk, a cherry oak creation with silver scrollwork inlaid along its base. A bay window on the far wall looked out on the main courtyard from which all the roads in Hillside began, and on the floor beneath the window, a thick patch of clover grew in a deep trench filled with soil. The warm musk of the clover flooded over him and made his eyelids droop, so he leaned back in the chair and grinned. Every aspect of the study radiated the power and security of her kingdom.

Someday, it would be *his* kingdom.

His smile widened at the thought of being the Blood, of resting the weight of his people on his shoulders and knowing that everyone would look to him for answers and guidance. He stood and spun the sword in the air, focusing his mind on the green metal in an effort to make it change form as it so often had for his mother.

He held the tip of the sword hilt in his palm, so that the blade pointed to the ceiling. It twirled on its head as he glared at it, spinning faster the longer he bent his mind around the image of an axe. It flickered as it spun. The green curve of a battle axe darted into the blur of spinning metal, but quickly disappeared. The blade slowed and began to tip, so he grabbed the hilt to keep it from hitting the floor.

He shrugged. There was still time to learn.

Sunlight darted through the window as a cloud passed by. He swung the sword once, twice, savoring the way the light turned red when it passed along the surface of the Sartori.

But on the third swing, the sword shot from his hands into the bed of clover.

The hilt disappeared into the dirt, slicing the heads from the plants in its way. In the seconds it took for him to race over to the patch of dirt and decapitated weeds, the blade had submerged itself. He dug through the soil, but it was gone.

"What did I just do?" he asked the dying heads of clover.

An unrelated panic raced through him and jolted him into a frenzy. Sweat poured down his back, and it was difficult to breathe. He rubbed his face until his cheeks were red from the friction. It was more than the thought of losing the blade; this burned deeper. Something terrible was brewing. His mother was in danger.

He grabbed his own sword from the cherry oak desk and ran out the door, down the stairs, and behind the castle. There were gasps, whispers, and even screams, but he ignored them all. His only purpose was to find his mother.

His feet led him to the stables, where he flung open the double-doors to the Queen's private wing and hurried along the stalls. The animals were all in an uproar, flailing around in the same panic that was slowly numbing every other thought in his mind. He stopped when he came to his mother's favorite mount: Mastif, her massive gray wolf.

The creature was the only steed in the hall that was not pacing or running or screaming. Mastif sat with its legs apart, braced to bolt with its haunches high in the air. The corners of its mouth quivered, exposing its sharp white teeth in its rage. Gavin threw open the wolf's stall door.

"Take me to her!" he commanded.

Mastif knelt. Gavin dug his hands around the long fur and pulled himself on without pausing to find a saddle. The wolf waited only long enough for Gavin's weight to fall onto its back before it tore through the stables and into the streets of Hillside.

Gavin didn't notice the countless citizens he passed as he and Mastif sprinted over the shifting roads of the market quarter. He didn't hear Richard rallying the guards and troops of all Hillside, or notice the fear which racked every face he passed. But most of all, Gavin didn't notice the one twisted soul, settled in the alley by a glove vendor, who was smiling at her handiwork from behind a face that was not her own.

※

Lorraine lunged at the Stelian king, her sword now in hand. She had only a fleeting moment of his surprise to leverage against him. It needed to be used well.

Carden parried her attack, spun, and threw an uppercut to her jaw. She buckled under the hit but stood just as quickly, already healed, and shot her hand toward his face. A trail of thorns and ivy burst from the ground at the gesture, flying and turning and twisting in any direction she chose. The thorns wrapped around his face and neck, slicing apart whatever skin they touched. Black blood oozed over the thorns.

Her heart skipped a beat. Black blood: this truly *was* Carden. It hadn't been real, even after seeing the Sartori, until she saw his blood.

Her thorns twisted and tightened the more he fought, but a black fog whistled from the pores on his arms. It warped the thorns, bending them as they dissolved with acidic pops and hisses. The vines drooped and broke off, falling in limp streaks of green to the charred grass at Carden's feet.

She swung for his neck as the hundreds of oozing black wounds congealed and shrank away, healed. He parried and hit her hard in the chest with his palm, drawing the wind around him in a rush of hot air that shot her backward a dozen feet. Her body skidded and rocks scraped away layers of skin, but the wounds stitched themselves together as she stood and dove for him once more. They attacked and retreated in this deadly tango, leaving curving trails of broken meadow grasses as they fought and ducked and rolled.

Lorraine tripped over her long skirt and fell, rolling away from Carden mere seconds before he stabbed the ground where she'd just been. She grabbed the edge of her skirt as she ducked beneath another swing and, with three mighty rips, made her elegant silk gown a knee-high dress without sleeves.

Carden grinned. "I am pleasantly surprised. I was under the impression that this would be too easy."

He twirled his Sartori in his hand and the blade shimmered, blurring until it became a spiked mace with foot-long barbs that reflected the sunlight. She resisted the instinct to match his weapon and shift her own Sartori, since she was best with a sword. If he'd known enough to lure her away from Hillside while she walked her favorite trails, he probably knew her strengths and how to play around them.

"I already knew the truth about your son," the Queen said, using the truth in an effort to throw him off-guard. "I've known from the first night, when Braeden changed form in his sleep."

Carden raised his eyebrows in surprise and paused. He grimaced and laughed darkly, shaking his head. The air around him vibrated and hummed as his body stretched higher and his skin faded into the same dark charcoal gray Lorraine had seen the night Braeden had been brought to her. Carden sneered.

"This is what you saw?" he asked, his voice deeper than before.

A rush of memories made her stagger: Braeden shifting to his Stelian form, fast asleep and only twelve; her Sartori blade hovering over the boy's neck as he slept; her throat catching as he reached for her hand in his sleep. She'd pulled the sword away, wondering if Richard would understand while simultaneously knowing that Gavin never would.

Lorraine took a deep breath to bring herself back to the meadow. Her body warmed and the magic took over, clearing her mind while dissolving the fear and shame into a rush of glee. The burning current of power— Father had called it the daru when she was little—churned beneath her skin, begging for release, but she wasn't yet sure if she needed to tap this deeper power. It would give her added strength and speed, certainly, but its cost was control. She would be lost to the bloodlust of the fight.

She swallowed. Against Carden, she would likely need control and cunning over strength. She hoped he was too arrogant to tap into his own daru, and since he'd come alone to face her, that was likely the case. Whatever he'd done to Braeden had scarred that boy for life, so she would end this. She would end *him*.

"Braeden deserves better than your bloodline," she said. "I have always loved him, though, regardless of what he is."

"You're lying," Carden snapped. "You would never have allowed him into your home if you knew."

"I never lie. He will be more powerful than me, someday, and is already more skillful than you if this is the best you can do. I saw his potential. He is capable of good, even though he was bred to destroy. He needed a second chance."

"This is a surprise, I suppose, but irrelevant. I need my son to return to me, my Queen, and I have reason to believe that your son isn't as wise as you are. When he reigns, he will send Braeden back to me."

The Stelian king swung the mace and missed her jaw by inches. She rolled away and tightened her hands around her sword's hilt.

"Gavin will surprise you."

Blood Carden swung again at her neck, but she ducked her head beneath it. It sailed overhead, and a spike sliced off a trailing lock of her hair, which fell, smoking, to the ground. Carden continued twisting until he spun around completely. He aimed his left fist toward her jaw.

She pressed her hand to the ground and the soil convulsed at her touch. A wave of dirt and rocks melted beneath him like an ocean, twisting as it swallowed his legs. The forest rumbled and the wave bent with his weight, pulling him into the earth as Lorraine lunged for his neck. She swung as he was pushed off balance, but he managed to twist just out of her range. She missed his neck, but the blade dug deeply into his wrist instead.

He yelled in agony. Her Sartori's poison seeped into his blood and settled deeper along its deadly course. She could feel its movement as if she directed it: deeper, deeper through his veins, headed for his heart.

This would all be over once it found his tiny, black heart.

The wave of soil and dirt froze, but he broke through it like a hammer through ice. He rolled onto the grass beside the chasm, cradling his hand, and even though he had overcome the liquid rock which she'd used against him, she smirked.

"At last, you prove your worthlessness," she said, sword point to the grass. "A quick battle is all it took? You should have known not to underestimate your opponent, however fragile she may seem."

Lorraine lunged for the Stelian king's chest, certain, now, that this was the end. Braeden would become the Stelian Blood, yes, but she could teach him to master the darkness. He would learn to control the rage and then, once he was ready, she would tell Hillside. Her adopted son would no longer have to hide who and what he really was.

But as she charged, she fell into Carden's trap.

Carden spun with a sudden force and knelt, catching her arm. He stood, pulled her around, and slid behind her. His Sartori shifted into a simple black dagger that he sank into her lower back. Its handle pushed against her spine. Nerves snapped. Bones shattered. Her blood raced to the wound, but the poison kept the healing stitches at bay. Her senses quickly faded, and numbness seeped into her fingertips until all she could feel was the soft wind on her dry lips.

A thick hand cradled her jaw. Her eyes shifted, slow, to see the Stelian king's thick black gaze so close to hers. He brushed back the hair hiding her ear.

"You failed to take your own advice, pretty little Queen. Never underestimate your opponent," —he chuckled, the noise rumbling in his chest—"or his tolerance for pain."

He released her face and yanked his Sartori from her back, letting her crumble to the ground. There was a dawning thought that her hands were empty, her Sartori gone. She heard a sizzle. Carden held the green sword with a grimace as his skin burned on the hilt he was not meant to touch. She wanted to scream at him, but her throat was dry. Parched.

None should touch the Sartori but its master! I am its master. I am not yet—I am not yet—

She meant to think *"dead,"* but her mind went blank as she watched the Stelian Blood retreat. His breath came in ragged gasps, and his jaw was tight from the poison seeping through his veins. His entire hand was soaked in black liquid that dripped over the hill, hissing as his acidic blood burned away the rich meadow grasses. He paused and looked back over his shoulder, turning toward a sound she couldn't hear.

"Your son is quick, but not fast enough." He winked. "How sad that your senses are almost gone. You will barely hear his voice when he does arrive. Still, try to tell him that I send my best."

He peered once more into the woods beyond her vision before he turned away. Something scampered onto his shoulder—or was that just a play of the light? The air around him cracked after a few limping steps, and a thick black mist erupted around him, swallowing him entirely. The smoke engulfed him, marring the summer morning like dark dust tumbling from a fan. When it cleared, he was gone.

Lorraine sank her cheek into the grass. The light began to dissolve into white spots across her vision.

✠

Gavin caught only the sinister glare of his mother's attacker before the man limped off and disappeared into a thick black fog. The wind blew it away in a matter of seconds, so that all that remained in the meadow was bright sunlight and his mother's labored body.

He leapt from the wolf before it stopped and ran to her. Mastif crept up behind him, whimpering, as Gavin knelt and lifted his mother's head into his arms. The whites of her eyes flickered beneath her eyelids as she tried to see him.

"Gavin," she whispered. Her voice broke on his name.

He shushed her as the wolf lay down and cried again, setting its nose gently by its master's thigh. It whined and nudged her.

"Mastif, good boy—" She lifted a hand, and the wolf set his massive nose inside her small palm.

"Mother..." Gavin began, but he couldn't think of anything else to say. He moved her hand away from her wound. Her blood bubbled, reacting to the poison left behind by what could only have been a Sartori. Tears bruised his eyes. He fought them back so that he could see and hear her.

"Mother, who did this? Who was that?"

"Carden." She was weak, her voice soft.

He pulled her in tighter and stroked her hair, but she set a finger on his nose to get his attention.

"I cut him, so he took my—*your* Sartori. In each sword lies the antidote to its poison. He has your blade. You must retrieve it." Her voice became softer and more distant with every word.

Gavin just nodded, without the faintest idea of how he was supposed to do that.

"How can we heal you, Mother? Is there anything but the Stele's Sartori? Anything?" The pain in his throat burned his words. Tears snuck by, unbidden.

She just smiled.

"Tell Richard that I will wait for him."

"You can tell him. Just hold on. Hold on for me."

She shook her head, eyes closing.

"I knew this was—" She sighed. "The world is changing. I am not strong enough, any longer, to survive it."

She licked her cracked lips and paused, so he stroked her hair and held her tighter. There was nothing else he could do.

"You are worthy, son. You will make me proud." Her voice trailed off into a whisper, and she smiled again. Gavin laughed along with her, the sound broken and humorless.

Her eyes snapped suddenly into focus, as if she'd remembered something crucial, and she tried to speak, but her voice came out too soft to hear. The sound was just a rush of air through her lips, which Gavin could barely read. All he caught was his brother's name.

"What about Braeden?"

She nodded and continued to mouth broken words. He tried to follow, but the movement ate the last of her energy. Her lips slowed, she closed her eyes, and she faded. He cradled her until her lungs stopped.

When her last breath left her, it seemed that his next breath burned him more than any fire ever had. His lungs stung, as if filled with needles that tore through his body with a life of their own. His veins melted. The echo of his yell rang through the forest before he realized he was screaming. The woods were quiet after his noise: breathless, waiting, lost to his agony as he became Hillside's next Blood.

He curled around himself in the meadow. The charred, broken grasses brushed his face for what seemed like days until the searing blister abated. Even then, he couldn't move. He lay there, wishing he could still cradle his mother, but unable to budge. He was somehow determined that he could bring her back out of sheer will if he could only *touch* her.

A dead leaf tickled his wrist as he pulled himself to his hands and knees and crawled back to his post at his mother's side, pushing through the rippling pain that cascaded through his body at each movement. But as he reached her, as he finally brushed her face and could no longer control the wet splotches at the corner of his eyes, the first bits of her began to dissolve into the wind. Flecks of green, shimmering dust chipped off of her face, revealing a second layer of skin that glowed with a dark green light. A single piece of her dust floated away here and there as the wind picked at her body and drew it away, grain by grain.

She was dead.

Footsteps crunched the grass behind him. He spun around with what energy he had left, but saw only Richard. His father stood at the head of an army, his face twisted in a mask of sorrow, and forced himself to close his gaping mouth as a single, thick tear coursed down his nose.

Richard helped him to his feet as Gavin tried and failed to stand. He leaned in and choked on his mother's last words.

"She said she will wait for you," he muttered, his fingers and toes and chest all numb. "But you can't leave me yet."

Two hours later, Gavin waited in his mother's study to bide his time before her sunset memorial, tormenting himself in the silence.

Things might have been different had she not needed to summon the Sartori. He wondered why she'd been so far from home, why she had chosen to fight instead of retreat. Guilt ate at him. Had he pushed her from her throne? His daydream of being Blood had been just that: a daydream. This was too real. This was life and death. He was not ready.

An uncomfortable calm had settled upon him. As he'd ridden home on Mastif, he hadn't said a word to Richard or to anyone else. He'd expected to go into a fury when he returned to the castle, to burn and break and destroy. Those who manned the castle halls had prepared for this as well; the paths to his room and to his mother's study had been empty.

But he was calm.

He didn't have any desire to yell or throw things or eat. He sat in his mother's chair, watching the sun through the bay window as it retreated from the empty, mourning city. When the smoldering horizon ended the day, he would be expected to deliver an old adage to the kingdom:

Through the darkness of this night, there will be no master. There will be no light. All will mourn so that the morning might shine brighter for our loss.

Tomorrow, he would be their Blood. They would celebrate. He would grieve.

Gavin ran his fingers over his mother's books, reading and rereading her half-written speeches. He even savored the lingering smell of the powdered sugar from the three lemon cookies still sitting on a plate at her desk, awaiting her return.

He glared at the flowerbed into which the sword had vanished. He now understood why she kept an open garden in her study, where she'd always stowed her Sartori. She must have summoned it somehow through the soil. Hillsidians preferred to draw their energy from the earth. It made sense. He crossed to the headless stalks of clover and knelt.

The dirt was hot and stuck to him when he dug his hands into the soil. It was soft and light. He wriggled his fingers and thought of the blade, envisioning the sword in his mind: the hilt's emerald base and leather handle; the ivy scrollwork etched into the thick steel. He remembered its weight.

But when he pulled his hands from the flowerbed, the only thing in his palms was dirt.

He hurled the clumps of earth against the window and screamed at the top of his lungs, releasing for the first time the true depth of his hatred for the Stele and for Carden and for anything else with the black bloodline. He fell on his hands and wept into the flowerbed before he could find his voice.

"You will pay for this, Carden," he whispered, the sound nothing but a hushed crackle. "I will kill you and your family for taking her from me."

Someone knocked on the door. He hesitated on the flickering thought that he should open it, but the door hurled itself open in response and slammed into the wall. He couldn't control his magic or his mind in this rage.

Richard stood at the threshold, dark purple circles under his eyes. Gavin tried to bury his own anger to respect his father's. The retired king walked to him and knelt, wrapping him in a deep, long hug.

"The world goes on, boy, despite how desperately we may want it to stop for just a moment so that we can catch our breath. Your people want you speak to them, to comfort them, and you need to uphold that tradition. Many before you have wept for the dead and still delivered a speech."

"I can't say anything that's good enough to even flatter her, much less remember her. Richard, I disagreed with her often, but I'm not ready." Gavin wiped the dirt from his face and sat on the floor.

"Ready or not, this is yours. You must take what you have been given and do with it the best you can. Whether or not you stumble, you must do your best to walk in the same wise steps she took. Our family does not sit idle, nor do we grasp for memories. We continue on, always forward, never back." Richard's steady eyes burned, giving Gavin the thinnest ember of renewed vigor.

Gavin nodded. Richard helped him to his feet and stepped aside to let him through the doorway. They started down the hall, Gavin bracing himself for the speech he was neither prepared for nor wanted to give.

They turned a corner and came to a balcony, its doors open and waiting, and he stepped onto a terrace that overlooked the courtyard. Hillsidians gathered on every inch of the cobblestone and pooled down along the roads, even farther than he could see in the growing dusk. All were quiet. The roads were dark.

There will be no light.

Gavin grabbed the balcony for balance and listened to the silence of the kingdom beneath him, focusing on the deep sadness before he spoke. It wasn't necessary to tell them that which they'd memorized from birth. Why should he recite a tired adage that everyone knew? He ignored custom and instead told them the truth.

"We were unable to see just how dark this era is," he began, thinking of Carden disappearing from the meadow. "The world is more evil than it has been in centuries. The truth is that our beloved Queen was killed by Carden, Blood of none other than the Stele. The Stelians, isolated as we thought they were in their banishment, have grown strong and want to rip apart the world which we hold precious. I will not let them succeed."

A thought struck him: *the Grimoire.*

He paused as he looked out over the crowd. There was hope yet. He made a fleeting decision without knowing where it would take him. Never once in the years to come would he pause again to question his choice.

"Alone, we aren't strong enough to win a war against the Stele," he continued. "Not even with all of our villages pooled together. That is why, for the first time in a thousand years, I will try to bridge the gaps of mistrust and disloyalty that divide us from our cousins in Kirelm and Losse. I know that our good friend Aislynn will join us, too, and bring her warriors and seers from Ayavel.

"This, my people, will be a time of war greater than we have ever known. This will change the tide of the yakona race. We will fight for peace by uniting against Carden this once, destroying the bloodline that has always caused unrest, and laying down our weapons and prejudices forever."

His people applauded. There was no light, but there *was* an uproar as the first hint of excitement and renewed life brewed in the crowd below. Gavin turned without another word and retreated to his room.

※

A waning moon began to rise in the sky and peeked through the partially-drawn shades of Gavin's bedroom window, bleaching the darkness with its pale blue light. Shelves stacked with books covered much of the walls, and some trinkets lined the mantle above the hearth: a medal, a few daggers, framed portraits of his mother and Richard. The dead, black wood of last winter's fires sat idle in the dark fireplace. A dragon sculpture sat curled around itself on one of the shelves, its eyelids barely containing their red glow. Thin smoke drifted from its nose and mouth with each tiny breath.

A hidden door grated and slid open in the wall farthest from him to reveal a thin body that stepped out from a secret passage. Soft footsteps tiptoed into the room, but Gavin did not acknowledge them.

His bed was next to a wall of windows. He sat on the edge of his mattress, the blanket curled in his lap as he stared out into the night. His eyes were hollow as he gazed into the sky, reaching out to the stars for the answers he needed even though he knew they would never come. Still, he glowered as if doing so long enough would achieve something.

The footsteps stopped beside him.

Evelyn of Ayavel stood by his bed, her sleek silver skin glistening in his peripheral vision. She bit her lip and watched him for a moment before the air around her shimmered, and she shifted into her Hillsidian form. Her long hair darkened to an ashen blond color, and her skin faded until it was pale and freckled.

She wrapped her robe tighter about her and nestled beside him without a word, placing her head on his shoulder and wrapping her arm around his waist. He could feel the soft silk of her clothes slide against his arm, but for a while he couldn't move or speak.

Finally, he raised his hand and rubbed her neck without looking away from his window. She pulled him tighter. Amidst all the chaos, he was glad to have his Evie, even if no one else could know of it.

"Over time, the pain of losing her will fade," she said. Her voice was as angelic as her face and lined with an old sadness. He couldn't help but turn and watch her large brown eyes as they looked up at him. Her sweet gaze made him smile, and he brushed some loose hairs out of her face.

"I think I'll go to the study."

"Stay with me a while first," she pleaded, hugging him tighter.

She inhaled and held the breath on her tongue as if to speak again, but she hesitated. He knew better than to ask what she was thinking. If she was holding back, it was her choice. He had learned *that* lesson from the many flaring fights that arise when two hot-tempered minds are somehow drawn together. He lay down on the comforter and pulled her with him, curling his arm around her shoulders.

"I think Hillside has a traitor, Evie."

Her doe eyes widened as she looked up at him. "Who?"

"I don't know. But someone told Carden where Mother would be and when she would be there. This was a trap set by someone in my own kingdom."

"Oh, Gavin, you need sleep. If you think of it endlessly, you will act rashly. Sleep."

She slid her cool fingers over his cheek, and he closed his eyes at her touch. He lay still, letting her massage his temples.

"What does it feel like, to be Blood?" she suddenly asked, breathless. He flicked his eyes open. The curiosity ate away at her expression. However much she might have wanted to mask it, she couldn't contain her lust for the knowledge of what was to someday be hers as well.

"It's heavy," he admitted. "I feel old. Every inch of me burned when it happened. It was the worst pain that I've ever felt in my life. I even somehow felt Mother's agony when Carden stabbed her, and that paled in comparison. There are still flares here and there, but I'm getting used to the ache."

He looked away without trying to gauge her reaction. He'd told her the truth. If she still wanted the Ayavelian bloodline after learning how painful it would be, that was her choice. Leaving *him* for the duty her aunt pushed upon her would be her choice.

Neither spoke. He watched the smoke rising from his dragon figurine and lost himself to fitful thoughts of guilt and traitors and treason before he felt her cold finger run along his chest. She spoke in a soft hush.

"I've heard rumors of this new Vagabond. What do you think of her?"

He laughed. "You have nothing to worry about. She is a human and a weapon, nothing more."

Evie smiled, and he kissed her forehead. Her eyes fluttered closed. He waited to leave until she was fast asleep, but as he stood, there was a knock at the door.

Richard waited in the hallway with a cushion in his hands. An ornate and familiar crown rested on the cushion's plush silk, and a knot caught in Gavin's throat. It was midnight, then. The door clicked shut as he closed it behind him to hide Evie, but Richard didn't notice and instead held out the crown.

"This was your grandfather's, once, and it was mine while I sat beside your mother. The reins have fallen to you now, my son, and this is yours alone to wear."

Gavin lifted the crown with both hands, examining the rosy gold and elaborate emeralds. His throat tightened as he dusted one stone with his thumb, watching it glisten in the moonlight which peered through the windows on either end of the hall.

"My boy," Richard said, clutching Gavin's shoulder. "Be merciful and kind. Your mother always had compassion for those who deserved it. Rule as she did and you will be a strong king."

Gavin nodded, but in his heart, he knew that he would give Carden neither mercy nor kindness. He would punish every living thing in the Stelian bloodline. That, he knew, was justice.

❋CHAPTER SIXTEEN
AFTERMATH

Braeden led Rowthe through the dark forests that shrouded Hillside from the rest of Ourea. A thick fog curled through the fields and underbrush. The muses had called the flaer for them so that they could return faster, but Braeden's stomach churned more fervently the closer they came to the city. He didn't want to go back.

Kara sat behind him, her hands around his waist as they trotted through the woods, and he tried to ignore the way his heart skipped beats when she shifted her weight or wound her hands tighter around him.

His wrist still stung, but the pain had mostly subsided. There was no scar, no blood: only the lingering throb of a cut that wouldn't heal. He had sparse clues as to what had happened, but the strongest was the wave of Carden's hatred which had throttled him in the clearing. It had washed over him with a single thought: *Lorraine.*

They continued through the quiet forest without speaking as he reasoned with himself. The only way for him to have felt a phantom pain like that from so far away was if Carden had been stabbed by something truly powerful—like the Hillsidian Sartori. Braeden's sweating palms stuck to the hair on Rowthe's neck as he pieced together his theory and hoped he was wrong.

He glanced down at Kara's hands around his stomach, and tried to keep his breathing normal. He couldn't. Her touch made his skin smolder, even through the cotton of his shirt. There was no telling when that had started, but he both hated and loved the feeling. He patted Rowthe to distract himself from the sensation and pulled to a stop in front of a massive, gnarled oak.

"Kara," he whispered. She lifted her head from where it lay against his back. "Do you want to see how to enter the kingdom?"

Her eyes lit up, but she pursed her lips. "Won't you get in trouble?"

"I happen to be a dashing prince. I can get away with anything." He chuckled and shot her a mischievous grin.

He dismounted the flaer, and she laughed at his joke, but her smile faded just as quickly as it came. She glanced around the forest, and he followed her gaze. It was too quiet. The birds and crickets were silent. The canopy was still. Nothing in the woods breathed, as if everything was waiting for an unseen hunter to kill and be gone.

His smile dissolved as a creeping chill wound up his neck. He shook off the feeling of being watched and crossed to the mangled oak. It was covered in knobs and bumps, one of which had the small black outline of a tree branded into it. He whacked the knob like it was a button, and the hollow covering popped open to reveal a small keyhole beneath it. He pulled the Hillsidian key from the long chain on his neck, set it in the lock, and turned it.

A broad ray of green light cascaded across them. Kara shivered. The edges of the forest blurred. A new, greener avenue of pine trees and a cobblestone road appeared before them where decaying trunks had been before. An intricate metal gate with no visible door towered at the end of the path, its thick golden rods carved to look like vines of ivy. The vines untangled themselves in welcome, whistling and grating as the metal plants slid over each other. They unwound to create an opening just wide enough for the small party to walk through.

Braeden remounted behind Kara, and they hurried through the gate. The gold metal rewound itself behind them as the small group trotted through Hillside's empty streets.

The colder air of the city sent chills racing down Braeden's back before he could quash them. The flaer stepped along the vacant cobblestone road on the balls of its feet, its footsteps light and ready to bolt.

Braeden held his breath. Every door and window was closed and dark. The lamps had been extinguished, forcing him to maneuver the streets by memory and moonlight. Even the once lively, shifting cobblestones were still.

Kara reached absently for his hand as she examined the quiet houses. He swallowed hard at her touch, his stomach jumping at the warmth in her palm, and squeezed back.

"How did you know about this, Braeden?" she whispered.

"I know who it involves."

"Tell me."

"I—" He paused. "I want to be wrong."

"Please tell me."

He sighed. "The Queen. I think she's dead."

Kara shifted around to look at him. Her eyes were wide and her lips parted slightly, which, for some reason, made his stomach twist even more. He swallowed and pretended to appraise the rows of silent homes and shops, hoping she hadn't noticed the way his hand tightened around hers without his meaning it to.

"But how is that even possible?" she asked. "I thought Bloods could heal."

"They can, but everyone has a weakness. A Blood's greatest weakness is a Sartori," he explained. "Every kingdom has its own blade, which is coated in a poison that was specifically designed to keep Bloods from healing. It's the only weapon from which a Blood can almost never recover."

"So you think someone killed her?"

"I think Carden did."

"Why do you think it was Carden?"

He shook his head. He couldn't say it out loud, but only one walked away from a fight between two Bloods. No prisoners. Since he hadn't become the Blood to the Stele, Carden was still alive.

"I'm so sorry, Braeden," she said. "She must have been like a mother to you."

"I think she tried in her own way, but we were never very close," he said, hating himself for admitting it. "She was kind, and I will not deny that, but she always watched me from a distance, observing how I interacted with others, how I sparred. I'm closer to Richard, just as she was closer to Gavin, and I think that's what she wanted."

Kara squeezed his hand tighter in support and turned around again, letting go as she did. The skin on his knuckles grew suddenly cold, and he wished she hadn't moved away. He said nothing.

Rowthe stopped when they reached Hillside's castle. It loomed above them, no guards on the front steps and no lights in any of the castle's thousand windows. Braeden rested his hand on his sword out of instinct and dismounted. He hated quiet.

"Thanks, buddy," he heard Kara whisper to Rowthe as she dismounted. He turned back, but the flaer was gone.

Kara sighed and nodded toward the closed main doors.

"Shall we?"

The two of them took the stairs slowly, not wanting to know the truth, and pushed open the doors. Only a thin stream of light poured into the dark hall from behind them, so Braeden lit a gray flame in his hand. It cast long, broken shadows onto the closed throne room doors as they passed. He stopped abruptly to watch them, half-hoping the sconces in the room beyond would blaze to life so that he could believe for even a second that everything was fine.

"This can't be real," he whispered.

Kara set her hand on his back, but even her touch couldn't chase away the numb disbelief. After all, the woman who had unknowingly given him a second chance had been killed by his own heartless father.

"If I'd been here, Kara, I could have helped."

"We both know that's not true."

The flame in his hand cast gray light across her face, which froze her expression and made her look like a black and white sketch as she glanced up to him. Her frown said everything: if he'd been here, if he'd seen Carden at all, he would've been discovered.

"We should find Gavin," he said, ignoring her so that he wouldn't have to admit she was right. "When we do, let me speak to him alone first. I'm not sure if he's safe to be around quite yet."

⚜

Braeden knocked on the study door after he found Gavin's bedroom empty, though the small silk robe left on the bed suggested Gavin hadn't kept to himself in his grief. The study lock unlatched with a click, leaving the door just slightly ajar. Braeden pushed it open and walked inside.

Gavin paced by the mantle, where a fire fumed despite the warm summer night. The crimson glow highlighted the Blood's sharp nose, deepening the brooding scowl that made him look ten years older.

"Shut the door," he commanded.

Braeden turned to obey and caught Kara's eye from where she leaned against the doorframe, waiting. He smiled humorlessly and left a thin crack in the door. He did this for several reasons, the most significant of which involved the fear that his adoptive brother had somehow connected him to the Stele. It was a very real possibility and depended solely on how many clues Gavin had, so he didn't want to lock himself in the room with a new, hot-blooded king if his brother had somehow discovered the truth.

Braeden walked toward the desk, but Gavin didn't look up from his pacing until he turned toward the fire with a sudden grunt and threw his hands in his pockets.

The fire crackled as they both stared into it. Braeden set his arms behind his back, his right hand free to grab his sword if needed, but Gavin didn't move again until he draped his arms over the mantle and leaned against it for support.

"I watched her die, brother," he finally said. "Blood Carden killed her. I missed him by seconds."

He called me brother. It was selfish, considering the rest of the news, but Braeden's heart melted with relief. For now, he was safe.

"I'm sure there was nothing you could have done."

Gavin stared into the fire without answering. They stood in silence like this for a few moments, long enough for Braeden to lose track of how long the crackle of the fire had been the only sound.

"I want revenge," Gavin muttered.

"I don't blame you."

"I know how to get it."

"How?"

"Peace."

Braeden paused. "What?"

"We're squabbling with the other kingdoms, fighting and warring with them in tiny battles that gain nothing while Carden grows ever-stronger because we ignore him unless his minions cross our paths. Think about it. Instead of fighting, we should unite against him. Tell them that Carden and his Heir are the real enemies. Pull everyone into a war in the name of unity and kill everything in the Stele."

Braeden's body tensed, and his muscles ached from the immobility. Gavin continued to stare into the fire and, thankfully, didn't notice.

"That's manipulation, Gavin."

"It's the truth," the Blood snapped. "The Stele is a melting pot of vile scum, but it's a large one. Alone, we have no chance at destroying them. But with the other kingdoms, we have a real army. We can extinguish every light in the Stele."

"If you want revenge on Carden, take it, but don't start a war."

"He already started one."

"Gavin, the Queen would not—"

"She wasn't your mother! Don't tell me what she would have

wanted!"

Braeden's mouth twitched with shock. He didn't know how to respond.

"Carden could return here to finish what he started," Gavin said after a short pause. "Even if he doesn't, Losse and Kirelm are likely to be attacked next. The Stele is a threat. If we want to survive, we must take action. Am I wrong?"

He was not, but Braeden didn't give him the satisfaction of knowing it. Gavin continued without waiting for an answer.

"Losse and Kirelm are stubborn. They will not care about what I have to say, but Kara can help us. I arranged for her to leave for the other kingdoms in the morning, starting with Kirelm. I simply hope that she will be willing to speak for us."

Braeden quelled his annoyance with a sharp breath. Even after losing his mother and becoming a Blood, Gavin still couldn't stop manipulating those around him. The warm memory of Kara reaching for his hand flashed across his mind.

"Kara isn't a weapon, Gavin, nor a tool. We can't control her."

"Not a tool, no." Gavin waved away the idea. "She trusts you, so just ask her."

"I think it would be best if you did that."

Gavin glared at him, his eyes narrowing. The fire played with the lines on his face and cast his shadow across Braeden's feet until he stepped back from the fireplace and folded his arms. Then, as quickly as they had tensed, his shoulders relaxed. His breathing slowed.

"Very well. I will ask her myself."

Braeden took a deep breath. The storm had passed. Gavin tried to continue, but his voice broke over several half-formed words.

"Did you know he came alone to kill Mother?" Gavin finally asked.

"I did not."

"He lured her through a hidden lichgate, though we're still not sure how. He ambushed her. He was *alone*. He didn't even think Mother would be a challenge."

Braeden's jaw tightened, and he looked to the floor. Carden *was* crazy, then.

"I will kill off Carden's bloodline," Gavin said. "For all the suffering that kingdom has caused, none should survive. I just have to find the castle and that Heir of his."

Braeden stopped breathing.

"Is Kara waiting in the hall?" Gavin asked, rubbing his face with his hands, apparently too tired to notice the panic flash across Braeden's face.

"Yes."

Gavin gestured to the door, which swung open to let Kara into the room and closed once she was through. Its latch clicked, sealing them inside. She stopped beside Braeden as Gavin nodded to her in welcome. He sat at his desk and hunched in his chair, leaning his weight on his elbows.

"Vagabond, I have arranged for you to leave for the other kingdoms in the morning, as long as you are still willing to go," he said. "I would not normally have pressed you to leave Hillside, but times have changed."

She nodded. He glanced quickly to Braeden and continued.

"I'm certain you've already heard the news of Mother's death, so I must also ask—" His voice crackled with a suppressed sigh, but he recovered. "I must ask that you speak for us. Please tell them of our plight and use it as you will to unite us all once more. A war is brewing, my friend, and your voice must be a powerful one if we are to win it."

"I will," she said, nodding again. She was so calm, so relaxed. Had she even heard the conversation from before she was invited in?

"Thank you," Gavin said. "Captain Demnug is a good friend of Braeden's. I chose him as your guide because I knew that my brother would approve of the choice. The captain will take you to the Rose Cliffs and the Kirelm guard will later take you to the Villing Caves.

"Braeden, I need you in the Eastern villages as Mother requested, and you must leave as soon as you can. The isen there is out of control."

Gavin leaned back in his chair and stared out the dark bay window. The door opened on its own behind them, their meeting apparently over. Braeden bowed and led Kara from the study, but took one final look over his shoulder. Gavin glared through the window, no doubt already imagining the look on Carden's face when the Hillsidian got his revenge.

※

Braeden walked Kara to her room. Their trip was noiseless, and he had no idea how to fill the silence.

"He thinks he's using me," she said after a while. "But we're trying to make the same thing happen, just in different ways."

Braeden shook his head, grateful that she'd listened after all.

"I'm scared for you," she continued. "Some people can't see through their hatred, and Gavin is one of those people. You're in danger if you stay here."

"I'll be fine." He shrugged as they stopped in front of her door.

She looked up and forced a thin smile in response. So she didn't believe that either.

There were light, purple bags under her eyes, and it was hard to imagine that he'd been showing her the blades technique just that morning. He'd weaseled a few smiles out of her, then, but those were long gone. Whatever the drenowith had done to her had seen to that. He set his hands on her shoulders.

"I know that you have no desire to talk about what happened before I found you at the waterfall last week," he began. "And I know that you probably can't tell me what the drenowith told you today. But I'm here if you *do* ever need someone to talk to."

"Thanks, Braeden."

He opened her bedroom door for her and could smell perfume in her hair when he leaned for the handle. She hesitated on the threshold, but ultimately stepped through and peeped around the door as it closed.

"Sleep tight," she said.

❧CHAPTER SEVENTEEN
FLIGHT

The door clicked as Kara pressed it shut. She leaned against the paneled wood, unsure of what exactly had just happened but relishing the quick race of her pulse. Braeden sighed on the other side of the door and after a pause, the echo of his footsteps started toward the stairwell.

She sat on the edge of the canopy bed, her eyes stinging and begging her to sleep as blue moonlight bled through gaps in the drapes. The pale light splashed across the polished hardwood beneath her feet and left her borrowed room both bare and quiet.

She slipped off her boots, letting them thud on the floor, and curled her legs beneath her as she settled on the bed and examined the freckles on her hand without really seeing anything. Her shirt crinkled as she shifted, the dried sweat on the cloth cracking with the movement. She cringed and looked over at the bathroom, where a bath and clean towels hid beyond the light, but her eyes drooped.

All she wanted was sleep, but she was afraid of the dreams she might have after such a hellish day: she'd relived her mother dying; she'd been told she wasn't even worthy of Adele's or Garrett's friendship; Braeden had almost been found out. Carden had been so close, and if the Stelian prince hadn't gone with her to the drenowith—well, she didn't want to think about it.

Carden is starting something vile. I just wish I knew where he was going with this. I mean, why kill the Blood? Chaos for its own sake? It's not like Carden could ever rule any other kingdom but the Stele...right?

A memory flashed across her mind of the horde of wolves and minotaurs and trolls and the gray, smoking yakona which had tracked her after her escape from Carden's throne room. She shuddered and summoned the Grimoire.

The warm musk of its leather filled her nose, and she smiled for the first time since Braeden had shown her how to pull a blade from the air. She flipped open the cover, brushing her hand along the first, empty page. If nothing else, she had the Grimoire. It was constant. Steady.

Smart.

"What is Carden up to?" she asked.

Flick, flick, flick. The pages stopped on a block of text:

I know only of the past, never of your present.

"You are the worst Ouija Board ever," she muttered.

Someone knocked on her door. She flinched and listened. The hollow thud of footsteps raced down the hall.

She jumped up and yanked open the door to look for her visitor, but the portraits were her only company in the empty hallway. They each stared, peering at her through the dark hall. A few creaks broke the silence, floorboards bending beneath feet in the hallway above, but there was no one nearby. Her visitor was gone.

Intuition pulled her gaze to the floor. There, wrapped in a loose white cloth, was a blue stone. It was square, two of its edges jagged, and small bits of embedded gold glittered from behind the carvings which adorned its polished face. The Grimoire's clover symbol was engraved with delicate lines into the corner where the two smooth edges met.

Kara knelt and grabbed the cold blue stone. It was identical to what Braeden had given her. She peered around the hallway again, but it was useless. If anyone had stayed to watch her accept the gift, they were well hidden.

"Thank you," she said anyway as she retreated to her room. She leaned against the door once it closed and bit her lip. The hairs on her neck stood on end. Goosebumps broke out on her arms.

That was half of the puzzle completed, and she hadn't even left Hillside yet. She should be ecstatic. But a chill raced up her back and tickled her neck instead.

No one would leave a rare slab of lapis that obviously belonged to the Vagabond at her doorstep without an explanation—that is, unless they knew what the lapis was meant to do. Unless they wanted her to find the village.

She huffed and stripped off the nasty, sweat-stained clothes that had carried her through the day, trading them for clean pajamas before she slid beneath the covers. The slab of blue stone weighed on her fingers as she examined it, but there was nothing on it to distinguish it from the other one. This had to be the Hillsidian map piece. She desperately *hoped* it was, at least.

Her back slouched against the headboard in defeat. It didn't matter if someone had ulterior motives for helping her find the village; she needed to do it anyway. The Vagabond had told her that his half-finished projects would help. What with the crazy monsters and all the creatures that could shape-shift, those projects might even save her life.

Kara stretched her arm to the floor and after a second or two of reaching for her satchel, she dragged the bag onto the bed and pulled out the other lapis square. She weighed it in her hand before experimenting with the various ways they fit together. When she found the right fit, she touched their edges to one another.

A sharp burst of silver light erupted across them, blinding her. Spots dotted her vision. She cursed and squeezed her eyes shut. The light glared for a minute, but receded once more into the blue darkness before dissolving completely. She blinked until she could see shapes and colors again.

The pieces in her hand had fused together. There was only one jagged edge, now, along the top. The welded edges were perfectly smooth; there wasn't even a scar where they had once been broken apart. The map made slightly more sense now that she had half of it, but not by much.

In the center was half of a massive oval, which took up a third of the space. Both corners had the clover symbol carved into the stone in thin indents, and the entire map was framed with twisting vines and leaves, but there were no mountains or landscapes that she could recognize. For a map, it had remarkably little direction to it.

Something vibrated. It was short. Sudden. For a moment, she wondered who the text message could be from.

Then she laughed.

The vibration came from her satchel, where her little blue egg was nestled in the bottom corner. She lifted the little orb from the bag and slid the half-finished map back inside. The egg's inner light glowed orange, the hue more vivid than before. She rubbed it with her thumb.

"So what is this thing, Grimoire? What does it hatch into?"

The pages opened to a drawing of a small creature that resembled a fox. Red stripes lined the otherwise black fur in curving patterns. Its ears swallowed its head and its massive eyes glistened with curiosity. The drawing twitched. The sketched creature tilted its head and snapped its mouth once in a silent bark. She laughed, surprised, but the fox-thing didn't move again. According to the header on the page, it was an Xlijnughl.

"It's—" She played with the pronunciation, but didn't even know where to start. "It's a what, now?"

She reread the name several times and didn't get anywhere, so she skimmed the description. The creatures were considered good luck, and if one could find an egg and raise the thing from birth, the creature would be bonded to that person for life. They had many small powers and in lore were considered one of the most powerful omens of good fortune.

"So it's a miniature fox with massive ears, zebra stripes, random magical powers, and it hatches from an egg?" She paused and looked at her orb. "Why does anything here faze me anymore?"

The egg glowed brighter as she rubbed it, so she toyed with the little orb and lost herself to the thoughts of what would come.

"What are the Rose Cliffs and the Villing Caves?"

The pages flipped to a header that read, "Ourea's Wonders." The two-page spread was a collage of small sketches: a wall filled with diamonds that glittered despite the darkness; a cliff that overlooked hundreds of miles of forests; a tall volcano that stretched to the heavens.

She turned the page. Another two-page sketch portrayed a cliff range in stunning detail, from top to bottom. Thin vines with small blossoms covered the rock face, while a forest composed of tiny trees carpeted the hills and valleys along the bottom of the picture. If the scale was correct, the cliff had to be at least a few miles high. In the sky beside the rock wall were the words, "The Rose Cliffs."

The page turned on its own and revealed the same image, but drawn this time in gray pencil. Thick blocks of text were overlaid in dark red ink.

> The kingdom of Kirelm celebrates the Rose Cliffs as the birthplace of its race and the stronghold of its magic. Legends say that the first Blood of Kirelm was pricked by one of the hundreds of thousands of roses which span the side of the Cliffs as he climbed it in search of a better home for his tribe. In this moment, his blood was infused

with the magic that later developed into the Kirelm bloodline that is known today.

The Kirelm people once lived above the cliffs, but fear of discovery drove them away shortly after the yakona race's great divide. Still, its eleven miles of cliffs is often visited by Kirelm merchants, and one of their villages is rumored to exist in its forests.

Kara turned the page again to see yet another two-page spread, this one of a cave wall, its polished rock embossed with veins. She squinted. No, the rough lines had patterns to them: they were dragons. Many had beards, their mouths hung open in frozen bellows. Crystallized fire spewed from them, fossilized in the rock, and spiraled around a small being in the center of the massive wall.

She shifted into the moonlight to get a better view and figure out what this smaller thing was. Two legs. A face. He was a broad man, built like a tank and frozen in the rock with the dragons. His hands stretched to the curved, unmoving heavens above him, and one held a sword as tall as him. His face was locked in a roar.

Again, she turned the page for its description.

Now vacant to all but its immobile tenants, the Villing Caves were once a celebrated haven in the time of Ethos. Yakona would come from miles away to walk the endless grottos and explore the hidden caverns and lakes here. After the collapse of Ethos, however, the caves became favored by the Retrien Bloods: a yakona bloodline that preferred the heat of the caves' nearby volcanoes.

More than two millennia ago, a vicious breed of dragon infested the network of caves that compose the caverns. They killed thousands of Retriens. To save his people and his home, the Retrien Blood led a final, desperate battle against the dragons. When it was clear that his soldiers were losing, he called upon every drop of power he possessed and sealed the dragons and himself in a stony tomb.

His bloodline has long since disappeared, as his Heir did not awaken at what all thought to be his father's death. Instead, it's believed that the Blood lives still, trapped in the very stone which binds his enemies.

"Ourea is intense," Kara said, rubbing her face.

She nestled her head against the pillow, but tried to stay awake even as her eyes glazed over. Her mind would just replay the car crash over and over if she slept, like it had for a solid month after the accident. Her eyes closed even as she begged her body to stay awake.

⚜

Kara hadn't even realized she'd fallen asleep until she woke up. She tried to shake away the groggy hum of exhaustion.

At least there weren't any dreams.

The morning broke bright and sunny, as if there had never been a sad day in the city of Hillside. She stretched and crossed to the window. Dappled splotches of shade from the clouds above fell over the stables, where a figure with black hair walked by with two shoulder packs and disappeared into a stall.

She bathed, changed, wrapped the satchel—which she filled with her few possessions—over her shoulder, and headed for the door. She guessed her way through the hallways and somehow ended up in the kitchen twice, but eventually she found the dining hall and the door that led out to the stables.

Stone bricks framed each stall's thick wooden door. The top half of each door lay open to let in the sunlight, while the bottom half remained closed to keep the mounts and other creatures inside. In one stall, a fully-saddled black horse whinnied, its reins shaking around its neck as it perked its ears toward her.

"Good morning, Vagabond."

Kara turned to find Braeden behind her, a wide saddle on his shoulder. He rubbed the deep bags under his eyes with his free hand.

"You didn't sleep last night, did you?" she asked.

He shrugged and walked through a hallway she hadn't noticed before, which led to the center hallway of the stables. Each of the stalls she'd seen from the outside also had wooden, inward-facing doors that swung open on hinges.

The ceiling opened into rafters. The arched support beams curved and intertwined with each other, each one looping over and under a dozen different arches before it reached the other side of the roof. Birds twittered and sang to each other, flying from nest to nest as stable hands led horses and even a giant wolf through the hallway.

Braeden slipped into the stall next to the one with the black horse, so Kara leaned on the doorframe and looked in.

She gasped. "What is that?"

He threw the saddle on what looked like a giant, horse-sized Doberman with two heads, a short gray coat, and black stripes on its legs. Both heads turned when she appeared, their glossy black eyes looking her over while their drooping ears perked in curiosity. Each stretched its neck forward as far as it could without moving and sniffed the air around her.

"A drowng," Braeden answered. "They're incredibly fast and even more loyal. Most of the Hillsidians I know ride these instead of horses, because they actually attack instead of running away. No offense, Goliath."

The black horse in the stall next to them snorted.

Boot heels slapped on the stone hallway, and Kara peeked out, turning in time to see Gavin come around the corner. His mouth turned up as though to smile, but with the bags under his eyes, it looked more like a grimace.

"Are you ready, Vagabond?"

Kara nodded.

"Wonderful. I must thank you again for agreeing to speak for Hillside on your trip. I wanted to give you a parting gift." He patted the black horse's stall door. "This is Goliath. He was one of Mother's mounts, but he is now yours."

Goliath reached his nose through a gap in the stall bars and nickered, so she rubbed his soft muzzle. He licked her hand, leaving a hot trail of saliva on her fingers. She grimaced and wiped it on her pants before peeking through the stall door to get a better look.

He was as beautiful and toned as a racehorse. His shoulder alone was taller than her, and a white crescent moon peeked through the thick black forelock which fell into his eyes.

"Thank you, Gavin."

"I thought you would be more comfortable on a horse, even if they aren't as smart as our other mounts."

Goliath snorted again and stomped his foot, but if Gavin noticed, he didn't react. Instead, he bowed to her, nodded to Braeden, and strode from the stable.

Kara slid back into the drowng's stall and leaned on the doorframe, eyeing Braeden as he glared at the floor, lost in thought. His eyebrows overshadowed his eyes and made the bags look darker as he turned back and tied the leather bags onto his saddle.

"Is everything okay?" she asked.

"Of course not. You heard him last night."

"You really needed to sleep."

"Promise me something," he said, walking to her. He leaned one arm against the wall and looked down at her, lowering his voice to a whisper.

"Don't trust Gavin with *anything*," he said, frowning. "If you decide to make this your home, if you decide to come back here after you go to the other kingdoms, stay away from him. Stay away from everyone."

Kara paused, biting her tongue. She wanted to tell him about the Vagabond's village, but her gut twisted again at the thought. Her intuition flared. *Tell no one,* it said. She swallowed her words and forced a wry smile.

"What happened to kissing babies?" she finally muttered.

"Kara, no jokes. Not now."

"I was kind of being serious. If I'm here, I'm supposed to socialize. That's what you said, isn't it?"

"The Gavin you saw through the crack in the door last night was just a taste of who he truly is. If he wants you, he will do absolutely anything to control you. You can't trust anyone here."

"I trust you," she said, catching his eye. He tensed his jaw and sighed.

"I know." He forced a smile and set a hand on her shoulder. "Thank you."

Goliath nipped her shirt through a hole in the stall and pulled her away, nickering in glee once he had her attention.

She and Braeden laughed, the dark spell of their conversation broken, but they avoided eye contact. Braeden opened the stall door which led to the field behind the castle and pulled himself onto his drowng.

"We should get going," he said, ushering his mount into the sunlight.

Kara slipped into Goliath's stall. The horse perked its ears again and nuzzled his nose into her shoulder as she ran her hands down to the saddle. Up until now, Rowthe had simply read her mind and known where to go. She thought back to a horse camp she'd gone to in the eighth grade. Hopefully, she remembered enough to at least mount her horse without looking like a complete idiot.

She opened the outward-facing stall door and caught sight of Braeden as he waited for her under a passing patch of shade. Goliath stood still as she slid her foot into the stirrup and hoisted herself onto the giant horse. She muttered a silent victory when she didn't fall off the other side.

She lifted the soft reins until there was only a slight bend in the line between her hand and Goliath's mouth, gently tilted his head toward the exit, and tapped him lightly with her heel. He started a slow walk toward the Stelian Heir, who waited for her to reach him before he steered his drowng around the castle.

Together, they walked toward one of the roads which led away from the city. They were quiet. The memories Verum had pried from her swarmed in the silence, flashing and screeching and echoing with the lost sound of her mom's voice. She didn't know why she wanted to tell him, to confess, but she knew he would understand.

"Braeden?"

He looked over. "Yes?"

"My Mom died in a car crash six months ago. I was driving. It was my fault. That's why I was going to a therapist."

He watched her, even though she couldn't peel her eyes from the shifting cobblestone road, and didn't respond. She didn't want him to.

"I think about her every day," she continued. "The ironic thing is that I was just trying to get her to a hospital, because she was sick and my dad was out of town on business. I didn't know what to do. It had just rained, but who am I kidding? It's always raining in Tallahassee. I took the curves too sharply. I hit a ditch. Glass was everywhere—" Her voice broke.

"I am sorry you had to relive that, Kara."

"The drenowith said I was broken, that I couldn't help anyone until I fixed myself." She scoffed. "I don't even know how to do that."

"You aren't broken," he said softly. "You made a mistake and you can't forgive yourself for it. That just means you are normal."

She glanced up to him from the corner of her eye, and he shot her a reassuring smile.

"It gets better," he added. "The pain never goes away, but it does get better."

The gate came into focus at the end of the road, the gold of its metal ivy glinting in the warm summer sun. It was framed on either side by redwood trees, the metal ivy stretched between them and welded to their trunks. The vines slithered over each other as she and Braeden came closer, unweaving themselves to create a hole large enough for them to pass through. A stone path lined with pine trees led the way into a lush forest.

Six mounted Hillsidians, each sitting on a drowng, waited on the other side of the gate. They wore green uniforms with a golden tree in the center and swords around their waists. The tallest of them trotted forward to meet her as the ivy gate closed behind them.

Braeden smiled and nodded to him. "Good morning, Captain Demnug. Kara, this is the captain Blood Gavin mentioned last night. He will take you to the Rose Cliffs."

Blood Gavin. His title sounded too formal. It sounded wrong.

"It's nice to meet you, Captain," she said.

"The pleasure is mine. We will make sure you get to the Rose Cliffs safely, Vagabond."

"I will see you when you return, then, Kara," Braeden lied.

She glanced over to him as he steered his mount away. He winked, flashing the white shell necklace, and she had to remind herself that he wasn't really leaving. She wasn't really alone in this.

The incessant Hillside fog rolled into the lane, shrouding the distance in white mist. Braeden bolted down the path to the thundering sound of his drowng's paws and became a black figure in the vapor before he dissolved from sight completely.

The six Hillsidian guards closed in around her, making a circle with her at its center, and started forward at a slower pace.

A green flash surrounded them in a sudden blaze. An icy breath of frost blew up her arms, leaving goose bumps. She turned to look at the gates, but all that remained were closely-knit trees branching out into the forest, shrouded in more of the deep fog.

"What was that?" she asked.

"We passed through Hillside's lichgate, Vagabond," the captain answered. "I forget you aren't from Ourea. With most lichgates, you see a blue light and feel a kick in your gut. But we have perfected ours so that you feel only a slight chill. I must confess that the green light is just vanity on our part. We liked it."

"Ah."

The somber guards ushered her forward, but sat on the edges of their seats. Their stirrups rested on the balls of their feet as they examined every break in the forest they passed.

The sun crawled overhead, and her satchel rubbed against her lower back, making her think of the blue egg inside that was slowly turning orange the closer it came to hatching. A few names ran through her mind, mostly those she'd dreamt up for the Siberian Husky she'd never been allowed to get. One popped randomly into her head: Flick. She toyed with it.

I like it. Flick.

The sun warmed her neck and arms as they passed through the occasional beam of sunlight. The stone road faded into a dirt path that wound in and out of the trees. Birds sang and fluttered. Creatures— more of what she didn't want to assume were squirrels—tore through the tree branches above, scattering leaves onto the company like rain. The forest was alive and unafraid, so unlike the foreboding silence that had eaten at her nerves when she'd returned last night.

She tried to focus on the sunlight instead of the many memories which plagued her and instead watched the captain, who examined the forest. He kept one hand on the hilt of his sword.

"How far away are the Rose Cliffs?" she asked.

"A day and a half's ride if we don't take any detours," he answered before turning back to the forest.

All right. No conversation, then.

She decided to use the silence to practice the magic she'd learned thus far. She started with flames, focusing her energy on her palm and drawing a small fire. She made it larger, then smaller, and then made it flicker out completely. They walked like this for hours, listening and watching and waiting for something to happen.

Dark, brewing clouds covered the setting sun in the distance, making the evening come much earlier than it should have. The sudden darkness nudged Kara's eyes back into focus from whatever daydream she'd lost herself to on their boring ride. She sat up straight and looked around. The forest was thicker, now. They stood on a hill. A dozen feet off, the road sloped down and curved.

"A storm is brewing," the captain said. "This isn't the best timing, but we should still be all right. There is a lichgate up ahead, just beyond a river up there. There will be an inn of some sort in the human world."

She hiccupped in her surprise. "We're going back?"

"We must. We'll spend the night at the inn. It will be a safer place to stay than out in the woods."

The heavy clouds on the horizon stretched their way toward them. The sky was riddled with gloom. The darkness spread into the forest, plunging the road into a shadowed cave of leaves and bark as they walked along. The summer evening chilled. Thunder rolled. Gusts nipped at the hair on her arms. Leaves tumbled across Goliath's hooves, victims of the wind that darted through the tree trunks in spurts of fitful energy. Shivers raced along her neck.

The cool wind pricked her senses, and with her awareness came paranoia. The shadows became ghosts, moving only when they were in her peripheral vision. The guards saw it, too. The entire company flinched one way and then another. Every snapped twig became a threat, every rustle an enemy.

The wind brought the tickle of an oncoming downpour. The trees bent in the gusts, stretching their bases farther than she thought they could move as they became a single unit, swaying in unison through the dusk. The shorter trees' branches swept the ground. Leaves fell loose and billowed around in small tornadoes, scattering along the forest floor after a few short minutes of life.

Kara urged Goliath along, but had to continuously nudge him forward. The muscles in his neck twitched. Twigs and loose bark crunched beneath his hooves. He lowered his head and flung his ears forward, listening.

"Ready, men." The captain drew his sword. He kicked his drowng, pushing the creature faster along the road.

The guards followed suit with Kara still in the middle of their circle. She held out her hand and focused her adrenaline into her palm. A lavender flame erupted between her fingers. She didn't have a sword—not that she knew how to use one or anything—but the fire would work for now.

A thick branch cracked in the distance. Its ripping sinews tore through the growing tension and billowing wind. Kara spun, peeking around the rear soldiers at the sound, but all she could see was an empty forest. The sway of the trees and the whoosh of grasses drowned out all other sound. She wanted to think a tree's branch had just fallen, but her intuition screamed to her that she should run. There was something here with them.

Goliath pranced, itching to bolt forward. She tugged on his reins, holding him back. A frantically running horse was useless, especially if she was trapped on its back.

A pebble flew at her face like a bullet. She ducked, but it still grazed her temple. She didn't realize until too late it was a distraction, hurled to steal her attention from the massive branch coming at the back of her neck. When it hit her, she fell. Goliath reared. She did not feel pain until she awoke.

⚜

Kara heard yelling. Agony. Someone screamed. Hooves struck the dirt nearby. She couldn't see at first. The world was blurred from the rough pounding at the base of her skull. She reached around and patted the wet area. She cringed. It stung. She turned onto her stomach and glanced toward the noise, her gut twisting at what she saw. Her cheeks flushed. She had to swallow hard to contain the bile.

Hillsidians swung and ducked. Light erupted from their hands. Green mists and explosions billowed through the forest. There were much more than just six of them, too; dozens of soldiers fought on the path and more slid in and out of the tree line. Some Hillsidians were still on their mounts, but most fought on foot. Any drowngs not carrying a yakona growled and snapped, barking and tackling whatever wasn't wearing a green uniform.

But it was what the Hillsidians were *fighting* that made her queasy.

Stelians flooded every free inch of the path, their gray skin steaming. They towered over the Hillsidians by a good foot or so, their arms as thick as her leg. Their black eyes glistened in the low light. It was hard to believe that Braeden was part of such a frightening race.

A centaur bellowed and ran through the woods, tackling a Hillsidian as he charged. The monster's feral eyes flitted around, looking at everything and seeing nothing. His hands dripped with dark green blood.

Another Hillsidian fell in front of her, landing on the dirt with a sharp *thud*. She screamed in surprise. His eyes were fading, his mouth twisted in pain. His body dissolved into flecks of green dust, the gust billowing through his clothes and pulling away bits of ash as he rotted before her eyes. She screamed again.

Something nickered in her ear. She glanced up, ready to bolt, but

Goliath nudged her with a quick bump of his nose. The whites of his eyes were visible and his nostrils flared with his deep, panicked breaths, but he lowered his head beneath her hand and waited. His legs and rump trembled. His ears twitched at each new sound from the battle.

She jumped up and slid her foot into the stirrup, pulling herself on to his back even though her body shook as much as his.

There was a snort and a growl. Another centaur eyed her from behind a tree, and both she and Goliath froze. The creature looked her over and sneered, his wicked grin layering his face with deep lines. His pale upper body was splattered with dark green blood that trailed onto the brown fur of his back end. His nose was broken, and red streams of dried blood coursed to his mouth. The wild anger in his eyes choked the air from her lungs. He yelled, but she couldn't hear it. She couldn't hear anything. He charged.

Kara kicked Goliath hard in his side, but he wouldn't move. In fact, she had to kick him several more times before he would actually follow her "Run like hell!" command.

The centaur was only forty feet away by the time Goliath snapped out of his shock and bolted down the road she hoped led to the lichgate. Another roar bellowed from behind, but she couldn't look. She called on everything she could remember about horses and clutched the saddle with her thighs and knees, leaning forward and letting her horse gallop with all his might down the road.

She turned her head after a few minutes of running to get a view of the trail behind her, but she whimpered at what she saw. Goliath hadn't gained any kind of lead from the centaur, who was actually *gaining* on her. But now, the centaur wasn't alone. Wolves and a dozen Stelians riding drowngs had joined the chase. A teaming host of monsters chased her down the trail.

Goliath charged on. Sweat pooled on his neck. It stuck to her hands as she brushed it, making her grasp on the reins slip. It didn't really matter, though. She didn't have much control at this point. She wrapped her fingers into Goliath's mane and clenched the saddle even tighter with her knees. That horse couldn't have bucked her off if he'd tried.

They raced along the curving trail. For brief moments, she lost track of the horde behind her, but after each wave of hope that she'd really lost them, they would resurface around the next bend. She prayed the lichgate would be easy to find.

The trees ended. Mountains consumed the close horizon and stretched into the growing night above. And there, plain as day, was the white wooden outline of a lichgate built into the base of one of the nearest cliffs. Water rapids gushed close by, and she gasped after she had a moment to process exactly where those rapids were.

The river stood between her and the lichgate. The broken bits of a bridge appeared along the shore as they drew closer, the fragmented ropes clinging to their rotten posts. The channel was only about eight feet wide, but the sharp rocks and raging water would make swimming or jumping impossible. She pulled a rein to make Goliath turn parallel to the river. They could find another bridge.

He ignored the tug.

She pulled harder. He yanked the rein back. Her hand flew against his neck. His head centered on the gate. They were only thirty feet from the river.

"No," she whispered.

He sped up.

Twenty feet.

She clung to his neck.

Ten feet.

She closed her eyes.

Any second now.

He lifted his front hooves and arched his neck. Her stomach flew into her throat. Sweat made her palms slip down the reins. They hung in the air, suspended as the giant horse jumped the gorge. She let out a shaky breath.

Too late to change anything now. Whatever happens, happens.

Goliath landed on the other side with a thud. Her weight returned suddenly to her knees and the balls of her feet. Her head fell hard on his neck.

Kara twisted around in time to see the centaur attempt the jump. He fell on the sharp rocks bordering the edge of the river and split his head on the bank. The rapids washed him away, the water's white foam marred with the thick, red ribbons of his blood.

Two mounted Stelians jumped after him, unable to stop in time, and also crashed into the sharp rocks on the opposite bank. Their drowngs yelped, their heads cracking against the jagged shore before the riders and mounts alike fell to the same bloody fate as the centaur.

The rest of the host pulled to an abrupt stop on the opposite side, glaring at her with sneering faces that disappeared as she turned to look through the lichgate.

Through the gate was a forest. It was shrouded in a haze, like a coating of foggy glass. The faded green landscape looked foreign on the sheer mountain wall, as if it was painted on the mountainside with creams and pastels, and she could see the wind rustle through the branches beyond the lichgate. Goliath charged toward the gate, jumping again as they barreled through. As they passed, her gut twisted. A sharp blue light blipped in the corner of her eye.

She tensed as they bolted toward whatever was waiting for them on the other side of the lichgate.

❧CHAPTER EIGHTEEN
TRUTH

The scene from the other end of the lichgate would have been a staggering one if any human had been lucky enough to witness it.

The forest was calm. A subtle breeze skirted through the trees. A squirrel—a real one—ran along the path, lucking its way across a nut, when it stopped abruptly. It felt the ground, sniffed, and squeaked. A horse erupted from nothing, jumping through an unseen gateway into reality, and the petrified little rodent scampered into the underbrush.

Kara stormed along the path, adrenaline boiling her blood. It made stopping and breathing and thinking all impossible until she forced a shaky breath and leaned back in her seat. Goliath slowed from a canter to a flighty walk, where he snorted and glanced around at every crunched leaf with a fresh desire to bolt. Kara hunched in a similar flight response, but did everything she could to make him walk with long, slow steps.

The forest was almost identical to the one she'd raced away from: the trees still towered above, all of them close together. Years of rotting foliage shifted in the idle wind that crossed the deer trail. The sun was on its last beams of light here, its burning rays glittering through the leaves as the wind pushed through them.

The tree line thinned and a road stretched across her path: a real, asphalt road. She came up to it and stopped, not fully able to believe it even existed. A blue sedan rolled up the drive, puttering toward her as she froze from the shock of seeing something so normal.

The mounted figures of the small Hillsidian army emerged from the trees across the way as the car passed by. One or two of their giant dogs howled at the setting sun, but the young man driving the car was singing along with the stereo while a girl, maybe sixteen, played with her phone. Neither looked up.

The Hillsidians waited for the car to pass before crossing the two-lane road. The captain and five other yakona broke away from the rest and circled Kara, leading her along the side of the street as they had in the forest before the attack. The rest of the band hurried into the woods from which she'd just emerged and disappeared from sight, until she was once again accompanied by only six soldiers.

Captain Demnug walked beside her, his eyebrows furrowed as he scanned the road. His jaw was tight, his shoulders tensed, and she didn't know how to break the silence.

"What was that?" she finally asked.

"An ambush. Carden's company was small, so I suspect the demon sent his hordes to scour every inch of Ourea. They did not expect a small army to greet them."

"Neither did I, but I'm glad they were there. Why were the other Hillsidians hiding?"

The captain paused, but eventually turned to her. "We did not want to alarm you with the possibility of an attack."

Kara rolled her eyes. "How'd that work out for you?"

She glared into the silent forest, chewing on the thought that the now-motionless trees housed dozens of uniformed soldiers on mutated dog-creatures the people in the sedan hadn't even noticed. The captain didn't answer her, so she turned in the awkward silence to look for another car along the empty road.

"Why didn't the two kids in the car look up? It was almost like they didn't even see us."

"We may be riding drowngs while wearing full Hillside uniform, but if they'd glanced over, those humans would probably have seen horses and—what is that terrible fashion called?—*jeans*. Sometimes, your kind doesn't see us at all. What a human chooses to see is never all that really is."

"Amazing," she said. "I wonder how many giant, two-headed dogs I passed without ever knowing it."

"Here we are."

The captain pointed ahead to a large farmhouse with a wrap-around porch that sat at the edge of the road. It had a small gravel parking lot with a few dusty cars and a barn that was leaning on its last, crooked legs. An old, wooden sign out front said *The Mountain Ridge Bed & Breakfast* in faded red paint.

He pulled to a stop by the porch and dismounted while the rest of the company followed suit. An older woman pushed open the screen door and greeted them with a warm smile. Her curly gray hair framed her oval face and fell over the ruffled sleeves of a red apron that matched her old, faded sign.

"Welcome!" she called over the porch railing. "Do you have a reservation?"

The captain forced a smile. "No ma'am. I was hoping you could house us anyway. Do you have room?"

One of the drowng's heads nuzzled the woman's hand as she reached for the captain's reins, and a light, happy growl curled from its lips. She smiled and patted its nose while its other head—which she didn't appear to see at all—hugged in close, waiting for an opening so that it could sneak in for a rub. Kara suppressed a laugh.

"There are only four rooms left, but if some of the gentlemen don't mind sleeping in a bunk bed, I don't see a problem with it. Anyway, I'll get your horses fed, so don't you worry about them. I was just about to start a late dinner, too. Hope you're hungry."

"That sounds fine," the captain said.

Demnug and his men dismounted and headed for the farmhouse, so Kara dismounted as well and handed over Goliath's reins. The old woman felt the horse's neck and shoulders, letting out a disappointed sigh when she touched the damp, sweaty hair.

"Goodness," she said. "Have you been racing, girl?"

"You can call it that," Kara said with a nervous chuckle.

"Well, I'll take good care of this big guy. You poor thing. You tired?" The woman patted Goliath's nose, and he nickered as she walked him away.

The farmhouse's screen door creaked when Kara pulled it open, and the murmur of men talking bubbled down a thin hallway that was lined with mirrors and old photos. She skirted around an antique end table littered with unopened letters and headed for the kitchen, of which a table and a refrigerator were visible through the narrow doorway at the end of the hall. The Hillsidian guards all sat around the table, talking as they chewed on rolls from a small basket in its center.

The captain leaned against a counter, lost in thought as he bit large chunks out of a roll of rye bread.

"How did you know there would be a bed and breakfast with a barn right here?" she asked him.

"Yakona take care of the lands around the lichgates," he said. "Now, that woman has no idea what we are. She can't see our uniforms or the drowngs, but we will leave her with enough money to last her a while.

She will find hidden treasures here and there, and without her ever realizing it, our little blessings will be enough for her to stay and make a happy living helping us."

"That's amazing."

He chewed through a second roll. "Tonight, you are my daughter and those gentlemen are various nephews and brothers of mine. We are on a farewell trail ride before you go off to—dang it. What is it called? College."

"I can remember that, but have you ever wanted to tell her the truth?"

He shrugged. "We can't. The truth would be too much to handle. Even if she believed us, even if she did *not* forever bar us from this inn, which I happen to love, the treasures would go unappreciated. No, it has to be a subtle friendship, one neither she nor any of our other human friends will ever see."

Kara nodded and stood with him for a short while, but the conversation had run its course. The other Hillsidians were engrossed in their own discussions of the strategies they'd used and the friends they'd lost to the Stelian ambush. It was not a place for her, so she left them and trotted up the stairs.

There were eight doors and, of them, only the last door on the right stood open. Within, framed landscapes covered the little room's walls. A twin-sized bed sat in the corner, a thick red comforter neatly tucked around the mattress. A small fireplace filled part of the wall on the far end of the room, and above it was a painting of a cliff. A river raged beneath the watercolor mountainside, and a wide, wooden bridge scaled across it. She studied the canvas as she walked closer, recognizing it as the very river over which she and Goliath had just escaped. Someone had given the lichgate caretaker a painting of Ourea!

She laughed and became suddenly dizzy. She sat on the bed, waiting for the black and white spots to fade as the last of the adrenaline dissolved in her system. Her head reeled. She set her cheek on the soft pillow, which melted the tension in her neck, and pulled the far end of the comforter over her like a sleeping bag. She dangled her filthy, mud-drenched boots over the side of the bed as she fell asleep, but even the deep exhaustion couldn't suppress a dream that was too tormenting and violent to let her sleep.

The world was hazy, immersed in a thick layer of smoke. Without understanding why or how, Kara knew this was a dream. She was looking at the world through someone else's eyes, and it annoyed her that she knew this.

Several guards burst into her otherwise empty room, each of them so massive that they barely fit in the tiny space. They had large wings: some black, some white, some gray. They grabbed her arms and dragged her upright. She fought them, twisting and struggling out of instinct, but she was shackled within seconds. Sharp needles bit into her skin. The blurry outlines of the spiked cuffs which had confined Braeden in the Stele peeked back at her from her own wrists.

The world went dark until a single ray of unexpected light sprung into view. More sunshine appeared, radiating from the windows above, and echoed off the brilliant white stone walls. It burned her eyes as they adjusted.

Another of the winged yakona stood before her, his skin a pale shade of silver that glistened in the sunlight, iridescent and beautiful from beneath a white fur cloak. She recognized him, but couldn't think of a name.

A dawning realization crawled over her skin like a frost, icing her blood with a wave of panic—something terrible was about to happen.

The winged figure looked her over and sneered, as if he smelled something foul. "You call yourself a hero, but you're nothing more than a thief."

"I don't call myself a hero," she heard herself say. The muffled sound wasn't her voice, but in the hazy echo of the dream, she couldn't tell whose it was.

"You threaten the safety of my people and of my bloodline," the man said. "For this, you and your minions will pay with the very blood you stole."

A guard carried in a beautiful woman with dark skin. She was limp in his arms, and bright red blood trickled in rivers down her hands and bare feet. The guard tossed the woman on the floor as if she were garbage and not a real, breathing creature. Kara leaned in, breathless and afraid for the woman, who couldn't have been more than twenty. Dozens more yakona from every kingdom were brought forth in a similar manner, some of them unconscious, and all of them chained.

"You offered them freedom, but lies and heresy always lead to death. None should have the power you bestowed upon these strangers, these enemies of all yakona bloodlines. Your reign over our people will end here, tonight!" The winged tyrant pulled out a sword.

Kara sat upright in her bed and heard herself screaming.

She clamped her hands over her mouth and leaned into the pillow, hoping that it would help to settle her racing heart. The door burst open, shedding hallway light into her dark room. The captain ran in, wearing his uniform and gray socks.

"What's wrong?"

The five other guards followed suit, all dressed for battle and missing their boots. A few minutes later, the old woman raced in as well, draped in a black shawl that swept dust from the floor. Kara blushed.

"I'm sorry, it was just a nightmare. I'm sorry." But she was shaking, the dream far too vivid to have truly been just a nightmare.

"What happened?" The captain sat next to her on the far end of her bed, dismissing the other soldiers from the room with a wave of his hand. The old woman nodded as well, apparently believing that she saw a father talking to his daughter, and closed the door when she left.

"What did you see?" he asked again.

Kara just shook her head. Her entire body still trembled, the image of the winged man and his sword still imprinted on her eyelids. She was afraid to close her eyes.

Demnug cleared his throat and slapped his hands on his knees, pausing for a second before he pushed himself to his feet.

"Very well," he said. "Try to get some sleep."

She waited for the door to latch behind him before she wished forward the Grimoire and opened it. For a while, she just stared at the first, blank page.

That dream had been real and unlike anything she'd ever experienced. Who was that woman? She'd had red blood, after all. Since Braeden had black blood and Hillsidian blood was green, she figured that the woman had to be human. But, since the man had mentioned that they were all "freed," she thought again.

Were they the vagabonds? The first Vagabond's followers?

She doubted she could ask the Grimoire how the Vagabond died; after all, he wouldn't have been alive to write the entry. She could summon his ghost, like she had in the forest, but she wasn't sure how he would react to such a question. Her stomach twisted into a knot at the thought of asking him. How could she word that without sounding insensitive and nosy?

The edges of her nightmare were already blurring. She couldn't remember any faces, not even the tyrant's. Words faded until only the general understanding of what had been said lingered on her mind. But the wings—those weren't something that could be forgotten. She debated. They might have been a creative tweak her mind inserted into the memory, borrowed from her worries of meeting the Kirelm Blood.

Either that, or a Kirelm Blood killed the first Vagabond.

He was only trying to unite everyone. Why would anyone kill him? She rubbed her tired eyes with her palms.

She hunched forward and pondered all of her new questions, none of which the Grimoire could answer. It wasn't until the first rays of the morning told her to get dressed that she wished away the untouched book and peered out the window at the sunrise.

On a sloping hill below, the old woman picked up sticks from the thick patches of grass which covered most of her yard. The woman bent for another stick and paused, looking into the forests where dozens of Hillsidian yakona hid, but the woods were tranquil. Not even a leaf tumbled across the thin spaces in the trees. Still, she watched, half-frozen in her quest for the small branch beneath her fingertips. Then she was mobile again, snatching a few more twigs before turning back inside. She glanced up to Kara's room.

Kara's heart panged with the guilt of being caught spying, and she ducked away from the window. When she peered out again, the woman was gone.

A warm bath and a hot breakfast later, Kara was sitting on Goliath, waiting for the company to head off for the last leg of their trip. The sun stretched over everything, chasing away the dusk that still lingered between the trees.

Goliath no longer shivered, but his ears still twitched at sounds she couldn't hear. He was calmer, but not quite yet at peace with the summer morning that waited for the hot afternoon ahead.

The captain finally mounted and started off into the trees, the rest of the band following behind him. Kara looked back as they crossed into the forest, glancing over the sloping barn and giant farmhouse to see a gray head dart away from the very window through which she herself had been spying that morning.

They stopped in front of another lichgate after about ten minutes of walking. This one was smaller than the last and hidden in the farther reaches of the woods without any path to find it. It was made of thick thorny vines that spanned a tall bridge between the trunks of two oak trees. She would have missed the lichgate entirely, in fact, if the captain hadn't pulled back a few bushes to reveal it.

He ushered a few guards through first, and each of them flinched as they rode through. They looked like ghosts on the other side, hazy figures that crossed in and out of sight as they moved over the forest floor beyond. The captain tapped her shoulder and nodded, indicating that she was next, so she nudged her horse along.

The familiar kick in her gut made her cringe when she passed under the gate. The forest on the other side was lush and green, dotted with twittering birds that flitted through the branches.

"Where exactly on the Rose Cliffs are we supposed to meet the Kirelm soldiers?" she asked once the captain had joined them.

"They will meet us at the peninsula with a few men," he answered. "It's the point where the cliff stretches out the farthest over the valley below. Do you know the legend of the Rose Cliffs?"

"I read about it."

"Personally, I think they're just a great big set of cliffs and that the story is a fairytale for children, but the Kirelm take it to heart. Be careful not to make light of it or you might upset someone important. Here now, we're close."

A strong gust of wind ruffled Kara's hair, and the forest broke suddenly away to reveal an endless sky. A quarter mile away, a sharp ledge stretched around to the left and right, curving until it disappeared behind the tree line. A brilliant landscape dotted the distant ground, tiny and much too far away. Small mountains framed the horizon, mere hills compared to the massive cliff on which they stood.

The guards halted. A long stretch of cliff jutted several hundred feet away from the forest on a wide catwalk above the valley thousands of feet below. Balanced on this rock-peninsula were at least one hundred Kirelm soldiers, their broad wings tucked in tightly to their sides, silver skin glistening. They wore royal blue tunics and sleek black pants, and everything they wore was branded with an image of a silver sun with pointed beams radiating from its center.

"This is a 'few men'?" she asked, reclining toward the captain. He wasn't listening, his glare instead focused on the rows of Kirelm soldiers before him.

The rest of the Hillside soldiers filled the gaps in the trees, creating a wall of green tunics and scowling faces. Gavin must have sent this many soldiers to make a statement, not just to keep her safe. She glanced over her shoulder to look deeper into the woods, where a pack of rider-less drowngs hovered behind the troops, each tied to a mounted rider's saddle. Guilt stabbed her as she wondered how many yakona had died in the skirmish.

The nightmare resurfaced when she turned back to the rows of immobile Kirelm soldiers, but she forced a deep breath. Even if her dream *had* been the Vagabond's memory, these were different people. They wanted peace. She could make it happen.

She dismounted Goliath, who nickered and nudged her as she passed him, and walked alone to the silent party of Kirelm yakona on the jutting strip of rock. The ground on either side disappeared into a dizzying drop to the far-off valley, so she held her breath as she walked. If she fell, she would lose her voice screaming before she hit the ground.

A Kirelm soldier walked forward to meet her. His uniform was more elaborate than the rest; its hems were lined with silver trimming, and several medals were pinned across his chest. He stretched his pale white wings, which glowed in the sun. She squinted at the sudden influx of light, so he tucked his wings in close once more. He took a deep breath and sighed as he looked her over.

"I am General Gurien," he said, bowing. "I will warn you, we were expecting someone, uh—taller."

"No, you were expecting a big burly man," she corrected. "I've heard this already. Let's get on with it."

He chuckled and stepped aside to reveal a griffin covered in black fur and gray feathers. Its massive eagle head tilted as it saw her, mildly interested in the color of her hair, but it clawed at the cliff rock when it once more became bored. The general turned to Captain Demnug and arched his shoulders in what Kara assumed was a suppressed sigh.

"I can't help but notice, Captain, that several of your *dogs*"—he said the word with distaste—"are without their riders. May I ask what happened?"

"We were ambushed by Carden's men. The Vagabond will tell you the rest."

"Unfortunate," Gurien said, clicking his tongue in forced disappointment.

Kara turned toward the griffin, shaking her head and trying to avoid any more forced pleasantries. Someone nearby cleared his throat. She turned and caught the gaze of a Kirelm guard with rich black eyes, his brow furrowed with worry. He winked when she looked over, and it took a moment before she noticed his white shell necklace. She hid her relief that Braeden had found them and pulled herself onto the griffin.

Soldiers jumped off of the cliff at a silent command from General Gurien and one-by-one spread their wings to catch the drafts coursing around the edge. Gurien soared over her and waved for her to follow, but she peeked out over the cliff. A thick wind ran through her hair as the sheer drop below made her head spin. She clung to the griffin's neck and urged him over the edge with a timid tap of her heels.

The creature bolted as if she'd kicked it and jumped into the air, opening its wings as a draft caught them and lifted them higher. It took every fiber of her being to suppress the scream that so badly wanted free as she jumped off what had to be the tallest cliff on Earth on the back of a flying lion-eagle hybrid.

They flew into a thick cloud cover. Her griffin directed itself, weaving in and out of the flying soldiers until she completely lost sight of both Braeden and the ground. The swarm climbed in and out of clouds as a single unit, confusing her until she had no idea of where they were going. She gathered that this was the point of the whole show, though, so she just held on for the ride.

❧CHAPTER NINETEEN
THE KINGDOM OF KIRELM

Kara counted the hours she spent in the sky by the growing soreness in her rear. Luckily, the griffin kept its head high enough to block the wind, so all she could feel of the icy altitude was a quick breeze that tickled her elbows if she didn't tuck them in. The steady pump of the beast's wings beneath her made her legs go numb, and it wasn't long before pins and needles replaced all sense of feeling in her lower back. She was about to cave and ask for a break when two clouds parted and a glimmer on the horizon caught her eye.

It was a flicker of light, like the sun glinting off of a piece of glass. They flew toward it, and after a few minutes, the light became a spire. She could make out another tower, and another, each blinking into view with a spark. A floating castle bled into sight, peeking around gaps and breaks in the cloud cover until a vast, teeming city of spires rose out of the clouds.

The city was surrounded by a thick circular road paved with polished silver stones. The entire kingdom was covered by a huge dome made from millions of intertwining metal wires, each curled around its brothers in an intricate pattern. The wires were thin, woven loosely enough that they appeared invisible unless an onlooker was close. A tall wall enclosed the city and ended in a single, massive gate, its doors composed of the same curling wires as the dome. A hundred thick, sharp spikes fortified the top of the gateway in what Kara assumed was mere show.

The massive gates opened as they drew nearer. Kara expected to land—no, *needed* to land—but the army sailed through the gates like a flurry of snow. The swish of air over their wings echoed as they passed. The wind howled over her. The company breezed by houses and buildings too quickly for her to make out anything more than white roofs and gray streets.

General Gurien appeared above her, snapping his wings in sharp bursts, just out of reach. The army broke away after a few moments and pulled behind, so that she and the general led the way.

The sun began to set behind the castle, bleeding red light onto the purple horizon. Kara paused. They hadn't been flying *that* long. Then again, it was possible that the lichgate this morning had taken her to another "time zone," as Braeden put it. After all, the Stele had been snow-covered and bright; and yet, back at the rental in Montana only hours later, it was still dark and only hours had passed.

Anything was possible in Ourea.

Thin gold lamps lit themselves on the street below in the coming dusk, flicking on one after another as she flew over them. Eyes peered from the windows she passed. She caught sporadic glimpses of the Kirelms, all with the same silver skin that began to glow subtly green in the growing night. Everyone wore brilliant blue and silver clothes, and though the men wore their dark hair cut around their shoulders, the women seemed to never cut their hair at all. Every adult woman Kara passed wore a floor-length gown and had her hair braided behind her, its tip brushing the ground as she walked.

Kara's convoy rounded a bend in the road, and a second gate came into focus. It contained the towering castle and its glinting spires, as well as several taller and more ornate homes than those which she'd already passed. The gate and its walls were thicker than the first and bigger, with yet another dome that stretched just beneath the first one. Kara looked back toward the outer wall, but could only see the clear sky beyond. The bars of the first wired dome were invisible, giving her full view of the clouds burning in the sunset.

The general grabbed her griffin's reins and led it to the street. They landed with a heavy thud at the foot of the closed gates, his hand gripping the creature's bridle long after they had stopped. The second gate opened to greet them, its deafening grate of metal on stone drowning out her request that he let go.

He strode through first and dragged her along behind him, leaving her little choice but to just go with it and suppress the urge to roll her eyes. The rest of the army waited at the open doors in militant rows, staring ahead with their wings tucked at their sides, and did not move or try to follow. Her palms began to sweat. She couldn't see Braeden's white shell necklace anywhere.

The palace itself was made of a pale blue stone and loomed over her, vast and unending. Dozens of towers with blue and red stained glass windows battered the sky, blocking out bits of sunlight and casting long shadows over the road.

Gurien stopped in a small courtyard that led to the castle's main stairs, where the palace doors stood open. A stunning young Kirelm woman stood on the first step, her hands tucked in front of her. Her oval face was smooth, her large black eyes masked with thick lashes, and dots of black freckles brushed her silver nose. She smiled as they approached, the warm gesture wrinkling her eyes ever so slightly. Kara's heart settled.

"Welcome to Kirelm, Vagabond. I am Heir Aurora. Please, take a walk with me. Blood Ithone will be able to meet you tomorrow afternoon, but for now we hope that you will relax after what must have been a long journey."

Kara smiled. Relief washed over her. Sleep and a soft mattress were all she really wanted at that moment anyway. She rubbed her lower back and dismounted, readjusting the satchel around her shoulder before she headed toward the princess.

Her mind flickered back to the first Vagabond as he stood by the creek in all his wispy glory. "*I hid all of the map pieces in the various kingdoms' gardens,*" he'd said. "*It's best you look there first.*"

"Um, will you show me your gardens, Heir Aurora?" Kara asked, hoping she sounded relaxed despite the cool sweat forming in her palm.

"It would be my pleasure."

The princess gestured toward an iron gate in a nearby stone wall and began toward it. Beds of blossoming roses came into view through its gaps as Kara followed. Aurora held open the gate when they came to it, but thereafter, they walked in silence. There was no sound but the rush of the periodic breezes breaking over the walls and rustling through the garden.

Kara casually examined the vines and flowerbeds, looking for some sign of the map piece and occasionally stealing a glance at the princess. The young woman's eyes were deep in thought, and her cheeks puckered slightly, as if she was biting them. There was something on the princess's mind.

A golden glint shimmered in Kara's peripheral vision. It flickered out and then flitted across her vision again, so she scanned the garden, searching for its source. Vines covered almost every inch of the stone walls, and in one section of the garden, blue roses blossomed among them. In one break in this color, a blue stone glinted in the fading red sunlight. Embedded gold flashed in the rock.

Kara slowed, letting the princess walk ahead, and sauntered over to the wall. She brushed the vines to the side, trying to avoid the thorns, and all but threw her hands in the air with victory when she figured out what it was.

The map piece!

Her eyes flitted to the princess, who was still walking along the path and hadn't even noticed her move. The yakona's silver and black head disappeared behind a wall and drifted out of sight, so Kara dug her nails behind a corner of the stone and tugged.

It didn't budge.

"Vagabond?" The princess's voice rang from the other side of the wall.

Kara's heart skipped a beat. She bit her lip and dug her nails deeper into the wedge. A centimeter pulled free. The rock grated. A fingernail snapped. She took another breath, held it, and pulled until her cheeks flushed from the effort. The map piece popped free, falling into her hands like a five-pound dumbbell. She slipped it into her satchel and leaned against the wall in what she hoped was a leisurely slouch seconds before the princess rounded the corner.

"Is everything all right?" Aurora glanced to the rose wall with a puzzled look on her face.

"Yep. I was just—uh—admiring these roses. They're so—blue."

Kara wanted to hit her head against the wall at the dumb remark, but she forced a smile instead. Really? They were blue, huh?

The Heir narrowed her eyes. "I see. Well, I do hope my silence hasn't bored you."

"Not at all."

"I just—" Aurora's eyes slipped out of focus again and whatever had bothered her returned with a vengeance. Kara sighed with relief when the princess continued walking, apparently already forgetting the temporary disappearance.

"Is something wrong?" she asked, trying to nudge the conversation away from the wall and the secret map piece hidden in her shoulder bag.

"I pray that I am not overstepping any boundaries of propriety," the princess said. "But I feel that I must warn you for the reception you will receive."

"What do you mean?"

The nightmarish memory of the bleeding woman flashed in her

mind. She held her breath and looked back to the small wrought iron gate that was the only exit.

"What are you doing?" Aurora set her hand on Kara's shoulder, which only came up to the princess's chest. Even with her added height, the yakona was much thinner. Her frail hand blocked out Kara's peripheral vision with a silver blur, but the touch nonetheless soothed her panic.

"Is something going to happen?" Kara asked. "Do I need to leave?"

Aurora laughed. "Heavens, no. I must apologize. That was not the manner in which I should have introduced the subject. You are a creature of peace and should feel at home wherever you go."

"Then what did you want to warn me about?"

"Regardless of your gifts as the Vagabond, my father and his seers will only see that you are a woman. They will only see your dress, which will make tomorrow's meeting difficult for you."

Kara hesitated. "What does wearing a dress have to do with anything? I mean, you're a woman and the Heir. You'll be Blood someday. Why should they care if I'm a woman?"

"I'm the first female Heir in the history of our nation." The princess looked to the ground and took a deep breath, as if it was a shameful thing. "My father has betrothed me to General Gurien so he can lead when I am not capable."

Kara gritted her teeth and took a deep breath, resisting the urge to both laugh and scream at the same time. "That's—uh—interesting."

"Kirelms are simple," Aurora continued. "Men are warriors while women embody the art, beauty, and spirituality of our nation. With this balance, warriors will always have something to protect. It's basic and modest and our most cherished belief."

"I don't mean to be rude," Kara said, almost certain that she would sound rude anyway, "but you're meant to be a leader. You can't deny what you were born to be."

The words grated against her throat as they left her mouth, and she suppressed the thought of Braeden as quickly as it arose.

"One never knows what one was born to be," Aurora said. "Nor could you know what another is meant to do with life. I ask that you not judge us, Vagabond. If you do, you will not succeed here."

The truth in the princess's words made Kara swallow a sarcastic retort.

Aurora nodded to the gate. "I must leave, but a maid is waiting for you by the stairs just beyond the garden. She will lead you to your room."

Kara bowed her head in thanks, unable to speak for fear of saying something stupid in her rising annoyance. She headed back to the garden gate and walked toward the castle as Aurora set off in another direction.

The gate opened without a sound, and as she walked through it, Kara spotted a small set of stairs which led from the side of the castle. They curved out onto a side path, their bottom steps rounded out like the wave of an ocean. A broad set of doors stood at the top of the steps and opened for her as she took the stairs two at a time.

A Kirelm woman in a simple blue gown stood in the center of the hallway, barring the way as the doors swung apart. The maid flashed a thick grin, but Kara's aggravation at what Aurora had said was bubbling now, festering so that she couldn't contain it anymore. She walked around the maid without pausing or acknowledging her, but the woman's smile didn't falter. She spun and matched Kara's pace.

"My lady, may I show you to your room?" the maid asked.

Kara debated following her, but her stomach gurgled. "Actually, can you show me to the kitchen?"

"We will bring you a feast, Vagabond."

"I'd rather explore a little. Please just tell me where the kitchen is."

The woman's cheeks flushed green. She scuttled around and stopped just ahead of Kara, nearly toppling both of them in the process. The woman began to plead with her in a quiet, pitiful voice.

"Please, Miss! You must go to your room!"

"Oh my *goodness*, all right!" Kara put her hands up in surrender, the babbling too much to bear. The woman was like a moth dive-bombing her head.

The yakona smiled, relieved, and ushered her up the stairs. The sloping stairwell was covered in plush blue carpet, and its spiraled railing led the way to a hallway one floor up. Doors lined the left side of the hall every ten feet or so, but to the right was a railing that looked out over a courtyard. In the open space was an indoor waterfall, which began about twenty feet above and crashed to a lazy river below. Mist curled up from the black rocks that lined the stream as it coursed down the hall and out of sight.

The woman hurried Kara onward, trotting her away from the breathtaking falls with an urgency that could only mean she wasn't meant to be seen. The crash of the waterfall became a distant hum, but the river still wound in lazy curves below.

They finally stopped at a silver door identical to the rest. Kara suppressed a deep sigh and walked in when the maid opened it.

"Will you nee—"

"Just the food, thanks," Kara interrupted.

She slammed the door behind her and stretched her arms in frustration on her way to the window, where she glared out at the fading dusk. The stars were brilliant in the dark blue haze above, glimmering from their own worlds far away. She wondered if life beyond was as messed up as it was on Earth.

The door creaked open and latched closed again. Floorboards creaked. She turned to see a broad-shouldered Kirelm soldier looking down at her.

"Will you all leave me alone?!"

"Uh," he stuttered.

She glanced at his white shell necklace. "Oh. Sorry, Braeden."

He took a step closer. "Where have you been? I've been trying to find you. I was worried."

"I'm fine. I went on a walk with Aurora."

She watched him with a sideways glare. This was Braeden, sure, but it was too strange that he had a different face.

"So you were attacked on the way here?" He crossed the room and examined her, lifting her chin and checking her arms for injuries.

She was too tired and frustrated to pretend to fight him— truthfully, his touch was welcome warmth after the bitter wind from their flight over. He seethed and paused. He must've seen the gash on her neck from the branch that knocked her out in the ambush.

"Carden's guys," she said absently.

He pressed his thumb to the wound without answering. There was no sting like she'd expected; instead, the skin tingled. It seared and cooled in the instant he touched her. He moved his hand away too soon. The throbbing itch disappeared, and, when she rubbed her neck, so had the gash.

"Thanks for that." She craned her neck to look up at him. He frowned, his eyes shrouded with worry. Without thinking about it, she laughed.

"What—why are you laughing?"

"It's so weird talking to you when you look like this."

"This isn't funny," he said, but he smirked. "How was your detour with Heir Aurora?"

"Annoying." Kara stopped smiling at the thought of the princess. Her lip and eyebrow both twitched.

"I understand your frustration. They aren't fond of women here."

"Oh they love girls," she said, imitating Aurora's warm honey voice as she rolled her eyes. "But only if they sew and curtsey."

"Tomorrow is going to be interesting," he said, eying her. "I suppose I should let you get some rest."

"What are you going to do?"

"I told the soldiers that I come from one of Kirelm's outer villages." He grinned, cracking his knuckles. "I get to spar."

"Shouldn't you be, I don't know, lying low?"

"Nah." He waved away the thought. "I found them on the Rose Cliffs. I told them I was visiting my sister and would be leaving in a few days. They're kind, really."

"You didn't invite me to watch the sparring?" Her heart fell as she eyed his broad, black wings. "That sounds like a lot of fun."

"Sorry. Ladies have a curfew. However, I might have been inadvertently involved in getting you a bedroom that overlooks the sparring arena."

He grinned and retreated from the room, shutting the door behind him.

Kara smiled and shook her head, turning once more to look out the window. If she'd looked down as she pondered the stars, she would have seen the sparring arena. It was a large circular platform encased with more of the thin, woven wires that surrounded the city. Soldiers pooled in groups of two and three near it, talking or pulling off their shirts for the combat ahead. They each had tattoos on their right arms, just like Braeden. The sprawling works of art ran from their biceps to their shoulders, and some even had tattoos which climbed down their entire arms and finished on the backs of their hands. She'd have to ask the Grimoire about that someday.

Someone knocked, but it opened without a pause. The woman from earlier brought in a tray of fruits, bread, strips of red meat glazed with honey, and a glass of wine. Kara muttered her thanks and grabbed the wine before the woman set down the tray.

She turned back to the window and saw a group of ten Kirelms walking to the arena, but couldn't see any necklaces from this distance.

However, she did recognize one long scrolling tattoo that spiked along a soldier's chest, though no one else seemed interested in how different his jagged tattoo was from the others. She chuckled, pitying whoever agreed to spar Braeden.

He entered the arena first, and a much taller, much broader soldier followed him in. The door closed. Braeden turned and froze mid-stretch when he saw his massive opponent.

Kara grappled for the lock on the window. She had to hear this. The latch gave her trouble, and it took a few seconds before she heard the sharp pop that meant it was open. The window opened only about two inches, so she made do with what she had and folded her arms on the windowsill.

The two men in the arena circled as the audience cheered. The Kirelm soldier threw test blows to flush out weak spots, but Braeden watched and waited, ducking lightly out of the way of each blow. The jabs became faster, until the soldier feigned a punch and used the distraction to hurl his wing into Braeden's chest.

Braeden flew through the air and landed against the cage wires, falling to the platform with an audible thud, like bricks hitting cement. Kara gasped, but it was a stupid thing to do. He was an Heir. He'd be fine.

The disguised prince rolled beneath another swing and jumped to his feet. He delivered three jabs into the soldier's solar plexus, side, and chest before he shot a thick current of wind that knocked the soldier clear onto his back.

The Kirelm nodded defeat and limped out of the arena.

The audience cheered through the metals gaps in the arena walls, the general among them. Braeden tried to bow himself from the ring, but the crowd roared in protest and he was given another contestant: and another, and *another*, until the sun was completely gone and their only light came from lamps nearby.

"One more!" The soldiers laughed after Braeden shrugged to them, asking for his freedom with a sheepish grin. He ran his hand through his hair and nodded.

"One more!" he agreed.

The gate opened and General Gurien walked into the arena. The Kirelm spread his broad white wings, which glowed just as brightly in the lamplight as they had in the sun. Braeden's smile faded as the crowd applauded the new contestant, but he recovered after a second and bowed in welcome.

He adjusted the loose folds of his pant fabric and began to circle. The general, instead of matching his pace, walked to the center of the ring and slowly rotated, studying Braeden's movement. Braeden jabbed the seasoned warrior's side, which was open, but the general didn't react except to take a step out of the way.

Their dance continued like this for too long. Braeden experimented with the general's weaknesses while the soldier only moved to avoid contact, which apparently frustrated the prince to no end. He swayed and jabbed at anything that became open until finally, when he couldn't take any more, he launched into a wild, unfocused barrage of fists, wings, and black fire.

The general dodged the attack with a few light steps, wrapping his arm around Braeden's bicep. He lodged his foot at just the right angle and used the prince's momentum to take him to the ground. In another split-second movement, Gurien summoned two massive swords of ice and held one in each hand. He pointed them to Braeden's throat.

Kara grabbed the windowsill, but the crowd laughed and applauded as the blades of ice shattered, fractured shards landing in Braeden's hair as the swords broke apart.

The general bent and offered a hand to help Braeden to his feet, slapping the undercover prince's back as he laughed and mumbled something Kara couldn't make out. Braeden nodded, bowed, and walked as fast as he could out of the arena. He paused, turned to her window, and bowed once more before continuing off and disappearing from sight.

She laughed. *Show off.*

Gurien, having won the last match, waved to the crowds for another opponent. Kara grumbled and closed the window before jumping onto the bed. She had no interest in watching *him*.

She nibbled the meat, which had a peppery hint to it, and picked at the fruit. Her wine was long gone, and she wished she had another glass. This place gave her a headache. It would probably be simple to get another serving, but she decided against it. Dealing with the dive-bombing moth-woman would just make her headache worse.

The satchel rested on the floor by the window, so she pulled it onto the bed and poured its contents onto the comforter. The half and quarter map pieces slid out onto the linens, closely followed by the rolling tumble of the little blue and orange egg. Kara grabbed the orb and rubbed it with a finger, grateful that it had survived the trek, before she set it on her pillow.

She pushed the new map piece against the half-finished slab, experimenting with how they fit together. A silver flash of light illuminated the room when she found it, but she was ready this time and shut her eyes in time to block out the glare. When she opened them again, just a few black and white spots blurred her vision.

The map was almost finished, now, with only a single corner missing. Still, the only design on the map besides the intricate ivy frame was the partially-completed oval, which was really nothing more than an indent that took up most of the lapis. Its center was smooth, without any traces of landscape or anything else that would exist on a real map. She bit her lip and frowned.

Why would the Vagabond send her on an errand around Ourea for a map that couldn't take her anywhere?

She ran her fingers along the cold blue stone and tensed her jaw. He wouldn't do that. There was a rhyme and a reason to it—she just hadn't figured it out yet. Wherever the village was, it wouldn't be easy to get to. That was kind of the point, after all, and she wasn't sure she should go alone. Braeden would be an incredible ally on the trip. But anxiety twisted again in the pit of her stomach, as it had every time she thought of telling him.

He'd already proven that he would protect her, but what she couldn't figure out was why he cared in the first place. After all, he had nothing to gain from it, not really. Yet, he'd lied to his own brother—well, adoptive brother—about where he was in order to make sure she was safe on this journey. He was risking being exposed as the Heir to the Stele by shifting form and following her on an expedition where she would have otherwise been completely alone. He hadn't even pressed her for a chance to talk to the Grimoire. He hadn't taken advantage of her in any way.

Guilt churned in her stomach. Those weren't reasons to distrust him.

Whatever the ramifications, she would tell him about the village the next chance she had. Her gut panged at the decision, but she ignored it and threw the map in her bag. She grabbed her egg, massaged it until it was warm, and slipped it in her satchel as well. She stretched out on the mattress and stared at the ceiling.

The edges of her vision darkened, and she lost track of the time she spent watching the spackled roof above her. There was a conscious thought that she was falling asleep, but that couldn't really be happening. Usually, realizing she was about to fall asleep shook her awake. But here, now, the darkness grew until it consumed all the light in the room.

The temperature plummeted. Goosebumps chased across her arms. She couldn't see, even though her eyes were open, and the hair on her neck and arms stood on end. Shivers ricocheted along her body as she tried to keep warm, but aside from those unnatural movements, she couldn't even turn her head. She was frozen in place.

Move! She tried to twitch her knees, her toes, her hands: nothing obeyed. *Move!* She meant to scream it, to yell, but her voice was locked away in her throat.

Move!

Mobility returned to her with a sudden jolt that made her snap upright and rub her shoulders. The rest of the room had dissolved into unending blackness, leaving only her bed—which was nothing but muted shades of gray—floating in the darkness. There was no sense of up or down or distance. There were no dimensions.

Thin white wisps sped past her and congealed a short ways off, twisting and convulsing around each other like snakes until they became a tall man wrapped in a hooded cloak. He hovered in the darkness, the corners of his robe billowing without a wind. His hood veiled his face.

"What was *that*, Vagabond?" she demanded. "How was that necessary?"

"I'm sorry if I frightened you. I brought you into the Grimoire as you slept. It's the only place where we may speak freely," he said. His voice echoed, reverberating in the vast nothing which surrounded them.

"Warn me next time." She tried to forget the frightful paralysis that had kept her cemented to the bed, but shuddered as the memory resurfaced anyway.

"You are in Kirelm," he said. It was not a question.

"Yeah, how did you know?" she asked, looking him over. He clenched his fists but released them just as quickly. He ignored her question.

"How have you been received, Kara?"

"No one tried to kill me, so I guess that's a good start."

Her chest panged with regret and her throat caught on her words, but it was too late to stop herself. She glanced back to the Vagabond. If her nightmare had really been a memory, that had been crass.

"I'm sorry," she said. "I'm just so frustrated that I didn't think. They don't have much respect for women here."

"They have every respect for women," he corrected. "They simply don't believe that a woman should partake in politics or war, and you are meddling in both. Few here will ever be fond of you for that reason, and such is why you must act with restraint, patience, and conviction."

"That's complicated."

"As is life."

"Vagabond," she began, her voice quiet. She wasn't sure how to word what she wanted to say. "You said you're a spirit, right? A real ghost? So you know how you died?"

The hood turned to the floor. She wished she could see his face.

"Why do you ask?"

"I had this nightmare on the way here. I was lying in a bed and Kirelm guards grabbed and chained me. Was that the village? Is that where I'm trying to go?"

"That was indeed a memory of mine," he said softly. "But no, that was not the village. We were in what we thought was a safe house. It was a trap."

She was silent.

"What else did you see of that night, Kara?"

She told him everything she could remember about the dream, and he became unnaturally still when she described the stunning woman who bled over the white marble floor. Her voice died off when she finished. Neither of them spoke for a while.

"That was Helen," he finally said. "The love of my life."

"I'm sorry, Vagabond."

"Is there more to the dream?"

"No." She thought back to the blood dripping over the woman's fingers. "Do all vagabonds have red blood?"

"Yes. You will not stay here long, so don't be surprised if you are quickly ushered out of the kingdom. The Kirelm were never fond of our kind." There was no emotion in his voice.

"That memory—did you die that night?"

"That's irrelevant."

"No it isn't. I have a right to know what I'm up against."

"You have already seen that. To know my past will only cast doubt on your purpose."

That was *not* a real answer.

"Is that going to happen to me?" she asked. Her heart was steady and her breath calm, which surprised her. She'd just asked him if she was going to die, after all.

"No," he answered. "At least, not today. Not tomorrow."

"Ah. Well I feel better, then."

"This is sarcasm, yes?"

She laughed and rubbed her eyes without answering.

"Sleep well, Kara."

When she looked up, the room had returned. The lanterns by the arena were extinguished, so that the only light came from the brilliant moon hanging in her window. Its light cast a silver haze on her bed.

"Right," she said to the empty room. "Like I can sleep now."

The knock on Kara's door in the early afternoon was timid at best. She'd managed to doze off at some point in the early morning and slept far longer than intended, so in her tired delirium, she mistook the incessant tapping on the door for rain on her window. When she did finally hear the soft rapping, she opened the door to the same woman that had ushered her out of public view the night before. The maid held a tray of fruits and a cold omelet.

"You must hurry to be ready for your meeting with Blood Ithone," the woman said, her voice fluttering with nerves. She set the tray on the vanity and slung a long silver gown over the bed. She turned to Kara, waiting to help her dress.

Kara thought back to her conversation with Aurora. If she wore that dress, it would be all Ithone saw. He wouldn't listen.

"No." she finally said.

The maid froze. "I—I apologize, but what? No?"

"I would like pants, please."

"But Mistress, we have customs. We must all dress in a similar fashion. It's our way."

"I respect that. I am also not going to wear that dress. Hillside gave me pants and that's what I expect here as well."

Admittedly, the dress was beautiful. Even Kara, who ripped her prom dress falling down the stairs in her senior year of high school, could appreciate the silk. She knew it would flatter her body, and the fabric glittered in the afternoon sunbeams as if it were made of diamonds. But it was still a dress. At this point, she had to defend the principle.

The woman blubbered again, as she had in the hallway yesterday, but Kara was ready this time. She waved her hand to cut it off.

"No."

The woman scowled. Wrinkles twisted her brow, and her mask of timid blubbery dissolved into annoyance as she marched from the room. Kara closed the door behind her and without another word, summoned a small lavender flame to warm her omelet.

The egg was mixed with peppered tomatoes, which added a warm spice, and there was a hint of something sweet as well. She ate and bathed, wrapping herself in a towel afterward as she scrutinized her two clothing options: the dingy, tattered rags in which she'd come to Kirelm; or, the stunning dress that undermined everything she was trying to do. She grumbled, snatched the tattered rags, dressed, and opened her door to General Gurien, who was poised to knock.

He gaped and examined the mud-stained rips and splotches of blood left on her traveling outfit.

"My lady," he said when he found his voice. "You would certainly not wear that to speak to Blood Ithone?"

"Unless you have a set of pants I can wear," she said, with a warm, fake smile.

He scoffed, and she brushed past him without a clue of where she was going. The rush of the waterfall grew louder in the few steps she was allowed to take before the general stopped her.

A sheet of ice crackled across the wall. It raced past and licked the floor in front of her, creating dark, frozen pools that stopped her in her tracks. The frost bent and split, growing to cover the entire hallway like a thin, frozen wall. Icicles dangled over the railing, frozen daggers that reminded her of Christmas and home and everything she was giving up for the yakona who made her life in Ourea so difficult. She glanced over her shoulder and cocked an eyebrow.

The trail of ice stemmed from where Gurien rested his outstretched hand against the wall. He frowned and sighed, but it came out as more of a growl.

"I have a compromise, Vagabond, if you will just *listen*."

Fifteen minutes later, she was wearing a child's small gray traveling suit—the only outfit Gurien could find that fit her. Its simple bodice had only minute décor along the sleeves, and the suit was rimmed with a knee-length, blue satin skirt. However, and much to her liking, black pants were involved beneath it all. She glanced herself over in a mirror and grinned.

"I misjudged you, General."

"At least you're in a woman's clothes," he said, apparently still not entirely happy with the arrangement. She glared at him over her shoulder, but he didn't apologize.

"Your people are different." He shrugged. "I understand. But you aren't with them. You are in a nation of a different sort. You must learn to respect the customs where you go or you will offend those you try to help."

"We should get going," she grumbled.

"You can't expect us to conform to you. That's not tolerance. It's ego."

"It goes both ways, General."

He sighed. "Be careful what you say to Blood Ithone. He isn't compromising."

The hallway in this section of the palace had no waterfall or courtyard, but was instead wide and empty and open. Gray paneled walls lined with black wooden trim continued down the corridor and twisted out of view around a corner. Gurien, however, turned to the right and began down a set of silver stairs lined with blue carpet. Rows of feet appeared one after the other as she followed him, until a massive throne room came into view.

The room was filled with Kirelms, most of whom kept to the walls. Soldiers stood in a line at the foot of the stairwell, clearing a path for her that led to a set of three thrones at the far end of the room. A tall Kirelm wearing a thick silver crown sat in the center seat; Kara could only assume he was Blood Ithone. Aurora sat to his right, and an older woman, likely Kirelm's Queen, sat to his left.

Disdain wrinkled Blood Ithone's face. He looked her over and grimaced as she walked closer, unannounced. Kara examined the tile and windows as she walked, trying to decide if this was the room from her nightmare. It wasn't.

Ithone rested his chin in his hand and watched her, waiting to speak until she stopped at the foot of his throne.

"Were better clothes not provided? I was not aware that you were a twelve-year-old about to take her first flight beyond the walls," he said, looking her over while his audience laughed at his joke.

"A dress was provided, if that's what you mean," she said with a wry smile, catching his eye.

He smirked. "I will not lie to you, young lady. I am highly disappointed."

"As am I," she confessed.

The crowd hushed. He laughed, but the mirth was short-lived.

"How could a woman, brazen though you may be, unite warring kingdoms?"

"With all respect, I think your focus should be more on the Bloods and their ability to think about what's best for their people."

Another tense murmur bubbled through the crowd. She could see civilians and soldiers alike throwing glances at each other. Ithone hadn't laughed this time.

"I'm sure you know this, Vagabond, but our kingdom has always been wary of your kind. Especially so of your master."

The image of the blood-soaked Helen flashed in her mind, but she took a deep breath and clenched her fist to stay calm. He eyed her without blinking. She wanted to squirm, but held his gaze instead.

"Your master was a truly powerful man," he continued. "In fact, it seems the more he spoke of peace, the stronger he himself grew. My ancestors found this to be an odd correlation. But though we were cautious, he still managed to steal from us.

"Not only did he steal Kirelms from the very bloodline which defined them, but he stole our most prized possession. You recall the griffin that brought you here? He is of a race of beasts even older than my people. When the Vagabond lived, there was a stallion unlike any other that was stolen from beneath our noses."

The voice from her nightmare rang in her mind. *"You are a thief."*

Her body froze in a brief pang of terror. She shot her eyes left and right in what she hoped were subtle movements, but there was no exit. Soldiers lined every wall, and they'd even closed in behind her to block the stairs.

A thousand years ago, the Kirelm people had killed off the vagabonds. She was sure of that, now. They might have even killed the

Vagabond himself. They *still* hated him. He'd insisted that she wouldn't die today, but even the first Vagabond could be wrong.

She took a deep breath, held it, and let it slowly free. The only way out of this was convincing Ithone that she was on his side, so maybe she should've just worn that stupid dress. His voice boomed, pulling her from her thoughts to the throne room and its immediate danger.

"There are rumors that the first Vagabond sealed away our prized griffin in his book, as a *pet*." He bellowed his next words as an order. "Show me the Grimoire!"

Her back was rigid and unyielding to her attempts to relax, but she did manage to stretch out her palms. She didn't want to brush the pendant or betray where she kept the Grimoire, so she took another deep breath and focused on the image of her book instead. Ash appeared from the thin air, swirling and congealing in her palms as she summoned it. The Grimoire's red cover bled from the dust, and its weight settled into her fingers. The crowd gasped, but their king was unimpressed.

"Show me our griffin," he ordered.

Her heart skipped a beat, but his scowling face made it clear that he was serious. She looked down at the Grimoire and flipped open the cover.

"How do I bring out this griffin?" she asked too quietly for even her own ears to hear.

The pages flipped for several painful seconds, but they finally landed on the image of a griffin more regal than the one she'd ridden. The graceful curve in its neck continued to its beak, and it looked up at her from the drawing. There was no text to instruct her.

She traced the outline of its form. A rush of wind pummeled through her hair at the touch, stinging her ears and numbing her cheeks with its fury. White dust spiraled around her, pooling into a loose figure. The sharp curve of a beak appeared in the whirlwind, followed by a beady black eye. All at once, the rest of the dust blew away to reveal a griffin that peered over the silent yakona throng from where it towered above them.

It stomped its paw against the floor. The tile cracked. It inched toward Kara and lay down at her side, so tall that its head came to hers even when it was resting. The king laughed and stood, delight lighting his eyes.

"If you return our griffin to us, we will become your allies," he said with excitement.

The griffin cawed sharply. The painful bark shattered a window behind Ithone's throne and shook dust from the ceiling. The griffin turned to Aurora and shrieked again before lowering his head beneath Kara's hand. She swallowed hard.

"I don't think it wants to come back, Blood Ithone."

The king didn't answer. He clenched his fists and glared at the creature, stewing in his thoughts. He narrowed his eyes and fumed. Kara sighed.

"Majesty," she said, her voice gentle. "Blood Carden killed the Queen of Hillside. His soldiers ambushed me on the way here. It's safe to say that he at least knows the approximate locations of every kingdom. For whatever reason, he's going after the Bloods. He's after you. So don't start peace talks because you get a griffin. Do it because it's what's best for your people, for your nation, and for yourself."

Ithone leaned forward. "Have you spoken yet with the Kingdom of Losse?"

"Not yet."

"Then I have a challenge for you. If Blood Frine agrees to these peace negotiations, I will consider them as well."

He stood and left the throne room through a door on the rear wall of the platform. Aurora and the nameless woman followed him. The civilians dispersed.

What, was that it?

The griffin brushed the nape of her neck with its beak. It was smooth, like a river rock, but it pricked her skin with its sharp edges. She stroked its chin. It cooed.

"You're not so big and scary, huh?" She smiled and scratched the cool feathers on its neck. The beast squawked and rapped her shoulder in what she hoped was a love tap. She bent beneath it, a sharp pain searing her shoulder. It was gentle, for a giant bird-lion, but it would most definitely leave a bruise.

Someone cleared his throat nearby, and she turned to see Gurien glaring down at her. She swallowed hard at the frustrated glint in his eye.

"Vagabond," he said, "the Kirelm guard will lead you to the Rose Cliffs, but from there you will be on your own to find the Villing Caves. I'm sure with your vast knowledge of the Grimoire, you will be fine." He glared at the book, and she wished it away as he continued. "Had we known you had your own griffin, though, we would not have tired one of ours with the journey here."

He marched toward a set of doors that led to the brilliant day outside. She wanted to tell him that she had no idea about the griffin, but instead watched him leave and hoisted herself onto the creature with what she hoped was grace.

Once she was situated, the griffin stood and followed Gurien into the bright day outside without any need for guidance. She slouched and scrutinized her hands, unable to tell if the afternoon had been a victory or not.

She looked over her shoulder as they passed through the castle's shadow and, in a lower window of the front-most tower, saw Aurora's flawless silver face. The princess waved once, and Kara returned the gesture.

❧CHAPTER TWENTY
LESSONS

W ind blew over Braeden's face as he flew toward the Rose Cliffs with the Kirelm guard on their way to return Kara. He pulled behind to let the other soldiers glide on a draft ahead of him, but they moved at a slow pace and beat their wings only hard enough to coast. None of them joked or laughed like they had in the sparring ring. They focused on the sky ahead, as if only what lay before them had any importance. Apparently, there was no fun while on duty.

He was torn. Kirelm as a kingdom had failed Kara by refusing to take her safely to the Villing Caves. If she'd been attacked on the way to the Rose Cliffs, it was inevitable that it would happen again. However, the truth was that he'd *never* had as much fun sparring with Gavin as he did in the Kirelm arena with complete strangers. He hadn't even caught most of the soldiers' names, and yet he'd been welcomed like a brother and friend from the moment they found him. They snickered and teased like a family. He'd even become a legend for his ability to take a hit in the ring.

"My friend," a voice nearby said. "We must speak."

He glanced to his left as a Kirelm soldier he didn't recognize pulled just above him, flying with steady ease.

"You're leaving us at the Rose Cliffs, is that right?" the Kirelm asked.

"I was going to drop off a few miles sooner, so I suppose you could say that."

"It's close enough. The general has an assignment for you."

Uh-oh. He took a shallow breath to keep his voice steady, but his mind raced at the thought of which pants-wearing vagabond it likely involved.

"What would that be?" he asked.

"Follow this new Vagabond. Stay out of sight if you can, since Blood Ithone didn't tell us to help her, but see that she arrives at the Villing

Caves. Send word once she's been taken by the Lossians." He slipped a smooth pebble into Braeden's hand. The rock glowed blue at his touch, and a silver rune materialized in its center.

"What is this?"

"Break it when you arrive. The general will know, then, that she's safe."

"Word is that we aren't fond of the Vagabond," Braeden said, doing his best to sound nonchalant. "Why has the general asked that I watch her?"

He'd heard the gossip bubbling through the city as they left. The rumors claimed that the new Vagabond was little different from the first. She'd refused to dress in the city's custom and insulted the general by withholding her griffin, even though the flicker of panic that crossed her face in the throne room meant she hadn't known about the creature at all. He hoped no one else had seen that.

Still, because the general didn't seem fond of her, none of the soldiers were taken with her either. If they'd been ordered to kill her instead of send a scout after her, he had no doubt that they would've done it without a second thought. It therefore made no sense that Gurien would want the Vagabond kept safe.

The soldier winked. "That's another reason you were chosen— none of us would volunteer. But you aren't a member of the guard, yet. Doing this will put you in Gurien's favor."

"Then I'll do it."

"We suspected as much."

"I'm honored," Braeden said after a pause. "But why was I really chosen to do this?"

The soldier looked down at him. "No one has ever spent for more than five seconds in the ring with Gurien. You lasted over five minutes."

Braeden laughed.

"Now listen," the soldier continued, "If she's attacked again along the way, don't sacrifice yourself to protect her. You're a good man, and the many others who rallied for her cause in the past died for it. We want you to make the city your home, so come back when you're bored of that rural hole of a village you come from."

The Kirelm slapped him on the back in farewell and pointed down to the valley below, implying that this was where Braeden should leave. He twisted his wings and pulled upward, back into the cloud cover with his brothers.

Braeden watched the soldier disappear and shook his head in disbelief, laughing. He'd just been assigned to do the very thing he'd infiltrated the Kirelm kingdom to do. If Hillside ever became unsafe, at least he had a second home.

The valley whizzed by below, nothing but streaks of color in his peripheral vision until he focused his eyes. A herd of deer ran through gaps in the tree canopy, appearing for only a second as he passed them. He grinned. It was easy to appreciate the Kirelm body. Its wings were two extra weapons at his disposal. His sight, hearing, and sense of smell were all sharpened. Even his skin was thicker; he should have been cold, soaring at this speed, but the air ran over him like a warm breeze.

The sweet, biting aroma of roses flooded his nose, so he dipped beneath the clouds. Sure enough, the Rose Cliffs towered over the silent valley, much closer than expected. Rosebuds blocked out sections of the brown rock, blooming wherever there was a gap or crack.

Kara blurred through a break in the clouds ahead. She still flew at the front of the line on her griffin, with Gurien close in tow. The general eyed her, but shifted his gaze away each time she glanced over her shoulder. Braeden groaned. She should have just worn the dress.

The cliffs were only a few hundred feet off, now. He tucked his wings tightly to his body and dove, falling like a rock. The woods loomed closer. Wind poured over him, stinging his cheeks as he picked up speed. The forest pulled closer. He could see the veins in the topmost leaves of the trees.

He spread his wings to slow his fall and slapped them against the air, but he overestimated his own strength and crashed through the canopy. Twigs snapped. Leaves scattered around him. Branches flew by as he maneuvered and ducked. He finally hit the dirt with a thud, knees bruising from where they dented the soil, but the bruises healed as quickly as they appeared. Radiant light shone through a hole in the branches of the tree, marking his tumbling path. He'd have to work on his landings.

Gurien's distant outline was visible through the hole as he flew with Kara's griffin to the Rose Cliffs. The company hovered in the sky, beating their wings in quick bursts to keep themselves stationary as they waited. Gurien floated above Kara when she landed, said something inaudible, and returned to his fleet. The swarm of Kirelm soldiers flew off into the distance.

Braeden waited seven minutes before he finally lost sight of them. He looked down at the little stone and rubbed the glowing silver rune before he shoved it in his pocket. The tree limbs were unbroken and sturdy, so he climbed to the highest branch that could support his weight and jumped off. He caught a draft once he cleared the tree top and turned upward, toward the rocky peninsula above, always keeping his distance from the thick clumps of roses blooming across the rock. The origin of the Kirelm bloodline might have been nothing more than a legend, but he wasn't about to risk anything.

The edge of the cliff came sooner than expected. He scaled the curve and stumbled into his landing, skidding a few feet on his heels and flapping his wings to maintain balance before he managed to stop.

Kara sat on her griffin, looking him over with cocked eyebrows for a moment before she recognized him. She laughed.

"You're not a graceful bird, huh?"

He shrugged, grinning.

"It's good to see you, Braeden. I was beginning to think you got used to all the pretty ladies and the bowing and that you left me to fend for myself."

"I was already bored and we were barely there two days," he lied. He stretched his wings and yawned. He wasn't about to admit how much fun he'd had, not when she still looked so irritated.

"How did they not see you just then?" she asked, eyeing his broad wings.

"They told me to leave, Kara. Gurien assigned me to look over you. They aren't all bad."

"The entire experience was still annoying."

"They weren't altogether fond of you, either. You'll have to work on that."

She grumbled, and he decided not to press the issue. Instead, he looked out over the cliff and eyed a waterfall at the edge of his vision. Behind it was the lichgate they needed to take them to the Villing Caves.

"How do you like the view from up here?" he asked.

"I'm not a fan of heights, actually."

"Excellent! Because we have to go that way." He laughed, pointing over the steep drop. "The only lichgate around here that will take us to the Villing Caves is behind that waterfall in the distance."

"I don't even see a waterfall."

"Exactly," he muttered, walking closer. "It will be a trek, so let me change and then we can go."

He trudged into the tree line and pulled out the fresh change of Lossian clothes from the pack he'd hidden behind a tree trunk. He paused over his Hillsidian tunic and compared it with the thin pair of trousers from a village just outside of Losse called Atao.

Fact was he missed his Hillsidian form, even with the added power of the Kirelm body. It would be safest to travel as his Hillside self anyway, since he was most comfortable with it, so he switched without bothering to take off the Kirelm uniform. It would be too big for him once he changed.

His muscles tingled and numbed, his body shrinking as he focused on the olive skin tone that he'd grown so fond of over the years. The stretching ended almost as soon as it began, and he looked down to see his familiar tanned hands. He threw on his Hillsidian clothes and stuffed the Kirelm and Lossian fabric into his pack before returning to Kara. She lounged on the griffin's back in the shade of a tree, waiting for him.

"That's better." She smiled and offered her hand to help him up.

He grabbed her hand, a spark igniting in his fingers at her soft touch. Ignoring it, he hauled himself into the seat behind her without pulling on her at all.

"Onward!" He pointed toward the horizon and noted with a sad pang that he could no longer see the waterfall in the distance.

The griffin bolted for the cliff. Kara tensed and grabbed the feathers on its neck, which made him laugh as he reached around her to balance himself. His arms brushed hers as he did so, the satin bodice of her traveling clothes both cool and soft. He swallowed hard and looked at the sheer drop ahead of them, trying once more to ignore the way he had trouble breathing when he touched her.

The griffin jumped off the cliff and spread its wings, curling them after a second to dive into the forests below.

Kara screamed at first—a lot—but the terror became uncontrollable laughter not long after the griffin rolled out of the dive. They had no reins and no saddle; there wasn't anything to hold on to but the beast's feathers, which he noticed were already quite rumpled from her grip.

✢

Three hours later, they landed to make camp before the sun set. Braeden leaned against a tree with a loaf of bread and watched Kara scratch the griffin's forehead. The beast squeezed its eyes shut like a puppy at her touch. He chuckled and closed his eyes, too, basking in the last of the day's hot sun and relishing the breeze as it rolled through the forest.

"I want to name it," Kara muttered.

He peeked through his eyelids to see her sit against his tree. She scooted closer, until her arm brushed his. He grinned.

"It's not a poodle."

She opened her mouth to speak but paused as a different, unknown thought seemed to consume her. He eyed her and finished the last of his bread, wondering what she wanted to say, but he remained silent while she formed her words. She wrung her hands and stared at the griffin, eyes out of focus. When she finally spoke, her voice was almost too soft to hear.

"Why are you really here, Braeden?"

"If I recall properly, I'm protecting you," he said, smirking as he leaned his elbows on his knees.

"Yeah, but why?"

He ran his hand through his hair. "Okay, we can do the heart-to-heart thing. I won't lie to you. At first, it was only because I wanted to ask the Grimoire a question."

"What question?"

"It's more of an inquiry, really. I hoped the Grimoire could break my tie to the Stele."

The griffin squeaked and twisted its feathered head to glare at him. He assumed the noise had been a gasp or something to that effect, but it had sounded more like someone stepped on a mouse.

"But that would make you a vagabond. And everything in yakona life is tied to the Blood, right? The people's power fuels his power. Everything here seems to need that kind of balance. I get the feeling that making you a vagabond would break that. There wouldn't be an Heir. What would happen when your father died?"

He cleared his throat and went silent, shifting his gaze as he toyed with his words.

"There is a legend that, when a Blood dies without an Heir, all of his people die as well. Everyone with the blood loyalty."

There was silence. He peered over to her, but regretted it. Her mouth hung open in horror. She furrowed her brow, but her shock melted into revulsion as she seemed to realize that he was entirely serious.

"I can't believe you!" Kara pushed herself to her feet. He reached for her arm, but she batted him away.

"Kara—"

"That was your plan, wasn't it?" she interrupted. "You just wanted to use me to kill all of those people? You're no better than Gavin! There have to be hundreds of thousands of Stelians!"

"Seven million if you count the villages," he corrected. "But don't compare me to Gavin! He wants revenge. All I want is to be free. Besides, you've met Stelians. You know what they're capable of. They aren't the nicest—"

"They're still people! Well, yakona. But it's the same idea," she said, pacing. Her eyes roamed the forest, looking at everything but him.

"Kara, sit down for a minute and listen to me." He snatched her wrist when she walked by and gently pulled her back to sit on the ground beside him. She still wouldn't look him in the eye.

"It's wrong and—"

"Think about it, Kara. Think about what Ourea would be like without the most vicious race in this world. Stelians rule the evil things here and enslave everyone else."

He curled a finger under her chin and turned her to look at him. She still scowled, which cast a small shadow over her gray eyes. Her look of disgust made his stomach churn. He wanted to be ashamed of himself, but as many deaths as this would cause, he was right. The Stele had nothing good left in it to save.

"Just listen," he begged as he released her chin.

"I'm listening."

He took a deep breath to steady himself. Richard had taught him that if he fought hard enough, he could have whatever he wanted in this life. Well, he'd dreamt of the day he asked the Vagabond for his freedom since he was twelve. This was it.

"Think of that world, Kara, where there is no crime, where everyone is safe and we can walk out and about like this all the time, anywhere, without ever being afraid. You would never be hunted. If we can kill Carden and break my ties to the throne, that can happen. Exactly that will happen."

"It's murder." Her soft voice cracked. Her eyebrow twitched, and she glared at the ground as she ran her fingers through the grass. Her frown melted into deep thought.

"Kara, please," he said, setting his hand on hers.

A shiver of excitement raced through him when he touched her, and for once, he didn't try to ignore it. His heart beat faster. He finally admitted to himself that he liked it, but she didn't look up. He scooted closer until his knee brushed hers. He slouched and leaned forward in an attempt to catch her eye.

"Ourea can be a safe place," he said. "Ever since I first listened to Richard's stories about the Grimoire, I knew that it was everything I needed to bring peace to this broken world. This is what you have to do to get that peace. Please help me with this." He leaned closer, until his head was less than an inch from hers. She still smelled like the roses from the cliffs.

She twisted her gaze to him, and he held his breath at her intense stare. She watched him for a moment, but the glower dissolved as she once again lost herself to her racing thoughts. Her fingers toyed with the two pendants around her neck, such that they clinked against each other.

Blue ash swarmed in the air before her, twirling and pooling on the grass. A few loose strands of the dust flew off in the wind, but the Grimoire appeared at her feet in a sudden flare of light without them.

He grinned. Kara ran her hand along the cover, her face smooth and unreadable.

"I had no idea this book could kill like that. It's supposed to be for learning. For knowledge."

"Peace doesn't come without bloodshed."

She shifted her gaze back to him. "Sure it can. It's wrong to destroy an entire race of people, Braeden. It makes you no better than your father. I'm going to look, but not because I promise to help you. I'm doing it because I need to know if it's even possible. Can you understand that?"

"Kara, they deserve it!"

"Neither of us gets to decide that," she snapped. She turned to the griffin, who perked at her movement. "Keep watch, buddy."

She opened the cover and let it flop on the ground. Her fingers inched to the first, blank page, and she closed her eyes. Her lips mouthed words he couldn't understand. The pages flipped as she whispered, turning one after the other like a gale was ripping across them. His heart raced, but he pinched his wrist to stem his excitement. She hadn't promised him anything.

The pages stopped turning and fell open to an image of a hooded figure that Braeden recognized from Richard's storybooks—it was the Vagabond. The cloaked man stood on the right side of the page with his hand outstretched, and to his left were blocks of red text that shifted as Braeden scanned them. He managed to catch a word or two that he recognized, but they blurred into illegible runes just as quickly as he read. He squinted, trying to make sense of the words, but they evaded him.

"How can you read that?" he grumbled.

She shrugged. "It looks like English to me."

She ran her finger along the text as she read. She frowned, looking briefly at the next page before she reread the section.

"What?" he asked. He squared his jaw and held his breath.

"You aren't going to like this."

"Tell me."

"Don't get mad."

"I—I'll try."

She pursed her lips and read the passage aloud. "'A vagabond may never break a Blood's tie to the throne. Be he good or evil, his duty to the balance of our world is too crucial to break. While his people may be free, the Blood is forever a slave to the bloodline with which he rules.'"

The air left Braeden's lungs.

"'Life requires balance,'" she continued reading. "'Though a dandelion is never as stunning as an orchid, we would never appreciate a flower's beauty without also appreciating a weed's simplicity. Therefore, we must accept that there is evil if we are to understand what it means to be good. Even if a Blood or Heir was to become a vagabond, it's useless. The bloodlines of the yakona people will forever find a way to return, to survive, despite how we may strive to destroy them.'"

Braeden leaned against the tree for balance and stared into the forest without absorbing anything but his own panic.

"Are you—?"

"I can't be free?" he interrupted.

She shook her head. "That's all it says. The next page is about fruitcake."

"There must be something else."

"Braeden, I looked. I promise that it's legitimately about fruitcake."

"That's—you—"

He stood. His hands tightened into fists. Knuckles cracked from the force. A memory resurfaced of the impenetrable white wall in Ethos, and that same wave of helplessness washed over him.

He was *never* helpless. He'd spent his life training, learning, fighting—*anything* to never again be the little boy trapped in a carriage, at the mercy of a stranger. And here, now—he glared at Kara. Hatred burned in his gut, churning the smoldering rage that would always and forever burn within him. After everything he'd done to be good, he was still at the mercy of a book that wasn't anything more than the lifeless shell of a dead man.

The last ounce of his will dissolved. His control over the dark magic that ruled him snapped.

"Braeden—"

"YOU CAN'T DENY ME!"

Kara pushed herself against the tree at his outburst, her eyes wide and afraid. His form rippled. Beneath the rough Hillsidian skin shone bits of the ashen gray he so despised. And yet, as it covered him, he sneered with pleasure.

The rage scorched his veins and ignited the depths of his fury. His chest rose and fell in short, quick bursts. Red flames roared to life in his palms and turned black as they engulfed both of his hands and raced up to his neck. The fire seared the sleeves of his shirt. The stench of melting cotton stung his nose. He laughed. The sound was like rocks grating.

Kara whimpered. He could hear her racing heartbeat. Sweat licked her forehead, neck and palms; he could smell it. Her breath caught on quiet sobs. He took a deep breath and smirked—*fear.*

He *missed* that.

His neck cracked as he twisted to see her. Her body trembled, and she watched him, apparently too afraid to run. Good. She wouldn't have gotten far, anyway. A thin trail of blood streamed down her fingers from her grip on the trunk's bark. That fueled him—that is, until a slow understanding spread across her face.

She could see what he was, now—what he really was. She finally saw the true depth of what it meant to be in line to rule the Stele. Her realization quelled the hatred long enough for him to regain some sense of control.

He remembered the tingling rush of heat that raced through him every time he touched her. He tasted the way his breath was always hard to come by when she caught him with her clear gray eyes. She would never look at him the same way again, not now that she'd seen *this.*

Guilt and shame reignited his self-loathing. The fires raged across his body, stronger now. His flicker of lucid thought was gone.

Smoke hissed from the pores along his neck and arms, the steam turning black as it stole the oxygen from the air, and he gave himself over to the depths of his Stelian power. His legs and arms and spine stretched. The threads in his clothes strained. A shadow fell across Kara's body, and it took him a moment to realize that it was his. The darkness within him grew.

Heat welled deep within. His chest burned. The hair on his arms prickled. An icy fire raced through his blood. Red and black and gray flames coursed over his gray skin, fighting for dominance.

He hurled a ball of fire into a tree to relieve the tension. It cracked and toppled, smashing into the underbrush. The charred bark smoked and popped. Evil glee consumed him. Twelve years of suppressed resentment bubbled to the surface. He yelled into the sky, but it became laughter. The sound echoed in the trees.

A wave of cold air fell suddenly over him, like a storm front before a blizzard. It froze his racing blood. His head cleared. His mind was heavy. Exhausted. He sank to his knees and peered around the clearing.

Kara stood above him, shrouded in a wispy black fog that clung to her like a hooded robe. The makeshift cloak grew deeper and fuller until she was just a hazy outline within it, staring vacantly at him through its gaps.

"Heir Drakonin!" Her real voice—the soft sound he recognized— was a murmur behind a second, deeper tenor. His eye twitched at the use of his formal title and his father's last name. His palms pooled with heat. He seethed.

"Don't call me that!"

"Braeden," she whispered.

The final threads of his glee dissolved when he heard the gentle undertone of her voice. His pulse slowed as his control returned. He was so *tired*.

"Kara, is that even you?"

"You speak to the first Vagabond now, boy," she said. "And when you seek my wisdom, you will obey what you find. I won't negotiate, even with you. If a Blood dies, so do his people—that isn't a legend. It's a fact. Neither my vagabonds nor I will have a part in genocide. You must accept that."

It wasn't a request.

Braeden sat on his heels and looked at the grass. Clumps of ash clung to the thick layer of clover which carpeted the hill. The last fire in his palm burned out with a violent hiss.

"I understand," he said.

"Then there is still hope for you. You must learn to control your rage, prince, and not be governed by it. You have made a valiant effort all these years, but you still have so much to learn."

Braeden bowed his head and shrank into his Hillsidian form. His hands faded back to the familiar olive tone, but the darkness still smoldered within him, as it always had. He would never extinguish it.

"Think of it though, Vagabond," he pleaded. "My father killed the Blood of Hillside. He doesn't care about the balance of the bloodlines. He's a murderer."

"He is. But you can't kill many for one man's folly."

"But—"

"No! You must accept that it will never happen. In the coming years, you will have the single most important role in restoring the long-overdue balance to this world. You must be strong enough to face what is coming. You will be more important even than Kara."

"Me?"

"I see more than you might believe, prince, and learn more every day. Kara will need you before this is done. All the world will."

"Where do I even start?" He sighed with the hope that Kara wouldn't remember any of this when she came to.

"The muses will guide you. But, my boy, you need a reason to fight. Without a purpose for the bloodshed in your future, you will only fail."

Braeden looked up, confused, but the misty cloak of the first Vagabond was already thinning. Patches of Kara's pale skin appeared beneath the fading wisps, and her eyes snapped back into focus as the last of the haze evaporated. She blinked, glancing around and holding her head as if it ached.

"Huh. Wasn't I sitting down a second ago?" she asked.

She doesn't remember anything from during the possession. Braeden sighed with relief. Still, she probably remembered a fair bit of his outburst. He sat on the charred grasses and rubbed his neck, brooding over what the Vagabond had said.

"Braeden, what happened?"

"The first Vagabond took over your body." He bit his cheek, his anger making it impossible to say anything more.

She walked over and knelt in front of him, but she didn't try to touch him. He pushed himself to his feet.

"I need to be by myself," he said. "Just—just stay here."

He walked into the forest. A whisper came from behind him, nothing more than a soft, hurt word he couldn't make out.

This wasn't her fault. He knew that, and it wasn't fair to treat her this way. But though she could stop his breath with only a look, there were some things he just couldn't admit to her. Not yet.

❧CHAPTER TWENTY ONE
REFLECTIONS

Kara snorted in annoyance and sat under a tree, resting her elbows on her knees as she took a second to think. She didn't know what to do. She weighed her options: run after the bipolar prince who was probably already out of earshot, or wait.

He would come back—right?

She replayed the episode in her mind and trembled when she remembered what Braeden really looked like. In the Stele, she caught only a glimmer. Carden had forced him to change form for a moment, long enough for her to see his skin go gray. But this had been worse. His skin had been gray, sure, but his eyes—his eyes were red, swallowing the irises until they were a glowing wall of hatred and blood lust.

He'd sucked the life out of the forest and out of her. Her circulation had slowed. Her fingers and toes had gone numb, and the color faded almost entirely from the woods. Whatever he'd become, it wasn't just Stelian. It was something more. Something darker.

No—she didn't want to think about it.

The sun gave up its last efforts to animate the forest and burned on the horizon, letting the dusk settle on the growing night. The canopy hid most of the stars as the night grew darker.

She shifted her weight and looked around. Nearby was a meadow, with tall, delicate grasses that rustled in a hushed chorus as the wind blew through them. An owl hooted. A bat fluttered somewhere above, blocking the dim and distant starlight in flitting darts of movement. The trickle of a riverbed joined the night's melody. At first it was just another noise, but the rushing water became louder as she grew thirstier.

Kara pushed herself to her feet and made her way toward the brook, which was easy to find thanks to its loud, bubbling current. A break in the treetops let in the rising moonlight and illuminated the snaking trail of water. The creek was only about four feet across, but it was deep.

She knelt on the bank and dipped her fingers into the cool water, relishing the chill that crept through her hands and up her arms. It flowed over her palms, as clear as the sky. She drank what she could and leaned back against the willow trunk, watching and waiting for Braeden to come back.

There was no way to count the time that went by while Kara lingered. Her anxiety grew worse with each passing minute, and she couldn't shake the growing fear that Braeden had left for good.

She glanced out onto the stream to distract herself. The reeds along the creek's bank reminded her of Twin's animated water-effigy of her sister. The selfish desire resurfaced. Kara was alone out here, and there was nothing stopping her, now, from seeing Mom.

No. The Grimoire said I couldn't bring Mom back. The dead are gone. Balance and all that.

Still, she eyed the water. What the Vagabond didn't know wouldn't hurt him. This was Mom, after all. Kara needed closure. Even if she did end up getting a lecture, it would be worth it.

Kara took off her boots, rolled up her pants to the knees, and stepped into the brook. The wind picked up. Leaves swirled on the bank. Branches danced, making the riverbed glitter in the moonbeams that broke through holes in the trees. The water nibbled at her skin, freezing at first, but she walked until the creek lapped at her knees. Smooth river rocks shifted beneath her bare feet and tumbled farther along the riverbed, caught by the strong undercurrent.

She cleared her throat, unsure of what she was supposed to do. Twin sang to the water and was crying by the end of her episode, so maybe any emotional connection would work.

Kara thought of Mom buried in gauze on the hospital gurney. In those last days of life, Mom had recognized her only once—the moment before the heart monitor screamed. Mom had held her hand and whispered inaudibly, eyes wide and afraid and unsure.

"Mom—" Kara choked and lost her voice. Tears stung her eyes. The vengeful sadness clawed at her throat.

"I'm sorry."

The pool bubbled at her feet. Her heart leapt with excitement and fear. If she saw Mom, she had no idea what she'd say. Nothing would make it right again, words least of all.

"I'd give anything to have you back," she whispered. The water bubbled in larger, fitful bursts. "I feel like I don't deserve the second chance I was given. I'm—I'm so sorry, even though I know that's not enough."

The water went from bubbling to churning before a small whirlpool appeared at her feet, but Kara never once stopped talking and spoke without listening to the words. Hope made her heart race. Guilt made her sweat. Twin had warned her that this was dangerous. It probably was, but she didn't care.

A face appeared in the whirlpool. Features appeared on this new figure: a sharp nose, two gentle eyes, familiar ringlets of curly hair. Water dripped from this sculpture of the face Kara was slowly forgetting. She reached out to touch its cheek.

Her voice faltered. The words died off.

The familiar curves of her mom's face bent into unnatural angles when she stopped speaking. The kind eyes went dark. The teeth sharpened. This new—*thing*—screamed. It had a shrill voice, like a banshee, and the terrifying monster sprang toward her. It crashed into her and broke, falling back into the river as nothing but reeds and pebbles. Droplets of water splattered across the river and onto the bank.

Kara threw herself onto the shore and crawled back to the willow, where she hugged her sopping knees. The night was biting and icy now. Every breeze set her skin aflame with the painful cold.

Flames flickered and sputtered in her hand as she huddled against the tree, shivering and trying to light a fire to get warm, but she couldn't focus her mind enough to light a fire. The jagged teeth of the creature flashed again in her mind every time she summoned a spark or a puff of smoke. Its shrill scream rang again in her ear.

Something brushed her shoulder. She jumped, but it was Braeden. Through the deep cold from the water and the still-raging panic of creating the water-demon, she managed a thin smile at the relief that he'd come back.

His pack shifted on his back as he knelt over her, eyebrows pinched with concern. His lips parted to say something, but she shook her head.

He nodded and opened his bag, pulling out a blanket to drape over her shoulders. Once she was wrapped tight and starting to get warm, he set his hands on her neck. A wave of heat flooded her body, but it was more than just the unconscious thrill of his touch. The water evaporated from her skin, and the wind's chilly bite faded, her clothes and hair now dry. Her fingers twitched, their feeling returned, and she sighed with contentment.

His strong hand reached for hers as he helped her to her feet and led her back around the willow toward the griffin, which she'd forgotten was even there. She glared at it, wondering where the useless thing had been during the fiasco with Braeden.

They sat on the grass underneath a tree. She curled into the blanket Braeden had given her even though she wasn't cold anymore, since it gave her an excuse to not look at him. He leaned against the tree for a few minutes before he said anything.

"Are you going to tell me why you were soaking wet?"

"No."

She wanted to bury the image of the demon thing that had destroyed her last memory of her mom. She shivered, despite the warm blanket, and suppressed the urge to cry. Her mom was dead. Her dad was gone. She wanted to go back in time, to forget everything that had happened and stop the crash and live a normal life. No yakona. No Ourea.

No death.

She glanced at Braeden out of the corner of her eye. He stared into the night, his hands ripping apart already torn blades of grass. One elbow rested on his knee as he stared off into the dark woods. The silence grew heavier with each passing second, until she couldn't bite her tongue any longer.

"You're terrifying when you're angry."

He took a deep breath and rubbed his face. "You definitely never want to spend much time with Carden, then."

"I've seen you as a Stelian, but that wasn't what I saw today. You became something else."

He sighed and looked at his hands, dropping the shards of grass.

"That was my daru," he said. "Every Blood and Heir has the ability to harness that untapped power, and when we do, we become exponentially stronger as long as there is a source of energy around."

He looked over to her, but shifted his gaze to the grass as soon as he caught her eye. The whoosh of the trees drowned out Kara's thoughts, and a humming sound replaced them until he continued.

"Most of the time, the other kingdoms need their subjects nearby to summon their daru. The Stelian Bloods, though, can absorb energy from almost anything. The air, the earth, breath. I'm even more powerful around something evil, as long as I'm stronger. That's why Carden can always control me, because he's more powerful. But sometimes, when there's no other choice, I can pull strength from just my own hatred. There are legends that the daru is the Blood's soul in its rawest form. If that's the case…"

If so, his soul was a dark and twisted thing. Kara forced herself to swallow and hold his gaze, even though her heart raced at the memory of his blood-red eyes.

"Yakona fear me, Kara. This is what I've spent my life running from. It's why I needed your help. I've been searching for the Grimoire because I wanted it to free me from what I am."

"That's all in the past tense, Braeden. You don't want it anymore?"

"Of course I want it. You just can't help me. The Vagabond won't allow the Stelian bloodline to die out." He picked up the shredded pieces of grass, which started smoking from just the heat in his palm.

The reality of Ourea sank in, and a weight settled on Kara's shoulders. Magic could kill. The Grimoire was far more than a book. It could kill an entire race by turning just two yakona into vagabonds. Two powerful people, granted, but still. She watched him. He hung his head and slouched, refusing to look up from the ground.

"That daru thing isn't really you," she said. "I don't think your soul is evil. You saved me from an isen. When you asked if I wanted to see her dad, you were only trying to give me the opportunity you never had with your mother. I haven't known you too long, but I'm not a bad judge of character. I think you're a good person."

"Thank you." His voice was thin and quiet, and it was obvious that he hadn't believed a word she'd said.

"There's something I want to show you," she continued. She reached into her satchel and pulled out the partially finished map. It was missing only one piece.

"Is that—?"

"Yeah. Remember the little blue square you gave me? It's pretty important. It's one of the pieces to a map that's going to take me to the Vagabond's hidden village. The last piece is in Losse."

"What happens when you find that one?"

"I'll go wherever the map takes me." She took a deep breath and looked at him. "I trust you. I meant it when I said it before. You're the only one who knows about this map. If you're willing, I want you to find the village with me."

He nodded, but still would not look at her.

"Braeden, I might not be able to make you a vagabond, but I'll do whatever else I can to help you."

"Thanks, but I'll help even if you can't fix me. I'm different from my father. I can protect something because it's more important than me, not just because I can benefit from it in some way."

She smiled, and he returned a thin grimace, but they let the quiet settle on them once more. Her hands sweated from the heat of the blanket, so she let it slide down her back and took refuge in the melting chill of the woodland night.

Not too long ago, she was pulling up to the rental house in her beaten old Camry, pretending that the sunken library and the Stele and the random magic book she'd discovered were just a long and vivid daydream. But Deidre had ruined everything. Her dad had taken over the isen's body only long enough to say goodbye and tell her about—

"Dang it!" Kara leaned forward, rubbing her temples. "I'm so stupid! I completely forgot—well, we can't go back now."

"What?"

"My dad," she explained. "He told me to get something out of the house. He took over Deidre when she—" Kara stopped, trying not to remember.

"Your father took over Deidre after she stole him?"

"Is that not normal?" She wanted to laugh as soon as she said it. *Normal?* Really? Nothing was normal in Ourea.

"No, that's incredibly rare. You have a strong family, Kara."

"Why?"

"When an isen steals a soul, there's a brief moment of struggle where neither can dominate the other. It's the soul's one chance to escape, and only a few ever have. But I've never heard of a soul taking over the isen to speak through them. Your father didn't get away, Kara. He chose an eternity of slavery to talk to you. Do you know what he wanted you to find?"

"No." Guilt chewed at her stomach. She shook her head, trying to remember, but the whole night was a fragment marred by blurry figures. She curled against the tree, her hatred for Deidre growing in the pit of her chest.

"We should go back, Braeden."

"Absolutely not. That house has to be monitored by Stelians at this point. I doubt they expect you to return, but Carden will have scouts there just in case."

"If Dad's still caught in Deidre," she continued, not listening, "what happens if she dies?"

"All the souls she has trapped will be released."

"Then I'm going to kill her."

He took a shaky breath. "I understand that hatred. I really do. But it can be consuming. Trust me. Deidre is also incredibly strong. To put it in perspective, she's the only isen I've met and not killed. Ever."

Kara wasn't listening.

The two of them sat in silence for a while, watching the grasses dance in the night breezes. She massaged her temples.

"So isen can change their shape to be anyone, right? Anyone they've stolen?" she finally asked, trying to piece together the new information with what she already had.

"Yes. If an isen steals your soul, it takes your skills, your looks, your powers—everything, right down to the last thing you wore. They can take on your appearance at will and use your magic at any time. They are the worst kind of enemy."

"Are they all evil?"

"Most of them are just insane. They have to steal a soul every decade or so to maintain their immortality, and if they ever stopped stealing, they would eventually grow old and die. But having all those souls in one body makes them go slowly crazy. All of the eldest isen are mad, simply because they store so many souls within them. A lot of isen don't last longer than about a thousand years, because they accidentally kill themselves doing something stupid. Niccoli is the exception. I don't know how he has maintained his sanity enough to still lead a guild."

"Maybe he hasn't." Kara shrugged and lay back on the grass. "Why aren't there legends about these things?"

"There are plenty of creatures based on isen, just nothing quite like them. Anyone who sees an isen is stolen or killed, with a few rare exceptions"—he glanced over to her to prove his point—"so there isn't much to go on."

She whistled and stretched out, the soft grasses by the tree tickling her neck. Ourea was one hell of a place.

❧CHAPTER TWENTY TWO
THE KINGDOM OF LOSSE

Kara didn't sleep.

The bright moon broke in speckled waves across the meadow, illuminating the freckles on Braeden's face. He tossed and turned in his fitful dreams, half waking each hour to murmur and turn over, but at least he didn't change form again.

The griffin moved closer about an hour after Braeden fell asleep and now sat at Kara's feet. Only its feathers and fur, which bent in the wind, moved. It watched the forest as if something was coming, its neck arched toward a silent threat she couldn't see. Her muscles tightened. She thought she could sense the lingering tension, too, but figured it was probably just the motionless beast in front of her that made her uneasy.

A thin halo of the morning sun appeared on the pink and yellow horizon and its first ray fell squarely on Braeden's forehead. He opened his eyes as if it had poked him.

"Did you sleep?" he asked, stretching.

"No."

"I would've taken watch, if you were worried."

She stood without answering and rolled up the blanket he'd given her the night before. Her exhaustion was biting, but somehow refreshing. For the first time, she began to truly feel the weight in the woods, the strain on the sky, but the sun didn't dissolve all of the tension like she'd imagined it would. The world was prepared for something she still couldn't see, and that understanding both unsettled and calmed her.

They packed without speaking, and it wasn't until she pulled herself on to the griffin that Braeden spoke again.

"Kara, you don't have to do this."

"Do what?"

"Trudge through these hoops as if you care about our problems. These are our battles, not yours. I know you feel responsible, since you're the Vagabond, but that doesn't make you a slave to a world that doesn't want you."

"I have nothing to go back to," she said, her eyes stinging from the lack of sleep. "Ourea really is all I have left. This place is haunting, and even if I could somehow go back to my old life and never be hunted again, I could never stop dreaming about it. This is my home now. I'll fight to keep it safe if that's what it takes."

"We're lucky, then." He smiled and patted her ankle before jumping into the seat behind her and leaning against her back for balance. The griffin took a running start, beat its wings, and lifted them into the air.

Kara and Braeden flew until midday, long after a massive waterfall dissolved into view. It fell in a thick sheet over the sheer cliff, consuming at least a half mile on the broad mountain side, and even though they flew for hours, they seemed to never get any closer. The roar of its cascading water beat on the wind, drowning out the whistle of the air with its deafening thunder. Braeden tapped her shoulder when they were finally close enough to land and gestured to a wide walkway that led behind the waterfall.

"That will take us to the caves."

There wasn't enough space for them to land on the walkway itself, so the griffin flew to the top of the cliff to let them off. It nudged Kara's back and lingered, so she scratched its chin again. It dissolved into a thin funnel of dust at her touch and disappeared into the afternoon light, leaving her to hope that it had returned to the Grimoire and not disappeared forever.

They walked down the path that led behind the waterfall. There was no cave like she'd expected—just solid rock behind the pummeling water. Nestled into that rock was a lichgate, woven from thin, sprawling vines rooted in the cliff. The entry was small, about the size of a doorway, and its vines sloped without purpose in an odd, crooked frame that led to the muted gray depths of a cave. They walked through and she tried to ignore the telltale flash of blue light and the kick in her stomach.

The cave wound on for what felt like ages, growing darker with each echoing step. A small gray flame erupted in Braeden's palm and illuminated the lifeless tunnel when the light from the lichgate disappeared behind them. Kara hung at his side, close enough to feel his body heat through his sleeve. She was trying to think of something to say to fill the echoing darkness when they turned a bend, and the tunnel opened out onto a brilliant morning. She blinked in the sudden sunlight and lifted her hand to shield her eyes until they could adjust.

Their tunnel continued, but one side had long ago broken away to reveal another stunning waterfall that pulsed overhead. A four-foot wall was left to act as a guardrail between the walkway and the falls, but it was thin and mostly useless. Water pooled in tiny, unavoidable ponds along their path, soaking their pant hems with the waterfall's excess. Hundreds of feet down, a river tumbled away from the base of the waterfall, flowing its way through a teeming forest. After a few miles of green canopy, a thick line of white beach spread beneath them, and from there, an ocean stretched to the horizon.

"It's beautiful," she said. Braeden nodded in agreement.

They walked in single file along the far side of the wall to avoid slipping. The falls drowned out conversation, so she enjoyed the view. The salty zing of the water vapor snapped her from her exhaustion, and she was too consumed with her sightseeing to notice that Braeden had stopped. She bumped into him and teetered off balance, leaning toward the open tunnel wall, but he grabbed her waist to steady her. She blushed as he pulled her back on her feet, and she hated herself for the heat that raced to her cheeks. He didn't seem to notice.

"This is it, Kara."

He let her go and pointed down another tunnel. A faint green light radiated from hundreds of tiny crystals lining the passage walls. She went in first. As they walked deeper into the mountain, the sunlight and the roar of the water faded. The crystals were more than enough to light the way.

"Kara, stop for a minute. Don't look behind you."

"Um—okay."

Naturally, a tingling sensation burned through her like a finger poking her head, begging her to look because he told her not to. The hair on her neck tickled, and she longed to turn around to see why he was shuffling about behind her.

"All right," he finally said. "We can keep going."

She relented to her urge to turn around. A tall, thin, and very blue creature with a white shell necklace blinked down at her, his giant green eyes the color of seaweed. Her chest panged in surprise.

"A warning would have been nice, Braeden."

He made a gurgling noise that she figured was laughter. It was faint and soothing, like shallow water over river rocks.

"Sorry," he said, starting again down the passageway.

After only a few more minutes of walking, the tunnel bent around a corner and opened into a vast cavern. Kara whistled and craned her neck to see the ceiling, which loomed more than a mile above them. The massive space echoed with disembodied whispers.

Hundreds of small breaks in the roof served as skylights, illuminating the breathtaking scene frozen into one of the cavern's walls. The Grimoire's drawing hadn't done the real thing any justice.

At least a hundred dragons circled a single man, all of them embedded so deeply in the rock that they looked like carvings. They rose to the ceiling, circling and snarling. Bubbles of rock rose from the wall in immobile flames that roared from the beasts' gaping mouths. Tails curled around claws, teeth shone in jagged spikes, and lidless eyes glared down at the newcomers in the tomb.

Kara stepped into a puddle, which snapped her attention away from the wall. Dozens of small streams burrowed through the cavern, bubbling and churning on their way through their shallow riverbeds. They intertwined here and there, so that the end result was an elaborate combination of raised islands amidst foot-deep water that ambled toward a wide lake. The lake spanned the width of the cavern, its water deep, but more of the green crystals illuminated its depths where the sunlight failed.

"That yakona was the last Blood of the Retrien kingdom." Braeden nodded to the man frozen in the middle of the dragons. The Blood's sword was raised above him, and a thin beam of rock ran upward from the blade's tip into the dragons above. His face was a snarl, all the color and life long gone.

"Yeah, I read about him," Kara said

"His entire bloodline was lost when he fought the dragons, so I doubt he meant to freeze himself in there."

"Where did his people go?"

"Those that survived the battle vanished." He shook his head, disappointed. "They were brilliant fighters and yet, they advocated peace and understanding. Force was always a last effort. Of all the kingdoms, they should have been the last to disappear."

The hair on her neck prickled, like someone was watching her.

"Maybe they're not altogether gone." She glanced back at the lake, the watched feeling seeping into her shoulders and down along her spine. Shadows flickered through the green glow in the water.

"What is that?"

"The Lossians are here," Braeden said. "They must have been waiting for you."

More and more bodies blocked the rich green glow, until the lake's clear depths plunged into darkness. The giant blue orbs of Lossian heads—some bald, others with shoulder-length black hair—began to break through the surface, all with identical seaweed-green eyes.

The army waited while a single Lossian swam forward and walked onto the shore. He was about Braeden's height, his thin form slightly more defined, and his bare webbed feet dripped over the rock as he approached. He smiled and the pointed grin of his mouth stretched from ear to ear in a long, curved line that reminded Kara of the Cheshire cat. His uniform was tight and gray, just one solid piece of fabric that reached from his elbows to his knees. Black stripes ran diagonally across his arms, and a matching black belt with a pack on it looped around his waist.

"Welcome, young lady." He glanced to Kara, his eyes passing her over just as quickly as his words. He bowed to Braeden and smiled. "And welcome, my brother! I am Duke Trin, and I've come to see the Vagabond to the kingdom of Losse. Tell me, has he been delayed?"

Kara forced a stiff laugh and resisted the deep urge to sigh.

"I'm the Vagabond," she said.

"We—" Duke Trin lost track of his words and froze, his mouth unhinging to gape at her for a few long seconds before he recovered and reigned-in his jaw.

"Please forgive me."

"That's all right."

"And what is your name, brother of Losse? How did you come to travel with—" The duke paused, shifting his large, disbelieving eyes back to Kara. "With the Vagabond?"

"I am Asealo, my liege," Braeden lied, arching his back to bow. His voice was twisted with a slight accent that hadn't existed until the duke spoke. He pulled a small blue orb from his pocket—the Lossian key Adele had given him—and offered it to Trin as proof of who he claimed to be. Trin nodded, apparently satisfied, and Braeden put the orb away as he continued speaking.

"I live in the bordering village of Atao and came to see the Vagabond safely into the mighty Losse."

Wow, Kara thought. *Lossians talk a lot.*

The duke smiled. "You have done well, then. You may return to Atao."

"I asked—um—Asealo to join me in Losse," Kara said, interjecting in an effort to get them both to stop with the pleasantries. She just wanted to get this over with, but the duke snapped his wary eyes to her. His squint made her fidget.

"I shall need proof of who you claim to be before I show you our home," he commanded. "You'll understand, of course."

"What do you need me to do?"

"I should very much like to see the Grimoire." He sneered, his kind smile suddenly gone, and huffed as if it only an idiot couldn't have guessed that much. "I've seen the drawings and will know it when, or if, I lay mine eyes upon it."

She nodded, trying to ignore his tone, and wished the book forward. The cloud of blue dust swarmed around her, and the heavy red cover materialized in her hands. A chorus of bubbles rose from the lake as more heads popped up to witness the Vagabond and her book, but she wished it back into its hiding place after Duke Trin was satisfied.

"Anything else?" she asked with a smirk.

"No. Thank you, Vagabond." He pursed his lips. "But you must understand if you're still not permitted to see the path which we take to the kingdom." He pulled out a thin strip of black cloth and a great, pink starfish from the pack on his belt.

"What—?"

"You must wear these," the duke said.

The starfish wriggled in his palm, its limbs twitching, and he lifted it to her mouth before she could refuse. It wrapped around her jaw and nose, its suckers clinging to her chin and cheeks. She gasped for air, but found that breathing came naturally despite the slippery suckers bruising her face. The duke tied the sash around her eyes. All was dark.

A small cracking sound came from behind her, as if Braeden had dropped a pebble and stepped on it.

"I will guide her, Asealo," the duke said. A wet hand grabbed Kara's arm and quickly ushered her through the thin streams. Water splashed over her boots.

The floor sloped. The lake seeped through the seams in her shoes. Water lapped on the shore nearby as ripples broke across each other. Another distant whisper echoed somewhere in the recesses of the cavern. She walked forward, inch by inch, but the panic didn't hit her until the water came up to her waist and the slope grew steeper. It was up to her chest, now. Her neck. She held her breath as the surface licked her ears and covered her head.

The grip on her arm steered her when the ground disappeared. Her throat burned with the breath she'd trapped there. She couldn't hold it any longer.

Air pumped from her lungs, and she inhaled out of instinct, expecting a flood of water and the panic of drowning. But instead of terror, she breathed in relief. Oxygen filled her lungs, though it tasted like salt. She took deep breaths until her pulse slowed.

The fingers holding her arm pushed and tugged, directing her around the obstacles she wasn't allowed to see. They could have travelled for minutes or hours; she had no idea. She lost all track of time. Eventually, there was a sharp tug at the sash on her head, and it fell away.

She gasped through her starfish.

They swam through an open ocean, long gone from the submerged tunnels of the Villing Caves. The city of Losse was built into a string of reefs and sediment only a few hundred feet away. A tall and massive dome of golden light sprawled over it, running for miles over the ocean floor. A swarm of sharks circled the outskirts of the light, swimming just beyond the radiance so that its warm glow barely illuminated their underbellies.

The duke's grip on her arm tightened as they entered the swarm. The sharks rolled their eyes to watch her pass, swimming closer. One brushed her with its fin, leaving the numb trail of its touch on her forearm. Another stalked her, matching her pace with the slow flicks of its tail. Trin's grip on her arm tightened even more. *No sudden movements*, it said.

She peered over her shoulder. The army swam just behind the duke, blocking out the view of wherever they'd come from. Braeden was with them, but she couldn't catch his eye. His gaze flitted from shark to shark as he brushed their noses, pushing them away with his palm if they came too close. The other soldiers did the same, though without the nervous expression.

The duke descended toward the base of the glowing arch, which gave Kara the chance to peer through the golden light to see the buildings within as they passed the city. Tall houses and shops, maybe a dozen or so stories high, lined the many streets. Rivers and small waterfalls pummeled over grass-covered hills and miniature cliffs in the distance. In the center of the city, stretching almost to the top of the vaulting light, was a glimmering palace built from the brilliant blue and red reef coral.

Duke Trin drifted on the cold current and settled onto the ocean floor, pulling her down with him. Thin puffs of sand billowed from beneath their feet as they landed. A paved road began on the other side of the dome. The duke walked through the wall of light without hesitation, dragging her through behind him.

There was a draft of wind and, as it passed over her, the water clinging to her hair and clothes dissolved in a hot steam. The air inside the dome was perfect: cool, damp, and still. The duke removed the starfish from her mouth, and Kara touched her face tenderly until her cheeks regained their feeling.

A twitter of voices rushed around her as she entered. Dozens of Lossians lined the streets, all staring at her with their wide, green eyes as Trin marched her through the city. Those who had baskets set them on their hips as they gawked, while others tapped their neighbors' shoulders, whispering as they stared at her. Nerves fluttered in Kara's stomach, and she wanted to wave and laugh and leave all at the same time.

Trin released his hold on her arm, guiding her now with a light pressure on her back, and escorted her along a road paved with polished shells and lined with buildings constructed from pointed bricks of coral. More blue heads crowded the windows as she passed, pushing each other for the better view.

It was at least a half hour's walk to the palace, though she could easily see its turrets after her first step on the shell road. The endless avenue was lined with yakona, all of whom muttered in hushed tones as Kara and the Lossian army passed by. She began to ignore them after a while, her eyes locked on the castle instead.

What a welcome.

Finally, the front doors of the palace came into view. A massive flight of stairs led from them, glistening in the tawny dome's warm glow, and thick railings curled away from the large, open doors in sloping arches.

The main entrance led to a throne room with walls that glinted like mother of pearl and a ceiling that rounded out several stories above. Four pillars made of brightly-colored coral branched from the corners of the room and arched to meet in the center of the roof. They glowed in greens and reds and blues, casting a kaleidoscope of light across the walls and yakona below.

There were three polished thrones raised on three separate platforms in the center of the room, each with a set of stairs leading to them.

Three thrones, same as every other kingdom I've seen so far. For a race of creatures that claimed to be so different from each other, there were plenty of striking similarities in their cultures.

A Lossian sat in the center throne, too tall for his chair—the nape of his neck rested against the throne's high back. This had to be Blood Frine. His coal-black eyes accented his bald head, and his blue skin was wrinkled and dull. The yakona to his right was younger and almost identical, with the same dark eyes. They were so dark that she couldn't see them move. Her skin crawled.

A Lossian woman sat to the Blood's left, her dress flowing over the steps at her feet in white trails of silk that looked like foam on an ocean wave. She smiled at Kara and nodded her head once in welcome. Kara smiled back, relieved at the kingdom's first sign of kindness.

The pressure on her back disappeared as the duke and Braeden both sank to one knee, bowing their heads so low that she couldn't see their faces.

"Welcome, Vagabond!" the Lossian in the center throne said. "I am Blood Frine, king of Losse."

She bowed. Her eyes stung. The adrenaline from breathing through a starfish and swimming through a hoard of sharks was fading. All she wanted was sleep.

The Blood stood and walked down the steps to his throne. "I know you must be exhausted, but before you may sleep, I must know that you are who you claim to be. I assume that you showed Duke Trin your Grimoire. Show me as well."

Kara hesitated at the order, but wished the Grimoire forward anyway. Its weight fell once more in her hands. It was then, in the silence, that she realized there was no crowd to murmur and gape— only the duke, the royal family, and Braeden. The doors were even closed. She must have been more exhausted than she realized if they could close those massive gates without her hearing.

"That it is," Blood Frine said, more to himself. He continued walking toward her.

"Is that all you needed?" She wished the book away once more.

"Seeing the book is a start, but it isn't enough. Since I heard of your return, I've dwelt on how I would make you prove yourself to me."

She didn't like the sound of *that*.

"When the first Vagabond visited my ancestors, he proved his own power by wielding my grandfather's Sartori. Have you heard of the Sartori blades?"

Her mind flickered to the Queen's death. Braeden's blood-curdling scream had scared birds from the trees when his connection to his father made him feel the sting of Queen Lorraine's blade.

"I have," she answered.

Frine stopped only a few feet in front of her and unsheathed a sword at his waist. The dark blue blade glinted in the dazzling blue and green light, and its silver handle twisted in thin curves that covered the Blood's hand. Illegible white runes ran down the blade, such that it looked as much like a scroll as it did a weapon. There was a small, sharp breath from behind her, but she didn't dare turn around.

"If any but the Vagabond, my son, or I touch this sword, his hands will burn beyond healing. He will never again be able to use his fingers." Frine held out the hilt to her. "Prove yourself."

She reached for the handle and hovered over it. This could be a trick. She listened for Braeden, waiting for a clue, a hint—*anything*—but he was quiet. There were few choices here, so she took a deep breath and wrapped her hands around the hilt.

The weight of the sword shifted into her hand. Her shoulders tensed and complained as she tried to hold the unnaturally heavy weapon. The cool metal tickled the bones in her knuckles with a rhythm like a pulse, but there was no fire, no burning, and no pain. She let out a small, shaky breath. Frine took back his Sartori and slid the poisoned blade back into its scabbard.

"You are indeed the Vagabond, then," he said, but she wasn't certain he was pleased by the fact. He turned back to his throne and continued to speak as he walked. There was something sinister in his voice.

"I must ask, dear girl, how went your stay in Kirelm? In Hillside?"

"If you haven't heard, there was an attack on Hillside," she said.

"Carden killed the Queen and now her son, Gavin, is the Blood. He wants to negotiate a peace treaty between the other kingdoms, so that we can stop Carden before he finds the rest of you."

"No," the Blood said, sitting back in his seat. "He wants revenge and is too weak to do it himself."

She scoffed, but didn't answer.

"Tell me, has the Vagabond been reduced to a messenger between the kingdoms? Or are you just a pawn?"

"Don't insult me."

He raised his eyebrows. "And why shouldn't I?"

"If you know anything about the first Vagabond, you'll recall his purpose was always to promote peace. I'm just trying to do the same."

"That did turn out so well for him," the Blood observed with a sarcastic smirk. His lip twitched and his eyes never left hers.

"It's a different era. I'd hoped you all have grown a little wiser after a thousand years."

He chuckled and rested his head on his fist. "Well spoken, but I won't decide our place in this matter yet. I pray that you'll stay with us as I debate the consequences of such an alliance."

Kara bit her lip. Her eyes drooped. Sleep would help her think of a better argument, since uniting for his own safety apparently wasn't doing it for him.

"If that's what you need," she said.

"We have prepared a room for you, but we weren't expecting your companion. Tell me, who is this?"

"Asealo of Atao," she said after a short pause, proud that she had remembered the name at all.

"I have not been to the village of Atao for thirty years, my boy," the Blood said. His eyes shifted out of focus as he seemed to recall something. "Is that willow tree still alive?"

"I must apologize, my liege," Braeden said, "but I don't know of such a tree in my village."

"Hmm," the Blood muttered. "I must have your home confused with another's. Will you need a room during your stay?"

"I should very much appreciate it, my liege." Braeden's voice trembled with a submissive tenor. He didn't once meet the Blood's eyes. He was putting on a good show.

"Very well." The Blood motioned to the woman to his left. "Queen Daowa, escort the children to their rooms."

Kara bit her tongue and suppressed the sarcastic rebuttal that festered in her throat at his careless order, but Daowa nodded to him and stood with a sweet smile. The Lossian's dress tumbled over the stairs as she glided toward them.

"It's an honor to host the Vagabond," Daowa said. "I'll show you to your rooms. But if you aren't interested in sleep, you must stroll through our gardens. There are none like them in all of Ourea."

Oh, Kara would be visiting the gardens, all right. There was just one map piece left to find.

⚜

Kara gave up trying to sleep after an hour or two of tossing and turning. Without any curtains to cover the windows, the glowing golden light was too bright. So instead of getting the rest she needed, she grabbed her satchel and meandered through the gardens, which had been easy to spot from her room. She followed her feet once she found the entrance to the grassy park and began hunting through the endless array of bushes, flowerbeds, and ponds for the missing map piece.

She wasted *hours* scouring the garden's few stone walls, but she didn't find anything. The tall hedges were too frail to support a slab of lapis. The sparse, blossoming trees had no hiding places, and she would've looked like a crazed idiot if she'd started sifting through the dirt around the flowers. It was starting to seem like a good option, though—she wasn't going to leave Losse without that stupid map piece. But what if Frine had it? What would she do? He didn't seem like the type of king who would just hand it over.

Lost, frustrated, and without a clue of what to do next, she stopped at a shallow pond at the edge of the dome of light. It looked out over the endless ocean beyond Losse, giving her a view of the black depths. There was no telling how far down they really were.

She sat on the edge of the small pond and draped her feet into the water so that they scraped along the bottom, brushing the smooth white sand on its floor. A small red and white koi fish swam over and took a fancy to her toes, nibbling them periodically and tickling her until she giggled.

A blue sparkle caught her eye from the depths of the pond, so she reached her hands into the water and brushed away the sand. Beneath the layers of grit and nestled into the rocky bottom was the lapis cornerstone to her map.

She huffed. *Finally!* At least she'd found the dumb thing.

She dug her fingernails into the crevices, pulling on it until it came free. The flecks of gold were bright in the warm glow of Losse's dome, making the map piece glimmer like the night sky she couldn't see.

"There you are!"

A Lossian clambered up the small grassy hill to the pond. He glanced down at the map piece in her hand, and she panicked. She quickly slid the blue square into her satchel, wondering what she could say to explain her theft when she noticed the Lossian's white shell necklace.

She groaned inwardly at her needless anxiety. She needed *sleep*.

"Hey. So, I found it. The last piece." She smiled, trying to hide the ebbing tide of alarm that still lingered in her gut.

"When are you going to put it together?"

"I don't know what will happen, and I don't want anyone else to see it. I'll wait until we're alone."

"Good idea."

He sat beside her and dangled his scrawny Lossian legs into the pond. She had to look up to see his face, even though he was sitting, and his long mouth twisted downward. Wrinkles drooped under his eyes. She was still getting used to the Lossian features, but she was pretty sure that was a frown.

"What's wrong?"

"Remember that question about the willow tree?" He leaned in, whispering. She could barely hear him.

"Yeah. That was random."

"There *is* no willow tree. Atao is entirely underwater, just like Losse. The only village with a willow tree is Lotvine, which is in a marsh. He was trying to trick me." He cursed under his breath and shook his head. "If I hadn't been hunting isen there this year, I would never have known that. He knows something is wrong about me."

"Chill out," she said.

"What? How? It's important."

"If you work yourself up, he'll definitely know something is wrong. Lie low."

"How are you so relaxed? I thought you were going to fall asleep in the throne room. How are you even awake?"

She shrugged, not quite knowing the answer. He ran his fingers along the surface of the pond, his shoulders relaxing as he shooed away the little fish.

"You take this nonsense well," he finally said.

She sighed and leaned back on her palms, staring out into the dark depths of the ocean.

"A little over a month ago, I thought my biggest problem was deciding whether or not to go back to Arizona State. My little dramas seemed so important then, but now they'll never matter. Sometimes I still think that I'm going to wake up, propped against that stupid door in the mountain, and realize that I just hit my head."

Braeden pinched her arm.

"Ow!"

He leaned back and snickered. "You aren't dreaming."

"Did you really just pinch me?" She grumbled and rubbed her arm.

"At least you know for certain, now."

Another voice chimed from behind them. "May I sit with you, Vagabond?"

Kara turned. Queen Daowa stood on the small grassy knoll, her hands clasped in front of her long, flowing dress. She wore a graceful smile and a crown littered with brilliant sapphires.

"I shall leave you ladies to your thoughts." Braeden stood and bowed to the Queen, averting his eyes in what Kara assumed was Lossian custom. He winked at her once he was out of Daowa's sight and disappeared into the garden.

Queen Daowa knelt beside the pond, the blue and white fabric of her dress scattering in all directions as she did. She watched the ripples in the water for a few seconds before speaking.

"Do you enjoy your role as the Vagabond?" she finally asked.

"It's fun when I'm not being chased by something."

Daowa laughed. "What have you learned of magic thus far?"

"A few things here and there. Blades, a flame. Just the basics."

"May I share a few thoughts?"

"Absolutely."

"Magic is a union with the life in all things around you. By sensing the energy in even inanimate things, you can channel it and manipulate your environment. The Bloods, our most powerful yakona, can even control the elements when they don their daru. Have you heard of that?"

"Yeah—" Kara dropped off for a moment, the memory of Braeden's red-eyed daru consuming her. She blinked it away.

"So, the king can control the ocean?" she asked.

"If enough of his people are near to fuel his will, then yes," Daowa spoke softly, as if not to upset the air around her. "It's a breathtaking sight to see."

A short, young Lossian maiden scampered over the hill. Her dress covered her toes, but the patter of her bare skin on the grass reverberated across the garden. Once she neared them, she kept her eyes to the ground.

"My Queen, my Vagabond," the girl said. "Blood Frine has asked for your presence, if you please."

"Of course," Daowa answered. She rose to her feet, her billowing gown never once falling into the pond, and began walking toward the palace. Kara stood and followed.

"Do you think he's reached a decision about the treaty?"

"That's unlikely. He is slow to make these important decisions, because they can't be unmade. No, I suspect he will discuss your tenure here, Vagabond. We have many things for you to learn."

"Losse is beautiful, but I can't stay long. There's no telling when things on the surface will escalate. I need to be there."

Daowa eyed her with the same brooding glare Frine wore when he'd unsheathed his Sartori. A chill crept along Kara's neck, and the sudden wish for Braeden gnawed at her.

"I think you'll find both my husband and his kingdom very convincing."

She let Daowa lead and kept an eye on the castle as it neared. It didn't matter where she was in the kingdom; the palace was always visible. It loomed before them, and she wondered if anyone in Losse could ever feel safe when the fortress watched everyone constantly.

❧CHAPTER TWENTY THREE
TRAINING

Kara followed Daowa into the throne room, where Blood Frine and his Heir sat in their thrones. The two men watched them enter without blinking and sat motionless until the Queen bowed to her husband and took her seat beside him.

The four of them were alone in the massive hall: no guards, no on-lookers, and no witnesses. The only visible door was the one Kara had just come through, which had somehow closed once again without her noticing.

"Vagabond, is your room adequate?" Blood Frine asked, his voice thin and tense.

"Yes, thank you. Have you decided to start the peace negotiations?"

"You are so very much to the point," he said with a grumble. "But no. I've been preoccupied with another matter, one I suspect you'll quite enjoy."

She smothered the urge to sigh.

"And what's that?"

"Losse is home to the six greatest tutors in Ourea. Their parents trained me as a boy, and they themselves have taught my son. I asked them to also train you whilst you're here. This gift has never been granted beyond those who live in the palace, but I've done this with the hope that you'll see our natural honor. We are simply slow to join a cause, no matter whose name is attached to it."

Her stomach tightened with excitement. She would have formal training, and by the best! But training took time. Her heart fell as quickly as it had jumped into her throat. Carden wouldn't stop killing Bloods while she learned to fight. She wasn't the warrior the first Vagabond had been; she was the messenger, the one who brought the best fighters onto the same side of the war, and she needed to get back to the surface.

"I'd love to take you up on that in the few days that I'm here. Once the treaty is signed, I hope that you'll let me return to complete the training."

"When did you plan on leaving my beautiful city?"

"In three days, sir."

"That simply isn't long enough. You must stay longer."

"I'll come back. I can't thank you enough, and I'll gladly train with them. But I just can't do it all right now. I'll have to return another time."

"No," he said, firmly.

"Blood, thank you. But—"

"No," he repeated. "If you want a treaty, you must prove that you can lead us. Train, and I'll consider the negotiations. Leave, and I shall not."

Kara's mouth hung open, lost for words. In Losse, she was trapped under an endless ocean. There was no fresh air and no sky, just sharks and hundreds of miles of water. She had her puzzle piece. She could just leave.

No.

Peace was the Vagabond's purpose—her purpose. It was the reason she was in Losse to begin with. The treaty between the kingdoms was the first step on a long road. If that meant she was stuck underwater for a while longer, then *fine.* She sighed and bit her cheek to keep her voice steady.

"I'll stay, then. But we have to compromise on how long I'll be here. It can really only be for a short while."

"Excellent! You'll begin now!" Blood Frine clapped his hands, ignoring her conditional acceptance. He looked past her to the doors and opened them with a wave of his hand. They swung apart with a shuddering boom.

A line of six Lossians walked in unison up the stairs from the seashell courtyard outside. They stood on the threshold like statues, as still and watchful as the Blood and his Heir. Kara forced her mouth shut and swallowed hard, suddenly wishing she'd chosen to leave.

Four of the Lossian tutors were stocky bald men, taller than Braeden but still skinny when compared to the Hillsidians and Kirelms she'd grown accustomed to. Their thin limbs hung by their sides, and a solid black suit covered each man's entire body to the neck, wrists, and ankles. Only one of them carried a weapon, which looked at first glance to be just a very tall walking stick. That is, it did—until she saw the sharp dagger in its tip.

The other two tutors were women, their hair tied behind their heads in tight braids. Their black suits accentuated curves otherwise hidden in the flowing gowns of the other Lossian women. They glowered, their faces riddled with more scars than the men's. One of them smirked and gestured for her to follow.

Kara's training lasted for three weeks. She debated quitting with every blow to her back or shoulders or neck, the dangling promise of peace only enough to fuel her for so long.

She wanted to scream after every disappointed shake of her tutors' heads, or when they barked that she was a sorry excuse for a soldier. She wanted to yell back that she wasn't anything but a college sophomore who liked to hike and found the Grimoire on accident. Still, after a while, that excuse lost its power. She was the Vagabond, no matter what she'd been in the human world. If the Vagabond was supposed to be a warrior, then she would become one.

There was no sunlight in Losse. Instead, the golden glow of the dome faded to pale blue at the end of the day. There were no curtains to block out the brilliant golden glow when it returned in the morning, so she would force herself out of her warm blankets to begin her next day of training. She slowly adapted to their world.

She kept her satchel always slung over her shoulder. Though it sometimes limited her movement, it contained her little blue egg and the still-unfinished map, and she never once let it out of her sight.

Kara always meant to connect the final pieces before bed, to finally see where the map would take her, but each evening, she fell into a deep, exhausted sleep the moment she laid down. In the three weeks she was there, she never once had the chance to complete it or to even open the Grimoire.

The training toned her muscles. Her hand-eye coordination improved until she could swing basic weapons with accuracy. She mastered whirlpools and a dozen other techniques, and even cut a tutor on his cheek once with his own staff during a sparring match.

Each day, she ate with the still-disguised Braeden during her dinner break, telling him everything she'd learned—which he usually critiqued—before she visited Blood Frine in his throne room as a synthetic darkness fell over the city.

Every night, she asked the king to consider the treaty. And every night, he said, "not yet."

It was on the last night of the third week that she didn't leave the throne room when he refused to give her an answer. Braeden had missed dinner, and in the quiet hour she'd spent alone in the dining hall, she debated how much longer she could force herself through Frine's lessons.

She watched the Blood with narrowed eyes that had only hours ago been bruised and swollen from yet another beating in the sparring ring. She'd healed herself despite the tender pain and without her healing tutor's help, but the ache still hadn't completely subsided. Her torso, legs, and arms were riddled with at least a dozen scars collected during her short tenure with the battle masters. She was very much done with Losse.

"Blood Frine, people up there need my help!"

The Blood cocked an eyebrow.

"I appreciate this training," she continued, "but I'm leaving in the morning whether you negotiate that treaty or not."

"No," the Blood said after a short pause.

"What do you mean, 'no'?"

"You must stay here and learn. I vow to return you safely once you're ready."

"That's the thing," she retorted. "It's not your decision to make."

"Vagabond, please," Daowa said. "Watch your tone!"

"I'm done, Queen Daowa, and I'm leaving."

Blood Frine held up a hand to silence them both. When he spoke, his voice was heavy and disappointed. "Dear girl, I wasn't offering you a choice."

Kara furrowed her eyebrows, confused until his words sunk in. She had never been a guest. She was a prisoner. The training was a distraction. She backed away and walked toward the main entrance, but the entry broke open with a boom. A dozen other hidden doors opened, each ushering in a thick line of soldiers. They blocked the exits.

She was surrounded, with no choice but to turn back to the Blood. Frine pressed his fingers across the bridge of his low nose and scrutinized her with his coal-black eyes.

"Are you crazy?" she demanded.

"Only wary," he answered, calm. "You aren't ready. You will get yourself killed and lead those that follow you to their deaths if you leave now. You'll thank me, someday, for keeping you here."

"I don't want to stay!"

"It's hardly a matter of desire. These are facts. This is the safest kingdom, most hidden from Blood Carden's treachery. It's the safest place to hide articles of power—" He paused. "And Vagabond, you are nothing but an article of power. You don't yet realize how many worlds will plummet if you don't master yourself. I assure you that this is a favor for which you will someday repay me."

"I doubt that!"

"Curious," he said. "But your friend, I believe his name is Asealo? He seems to disagree with me as well."

Her heart fluttered. Is that why Braeden missed dinner?

"What did you do to him?"

"We merely spoke, but I'm grieved to discover that you have already begun to build your own army. Vagabond, I know he is free of his loyalty."

Frine glared at her, and for a brief moment, she had no idea what he meant. But it clicked, eventually. Braeden never had loyalty to Losse, since he'd merely changed form. Frine never had power over him, but the king had no idea what Braeden truly was. Instead, Frine thought that Kara had broken a Lossian subject's blood loyalty.

Neither explanation was really in her favor.

"Bring him!" Frine bellowed.

Another door swung open, and four soldiers dragged Braeden, still in his Lossian form, into the room. Two soldiers pinned his arms behind his back and pushed him forward while another guard held his head so that his throat was exposed, but the disguised prince caught her eye and winked. He nodded once to the door behind him, which still stood open. Just those four guards stood between her and freedom. She tensed for the escape.

"Blood Frine," she said, her shoulders tight and ready for the spell she was about to cast. "This is your last chance to let me leave as your friend."

"You aren't yet my friend, Vagabond."

She nodded, smirked, and spun around.

Lavender flames poured from her hands and engulfed the room, boiling the air with thick currents of heat. Soldiers flinched away. Kara bolted through the fire—it couldn't hurt its master—and barreled into the guards closest to Braeden. The guards broke away like bowling pins. Her friend shook free and grabbed her hand before he tore off down the empty hallway beyond the throne room. He waved a hand once they were through, and the doors shut at the gesture with an echoing boom. Blood Frine roared orders from behind the thick walls.

The hallway was wide, meant for massive armies and not two winded travelers in over their heads. They sprinted along without direction. Braeden shouted over his shoulder as they ran.

"Really?" he panted. "This is a submerged kingdom that's practically made of water and you shoot *fire* at them?"

"It's all I could think of!" she said with a huff. "Shut up!"

He tugged on her arm and pulled her into a stairwell without another word. His hand wrapped around the handle, and he closed it with a quiet click before he turned and took the stairs three at a time. Kara did her best to keep up with his pace, but she couldn't survive much longer on adrenaline alone. The endless, brutal training left her sore and exhausted, as Frine had apparently intended. After a few flights, she limped up only one step at a time.

The door crashed open below. She leaned over the rail. Dozens of blue heads stormed upward. She ran a little faster, driven by a fresh wave of panic.

Braeden stood at the next landing, peering through a small crack in a door. She came to a stop behind him, panting and trying to explain the soldiers running up the stairs, but he grabbed her arm and pushed her through the door.

Thick pillars supported the roof in this new hallway that looked out over a row of curved balconies with ornate railings, each carved from glistening mother of pearl. They were easily a hundred feet in the air, the balconies casting long shadows over the hushed city below. The city's gold dome was closer here, but still nowhere close enough to touch.

"Okay, come on." She grabbed his wrist and headed for one of the columns, but Braeden didn't budge. She peered over her shoulder. He forced a smile and slid out of her grip.

"I'll head them off," he said. "You need to figure out a way to escape."

Voices echoed in the stairwell.

"Stop playing hero," she said. "We're getting out of this together."

Footsteps clamored, ever closer.

"Sorry," he muttered. "I win this one."

He brushed the hair out of her eyes and smiled, holding her disbelieving glare for a second before he pushed her back through the door and shut it behind him. The door was solid, with no windows to betray what went on inside, but she heard him tear up the stairs with loud and purposeful steps. A stranger's voice hollered from the other side, just a few feet away.

She cursed and ran for the closest support column, sliding behind it on the smooth floor as the door rattled. Her hand shook as she rubbed the clover pendant and wished forward the Grimoire. It settled into her hands, its weight bringing back half-forgotten memories of black wisps and unanswered questions. She tore open the front cover, hoping that she wouldn't rip anything in her haste.

"How am I going to get us both out of here?" she asked the first blank page.

The Grimoire's pages turned and turned. Her breathing quickened, but she stopped breathing altogether when the door to the stairwell flew open. Voices flooded the hall. Footsteps echoed on the shell floor. Her voice caught in her throat.

Finally, the pages stopped on a panoramic illustration. Her lips twitched in a wry smile, despite the flurry of dread in her gut, when she realized what it was.

"It's perfect."

❦CHAPTER TWENTY FOUR
ESCAPE

Braeden raced up the stairwell until it ended in a plain, white door that led out onto a flat stretch of roof, where the golden dome that surrounded the city was close enough that he could see the sharks circling through its light. They passed by, the whites of their bellies glowing in its radiance. A rod extended from the ground in front of him and up to the edge of the dome, where a yellow orb flashed like a tiny sun.

Voices echoed in the stairwell behind him. He slammed the door shut and pressed his hands against it, focusing on the boiling adrenaline in his blood until black vines crawled from under his fingers and lodged in the cracks. They curled through the stone door, locking it with their thorny roots to buy him some time.

He hurried to the edge of the roof and peered over the waist-high wall. The city glimmered far below in the false sun, beneath rounded balconies that extended from the sides of the palace. These terraces alternated for several stories so that he could see one through the gap between the two above it. Hopefully, Kara had escaped.

The door crashed open to the ripping snarl of vine roots being torn apart. Duke Trin ran through the narrow entry, followed by a flood of skinny blue soldiers. He spat on the polished shell roof and grabbed Braeden by the collar.

"Where is she?" he asked. White twists of light danced through the Lossian's seaweed-green eyes.

Braeden shrugged. "Far away by now."

The duke broke his fist across Braeden's jaw. The disguised prince sank to one knee, his neck numb and bruised. Somehow, the skin hadn't broken; he was, by some miracle, not bleeding. His body began to heal internally, but it was slow. It had been an incredible, impossibly hard hit.

"Vagabonds always come back for their kind," Trin said, disgust wrinkling his face. "Seal the doors! Move to the lower walls and for the Blood's sake, spike this traitor!"

Braeden pushed himself to his feet as a soldier with a set of poisoned shackles ran toward him. His options were limited. The Lossian army far outnumbered him, so fighting his way back down the steps wouldn't work. Tapping into his daru would expose him for what he truly was, which would mean certain death when he was overcome by the sheer number of soldiers at Frine's command. He peered over the castle's edge once more, his head dizzy from vertigo. His stomach churned as he estimated the distance to the courtyard below, uncertain as to which fate would be less painful: months in the spikes or a fall to the ground. Both would end about the same.

A rush of wind billowed over him in the otherwise still air, and a black streak sailed overhead, landing on the roof with the heavy crack of snapping shells. It was a black beast with three legs, vein-ridden wings, and a massive, spiked tail. Its long neck craned and came to a massive head, which was adorned with a thorny crest made of the same spiked bone as its tail. It moved like a lizard over a hot rock, darting to bits of the roof with the fewest soldiers and herding them into a huddle far away. The thing snapped its head toward Braeden and scuttled closer, flashing him a sharp grin. Its massive fangs had no lips to hide them.

"C'mon!"

He heard Kara's voice, but shock froze his body for a second longer before he could glance to the creature's back. There she was, hand outstretched. Her face was white.

"Hurry up!"

He jumped up behind her and wrapped his hands around her waist, but the added height of the Lossian form made him slouch over her head. The beast jumped and soared straight toward the circling sharks, its leathery wings beating so quickly that all Braeden could hear was the sharp snap of its skin hitting the air.

"Hold your breath!" Kara yelled over her shoulder.

He looked up as they broke through the dome and took a shallow breath seconds before the cold water bit every inch of his skin. Golden light stretched to cover the hole they made in the dome, and only a thin stream of water poured through, falling like a spot of rain down to the city below.

The gathering sharks were roaches in the light, scattering as the monster tore through their ranks. They regrouped, pulling into a militant formation to speed after them with sharp flicks of their tails. Their bodies rippled from the force. A blurring rush of water coursed over Braeden's face, but he could still make out the duke and his men reaching their arms upward, twisting and turning their own bodies in coordination with the makos and great whites. The predators weren't just for display—they were a last defense as well.

Bleached rays of the dry world above refracted against the distant surface, too far away. Kara clung to the monster's neck, pinned, and Braeden shielded her from the rush of water as best he could. Her eyes creased from the strain of keeping them closed, and her mouth moved, as if she was whispering. Bubbles rushed sidelong from her lips. He reached a hand over her mouth to preserve what oxygen she had, but as he touched her cheek, he thudded against dry land.

He threw himself on his forearms and heaved. Water spewed from his mouth and ears, splashing on the grass. His vision blurred from the lingering saltwater, but there was definitely dirt and solid ground beneath him. He curled his hands along the earth, relishing the dry tickle of the dead leaves crunching beneath his fingers. Kara retched nearby.

His eyes stung from the salt, and he blinked until he could see. His hands were smaller and olive again. He cursed under his breath—he'd retreated to his Hillsidian form without realizing it. That was a careless mistake to make. His only hope was that it had happened when he was too far away for the Lossians to see.

He looked around, trying to figure out where they were. Thick rows of trees spanned every which way and blocked out the sky with their leaves. There was no water in sight; he didn't even hear a creek gurgle, but he couldn't hear much of anything through the hollow echo of the water lodged in his eardrums. He rubbed more water from his eyes and did his best to flush it from his ears.

The black three-legged dragon sat in front of him, its wings tucked at its side like a giant, scab-covered dog waiting for a treat. It grinned again as he looked up. A sunbeam broke through the treetops and glinted off its teeth.

At the sunny touch, the dragon broke into a cloud of black ash. There was no wind, so it settled on the thick air, shimmering in the light. The trees eventually sighed in a soft breeze that carried the remnants of the monster away.

"Summoned him," Kara said. "Apparently, the Grimoire has a pet store."

She was curled over her stomach, still coughing up water. Her hair clung to her cheeks and she had a green tint to her face, but she smiled at him.

"How did we get here?" he asked. "We weren't even close to the water's surface."

He knelt over her and lifted her neck so that she could better force the water from her lungs. She shifted her satchel over her back, but more water poured from it onto her already drenched clothes.

"I'm not sure. I got really dizzy there at the end, and I heard the Vagabond whisper something in my ear. I just repeated what he said over and over, knowing that it had to be a way out of that mess. Do you think it teleported us?"

"I have no idea what else could have happened. Do you remember what he told you?"

"No. I was panicking. He's never done that before." She shook her head and looked over to him, but started giggling.

"What?"

"I'm sorry, Braeden, but you look ridiculous."

"Oh. Well, thank you." He feigned a sarcastic curtsey.

His Lossian clothes clung to his body, constricting his chest and stomach, but the fabric was too long for his arms and slid back over his hands and feet every time he pulled it back.

He rubbed his neck with both hands and in a single, hot wave of air, he was dry. He repeated the technique on Kara so that she was comfortable and then ripped the too-long sleeves and pants until they fit with at least some comfort. He didn't have his pack anymore, so he couldn't change. He was just lucky that Frine hadn't found the Lossian and Kirelm keys he'd hidden in a secret pocket of his shirt. That would've been a disaster.

Something hummed. He glanced over to see the heavy Grimoire resting in Kara's hands and shook his head. The stupid book was more trouble than it was worth.

"Griffin, old buddy," she said to the open pages. "Get us out of here."

It took a few hours for the chill of their close call to fade away. Braeden wanted nothing more than to be in Hillside again, but after a few hours of flying, Kara insisted that she needed a break. The griffin descended into the forest and knelt for them to dismount.

They landed in a small clearing and walked to its edge to stay out of sight. Braeden scanned the woods with short twists of his head, ready for another fight and unable to relax.

Kara touched his arm, frowning. He flinched and forced himself to take a deep breath.

"I think we can calm down a bit, Braeden."

"No," he said with a shake of his head. "That's two out of five kingdoms that tried to kidnap you, Kara. And they had spikes—" His voice shook.

"We're safe." She forced a smile, but it fell short. Her eyes didn't wrinkle with relief like they should have.

"You don't believe that."

"No, not really. I was just trying to make you feel better."

"Don't console me. I'm supposed to be the one protecting *you*. We can take a break, but we need to leave soon."

She didn't answer, just sat on a log and opened her satchel. The two blue map pieces fell from the bag into her lap. They pressed into her skin, pinning her clothes against her legs as she slid the fourth piece into the empty corner.

A brilliant white light blazed along the map's edges, shattering the clearing with a blinding flare. Braeden squinted and shielded his eyes as the air buzzed. The glare sputtered and faded away, and when he could see again, flecks of gold glittered in the air above the map.

If it really was a map, it was unlike any he'd ever seen. There were no landmarks or directions on it, and its primary décor was a large oval indent that consumed most of the stone. Small carved flowers and tangled vines framed the map in a thick border, and in its center was a small carving the exact size and shape of the clover pendant. Aside from those few details, it was just a polished square slab of lapis lazuli.

Kara took off the clover necklace, and her fingers brushed the golden locket around her neck as she did. He noticed that she paused, hand shaking, and took a deep breath before she shoved the clover into the map until the cartilage in her thumb joints cracked. The pendant shifted beneath her hands, and there was a click as it snapped into place.

A ripple of air radiated from the space beneath her thumbs. The blue stone bent and stretched like the disturbed surface of a pond, and its golden flecks blazed with their own light, shining brighter until their glow engulfed the blue stone completely.

"Is it supposed to do that?" he asked.

"I think so. Come over here. It looks like it's drawing something."

A thin black line appeared on the now-golden map, moving as if drawn by an invisible pen. It sloped and curved, first drawing the crude slope of a mountain. A forest appeared beneath the summit and a stream appeared below that. A lichgate drew itself by the river, its roof sloping to a sharp point against the mountainside. A jagged line broke through the center of the mountain.

Braeden's heart skipped a beat. He groaned, rubbing his eyes out of frustration. He knew that mountain, and it was in the last place on Earth he wanted to go.

"Where—?" Kara asked.

"It's a mountain near the Stele," he answered. "It has to be, because I've never seen another mountain range with a crack like that."

"Awesome." Kara rolled her eyes. He guessed she was hardly eager to return, either.

The map drew more scenes in an ever-moving stream of black ink, sketching and then shifting away from what it had just drawn. The image revolved, zooming into the crack until it opened out onto a tunnel. Rocks fell from the walls, caving in and blocking the way ahead. The view turned sharply to the left and followed another tunnel until it spun and stopped at a door.

The Stele's coat of arms adorned the stone entryway, its thorn-covered vines twisted into a crude square. Silver daggers broke the shape in each of the symbol's four corners.

The door in the drawing opened as the sketch paused before it. At the far end of a shallow room was a pedestal that held a large oval amulet. It was set in silver, and the eight prongs that kept the stone in its setting dug into its large black jewel with sharp tips that bent like claws. Its silver chain dangled over the back of the pillar, swinging in the otherwise still room.

"No," Braeden said, seething.

"What is that thing?"

"That's supposed to be lost forever, not hidden in the Stele! I won't go back. I can't." He stood and paced the clearing, resting his hands on his head.

"Why would the first Vagabond want us to get some trinket?"

She stared at the map, the creases in her forehead illuminated by its glow as it replayed everything. The sketch was already zooming through the cracked mountain again, moving toward the sunken tunnel.

"I don't know. According to legend, it shows you where you belong," he answered.

Her eyes snapped into focus as it all clicked for her. Her shoulders drooped, and Braeden paused long enough to understand why she'd been asked to find it. If she was truly worthy of being the Vagabond, the amulet would show her the way to the village. Otherwise, the abandoned village would stay hidden.

"You don't have to come with me," she said. "I know that it's hard for you to be near Carden, or the Stele—"

"No, it's not *hard*, Kara. If he ordered me to stop breathing, my lungs would obey him and stop working. Hard is climbing a steep trail. Resisting a direct command from my Blood when he's near me is impossible."

"Sometimes impossible just means you have to try harder," she said, eyes locked with his. Her gaze challenged his lifetime of slavery to his father.

"You can't understand it, so don't judge me! You'll never have to endure such a thing!"

"I'm not judging you. But I did lose both my parents in the same year, so I think I know a thing or two about how difficult life can be."

"I know you haven't had an easy time here, but this is worse than losing someone you love. This is losing control over yourself."

"Like I said, you don't have to come with me."

"I would be a sorry bodyguard if I didn't."

"Well you're not much use if you suffocate yourself."

"This isn't funny."

"Sorry."

"I have a compromise," he said, sitting beside her with a sigh. "How about this—we go back to Hillside for now. Rest. Relax. We figure out what to do about Losse and only then do we go find the amulet."

"Oh man, *Losse*. What a disaster." She slid down the log and laid her head against it like it was a lumpy pillow.

A short laugh emanated from the clearing to Braeden's right.

"Can the two of you go anywhere without causing trouble?"

Braeden spun and instinctively reached for his sword—which was still in his room in Losse—but relaxed when he saw Adele standing in the grass with one hand on her hip.

"It's always an epic chase with you two," she said. The muse teased the pendant on her neck as evidence that something had gone wrong.

"It's good to see you, too, Adele," Kara said.

"What happened in Losse?" The muse sat on the log. Braeden crossed his arms and leaned against a tree, watching from a short distance.

"They weren't very agreeable."

"What an overpowering understatement," he said. "They tried to kidnap you!"

"And kill you," she added. "Regardless, Losse isn't interested now, and Kirelm would consider the peace talks only if Frine was involved." She glared off into the forest. "I'm starting to wonder if there's anything in Ourea worth saving."

"As long as there's evil, there will be good," Adele said. "You must watch for it and allow it to surprise you. For as many people that hunted the first Vagabond, there were just as many who fed him, hid him, and sent him safely on his way. These people defended the helpless and would have stood before a rising army to protect a stranger. They were true heroes. Don't lose your faith in life or the world. Millions already look to you for hope when they have none. You're one of those heroes, to them, so you must be strong."

Kara slouched against the log, looking off into the grass. Her eyes shifted out of focus. Streaks of grime covered her face, and there were deep purple bags beneath her eyes. Her eyelids drooped. Still, somehow, the sun made her skin glow beneath the dirt.

"I failed," she said.

"Not quite," Adele answered. "The Lossian Bloods have trusted Garrett for generations, as they are some of the few who openly speak with drenowith. We'd hoped we would not need to interfere, but we suspected what happened when we sensed you were in danger. He has gone to speak with their Blood to help him find reason."

"Why didn't he do this before?" Braeden asked. "Why make us go there in the first place?"

"The more we interfere, the more likely it is that the Council which forbade us from helping the Vagabond will kill us for treason," Adele snapped. "You must understand, then, why this wasn't our first course of action."

She had a point. Braeden huffed and leaned against the tree, avoiding her gaze.

"Will it work?" Kara asked. "Will Losse agree?"

"I believe so," the muse said.

Kara sighed with relief and leaned against the log, staring into the sky with a thin smile. Even Braeden's shoulders relaxed at the news. He hadn't trained with Kara, having not been allowed near her masters, but he'd watched to make sure she was safe and cringed every time she was thrown to the ground in combat. She hadn't learned, there. She had suffered. It was no way to train a new warrior.

He looked her over. She made him ashamed to think he was tired.

"I really want a bed right now," she said.

"You're only a few hours from Hillside." Adele brushed back a tangled lock of Kara's hair. "I'll go with you to the gates to make sure you arrive safely. We should leave now, while there's still a little light left in the day."

Braeden was closer to the griffin, so he mounted and reached out a hand to help Kara. She took it, wrapping her small hand around his wrist. A thrilling chill ran through him at her touch. He smiled despite himself.

"I'm going to sleep for days when we get home," she whispered to him once she mounted. She wrapped her arms around his waist for balance. His heart skipped a beat and for a moment, he couldn't swallow.

"Hillside is your home now, huh?" he joked when his breath returned.

Kara laughed, but didn't answer.

He turned toward Adele, expecting a snide comment, but the muse had already transformed into a griffin. Gleaming white feathers spiked along her neck, and pale beige fur covered her torso and legs, which ended in the sharp claws of a lioness. She preened, cocking her head when she caught his surprise.

Kara's griffin shuffled toward Adele. It curled its head and sidestepped, inching closer to her. Braeden nudged it with his heel, urging it away from the muse.

"Stop that," he muttered. "She's taken."

Kara laughed as the griffin batted Braeden's leg with its tail in revenge. It trotted forward, took a bounding leap, and they took off for Hillside.

Braeden was looking forward to his bed, but he knew that he

couldn't walk into Hillside with Kara. He couldn't keep her safe if all of Hillside knew he was her bodyguard, and he would be interrogated if anyone discovered that he'd somehow gone with her. He would sleep in the woods tonight and enter the kingdom through another gate in the morning. Even then, he wouldn't be allowed to go straight to bed if Gavin had his way. The Blood would want a report on the isen raid. And since Gavin always got his way, Braeden needed to speak to Adele to find out how it had gone.

❦CHAPTER TWENTY FIVE
PURPOSE

Just a few hours after Adele found them in the forest, Kara rode her griffin along a misty trail near Hillside. She was alone and not entirely sure if she was going the right way. Thick fog hung in the woods, blurring the path the muse told her to take before she'd shifted into a small bird of some sort and flown off. Adele the sparrow or nightingale or whatever was watching from the trees, small and overlooked.

Braeden had ruffled Kara's hair before he walked off to find his hidden drowng, whom he said was getting fat waiting for him in some remote meadow. She grinned at the memory, but the smile dissolved when she remembered that he'd be out in the unprotected forests overnight. She hoped he would be safe.

"Hello again, Vagabond!"

She wheeled around in her seat, trying to find the source of the voice. Captain Demnug stood behind her, half-submerged in the thick layers of fog. He bowed as she sighed with relief. The haze coursed around him, swirling through his beard and half-hiding him in the mist.

"You startled me," she chided.

"I was merely being cautious. You'll forgive me if I ask you to dismount your..." He trailed off and tilted his head. "Is that a griffin? To think, all we gave you was a horse."

"It's not a competition, Captain. Besides, he's mine."

The griffin knelt, letting her slide off, and nipped her shoulder once she was on the ground. She patted its neck, but at her touch, it broke apart into a cloud of dust with a small *poof*.

"You certainly are full of tricks," the captain said. "Now, please hold still for a moment."

He reached for her wrist and sniffed it. She eyed him, confused, as he did the same thing to her hair.

"Um," she muttered. "What are you doing?"

"It's a safeguard to check that an isen didn't steal your soul while you were away," he said with a lazy shrug, as if smelling someone's arm was absolutely normal. She really needed to rewrite her definition of ordinary.

"What are you looking for, exactly?"

"Master Braeden taught me to look for the scent of lilac and pine mixed together. It's hard to miss if you're ready for it."

She smiled wryly, knowing the answer to her next question before she asked it.

"Is he back yet?"

"No, but there's no need to worry. I'm sure he'll be back soon. Now you'll have to forgive me, but I can't show you into the kingdom." He pulled out a green blindfold. She sighed and let him tie it around her head, too tired to complain.

"Lead the way," she said with a grumble, reaching out her hands so that he could guide her through the gate she had already watched Braeden open.

⚐

Kara had been warned against thinking she could go straight to bed, no matter how tired she was. When the captain removed the blindfold and Hillside's markets bustled before her, she made a preemptive beeline into the castle and headed straight for Gavin's study.

She'd somehow remembered where the room was, but when she rounded the corner and found it, she couldn't recall which painting had previously hung on the hidden door. Whatever it had been, the late Queen's portrait had taken its place in the time Kara was away. The dead Queen looked down at Gavin's visitors with a thin smile, and though Kara expected the portrait to move like some of the Grimoire's sketches, it was still. She paused at the painting to rub a finger along the rough layers of paint before pulling the tassel which hung by the frame. No chime sounded, but she did hear a faint voice from within.

"Come in, Kara."

She shuddered and looked around for a security camera before she could stop herself. No, yakona just knew these things.

The door opened on its own with a soft click and closed with the same sound after she'd crossed the threshold. Gavin sat in a chair, reclined with his feet on a new, broad table in the middle of the room.

The table was covered with piles of maps, and a single plate of powdered sugar cookies sat at one end.

"Welcome back," he said without moving. "How was your trip?"

"Adventurous."

"I suspect that to be an understatement. Did anyone give you trouble? We thought you would return two weeks ago at the latest."

"I did run into a bit of an issue with Losse," she admitted. Her thoughts scurried over the weeks of brutal training, and she couldn't hide a relieved sigh that it was all over.

"We expected as much."

"However, I've spoken to the drenowith and they will see if they can change Frine's mind."

"I suggest you use his title to avoid offense," Gavin said, but his voice was distant and he seemed to speak more out of habit than real concern. His fingers resting on his chin as he watched her with unfocused eyes, as if lost in thought.

"What's wrong, Gavin?"

"It—the drenowith intervened?" he finally asked. "To help *us*?"

"Of course they did. Why does everyone have such a hard time understanding that? A drenowith trained the first Vagabond. A few of them want peace in Ourea as much as you do."

"I never knew," he mumbled.

"Well, now you do. We shouldn't advertise that, though." Kara groped for a suitable lie that would protect the muses without explaining why they needed protection. "They like their privacy."

"I won't say anything."

"Thanks," she said, sitting down across from him at the table. "Though the Blood of Kirelm is a bit of a pig, he agreed to talk with you so long as Losse agrees as well."

Gavin grinned, bringing his feet to the floor with a *thump* and renewed vigor. Whatever he'd been thinking about, he wasn't going to burden her with it.

"That is fantastic news!" he said.

"I thought so, too." She draped herself over two of the chairs, exhausted, and picked up one of the cookies sitting forgotten on their plate. The first nibble left crumbs on the corners of her lips, and the tart filling stung her sinuses. The bite snapped her from her train of thought.

"These cookies are delicious."

"You've done well, Kara. Negotiations will begin soon, then, and there will of course need to be a celebration when we sign the treaty."

"Here?" She took another cookie, unable to stop now that she'd started. They were *amazing*.

"No, it would be foolish to expose Hillside's location." He waved away her question and pondered. "Richard used to tell me of a Unity Gala that was held back in the times of Ethos. Each winter, they came together and celebrated light to give people hope against the cold. Sometimes, the Gala would last for weeks."

"Sounds like my kind of party."

"We could restart the tradition, but use it as a celebration of unity instead of light." He grabbed a cookie. "These were for me, you know."

"I was hungry. Besides, you shouldn't eat a whole plate of sugar." She shrugged, but he was smiling.

"Glad you could help, then."

"Just doing my part."

"We would need a neutral location."

She was confused for a moment, until she realized that his train of thought lacked tracks. They were back to the Unity Gala conversation. He leaned back in his chair as he thought aloud.

"What about Ethos?" he asked.

"Isn't it all in ruins?"

"Most of it, yes, but there's rumor of a central hall that survived. With the four armies together, we would have nothing to worry about in terms of security. It would be perfect, completely closed off, and neutral to everyone."

"Not to mention the symbolism behind uniting the kingdoms once again in the city where it all began," she added. "It sounds great as long as we can make sure it's safe."

"Absolutely. I'll send a company out to investigate. I'm in your debt, Kara." He smiled and took her hand in his. She flinched at the touch, but the movement was subtle enough that he either didn't notice or didn't acknowledge it.

"Thanks, but you don't owe me anything."

Relief sank into the pit of her stomach even as she tried to wriggle her hand free of his grip. Gavin might have been rash and a bit temperamental, but he seemed to have relaxed while she was gone. She had an ally in him. A cloud skirted around the sun and a beam of light lit the room, stinging her eyes. She needed sleep.

"You look exhausted." Gavin let her hand slide to the table. "I'm sorry to have kept you. Please, get some rest. Can we bring you anything?"

"I'm too tired for food, but thanks."

"But not too tired to eat my cookies, apparently."

She laughed. "I guess not."

He grinned. "To bed it is then."

She left, returning to her room without running into a soul along the way. The door swung closed behind her, and she traded her Lossian training gear for the loose shirt and clean pants someone had left for her on the bed. She collapsed into the mattress with no intention of waking up until the next afternoon.

✳

Someone knocked on Kara's door.

"Go away," she mumbled, two layers deep in the comforters. Smudges of dirt from her face stained the white linens.

"May I come in?" a soft voice called through the wood.

Kara tried to block the sun with her pillow as she searched her memory. The voice was familiar, somehow.

"Twin?"

"Yes. I'm talking to a door, which is awkward. May I come in yet?"

"Yeah, it's unlocked."

Kara sat up and wiped drool from her face. *Oh, gross.*

Twin opened the door and slid into the room. "I just wanted to let you know that Braeden returned."

"Thanks." Kara hadn't asked anyone to tell her that, but at least it was an excuse to be in the same room as Twin. She wanted to say something, anything, but the words wouldn't find their way to her mouth.

Where do I even start to apologize? "I'm sorry I made you relive your sister dying. My bad?"

The room was silent. Twin wrung her hands and examined the floor while Kara played with the edge of her comforter.

"Well, I'll leave you alone then," Twin mumbled, bolting for the door.

"Wait." Kara reached out to stop her. "Please. I'm sorry for what I said by that spring. It's not my business. What I said was just mean."

"It's okay, and I'm sorry I couldn't better explain the consequences," Twin said, stopping at the door with a sigh. "Just promise me that you'll never try it."

Kara's heart panged with the memory of the water demon she'd created on the way to Losse. Its sharp teeth seared her thoughts.

"Unless—" Twin gasped. "Oh *Bloods*! Did you—?"

"I won't do it again." Kara's jaw tightened, and she watched the floor.

Twin sat on the bed. "It's a dangerous addiction."

"If you know that, why haven't you stopped?"

"I have, actually. After you found me out, I could never bring myself to go back. You made me finally accept that my sister..." Twin trailed off and sighed. "She's dead."

"Is there anything I can do to help? Anything at all?"

"Yes." Twin laughed and stood, waving her hand over her nose. "Take a bath. You smell terrible."

Kara laughed and threw a pillow at her, but Twin caught it and used it as a shield against the barrage of pillows that followed. When the fluffy arsenal was depleted, Kara made her way toward the bathroom. A full tub, a change of pants, new boots, and a clean, green shirt were already waiting for her in the adjacent room.

"So," Twin said with a giggle. "I'm sure you missed Braeden after all this time. Are you planning on paying him a visit?" She batted her eyes mockingly from where she sat on the bed, and Kara wished she had another pillow to throw.

"Not really." She tasted the lie, but kept that to herself. "I'll see you later."

"He's just a floor above you," Twin called over her shoulder as she left. "Third door on the right."

"Uh-huh," Kara answered, trying not to sound interested. The bedroom door thudded closed, and she repeated the directions under her breath so that she would remember the way.

She heated the water by submerging her hands and lighting a flame in each palm. While the flames didn't appear underwater, the bath bubbled and warmed until steam danced along the surface. Kara grinned, happy with her progress since her first miserable bath in Hillside, and she treated herself to a long soak before dressing and heading off to find Braeden.

She knocked on his door when she found it, and he wrenched it open before she could knock a second time. His hair was clean but unkempt, and he'd managed to find fresh clothes.

"What a surprise," he said with a grin. "How was your chat with Gavin?"

"Astonishingly jovial."

"Come in." He left the door open and turned back to the piles on his bed.

"Is that appropriate?" she joked. "Don't I need a white-gloved chaperone or something?"

"And here I thought you were a modern American girl." He smiled again and continued sifting through the piles of cloth on his blanket.

"So, when are we going to leave? I figure—"

He interrupted her with a curt laugh. "You have no idea how to relax, do you?"

"It's kind of important that I find this amulet," she said. "I don't have time to relax."

"Don't be so boring."

Kara stepped inside as he leaned over several sharp, glinting weapons on the comforter. There was a cloth with several red and black streaks on it, which he used to wipe down the various knives and other sharp contraptions as they spoke. He cleaned each item thoroughly before setting it on a tall, crowded shelf across from the bed, as if he always had mundane conversations while tending to his small, well-organized armory.

"Braeden, come on. I know you don't really want to go, but—"

"It's not that I'm hesitant to go," he interrupted, pausing as he polished a sword with two curling blades that twisted around each other like a DNA double-helix. She shuddered at the thought of what it could possibly be used for.

"Then what is it?"

"If you work too hard for too long, you'll wear yourself out. Most normal people know that."

"Really? You're comfortable using that word? I have a glowing bluish-orange egg in my bag that's supposed to hatch into a mammal with superpowers. I don't even know what the word 'normal' means anymore."

"All right, all right. Still, you should relax. Eat, at least. We can take a walk, get some food, and then we can go. Will you grant me that?"

"Fine," she said with a mock sigh, smiling as he set the last of the daggers on his shelf.

He belted a sword around his waist and held the door open for her. Together, they walked into the hall. A young girl stopped on the stairwell as they left his room, frozen mid-step as she watched them. Kara caught the girl's eye, and the Hillsidian tore away in an unbalanced giggle-dash down the stairs.

"And the rumors begin," Braeden said with a chuckle. They headed down the same stairwell, but at a slower pace.

"Seriously, is the gossip here that bad? Maybe she was just—" Kara tried to give the girl the benefit of the doubt, but she couldn't think of an alternative reason for stopping, staring, and then tripping over oneself in an impish chortle.

"It's their entertainment. All Hillsidians have is shopping and gossiping about who's going to finally bond to each other."

"What?"

"Bonding? It's, well, it's our marriage, I guess. Yakona don't marry in the sense that humans do. We pick a partner and stay with them, sure, but there's no ring and there's no divorce."

"What do you use, then?"

"Maybe this is a topic for another day. If anyone hears us talking about this, the rumors are going to burn people alive." He shot a nervous look around at the empty stairs.

"I'll just ask the Grimoire."

She rolled her eyes as the stairwell ended, and they walked into the main dining hall. The room was loud, filled with Hillsidians who laughed and jeered at one another. Kara grabbed some fruit, honeyed ham, a loaf of bread, and a block of cheese before heading for the orchard through a side door.

Birds chirped as she and Braeden walked through the orchard on their way to the lakeshore, where they sat and ate. Kara lay back on the grass when the food was gone, listening as Braeden told her stories about his isen hunts, almost all of which ended with him in the human world. As he spoke, she let her mind wander and wondered if she would ever go back.

Even though she'd relaxed in the warm sunshine, Kara couldn't stop thinking about the village and the last obstacle in her way. She asked Braeden about leaving for the Stelian amulet at least once every thirty minutes for three hours until he finally conceded that they could go.

"But,"—he added—"we can go only if you promise that as soon as we find the village, we come right back here and do absolutely nothing for a week."

"Lazy thing."

"Promise."

"Fine. But as soon as we find the amulet, we're heading straight for the village. No stops."

"*Fine*," he said, mocking her tone.

They each took a half hour to gather food and water for the trip before they met back at the lakeshore. Kara adjusted her now-full satchel and stretched out on the grass while Braeden sat on a half-submerged boulder and stared out into the water, apparently lost in thought as he tore handfuls of grass to bits.

She whistled in the hope that it would catch Rowthe's attention—they needed him, since their route involved caved-in tunnels—and reclined on the grassy beach. She waited for Braeden to say something or to start another story, but he didn't move from his place on the boulder. She instead turned over onto her stomach and played with her tiny egg in the silence.

The little good luck charm warmed in her palms while her mind wandered. Her thoughts raced back over her conversation with Twin, back through the dining hall and to Gavin's lemon cookies. There was something she'd meant to ask the Grimoire, but she had entirely forgotten what it was.

She glanced over to Braeden. She'd meant to ask something that he hadn't wanted to explain. Ah. *Right.*

Marriage in Ourea was known as "bonding." She shook her head at the strange term and summoned forth the Grimoire, asking for more details with a soft whisper.

The pages flicked by, one after another, until they landed on a two-page spread of a pair of yakona. The male had no shirt, and his bare skin betrayed the tattoo that began at his shoulder and ended at his elbow. It reminded her of the sparring ring in Kirelm and how all of the soldiers had a similar, twisting line that ran along their arms.

The female yakona had a cloth wrapped around her chest, which hid everything except for her broad shoulders and arms. She also had a thin, spiraling tattoo along her right arm that ended on her neck. Kara leaned in to read the text besides the drawing.

> Yakona bond for life. It's an intricate, private ceremony that merges the lifelines of any two yakona such that they are eternally tied together.

So those weren't tattoos at all. They were lifelines. She shot a quick glance over toward Braeden before she continued reading.

> Yakona bond with each other by fusing their lifelines. The yakona's line crawls onto the arm of his or her partner, creating a new design that becomes an everlasting connection between them. When one is in danger or hurt, the other will always know where to find their lover.
>
> Only when a yakona dies does the lifeline disappear to allow the other yakona to find another mate. Usually, however, they never choose another, hoping instead that their love is waiting for them on the other side of this life.

As she read, the drawings demonstrated the ceremony. They held each other, the male lifting the female's chin with his fingers, and each tattoo spiraled down their respective arms. Soon, an entirely new design snaked over each yakona's right arm from their wrists to their shoulders.

Kara glanced again toward Braeden, whose elbow-length shirt covered his tattoo—well, okay, *lifeline*—completely. It was easy to remember, though: it had barely reached his bicep. That *had* to be the easiest way to tell if a man was taken or not. She laughed quietly, imagining a yakona night club. All a girl had to do was go up to a guy and ask him to roll up his sleeve. Or, better yet, take off his shirt.

A few short bursts of vibration buzzed on the grass around her. The little egg glowed brighter than ever and rocked back and forth, so she held it up to the sun. The faint outline of a tiny, bushy tail showed through the shell. It vibrated again in her hand, and she returned it to the grass.

Four tiny legs broke through the shell, though the rest of the body remained inside. It staggered a few inches and then fell, unable to see where it was going, so she set her hands on each side of it to keep it from running off. The four feet swung wildly, clawing at the shell with frail nails. The baby creature worked for a few minutes before another chunk of the shell came off, and another, and *another*, until the ground was littered with faceted shell fragments and a very wet, very small, very furry little creature.

It stared up at her with eyes almost as large as its head and a body no bigger than her palm. It had two large ears, a white splotch of fur on its forehead, and white stripes running down its otherwise red body. Its tail was longer than its torso, the hair matted with goo, and the thing had tiny clawed feet. It shook itself, trying to get the gook off, so Kara reached around to the lake for some water. She cleaned the bushy little thing and dried it with her sleeve to the buzzing hum of what she guessed was its purring. It nuzzled up to her hand.

"Hey, it hatched!" Braeden scooted in close and pressed his warm arm against hers. A jolt of excitement ran through her, but he was focused on the little thing and thankfully didn't notice her catch her breath. The furry, nameless creature wobbled toward him and sniffed him with a wary air.

"What are you going to call him, Kara?"

"It's a him?"

"I don't know. I was guessing."

"I was thinking I'd call him Flick. Do you like it?

"I do." He grinned. The tiny creature seemed to have quieted whatever silent worry had plagued him.

"All right, little guy," she said to her new pet. "What do you eat?"

Flick chirped and wobbled toward her when she pulled out some bread from her bag. He cozied up to her hand and nibbled a corner of the loaf with his back teeth, tickling her fingertips with his rough tongue as he lapped the salt from her hands in the process.

Soft footsteps on the grass made her glance up. Rowthe stood over them, the rocky mountain backdrop a sharp contrast that made him easier to see. He lowered his head and nibbled Kara's hair in welcome.

She cupped her hands around Flick and picked him up, and the little thing let out a long chirp and giggled as she did so. Braeden pulled himself onto the flaer and then helped her in front of him as she recalled the image of the small chamber that hid the Stele's amulet. Rowthe's ears perked back, and the flaer darted off into the mountain wall.

They suffered a few hours of the jolting kick of walking through cave walls, but Kara used the time as a chance to become acquainted with her new pet. As she tickled his tummy, Flick burped and chuckled and made all sorts of other noises she'd never heard before. She would dangle her fingers in front of him as he lay on his back and laugh each time he reached out to gnaw on her thumb. His small, dull teeth caressed the grooves in her skin, and his mouth wasn't even big enough to get half way around her fingertip.

They came to a cave with thick, black walls, where darkness permeated everything. Any light that did find a way in through small holes in the ceiling was swallowed by the hazy gloom. Goosebumps chased their way across her arms.

"I think we're getting close," she whispered. Braeden grunted.

Rowthe walked slower and passed through another wall into a small, dark hallway carved into the mountain. Thin streams of light broke through the crumbling roof and illuminated part of a stone door opposite them, which had somehow survived the countless years of cave-ins and ruin. Both sides of the hallway were blocked off by black rocks. The air was thin. White dots spotted the edges of Kara's vision from the lack of oxygen. They would have to make this quick.

Rowthe sniffed the hallway and stomped his foot, coming to a sudden, violent stop. The momentum threw Braeden against her back. She leaned, off-balance and about to fall, but he wrapped an arm around her to keep her on their skittish mount. Rowthe pinned his ears to his head and pranced, swinging his head around in search of something they couldn't see. The goose bumps spread farther along Kara's cold skin.

Braeden's chest warmed her back as he held her, one arm covering both her shoulders. He didn't let her go even when she regained her balance, and she realized with a happy pang that she didn't want him to.

"We should leave," he said in her ear.

"I can't leave without the amulet, Braeden. I know it's creepy, but don't you think you're getting upset over nothing? This is all in our heads. So far all we've done is find a door in an eerie hallway. Let's just have a look and then we'll go," she said.

He sighed, released her, and dismounted. The dark, brooding lines returned to his face as she slid off after him. Flick dug his feet into her sleeve and clung to the fabric, shaking. She pulled him back into her hand and huffed in annoyance at how Rowthe had gotten everyone worked up.

She grabbed the ancient stone door's rusted brass knob. She twisted and pushed it open, but the hinges shrieked in a tarnished protest. The door resisted, at first, and caught on the floor, so she shoved it open with her shoulder. A groan shook the stone, and it parted just enough to let her through into a pitch black chamber.

Whispered echoes of her own footsteps chorused around her. She lifted Flick to her shoulder and pulled a small amount of energy into her palm to start a thin fire. The pale flame offered just enough light to see by without burning much of what little air was available.

Though she could see the walls, she couldn't see the ceiling and very quickly came to the other end. The pedestal the map had shown her was the chamber's only décor, but it was empty. Crude writing covered the wall above it.

The runic script had been carved in deep and hasty writing with angry, illegible letters. At each crevice, flecks of the cave wall had been chipped away in the author's haste. The channels that comprised the mysterious lines resonated with the only language that had escaped her since she'd come to Ourea. Flick squeaked and dug his claws into her shirt as she scanned the wall.

Someone behind her forced open the door, and a gray flame cast her shadow over the letters. She turned back to see half of Braeden's face illuminated by the small fire in his hand. He glared around the room, unsmiling.

"We should go, Kara."

"I can't read this at all. Is this a yakona language?" she asked, ignoring him. The writing might be a clue to where the amulet had gone, and she needed to understand what it said.

"Yes. You can't read this because the Vagabond never made it to the Stele to learn its language." He read the wall with an expression of disdain.

"Oh." She stepped back. "What does it say?"

"No." He grabbed her arm and turned to the door, dragging her behind him. Flick twitched his ear across her chin.

"Braeden, what—?"

"We shouldn't be here. There isn't anything but evil in these caves."

"That's a little harsh." A new voice ricocheted from the shadows near the door.

Rowthe growled from the hallway and whimpered. The door slammed shut with a loud thud that shook the walls and extinguished Braeden's fire. He raced for the door, only to back up with slow steps as their visitor advanced.

A cloaked figure stepped out of the darkness and into the thin light of her violet-colored fire, pulling back his hood to reveal ash-gray skin that steamed with thick trails of smoke. Carden walked into sight, Kara's fire flickering and casting deep shadows across his face. He sneered, and the gray skin around his eyes creased. Flick squeaked and ran down Kara's side, into her satchel.

"I tried my hand at the Hillsidian form when I visited the Queen." Carden cracked his neck and frowned. "But I don't really see what you like in it, boy."

Braeden took a deep breath and moved in front of Kara, blocking her view of the Stelian Blood. She peered under his shoulder as Carden continued slowly closer, his boots leaving the hollow echo of his path in the still air of the chamber.

"That's hardly necessary, my boy. I'm not interested in your pet."

"Hey!" Kara said, bristling. Braeden pinched her sharply on the arm and cut her off with a fleeting glare. *Enough of that*, his look said. He inched toward the exit as his father circled. She followed.

"She has spunk, at least," Carden admitted. "It seems we share a weakness for those types."

"I'm nothing like you," Braeden said, but Carden's sneer widened.

"We're more alike than you think, son."

Carden pulled the missing amulet from a hidden pocket in his cloak and examined the black gem as he continued speaking.

"I figured you would come for this. I've researched the Vagabond as well, you see. It seems he always yearned to know where he belonged, since he was an outsider from birth, so it's only natural that he would send her after such a treasure. I'll give it to the girl, in good faith, if you do something for me."

"And what's that?" Kara pushed Braeden's arm down so that she could better see Carden. The Blood's lip curled in a half-grin that reminded her of a used car salesman.

"I didn't give you enough credit when we first met," he said. "You're far braver than you seem."

"Thanks, I think. But what do you want?"

"All I *want*" —he mimicked her frank tone—"is for Braeden to return to the Stele. You can go about your Vagabondish business and continue on with whatever little quest brought you here while Braeden returns home. After we talk, boy, I'll permit you to return to her if you choose to do so."

"Not an option," Braeden said. He continued toward the door.

Carden let the silence settle as they circled, the hollow *thump, thump, shuffle* of their dance continuing.

"You belong to the Stele, Braeden," he said. "Nothing can free you from that. There's no escape from what you are. Why fight what you were bred to be?"

"If you've showed me anything, it's what not to be."

The insult hung in the air.

"Stop inching!" Carden demanded. Even Kara stopped moving at the terrifying sound, but Braeden became rigid. His arms locked beside him and his face twisted with conflict, so that only his chest moved as he fought for breath in the thinning air. He gritted his teeth, and she could feel his body shake.

"I can't move," he whispered to her. "You need to run."

"Look me in the eye, Braeden Drakonin." Carden's eyes narrowed as he spoke.

He focused his trembling gaze on the floor. Anger and helplessness contorted his face, melting into hatred when he obeyed his father, and he lifted his head to glare at the Blood from under furious brows. Carden laughed.

"I'm glad to see that you're still loyal to me. I want you as my general, boy, but I want you to return willingly. This battle of ours is just a misunderstanding. You think I'm a monster, which is simply not true. I'm fighting to restore the glory of our people. I'm trying to end the banishment that we suffer at the hands of the hypocrites!

"The coming tide will turn swiftly, and the fate of all worlds on this Earth will change for it. I simply don't want my Heir to suffer with those who are beneath him. Return to me and your inner battle stops. You won't be forced to hide what you are any longer."

Braeden opened his mouth to speak, but stopped and looked back at Kara. Her hand had found its way to the hem of his shirt. She squeezed it tighter when she realized that she'd needed to touch him, to find some way to tell him to hold on. They could still get out of this.

"I learned a long time ago how to see through your lies. Let us leave," Braeden finally said, grinding his teeth. Relief flooded her heart without her entirely understanding why. They weren't free yet.

Carden sighed. "There isn't anything for you to see but facts, but you seem uninterested in such things. Fine, then. I must remind you of the life led by those who defy me. This is no longer a game."

The Blood made a small gesture with his fingers. Braeden's body, in response, wheeled around to face Kara in a motion that was almost too quick to follow. Panic ate away at his face in some realization she hadn't yet made. His arms moved like a puppet's, controlled by the Blood behind him.

He shoved her up against the wall and pressed her shoulders into the rock. She shrieked at the searing pain crunching her spine. Numbness chased down her back. She couldn't breathe for several seconds, and when breath did come, it was painful.

Braeden's face was the only part of him still left in his control, and his eyebrows twisted in fear when both his hands shifted to her neck and tightened. She wanted to scream, but the short bursts of air that did make it past the aching tension in her throat were reserved for her lungs. The violet fire in her palm flickered out as he suffocated her. Carden lit his own flame without care for the remaining oxygen, and it illuminated them all with a brilliant gray light.

"Braed—" She gasped, her voice breaking on his name.

His eyes snapped between horror and regret. He gritted his teeth, wrinkles of frustration and terror trailing from his mouth to his brow. But, when she caught his gaze, everything but remorse dissolved away.

"Stop!" he yelled over his shoulder to Carden.

The white dots along the edges of Kara's vision grew thicker, until she could see only flickers of movement without fully understanding what was going on.

"This is the world beyond my walls," Carden said as he walked closer. "If you disobey me, I will hunt down everything you love and make you destroy it. *I* am the fury within you that you'll never control. Your stubbornness will only hurt those who help you."

"No, please!" Braeden begged.

Kara's knees gave out. All that held her against the wall, now, were his hands against her neck. Carden's hazy outline lifted the amulet and slid it over her head. The king's next words echoed in her fading consciousness.

"Do you want to see where *you* belong, boy? Look into her eyes as the light fades. Once she's dead, look down to the stone to see the only world that wants you."

Braeden bit his cheek and choked on whatever he was trying to say. His eyes shook, and she saw a hint of wet in the corners. Carden stroked her cheek. His touch was warm, but she flinched until he pulled away. She fought through the vice grip on her neck to breathe.

"Vagabond, I regret that you were caught in this web," Carden said carelessly. "You might have been quite useful."

"Father, please! Stop!"

"Will you return to me if I spare her?"

Braeden didn't answer.

Kara couldn't see much of anything anymore, but she shuddered with unfocused disbelief and fought the surging wave of lightheadedness, trying to weigh both options. Neither was the right choice. She didn't know what she wanted him to say.

Something tickled her side, but she barely sensed it through the numbing tremors in her body. She couldn't pivot to see what it was until it jumped onto Braeden's arms and let loose a bark too vicious for something so small.

In one fell swoop, like a punch to her stomach, heart, and head all at once, her final breath in the cavern left her. The room went black, and her body hung in the air like she was floating. There was no sound, no fear. If this was death, then at least there wasn't any pain.

❦CHAPTER TWENTY SIX
SURVIVAL

Something cracked. Kara thudded on the ground. Air forced its way back into her lungs with a searing bite, forcing her to cough and sputter until her breath was normal again.

She gasped and turned over. At first, all she understood was the color green, but then the rough itch of grass irritated her skin. Flick scampered onto her shoulder, purring and whimpering. She picked him up and stared into his ridiculously massive eyes.

"You can teleport?"

The little thing chirped and licked her nose as Braeden walked into her peripheral vision. Flick squirmed out of her hands and stood on her head, growling at the prince with all his tiny might. She cupped him in her palms in an effort to contain his minute ferocity, but he watched Braeden with bared teeth from between her fingers.

The prince knelt over her, his eyes furrowed with worry and regret. He bit his cheek and looked at her with deeper concern than she'd ever seen in his face before, but her neck ached and her body shied away from him as she tried to make sense of what had happened.

"I thought—" She coughed again. "I thought I'd died."

He shook his head and pulled her into a hug. Though she wanted to kick him to the ground, she just burrowed her head into his chest until she could subdue the stinging threads of pain still lingering in her throat. Flick growled with useless twists of his body from somewhere in between them.

Braeden cradled her head in his palm, but nothing could make the sharp pain in her throat disappear completely. He rubbed her cheek with his thumb, and her skin prickled under his fingers. She pulled away, resisting the urge to run her hand over any bit of her that he'd touched.

She returned Flick to his place on her shoulder and looked into the forest to distract herself. A dirt lane curved through the woods, cresting over a distant hill before it turned down another. A tavern stood on the road nearby, the sound of clinking glasses escaping through the windows.

The amulet glistened on the ground a few feet from her, near where she'd landed after Flick had rescued them, and she preoccupied herself with lifting it off the ground and slipping it into her satchel. Flick snuck in after it.

"How were you going to answer Carden?" she finally asked.

He paused. "I don't know."

She glared over her shoulder, trying to catch his expression, but flinched and sucked in a sharp breath because he was closer than she'd expected. He looked at the ground in shame and stepped back, his expression twisted with the same searing pain that burned in her neck.

"Kara, even Aislynn can't always look me in the eye," he said. His voice was gentle, and he didn't try to touch her again. "I know that when she sees me, she remembers the most painful time of her life, even though she will never admit it. Carden wants me back in the Stele, but it's because he's after something that I haven't yet figured out. Richard and Gavin would disown me the moment they found out what I am.

"But you—you're the one person in this entire world who knows what I truly am and stayed by me without caring. You're the last person I want to hurt. We were lucky this time, but we might not be if it happens again. *When* it happens again. I need to fight this ba—"

"Oh, shut up." She rubbed her neck.

"What?"

"Save your 'I have to fight my battle' speech. I don't want to go around Ourea alone, and you're the only one I trust here, despite— that. I just don't want to be alone, not right now."

It wasn't the only reason she didn't want him to leave.

"Kara, when Carden gets that close again—"

"He won't," she muttered, but she looked to the ground when she tasted her lie. She nodded to the pub farther up the hill. "Now buy me a beer, and let's go to the village."

Braeden walked beneath an overhanging branch and whistled for Rowthe. "This isn't a time for jokes. I always held on to the belief that I could free myself from my tie to the Stele, but since that isn't an option anymore, I need to find someone who will help me control myself."

"You'll never be that close to him again."

"But I will! He's always hunting, always chasing, and I have no idea why!" He smacked a branch. Leaves shook off from the force.

"Braeden—"

"No! *Listen* to me." He marched over, getting so close to her that she could smell the oaky cologne on his collar. He whispered, his voice a breathy growl.

"I was going to kill you, not ten minutes ago, because he told me to. I was going to strangle you and watch you die because that was what he wanted at that moment. I need someone to teach me to be stronger than him, or Flick might not save you next time."

She held her breath and fought the impulse to shield her neck. His intense gaze froze her. Even as a Hillsidian, he was just as terrifying as his father.

He stepped away and watched the forest. "I think Adele will be able to help me. She and Garrett are the most powerful creatures I've ever met. When the Vagabond possessed you and told me off, he said that a muse would guide me. I think he was referring to them. I need to do this, and I promise this is best for both of us. I can be lucky for only so long. Once I take you back to Hillside, I'll set off for the drenowith."

She didn't answer, preferring to look off into the trees instead. Twigs crunched. Rowthe appeared behind a bush, barely visible in the bright daylight. His head hung low and his tail curved between his legs as he looked up at her with pitiful eyes.

"We know you were scared, Rowthe. It's okay." She scratched his ears and the creature let out a soft growl.

Braeden leaned against a tree. "Let's head back to Hillside. I don't think you should go to the village alone. Twin will keep you company until I get back, and then I'll go with you to find the village."

He gestured for her to get on Rowthe while maintaining an overly respectful distance from her.

She shook her head. "I'm not going to wait, even if it means that I have to go alone. I have what I need."

"Kara, no."

"You take Rowthe. There are other mounts in the Grimoire that can help me."

"Kara—"

"Go."

He tugged on her arm to make her face him. "Look, I apologize for putting you in this position, but I need you to wait. You don't know what's waiting there. Let me take you back to Hillside. Use it as a chance to relax or—or burn an effigy of me if you want. But *wait*. The village has waited a thousand years for you, and it can wait another month or two. There have to be more safeguards set up to protect the village. If you go in there angry and distracted, you'll fail." He paused before letting out a shaky sigh. "You might even die."

She glared at him, but he kept his gaze steady.

"Please, Kara."

"I'll do more than burn an effigy," she muttered.

He sighed and offered to help her onto Rowthe, but she mounted on her own. He pulled himself up behind her once she was situated. She shied away from his touch, and during the six-hour journey back to Hillside, they didn't say a single word to each other.

❦

Kara lay in her room, watching the roof of her canopy bed shiver in the subtle breezes coming in from the open window. Someone rapped on her door. She didn't answer. The door clicked open.

"I didn't say you could come in," she said.

"I don't usually have to ask permission," Gavin answered.

She looked over her knees to see the Blood standing with his arms crossed, watching her. He looked down over the brim of his nose.

"What's wrong, Vagabond?"

"Nothing."

"Lying isn't one of the gifts you acquired."

"Did you just call me a bad liar?"

"I did."

She sighed and sat up.

"Where's Braeden?" he asked. "I heard that he left you at the gates and tore off on what the guards believe to be a flaer."

"It is a flaer."

"Where did he go?"

She caught Gavin's eye and paused. She could give Braeden away right now. She could tell Gavin everything. The one person she'd thought was her best and only true friend left in the world had tried to kill her, after all. Even if it was at Carden's behest, he'd had the chance to save her and he had done nothing.

But she remembered the promise she made to Adele the first time she woke up in Hillside. She would protect Braeden as often as he'd protected her. Here, now, she would lie. Well, mostly.

"We ran into Carden. We only escaped thanks to that little guy." She pointed to where Flick slept on the mantle. "And Braeden needed to—um—I guess he needed to kill something after the experience."

"It's a miracle that you both survived," Gavin said. He sat on the edge of her bed and rested a hand on her ankle.

She swallowed hard as the memory of Braeden strangling her resurfaced. She clenched the sheets beneath her hands and glared at the floor.

"Are you all right, Kara?"

"I'll be fine. I should just relax." She had borrowed Braeden's words. Her throat tightened.

"What you need is a distraction. I'll send Twin to you immediately."

Kara laughed, but the smile faded as she remembered the way Carden sneered at her and lit his own flame when hers had petered out.

"I do have good news," Gavin said.

"What's that?"

"Ayavel, Kirelm, Losse, and Hillside have agreed on a peace treaty. We will have the Gala in a little over a month."

"That's amazing," she agreed.

"Now, since you aren't from Ourea, you might not know that each of the Bloods expect gifts at an occasion such as this. If you would like, I would be happy to help you brainstorm."

"Would you be helping me brainstorm your own gift?"

"Perhaps."

"You're shameless." She laughed, shaking her head.

"At least you're laughing." He squeezed her ankle and smiled before he left the room, latching the door behind him.

She stood and walked over to the window. The cobblestone road below was shrouded in the tree tops of Hillsidian houses, and in the distance, the market quarter boomed with life. She was safe in Hillside. This was home.

Someone knocked on the door. Before Kara could say anything, it opened with the swoosh of a skirt.

"Hi, Twin," she said without turning around.

"I'm so glad you're back! Try this on."

She turned to see Twin dump a pile of crimson fabric on the bed.

"What—?"

"It's your Gala dress! I hope you don't mind, but pants simply won't do for such a formal affair. Quick, slip it on! I had to guess your size, and I just know it's wrong."

"Do I get a say in this?"

"How ridiculous! Of course not. Come on! You have to try this on for me."

Kara lifted several layers of fabric off of the mattress, but couldn't for the life of her find the bedspread beneath it. Twin hoisted the fabric into her arms, and the sloping outline of a formal ball gown blocked out large chunks of the sunlight before it was dumped over Kara's head. A gap in the material appeared, and Twin grinned through it as the dress finally settled onto its victim.

When Kara's head was freed from the red fabric, she saw a different person in the mirror. Sure, her hair was still gritty and there was a streak of dirt on her chin, but the dress made her look like a princess despite all of that. It had silver trim on the bodice and hugged her waist, tumbling out from the hips to a long train that pooled around her feet. The fabric clasped at her elbows and her wrists with round silver buttons, while hemmed slits ran down the sleeves and tugged the neckline away from her shoulders.

She brushed her hair back and as she did so, two growing bruises on her neck that were shaped like hands became visible. Twin gasped when she saw them, but Kara cleared her throat and shook her head.

"Please don't ask."

"Are you all right, at least?"

"Yes, I think so. Twin, did you make this dress?" she asked, trying to change the topic.

The girl nodded and began to pin it so that she could better tailor it to Kara's body.

"I wanted to make it green and gold," Twin explained as she worked. "It would have looked great on you, but Blood Gavin told me I wasn't allowed to do that because the other kingdoms would take our national colors as a sign of possession. The thought! I merely wanted the dress to suit you."

"Well, it's stunning nonetheless. Thank you so much."

"This is only the beginning, because we get to go shopping for accessories tomorrow!"

Kara groaned at the thought of shopping as her friend helped pull the gown back over her head.

"Is that—?" Twin stepped toward the mantle, eyes widening as she caught sight of Flick. "Is that a—?"

"Yeah, I can't pronounce it, either."

"What an adorable little thing!" Twin giggled and rubbed her finger on Flick's forehead. He flipped onto his back to play with her fingertip.

"You really are a blessed girl, Kara! You have a gift from the heavens *and* the affection of a royal man!"

"You don't really think—wait, who are you talking about?" Kara paused, catching herself. There was no way Twin could know what Braeden really was.

"Oh I'm an idiot!" Twin slapped a hand over her mouth and set Flick back on the mantle.

"Twin, who are you talking about?"

"No one!"

"Twin!"

"No!"

"Twin!"

"I—" The girl gasped, sat on the bed, and stuffed her face into the yards of fabric lying there in all its pinned, pointy glory.

"You shouldn't—come on, don't do that." Kara tried to pull her friend's head out of the fabric. "Seriously, stop. You must have put a hundred pins in that dress."

"I can't tell you, Kara. I apologize. Blood Gavin would be furious!"

"Wait, are you trying to say that Gavin is interested?"

"Oh, *Bloods*!" Twin threw her face in the pile of cloth and pins again.

"Twin, that has to be a rumor. Even if the political implications of a Blood and the Vagabond weren't important, I'm not interested."

"Not interested?" Twin looked at Kara as if she'd just slapped her. "Not only is he the Blood, but he's a good person. How could you not be attracted to him?"

Kara raised her eyebrows. "Do *you* want Gavin?"

"Every girl in the kingdom wants him!"

"This isn't what I want to talk about right now," Kara said, her face flushing. "I need a bath. Just drop this."

"But there are a dozen rumors about his interest in a certain vagabond. You can't ignore that!"

"I'm the only vagabond."

"Well there you go. Mystery solved!" Twin giggled, Kara apparently catching onto the joke a bit late.

⚒

Kara escaped Twin's pressing conversation about Gavin's rumored affections long enough to duck out to the orchard, but she avoided the lake and chose instead to walk down the rows of apple trees. She passed a tree and did a double-take at its trunk.

Her heart skipped a beat before she recognized Garrett leaning against the tree, watching her with a sidelong glare. She sighed and cursed under her breath.

"Can't you just say hello like a normal person?" she asked.

"I am not a normal person."

"This is true. Why are you here?"

"It's a pleasure to see you as well, Vagabond." He bowed his head in welcome.

"Sorry. It's been a rough day."

"Understandably. Adele wished for me to check on you after Braeden told us of your brush with Carden."

"If Flick hadn't been there, I don't know what would've happened."

"You would likely have died," he said calmly.

Too many sarcastic rebuttals raced through her head for her to choose one, and the appropriate moment came and went without a word. She shook her head and sat beneath an apple tree, leaning against its trunk. Garrett did the same.

"I'm sorry that we couldn't help you," he continued. "We aren't supposed to help you, Kara, remember that. Every time we do, we disobey a direct order from the Council. We can't leave if we're with them. This was one of those times."

"I understand."

"I do have something else to ask you," he said, leaning forward. "Adele told me you consider Hillside to be your home. Is that true?"

"Yes," she said without a pause.

"Has anyone given you a key to the kingdom?" He was motionless, and she suspected he already knew the answer to that question. She shrugged.

"No, but Gavin's been busy. I'm sure he would give me one if I asked."

"Don't make excuses to avoid the truth," he said. "If Hillside was your home, you would have a key."

"Look, I'm sure it's—"

"You're comfortable here, is that fair to say?"

"Yeah, I—"

"They have their secrets, Vagabond, as dark as those of Losse and Kirelm. That you can't see them simply means they involve you."

She didn't have a comeback for that.

"You're comfortable here," he continued, "not because you're welcomed, but because in Hillside you fit in. In Losse and in Kirelm, you're notably different. There, you stand apart. You can sense it and feel it when they interact with you. You were an outcast before you had the chance to speak. But here, in Hillside, few acknowledge your human blood because they can't see it. To confuse that with the comfort of friends is a mistake."

Her stomach twisted. She blushed. The world she thought she understood rocked, and suddenly everything—her heart, her shoulders, her head—was heavier.

"I don't mean to shame you," he said. "It's a natural thing. But you must acknowledge it and push away from that comfort. It's a lie and it's a weakness."

"So where do I go?"

"For now, enjoy your rest in Hillside, but do so as a guest. It's deserved, though your fight is far from over. Find the village once you're rested, and that will serve you until each kingdom feels like home. When that happens, you will have succeeded in all the first Vagabond set out to do."

"Wait, how did you know about the first Vagabond's village?"

"Adele trained him," he reminded her, glancing around the empty orchard. "But I should leave. Braeden will be glad to hear that you're well."

"Punch him for me, will you?"

Garrett laughed and transformed into a hawk, his body shivering and shrinking until tawny feathers covered what had moments before been skin.

Kara thought back to the amulet and the finished map in the satchel sitting on her bed. She would leave them untouched for now, because the moment she put them together, she would know where to go. And as soon as she had the village's location, she would leave—with or without Braeden.

✤CHAPTER TWENTY SEVEN
THE AMBER TEMPLE

Twenty seven days passed without Kara really noticing them, even though she didn't do much of anything while she waited for the Gala to come and for Braeden to return. Flick grew bigger each day, until he was the size of a small cat and could just barely fit in her bag.

She kept her promise, leaving the map and amulet in her satchel, and distracted herself from thinking about the village by training near the lake. The Grimoire taught her to manifest a broadsword from the energy in the air, and she mastered it as the weeks passed. Besides that, the water techniques she'd learned in Losse consumed most of her time, though she practiced those more out of spite than a real willingness to learn.

Twin forced her to withstand one hundred and twelve more pinpricks as she tailored the masterpiece. It was by far the most beautiful thing that Kara had ever worn, and she could never quite stifle a coquettish giggle whenever she saw it.

At the final fitting, she grinned as Twin laced up the last string of the bodice.

"I have a surprise for you," her friend said, voice calm and not as excited as Kara would have expected. After all, the girl had spent hours tailoring the dress. Twin hustled back to a bag of supplies on the bed and pulled out a small present wrapped in brown paper.

"This is the finishing touch and completely selfish," she said. "I just wrapped it to make myself feel better."

"You still shouldn't have," Kara chided, but she smiled as Twin handed her the package. Inside the brown paper was a large black box that held a small silver tiara on a black cushion. The metal coiled and curved in an ornate pattern fitted with startling crystals.

"Twin, tell me you didn't actually buy this! Why would you get me something so nice? You know I'll just break it."

"Just try it on, will you?" Twin muttered. A nervous twitch pricked the corner of her lips, and her gaze shifted from Kara to the floor.

Kara's intuition flared. Something was off.

"Is everything okay?" she asked.

Twin nodded and feigned another smile, but didn't say anything.

Kara eyed Twin for a moment before she lifted the ornate metal work in her fingers. Twin would never hurt her. It was more likely that she was just keeping quiet about where she'd gotten it and who it was really from.

The metal was weightless, like holding a glittering feather made of crystal. Its gems gleamed in the sunlight from the window, drawing her eyes in and out of focus as she lifted the crown to her head.

"No, wait!" Twin said. Her voice dripped with panic, and she snatched the tiara.

"Huh—?"

"I can't be a part of this! It's just wrong!"

"What's going on?"

Twin's body shook. She leaned against a dresser and slid down its face until she hit the floor with a *thump*. Kara sat down as well, watching the tiara as it hung from her friend's thin, trembling fingers.

"I saw Gavin put a curse on the crown," Twin said, her voice shaking as she forced through her words. "Apparently, a servant heard some of your conversation with that muse, Kara. They know you have no intention of staying here. Blood Gavin, he thinks that the other kingdoms won't respect him if you leave. He told me to give this to you, but it will prick you with Hillsidian blood. Gavin would be able to control you."

A row of thin barbs glittered in the crown at this new angle, situated on the very front band of the tiara. Their jagged ends leaned inward to what would have been her brow if she'd worn it, their tips as green as the poisoned spikes on the cuffs Braeden so feared.

Kara held her breath, her chest tightening with the rapid race of her suffocating heartbeat. Garrett's warning resurfaced: *"They have their secrets, as dark as those of Losse and Kirelm. That you can't see them simply means they involve you."*

She leaned her head against the dresser and rubbed her face, her shoulders tensing as she realized the depths of this betrayal.

"The rumors about his liking me?" she asked in a terse whisper. "Did he start those as well?"

"I don't think so. No, I think those were just rumors. It might have given him the idea, though. Oh *Bloods*! Kara, he'll kill me!" Twin shook in violent twitches, her arms and legs inconsolable in her fear. It wasn't an exaggeration.

"I won't let him do that, Twin. You sacrificed everything to tell me this. I owe you."

"Then take me with you when you leave. I don't care where we go, but I can't stay here. Not now."

"I will," Kara promised without hesitation, but a flickering doubt hovered in her mind. This could be a trap. Twin had saved her from the tiara, true, but that could be part of the ploy. She was still a Hillsidian and still loyal to Gavin, and could just tell him where Kara went next. The only way she could really, truly trust her was if Twin became a vagabond.

Kara sighed. She didn't want to doubt Twin. The girl's fear was so real.

"You should head over to your room," she said, standing and offering a hand. "I need to speak with Gavin."

"No! He'll know I told you!"

"He won't," she corrected, winking. "I found it out for myself and chased you out of the room in a thundering rage, remember?"

"Please—!" Twin begged.

"I'll protect you, but Gavin needs to know he can't mess with me. He's gone too far."

"Please don't tell him it was me."

"I won't. Now, will you please get me the hell out of this dress?"

⚜

Once Kara had escaped the ball gown, she grabbed the tiara and its box and charged toward Gavin's study. She wished that Braeden or Adele or Garrett was there to tell her if this was even a good idea, but they weren't. This was hers alone to fix.

The study door and the dead Queen's portrait came into view as she turned around a corner. Blood Lorraine still smiled from her painting, but her eyes were steely in the thin morning light streaming through the windows above. Kara pulled the golden tassel to get Gavin's attention, avoiding the portrait's gaze as much as she could. When no answer came, she rang four more times out of sheer annoyance.

"Vagabond?"

She turned mid-pull to see Richard standing in the hall, his arms crossed. The lines on his face were deeper than when she'd last seen him, and she realized for the first time that she hadn't spoken to him since the Queen was murdered. There was a curious twist to his eyebrows as he examined her.

"Hi, Richard. I need to speak to Gavin. Where is he?"

"I'm not sure, though I would guess he's preparing for the Gala now that it's just a week away. Are you packed and ready?"

"Whether or not I even go depends on my next conversation with Gavin. Where is his room?"

"You can speak with him this evening," Richard said with a smile. He bowed to leave, apparently assuming that ended the matter.

"I need to see Gavin *right* now, Richard."

His smile became a glare. "You're a guest here, Kara. Don't confuse yourself as his equal. He is the Blood and not to be commanded. From what I can tell of my readings, even the first Vagabond always respected that."

"A lot of people tell me what the first Vagabond did or wanted, but these are different times, I'm a different person, and your son has gone too far."

"I'm certain that this is a misunderstanding," Richard said, but the shadows deepened in the bags under his eyes as he spoke. "What has he done?"

"Yes, Kara, please tell us," a voice echoed down the hall from behind Richard. Gavin walked down the hallway, his jaw tense and his expression as cold as his mother's portrait.

She tossed him the black box as he walked closer. Its clasp held tightly as it flew toward him, keeping the cursed tiara inside, but the way his back stiffened as he caught it suggested that he knew what it was without opening the latch.

"I know you only started peace talks because you aren't powerful enough on your own to get revenge for your mother," she said. Both men were quiet. "But the people around you aren't tools. You can't control me or the Grimoire and you never will. Hillside isn't my home, and I won't be returning here after the Gala. See? You didn't need your spies to tell you that."

The color drained from Richard's face. He snapped his head and stared at his son with disgust and a gaping mouth. Gavin furrowed his brows, unapologetic.

"Twin told you?"

"Don't touch her, Gavin. I happen to be smart enough to figure out curses on my own. Hurt her because I found this out and you'll be an even greater coward than I already think you are."

She shoved past him and left the silent Hillsidian royal family in her wake.

Kara retreated to her bedroom only long enough to grab the amulet and the map, pack some clothes, and find Flick. There was no way she could bring herself to wait for Braeden—not in Hillside, not now. She would have to come back for Twin, though; Kara had no idea what was waiting for her in the village and didn't want her friend to get hurt. She grabbed what food had been laid out for her and ran to the waterfall she'd so coveted as a peaceful spot just a few months ago.

She panted and sat down on the boulder near the waterfall, which seemed pathetic after seeing the thundering falls near the Villing Caves. The splash of the cascading rapids drowned out her thoughts, weighed as they were with the hurt and betrayal that made her throat sting. She didn't want to be alone, so she summoned the Grimoire and debated her options. There was the griffin, or maybe the black dragon from Losse. She flipped through the pages, but stopped when she came across the image of a tall, thin wolf with a thick black coat. It stared at her from the drawing as if it could see her. Chills raced down her spine as she read the text.

> Ryn the giant wolf can travel for days without rest. He is the fastest animal ever known to any world and can weave through forests, caves, and rivers alike without hesitation.

"Well, Ryn. I think you'll do just fine," she said. She rubbed her thumb across the drawing's face to summon the creature, and at her touch, a funnel of dust spun from the Grimoire and made the loose outline of a wolf in the air before congealing into the thick hairs of Ryn's black coat.

The wolf lowered its head to examine her with its gray, unblinking gaze, but instead of fear, a wave of relief crested along her shoulders.

She ran a few fingers along its muzzle and scratched its ear. The great, ferocious thing rolled its eyes back in delight before it lay down beside her to rest its giant head on her legs.

She pulled the amulet out of her bag and rubbed Ryn's ear again before she glanced into the cold, murky depths of the black stone. Gray smoke twirled within the amulet, billowing in fitful and violent bursts. It churned, settling only when a thick pillar appeared within the cold gem. The image panned out to show a large hall filled with dozens of similar support columns, and dark shadows lumbered between them. She shuddered.

"In the depths of Ethos, you will find the Amber Temple," a deep voice said in her ear.

The voice oozed into her ear, musty and dark. She wheeled around, but aside from Ryn and Flick, she was alone. The amulet shook in her hand as the voice continued.

"The Amber Temple is guarded by a lyth, a vicious creature to whom you must give this lapis key."

The amulet's smoke twisted into the outline of a cat-like creature the size of a tiger. Its teeth curved over its lips and down to its chin. Two orange eyes glowed from its face.

"Once the lyth lets you pass," the voice went on, "you must enter the temple and face its demons. The shadow demons have no master, and only the hourglass in the center of the chamber can contain them. As long as the grains of sand within it are still, the creatures roam free. When you turn the hourglass, they will be trapped within it once again, and a lichgate will appear. This will take you to the Vagabond's village, where you are needed."

The smoky images dissolved, and the stone became jet black once more. Kara took short, shaky breaths in her excitement. This was it. She was almost to the village.

"Flick." She pulled the little creature to her. He squeaked. "Can you teleport me to the Amber Temple?"

He cocked his head, chirping in his confusion.

"I guess that's not how you work, then." She sighed and set him back in the satchel. "Grimoire?"

The book's pages flipped to a picture of the same pillared hall she'd seen in the amulet. There was no title or text to give her any clues, but there was a map—a real one, with mountains and landmarks. She pulled the satchel over her shoulder.

"Come on, Ryn," she said. The wolf knelt, allowing her to hoist herself onto its back. After two quick, trotting steps, it bolted into the underbrush. She clung to its coat, but it moved with such an even gait that she could have slept without falling off.

They traveled for two days through forests and along steep cliffs that overlooked the sea, only stopping for brief moments to eat or stretch. Kara rarely slept because when she did, she was plagued by nightmares of the demons lurking in the pillars' shadows, just waiting for her to find them.

❦

Kara was lost in a recollected memory of her last dream—which was a murky concoction that had somehow involved Braeden—when Ryn came to a sudden stop.

It was dusk in the thick forest through which they walked, and the sun was setting somewhere beyond the rows of tall pines and oaks. The trees were riddled with dead limbs and leaves that would not relinquish their hold on the branches.

They stood on a wide, abandoned road carpeted with rotting leaves. The canopy thickened ahead and blocked out all light below it, shrouding the distance in a blackness that had no definition or depth. Ryn snarled, watching the shadows, and Kara lit a flame in her hand as she examined the empty trail. The lavender fire didn't dent the darkness before them, but it did usher forth a visitor.

Green light glinted off the air. It curved and twisted until a paw popped from it, hovering over the road without a body. There was a snapping noise, and a creature the size of a tiger jumped from the shimmying light to land on the path's dead leaves.

The creature was the color of ditch slime, and its teeth curved over its lips and down to its chin. Its orange eyes glowed with a light of their own, and it's tail twitched as it looked her over. It growled and walked closer, the noise vibrating in its throat like a chuckle. Ryn leaned back, shoulders hunched to spring.

This had to be the lyth.

"Well, a visitor! It has been many centuries since my last. He was quite delicious." The creature's teeth distorted its voice such that it sounded like it spoke with its mouth full.

Kara tightened her grip on Ryn's coat and sat up straighter. The flame in her palm ignited into a fireball that engulfed her fist.

"I don't want trouble," she said.

"How rude," it replied. "At least that visitor asked me my name. Do you have any manners, girl?"

"Not really."

It licked its lips and laughed another of its rumbling chuckles. "Such a tongue. You should be kinder to me. I am a lyth, after all—a guardian of the Amber Temple. I must assume that's where you're headed. There's no other reason to take this road."

Kara nodded.

"Why do you wish to find it?"

"Why should I tell you?"

"Because I guard the Vagabond's village. If you aren't his successor, I must kill you for knowing where it is."

She bit her tongue and tasted the blood. Her impulse was to tell him off, but with teeth like that, it seemed like a poor choice.

"I'm the Vagabond, and I have to find the village hidden in the temple. My map brought me here and told me you'd let me through."

"How convenient. Why must you find this village?"

"The first Vagabond told me to. There's supposed to be something there that will help me."

He clicked his tongue. "Nothing is learned if one blindly obeys. Still, I have long awaited the next Vagabond. I'll protect these roads once you enter the temple if you show me the key."

"What key?"

The creature narrowed its eyes and sighed. "The lapis map."

She blushed and pulled the blue slab of lapis from her satchel as the lyth brushed away twigs and branches on the road with its front paws, revealing a broken cobblestone path beneath the decay. A square indent the size of her stone map had been cut from the road.

"Come," the lyth beckoned.

She dismounted and took slow steps toward the creature until she was close enough to smell the pungent, rotting odor that consumed its fur. The lapis slab pulled on her hand as she walked closer, its weight leaning toward the gap in the road until she set the blue stone amongst the fragmented cobblestones and dead leaves.

The lapis glowed gold when it settled into its place in the cobblestones. Its light snaked through breaks in the road, kicking up leaves and patches of dirt as it raced away into the heavy shadows ahead of them. The darkness shattered like a broken mirror, dissolving into smoke and blowing away in the breezes of the growing night. The light continued to twist through the smoke, branching like veins through the air until it outlined a building.

The light flared, forcing Kara to cover her eyes. She peered through her fingers when the blinding glare receded and saw a temple with four rounded towers to mark its four corners. A giant dome curved to a point in its center, and its giant bronze doors arched at the top of a few steep steps.

"Tread carefully, keeper," the lyth said with a sneer. It turned and trotted down the road, dissolving into thin air when it walked through the first moonbeam of the night. She shivered.

"Come on, Ryn." She reached up to pat the wolf's neck, and it nudged her shoulder in return. She poked the satchel, where Flick slept, but he didn't wake up. Together, she and her small band walked up the stairs and paused at the door.

Kara twisted the knob until she could push the door open. Inside, rays of the growing moonlight peeked through the glass dome high above, but the light was lost in the room's gloomy depths.

It was exactly the hall the amulet had shown her. Dozens of pillars supported the roof in diagonal rows that had nothing but darkness between them. A pedestal glowed from its place on a raised platform about a hundred yards away, its body carved from rich orange amber. A hole had been cut through its center, and a rounded hourglass glimmered in the open space.

Ryn followed her inside, but dissolved into dust with every step that brought it farther through the doorway. The black ash rose into the temple air while the wolf's back legs continued forward, until Ryn was gone. She cursed as the last grain of his black sand settled at her feet.

Her bag trembled from its place at her side, and she peeked in to see Flick, wide awake and cowering in the corner closest to the door. He trembled and curled his head under his front paws, ignoring her touch when she brushed his back to console him.

The door swung gently closed behind her, the click of the latch echoing through the vast space and announcing her with a boom. The echo continued for several minutes, even as she began her walk toward the pedestal and the hourglass.

She kept to the sparse light as much as she could, shooting sidelong glances into the shadows clinging to the pillars. A huffing breath came from the darkness—a wheezing sigh that made her hair stand on end. She focused her mind on her palm, bending the heat which raced through her veins until a small purple flame erupted in her hand and shed its flickering light over the cracked pillars.

She walked quickly, but the room was still. Quiet. Tense. The shadows between the dark columns grew longer and darker the closer she came to the hourglass.

Feet shuffled along the dirt-covered floor just beyond her vision. Something growled. A sharp screech, like nails on metal, made her jump. Dust lingered in her nose and tickled her sinuses, but she held her breath until the urge to sneeze disappeared. Whatever these things were, they could make noises. She would not, in case they were looking for a reason to attack.

Hot air wafted over the back of her neck in an unnatural stream, but she didn't dare stop or look behind her. She was fifty yards away from the hourglass, now. The scraping became more frequent.

Forty yards—growls bled into grunts.

Thirty yards—the shifting became the swish of creatures pushing one another.

Twenty yards—the defined edges of the hourglass became clearer. All of the sand had pooled in the bottom of the curved glass, which reflected the golden flush of the amber around it. She was close enough, now, that its powerful light illuminated her shaking hands.

Her pulse raced. Breath was unmanageable. Fear told her to run toward the platform, *run!* and she could no longer dominate the impulse. She sprinted for the pedestal.

It was a mistake.

Something roared, and the nearest pillar cracked from the shrill bite of the sound. A fist the size of her head slammed into her ear and sent her flying. Her body fell against a column, and she tumbled onto the hard stone, shielding Flick's satchel with her body. Kara glared into the darkness to see what she'd let free. Her eyes went wide, and she gasped.

The monster was a giant shadow shaped like a massive ape. Its edges blurred into the darkness around it, so that there was no telling where it ended or began. The creature towered over her, hunched on its hands. It had no eyes, but roared and revealed the crooked white daggers that were its teeth. They jutted from every corner of its mouth, piercing its black gums and drawing bright red blood. It snarled and roared again.

Three more shadow demons bled into view from the gloom-drenched pillars, blocking her view of the pedestal. They bellowed. Panic raced through her. Warmth pooled in her hands from the adrenaline and magic, but she'd already drained a good deal of her own energy by summoning a fire without any wood nearby, and there wasn't any water to fuel her Lossian techniques. She was left with only the air, the darkness, and the little energy she had left.

She brought her hands together over her head, focusing on the air as she contorted it into sharp daggers that hovered in the space above her fingers. Ten, then fifty, then a hundred arrows surrounded her like a suit of razor-sharp armor.

Raging heat coursed through her as she focused and bent the air as far as she could. The blades circled, speeding around until they left streaks on the low light as they moved. The blur grew faster and thicker, and all she could see was the rush of sharp air. The demons chorused and chattered, each of them screaming.

The ground trembled. They were coming.

She threw her hands away from her body, a grunt escaping as she released the tension which had kept the blades near to her. The strain snapped from her fingers as the blades flew in every direction. They pummeled through the room, slicing through pillars and demons alike. Arms and heads and chunks of rock fell to the floor. The monsters shrieked, their voices shrill with pain.

Support columns cracked and toppled, forcing her to duck and dart her way around raining blocks of stone. Rivers of the demons' sticky red blood snaked across the tiled floor, the crimson streams the only color in the room besides the orange glow of the hourglass.

A gray hand larger than her head appeared from the shadows and swatted at her like she was a fly, knocking her onto her back. She skidded for a few feet. Another monster leaned over her as she came to a stop. It lunged, its claws ripping her clothes before she could roll out of reach.

Kara pushed herself to her feet and bolted toward the hourglass, throat stinging as she fought for breath, but another demon grabbed her and lifted her to its face. Its claws bit into her arm, the sharp nails ripping apart the skin as the thing clutched her tighter. She screamed in agony as thick lines of her blood ran down to her hands and dripped from her fingers, splattering to the floor. Her feet lashed out on their own, landing a solid kick in what would have been the monster's nose if it'd had a real face.

The shadow demon screamed and dropped her. She rolled across the ground, her arm still stinging from his grip. Blood bubbled from four holes in her arm, evidence of where the creature's nails dug into her. She held the wounds and dodged another demon's hand, trying to ignore the hot rush of pain. There was no time to heal.

This had to end now.

She knelt and set her hands on the floor. The heat from her palms seeped into the tiles, which rippled at her touch. The stone bent to her will, and she sensed poor supports in the ground beneath two of the demons to her right and another to her left.

A smirk spread across her face, the sudden control over life and death dissolving away her fear. A hum droned in her mind, blocking out the demons' snarling and heavy breaths. There was no pain anymore, no feeling: just the rush of life and magic and *power*.

Thick tension pulled on her fingers until it seemed they would fall off from the strain. She yelled like the demons she was fighting, and stronger ripples pulsed through the tile. The ground burst. Gray bricks lodged into the ceiling from the force. Deafening echoes of smashing and shattering rock broke through the hall as the ground disintegrated beneath the three unlucky demons. They screamed and fell into the unending blackness below the temple.

She grinned and glanced around for the next fight, but her smile faded. Her adrenaline dissolved into disbelief, and the power was gone.

Moonlight streamed through the broad dome above, now, brighter than before. The depths of the temple were finally illuminated, though the floors were still shrouded in a deep shadow that no light could ever penetrate. She could now see hundreds of rows of the demons surrounding her from wall to wall, allowing her only the small space in which she fought. They stood motionless, waiting for their turn to attack. They could have overpowered her at any time, but chose not to.

To her, this was life and death; to them, this was a game. She forced a hard swallow as the dread weighed her feet to the floor.

The hourglass waited on its brilliant pedestal, visible through gaps in the only row of demons which stood before it. She groaned, unsure of what else to do, and summoned the broadsword she'd mastered in her time training by Hillside Lake. She focused the air around her into one long blade that clung to her hand like a mist. The tension pulled on her mind, stealing energy and focus she didn't have, but this was her last attempt toward the hourglass.

At least the strain was a distraction from the hopelessness.

A cluster of demons nearest to the door screamed, their roars splitting the tense silence. The crowd surged and fluttered, their cries escalating as a collective frenzy rippled through them. Her adrenaline resurfaced as she prepared for the onslaught.

This is it.

Kara took a deep breath.

But the rows of demons ignored her crouching stance and turned toward the temple doors, which, she could now see through breaks in the monsters, stood open. Moonlight poured in and shed its murky spotlight on a small figure that charged toward her on a flaer. He had dark hair, olive skin, and the glare of someone about to kill something.

Braeden slid off of Rowthe at full speed, running to keep pace until he could get to the first demon on the outer edge of their circle. He jumped, drew his sword, and sliced the beast's head from its shoulders. The crowd bellowed again, but the sound became indignant hollers against the newcomer who was clearly cheating.

"Go!" he yelled.

Smog engulfed him. His skin faded to gray. The Stelian Heir erupted in black fire, and when he twisted around, his red eyes glowed from the temple shadows. He'd let his daru take over. A demon fell on its hands in front of him and roared into his face, sending a trail of saliva across him. But he laughed and roared back, lost to the fury and madness, before he erupted into even larger, darker flames.

Kara turned to the row of demons between her and the hourglass. Her skin prickled like she, too, was on fire, but the adrenaline contrastingly iced her veins. Her mind was calm and still, despite the chaos. She twirled the sword she'd created from the air and ran toward the creatures.

Her arms moved without instruction. She didn't watch the beasts as they fell around her or stop to guess what she was doing. The sword swung and sliced and spun, catapulting droplets of demon blood against her face in its torrent. She stopped only when she stood at the first step of the pedestal, her body and mind and satchel still all somehow in one piece.

Her ears rang, blocking out all sound but her breath. She walked up the stairs of the platform and scanned the hourglass as it hung, suspended, in the carved hole of the amber pedestal, reflecting the orange glow along its glass. The silver grains of sand waited at the bottom, where they'd lain useless for a thousand years.

The frosted glass stung her, cold as ice, when she grabbed it, but the hourglass didn't budge. She pushed harder, trying to turn it over.

Bit by bit, the hourglass inched over on its axis, hardly moving even after she threw all her weight against it. The grains of sand shifted, sliding along the glass without falling into the other chamber.

Movement in the corner of her eye drew her attention. The noise of the battle flooded her ears in a sudden rush, and sweat dripped along her nose. The sand shifted farther. Demons screeched, glaring at her.

A stampede began. They raced closer, galloping on all fours to stop her, to rip her to shreds. Braeden was nowhere to be seen.

She threw the last ounce of her strength into her chore, yelling and cursing at the old hinges until finally, with one last shove, the first grain of sand fell through the opening. It plopped without a sound onto the new bottom of the hourglass.

The demons screamed, some close enough that their hot breath fogged against her arms, but they dissolved into smoke as they ran. Light erupted from the amber pedestal and engulfed the room. The cold sting of the glass disappeared from beneath her fingers, and all sound, even the race of her heartbeat in her ear, faded away. There was nothing to smell, nothing to hear, and nothing to see in this ocean of light. The amulet had lied. No lichgate appeared, and Kara would have to face whatever was coming next alone.

❦CHAPTER TWENTY EIGHT
DISCOVERY

The sound of laughter came first through the intense light. It was the chorus of a studio audience, though occasionally Kara could hear the louder chuckles of two real people who reacted to a mumbling TV host. She smelled popcorn. Pizza. Leather from the sofa on which her dad had spent too much money.

She grinned. It was movie night at the Tallahassee house.

Colors bled from the white light around her, until the memory was visible and real and solid. Her mom and dad sat on the couch, watching television and giggling at the show's bad jokes. She had no idea what was on, but she didn't care. There they were, smiling as if the last year had never happened.

Kara laughed, but choked on a sob. She was elated and heartbroken and torn. They were so *real.*

"I'm impressed," a nearby voice said.

The Vagabond stood beside her, nothing but gray wisps of light. As she watched, though, he solidified. The shadows under his hood lengthened until he reached for it and pulled it back with two solid hands, revealing his weathered face. He was younger than she'd imagined, probably thirty, and had a scar on his cheek, thick blond hair, and dark eyes.

"Where are we?" she asked.

"Your mind. I know that you have often wondered what your most influential memory could be. Well, this is it. You realized how much you loved your parents on this night without ever fully understanding why. This is when you told yourself that you would love them forever, no matter what happened."

"Why are you showing me this?"

He shook his head. "I'm not showing you anything. You're stuck here. You can't leave this memory behind. This is your past, one that you'll never relive, and you can never succeed as the Vagabond until you accept that your family is gone. You must admit that they are dead."

She bit her lip and glanced back to the couch, her body tense, mind racing. Her mom and dad laughed again at the television, much louder than the audience. Her mom stuck a piece of popcorn up her dad's nose and giggled when he snorted it back onto her. Kara laughed through the sting in her throat.

She walked in front of them, blocking their view, but they looked through her. This was a memory. They weren't real. She stifled the tears that wanted so badly to be freed and wrapped them both into a tight hug, but neither reacted. The Vagabond cleared his throat.

"I promise that your father will be freed from the isen in the natural course of things, but only if you continue on as the Vagabond. Can you let them both go?"

She sat on the table in front of them and sighed, hanging her head in defeat.

"No," she said. "They're my family. I'd do anything to protect them, and since I failed at that I'll settle for the next best thing."

"Revenge?"

She scowled at the floor without answering. He reached out a hand, suddenly beside her.

"I need to show you something," he said. "I've seen your memory, so I feel you deserve to see mine."

She stared at his palm, and her eyes glossed over. It was difficult to move. Her rear was rooted to the table, and as much as she wanted to look back at her parents, she was unable to turn her head. Her hand inched out to the Vagabond's until the touch of his cold skin made her shiver.

The room flashed with another wave of white light. Her arms were pulled behind her. Spikes dug into her wrists, and she yelled in surprise and pain. Hot blood trickled into her palms. The room from her nightmare blinked into view. The world was clear and vivid, as her memory had been just moments before—there were no wisps, only vibrant detail.

A Kirelm soldier brought in Helen, the stunning woman with dark brown skin. She was limp in his arms, and bright red blood flowed in thin creeks down to her bare feet as she was tossed onto the floor like garbage.

Kara leaned nearer, living through the Vagabond's eyes and unable to control her movement. Helen looked over and moved her lips, but no words came out. Dozens more yakona—Hillsidians, Ayavelians, Kirelms, and Lossians alike—were dumped into the room in a similar manner. They moaned in pain and hung their heads, arms chained behind their backs.

The Kirelm Blood marched down the stairs from his throne, unsheathing his Sartori before he lifted Kara's chin with its poisoned tip.

"You offered them freedom, Vagabond," he said, "but lies and heresy lead to death. None should have the power you bestowed upon these strangers, these enemies of the yakona crowns. Your reign over the yakona people will end here, tonight!"

"Helen," Kara whispered to the girl, wishing with all her might that she could brush back the bloody hair from the flawless face.

"My love," she whispered back.

"I'm so sorry. I did this. I failed you," Kara said. The Vagabond's sorry flooded her heart with love for the stranger.

"I forgive you," Helen answered. "And I will wait for you."

Kara tried to speak, to lie and say that everything would be all right, but several guards grabbed her shoulders and pulled her away. They seized the roots of her hair and yanked her head back as she fought and resisted, so that her neck was exposed. The Blood walked closer.

"We make examples of traitors," the Kirelm Blood said. His eyes darted over her once and he scowled before he lifted his Sartori to her cheek and twisted the blade. It drew blood and seared her as the blade's poison bubbled and hissed in the wound. The agony stung and tore apart the veins in her cheek, but she refused to scream.

The Blood walked over to Helen and rested his sword on her throat. The girl's lips trembled. Horror settled on her face. Her chest rose and fell, her neck tensed against the blade as the Blood hesitated over his prey.

"You have polluted our world, Vagabond. You have ignited millennia-old tensions that will fester into war. Therefore, it's a given that you will die tonight. I can promise you that. But I want the world to know where your heart has truly been all this time—with the collective, or with yourself. You must make a choice. " He pressed the sword harder against Helen's skin. It sizzled. She whimpered.

"You must choose between your lover and your people. Whichever you choose, I will free. If you say nothing, I will rid Ourea of your kind completely, as it should be. Make your choice."

Kara snapped her head toward the other vagabonds, but they didn't look up from the floor. Her throat closed in her debate, making breath impossible. She glanced from her vagabonds to Helen, whose face was tense and wrinkled with fear as she bit her lip to keep the tears at bay.

"You're running out of time, Vagabond," the Blood said.

"Please, just take me. Let them all go, just take me."

"That wasn't one of your choices."

He pressed the flat of the blade harder against Helen's skin. The other vagabonds hung their heads, slouching deeper toward the floor as they accepted their fate. They knew what would become of them.

"It's as I thought," said the Blood. "You aren't a leader. You can't make difficult choices. Thus, I must make them for you." He pressed the sword closer to Helen's neck and drew a line of blood. Helen screamed and smoke from her burning skin billowed around her face. He lifted the sword and dug it into her side, beneath her arm. Her eyes went wide. She whimpered once before the life left her open eyes.

"No!" Kara shrieked. She forced her way to her feet, fighting the guards through the pain of the spiked shackles and the hissing wound on her face. One of them leveled her to the floor with a quick jab to her head.

Something pulled on the pit of her stomach and dragged her out of the Vagabond's memory. A figure wrapped its white, wispy arms around her, locking her in place as she continued to twist and fight. She opened her eyes to a dark world and floated in the nothingness, her hair weightless around her face.

"Kara, be calm."

She looked over her shoulder to see the Vagabond, his body nothing but wisps once more. The hood shrouded his face, but she was close enough to see the tortured wrinkles that contorted the corners of his eyes. He released her when she stopped fighting.

"I am imperfect," he said. "That was the moment I realized, too late, what it truly meant to be the Vagabond. I was unfocused. In my love for Helen, I lost sight of my purpose."

"How can you forgive Kirelm for what they did? How could you possibly care about yakona anymore?" she screamed at him, the rage from witnessing the ruthless murder still pulsing through her body, but the Vagabond's voice calmed her when he finally spoke.

"Yours is a different time from mine. Blood Ithone didn't kill my Helen, nor did his people kill my vagabonds. I won't forsake the peace of Ourea for the misguided hatred of a few."

"I—" She forced herself to swallow, and her heart settled. She hated his words, but he was right.

"You can't hate all isen because Deidre stole your father's soul. You can't hate yourself because of the accident that took your mother."

She shook her head. "So you *did* die in Kirelm. That's why you didn't tell me when I was there, because you knew I would have a prejudice."

"Blood Morden, the Kirelm Blood of my time, didn't kill me. He killed my people, but he didn't kill me."

"Then how—?"

"I asked my mentor, an isen named Stone, to seal my soul in the Grimoire. That way, I might be better prepared to help the next Vagabond learn from my mistakes. No one killed me. I sacrificed myself."

"But," Kara stuttered. "But Helen told you she would wait for you in the next life."

"Yes," he said, his voice almost too soft to hear. "But my task isn't yet done. I chose the Vagabond's duty, even though I didn't understand what that truly meant until I lost everything. If my spirit is ever freed, I hope to find her waiting still."

Kara covered her mouth and looked away, unable to process what he'd said. He'd chosen an eternity of slavery to the Grimoire over the woman he had loved and failed.

"Forgive yourself," he said. "Forgive Deidre. Focus on uniting the yakona kingdoms and know that your father will be freed without your obsessing over revenge."

He held out his palm and nodded toward her locket. She rubbed the golden oval on her neck with her thumb and glanced at the scarred groves on his fingers.

Her mom's face after the crash flooded her mind: the glass, the torn metal, the blood. Her dad's corpse on the floor of the rental house snapped into focus. She took a deep breath and shook her head, but the memories twisted in her mind until she unclasped the locket from around her neck. Then, there was peace.

She dropped the locket in his outstretched hand.

Light flared through the darkness once more. All feeling was gone from her fingers and her face, but she surprisingly did not care.

Sunlight trickled through Kara's eyelids, making the skin glow orange. She batted her eyes open, wiping away the stinging surge of morning light as it hit her through a window nearby.

Across from her was a stone sarcophagus, its lid carved in the likeness of the Vagabond without his hood. His hands were crossed over his chest, and enclosed in his stone palm was the tip of a small, golden locket.

It wasn't until she slunk against the coffin that she saw the black lump of Braeden's boot sticking out from around the corner. He lay on the ground, his skin gray and smoking in his natural, Stelian form, and he mumbled in his sleep.

She sighed with relief and moved to sit beside him, unafraid. A wave of exhaustion flooded over her. Everything, right down to her toes and fingers, ached. A tired impulse made her curl against him and close her eyes. After a short while, the only sensation was the rise and fall of his chest with each deep breath. Not long after that, she was fast asleep, and the world faded away completely.

❦CHAPTER TWENTY NINE
TENSIONS

Braeden woke in a tomb, his last memory nothing but a flare of light. The shadow demons had dissolved into the brightness as it engulfed everything. Now, he faced a coffin laid out in a stone room with a single, square window. Light flooded the room in sporadic rays, illuminating bits of the floor and leaving the rest in shadow. He clenched his fist and shifted into his Hillsidian form, pushing his back against the wall. He stopped when his hand brushed someone else's soft, warm skin.

Kara lay beside him, curled on her side and cuddled close enough that her cheek pressed against his leg. She murmured something and slid her hand under her head when he moved. A row of deep gouges in her bloodstained arm became visible. The wounds had scabbed around the edges but were still red in the center.

A breath caught in his throat, and he wrapped his fingers around her arm, already forgetting the coffin and stone tomb. Heat pooled in his hands as he focused what energy he could spare on the bloody scrapes, and it wasn't long until her skin glowed white where he touched her. The broken blood vessels and bruises began to blur and heal, slowly closing up the gaping holes. She whimpered. He held his breath, waiting, but she didn't wake up.

Four round scars, each just one shade lighter than her skin, dotted her arm. He rubbed one, wondering if he should wake her or just let her sleep, but something glimmered from across the room and caught his eye as he debated.

Her satchel lay on its side by the sarcophagus, its flap open. Flick's tail peeked out from a corner of the bag, which moved up and down with the small animal's steady breaths. The Stelian amulet was half-hidden beneath the furry creature's bushy tail, its black stone glinting in the muted sunlight.

Braeden walked over and knelt beside the amulet before he could question himself, his fingers hovering, uncertain, as he deliberated whether or not he wanted to know what the stone would reveal. Carden's words haunted him. *"Look into her eyes as the light fades. Once she's dead, look down to the stone to see the only world that wants you."*

His fingers twitched where they hovered. It didn't matter how much he'd trained with Adele or how far he'd come in his ability to control himself — if the amulet told him that he belonged at the Stele, it meant that he had accomplished nothing.

He grabbed it.

Gray smoke bubbled and twisted from the black depths of the stone, fueled by his touch. It thickened, pooling in dark layers until the throne room of the Stele appeared in the haze.

His jaw tightened. He dropped the amulet, letting it fall with a clatter on the stone floor instead of hurling it through the glass window like he wanted to. He stood in a frustrated huff and ran his hands through his hair, glancing back to where Kara slept on the floor. He sighed in defeat. No matter how much he fought it, the Stele chased him. It would never let him go.

He noticed a single door at the end of a short hallway and pushed through it into the sunny day outside. A set of stone stairs led to a paved courtyard, which was lined with a thick forest. Small, paved walking paths split and wound from the clearing into the woods, and a few cottages lined the intersections. Each stone-faced house was thatched with a straw roof and had a smattering of glass windows.

The village was nestled in a valley, and mountains scraped the sky in every direction. There were no weeds or cracks in the stone, and nothing had collapsed or rotted in the thousand years it had been abandoned. It was as if time had left the Vagabond's small world alone.

A three-story house stood at the other end of the courtyard, directly across from the tomb. Its porch wrapped around to the back of the mansion, and large, imperfect stones covered any part of the house that wasn't a door or a large window. A rocking chair on the porch moved on its own, swaying back and forth even though the trees were calm and still.

This is it. This is the Vagabond's village. Adele didn't do it justice with her description.

Braeden sat on the first step of the tomb's stairs. It wouldn't be right to explore without Kara. This was her home to discover.

His mind drifted back to the amulet, and his stomach churned with self-loathing. He belonged with Carden, even after everything he'd done to escape that fate. Anger and frustration boiled along his skin, like steam. He took shaky breaths until the heat faded and he regained control of himself, but a buzzing sound continued in his ear even after his head cleared.

His fingers reached into his pocket and fiddled with a small talisman before he realized that he'd touched it. There was still dirt on it from when he'd dug it back up after its twelve years of isolation, and he pulled it out without really looking at it. His eyes glossed over.

"You kept the key to the Stele?" The memory of Adele's revolted expression made him cringe.

He sighed and hung his head in shame, rubbing his temples. He hadn't kept it; he'd buried it by his waterfall in Hillside and left it, forgotten it.

"But you didn't destroy it, Braeden. That is all that matters."

He flipped it over in his hand. No, he hadn't. He'd never unearthed it again to try.

The small, black charm had been carved into the likeness of the Stele's coat of arms. It fit in his palm, its black jade thorns interwoven in a small square. Though it had nothing to do with Carden's hold over him, keeping it confirmed what he subconsciously knew: someday, he would go back.

The buzzing in his ear grew louder, snapping him from his thoughts. The noise was like a fly droning just out of reach: incessant and annoying. It was a sensation that had only ever plagued him whenever Carden was near, but he ignored it. There wasn't a doubt in his mind that this time, it was just severe and unyielding guilt.

"Why do you fight?" Adele had asked him once during a match, moments before she cracked the hilt of her sword over his head and sent him to his knees. He hadn't been paying attention to her like he should have; he'd been focused on the question. The first Vagabond had asked him that, too, when a possessed Kara had denied him the freedom he'd dreamed of for over a decade.

He'd always fought out of instinct and the fear of helplessness, but in his training with Adele, he'd thought of Kara: how the pulse in her neck had raced beneath his hands; how the life in her eyes flickered as she'd tried to choke out his name. The disgraceful rage that fueled him smoldered in his chest again, but he quelled it. It was easier to do, now.

"If you focus on your reason for enduring the pain, you will control the rage," Adele had often said as they trained.

The muse would beat him within an inch of his life, always gritting her teeth in annoyance when he let the daru consume him. Her tests were attempts to see how long he could withstand the pain and still control himself. He'd never passed. He hadn't finished training.

Kara was his escape from the daru. He would remember how clear her gray eyes were or how her hair always became honey-colored in the sun, and that would clear his mind. When she laughed, her face lit up and glowed with the sound. When she was petrified, she blinked a lot.

To the Bloods, she was a weapon, expendable when weighed against the lives of their people. But to him, her life and freedom meant more than even he could admit.

"Braeden?"

He shoved the talisman back into his pocket in what he hoped was a subtle movement and spun around, grinning when he saw her standing in the doorway. Her hair was a mess, frizzled and lopsided, and she patted it in a failed attempt to tame the tangles. She rubbed her eyes and adjusted the satchel on her shoulder before settling in beside him and looking out over the village.

"It's beautiful," she whispered.

"Yeah," he agreed, but he didn't look at the village until after he spoke. She rubbed the now-healed scars on her bicep with an absent look over to the mansion.

"Do you think that's the Vagabond's old house?"

"Probably. How are you feeling?"

"Better. I guess you healed me?"

"Yes."

"Thanks. And thank you for finding me. If you hadn't…" She trailed off and examined her hands, no doubt as a distraction from thinking of what exactly would have happened to her.

"Someone has to keep you out of trouble."

She laughed. He reached out and lifted her chin with a playful twist of his hand, but once he touched her, he didn't want to let go.

He'd meant to continue talking, to keep her laughing, but he forgot what he was going to say. Instead, he reached a thumb to her cheek without pausing to think about whether or not she would push him away.

She didn't.

The corner of her lip twitched into a smile, so he leaned forward and pulled her gently closer. He searched her face, looking for any hint that she didn't want him to do what he was about to do, but she closed the final inch between them and brushed his lips with hers. He held the back of her head and closed his eyes, grateful that she didn't flinch at his touch anymore.

She pulled away too soon with an unhappy breath and glared at the courtyard, avoiding his gaze. He bit his cheek and looked away, trying to figure out what he'd done wrong.

"I'm confused," he admitted.

She grinned. "No, I liked it. It's just that we can never happen. I mean, we're not even the same species."

"I never realized you were such a purist."

"Not what I meant." She laughed, but the smile quickly faded. "Braeden, we're going to get each other killed."

He sighed with mock relief. "If that is your biggest worry, then I can live with it. Some things are worth dying for."

"C'mon, Braeden, be serious," she chided, her voice quiet. She scooted closer to him and leaned her head on his shoulder, but he lifted her chin so that she had to look him in the eye.

"I wasn't joking."

A thought flickered across his mind and he paused before he continued, fearful of the answer.

"Are you still afraid of me, Kara?"

"No."

He took a deep breath and wrapped his arm around her shoulder.

"I forgive you for the incident with Carden," she said. "And I know why you left to train with Adele. I'm not angry, but it would be hard for me to live with myself if I got you killed. That's what happens to the people vagabonds care about. They die."

"You don't have to worry about me." He winked, weaseling a smile out of her.

She leaned into him, and in that moment, his mind went blank. The buzzing in his ear disappeared, and he was, for just one second, *happy*.

But that's the trouble with moments—they end. Kara shifted her weight and when she did, the buzzing returned in his ear with a vengeance. He became suddenly aware of the talisman in his pocket, and the amulet's smoky image of the Stele churned in his mind. Guilt twisted in his chest.

Kara's smile faded as she looked him over. "What's wrong?"

"I…" He trailed off as the last of her grin disappeared.

He wanted to tell her about the amulet, about the talisman, about the buzzing in his ear and the shame, but the words died on his lips. She looked him over and frowned, but he forced a smile and tucked a loose lock of her hair behind her ear.

"We should explore."

Her eyes narrowed, but she stood after a moment and seemed to accept that he wasn't going to tell her the truth.

"We can start with the mansion, I guess," she suggested, pursing her lips.

"That works for me."

He pushed himself to his feet and hurried down the stairs ahead of her, walking so quickly that he crossed the courtyard and walked up the steps of the mansion after just a few minutes. The wooden steps bent beneath his feet, but withstood his weight as he moved toward the door beside the still-swinging rocking chair.

He opened the door, but let Kara through first. He peered over her head as she hovered at the threshold, examining the mansion's foyer. The first floor hallway had only two doors: the first, on the left of the stairwell, had been left open to reveal the long wooden table and plush chairs of a war room; the second, to their right, was closed and had no handle. Its only décor was a small indent of the clover symbol in the center panel. A broad staircase consumed most of the entry and led up to an open hallway on the second floor, where a set of mahogany double-doors with thin silver handles sat at the top of the stairs.

Braeden walked into the mansion and stopped at the foot of the staircase, looking up to the second floor and its dark wooden doors that seemed to stretch farther away the longer he looked at them. The pit of his stomach tightened as he debated what could be behind them, certain that she would choose that room first, but Kara walked to the door without a knob and ran a finger over the small Grimoire symbol etched into its wood.

"Wait a minute," he said. "The first room you choose in a house full of doors is the one without a handle?"

She laughed. "C'mon. What else were you expecting? If I always took the easy way, I wouldn't be here."

❈CHAPTER THIRTY
THE GRIMOIRES

Kara glanced once over her shoulder at Braeden, who grinned and crossed his arms as he waited for her to open the only door in the Vagabond's mansion without a doorknob. She lifted the chain from around her neck and waited for her heart to pang as she remembered the locket was gone, but nothing happened: no fear, no sadness, no memories.

She slipped the Grimoire clover into the wood's engraved indent. The door melted around itself at her touch, and the weight of her pendant returned to the chain around her neck. Light burned from the hallway behind them, illuminating the small, empty room on the other side of the door. Its walls were bare, and a simple gray tapestry hung across the way, billowing in a weak draft that followed them as they walked in. She crossed to the tapestry and pulled it back, gasping when she caught sight of the next room. Braeden chuckled and shook his head in disbelief.

Beyond the plain, empty room was another, octagonal chamber filled with gold, chests, and weapons.

A window in the angled ceiling allowed beams of sunshine into the chamber. The light glinted off of the gold and steel and other glittering treasures in the room. Piles of gold bars, nuggets, and coins lay about the many corners. Chests filled with strings of pearls and crowns lay open, spewing their contents onto the floor nearby. There were even a few trunks of clothes. A black silk dress had been laid across one of these chests, as if someone had chosen the gown but left it behind on accident.

"This is incredible," Braeden said. "If you still want to go to the Gala, this room will make choosing the Bloods' gifts easier."

"Oh I'm going," she said. "We've gone through too much to miss it. I'm just not sure whether or not they've been good enough for presents."

He grinned and sat down beside a chest filled with swords, daggers, and other assorted sharp things, frowning as he rifled through it.

"This isn't how you store weapons," he grumbled. "It's disgraceful."

"They're yours to fix as you please, then."

He smiled and turned back to the piles of steel, biting his cheek as he focused. She glanced around the treasure chamber, but the glittering jewels just reminded her of the crystals on the cursed tiara in Hillside. She took a deep breath and headed back toward the mansion's foyer.

The stairwell drew her toward it once she walked through the treasure chamber's door-less frame and back out into the hallway. She took the carpeted stairs one at a time until she reached the vast double doors and paused, one hand resting on each of the handles. The latches clicked under her thumbs and she pushed them open to reveal a library.

It reminded her of the library where she'd found the Grimoire, really: shelves filled with thick, leather-bound books lined every wall, but at least there were doors this time. A wide oak desk with clawed bronze feet stood beneath a tall window, and a small shelf just high enough to reach the windowsill rested against the wall behind the desk. It was filled with dozens of crimson tomes that looked identical to each other—and to her Grimoire.

She pulled one from the shelf, horror inching into her chest as she examined a small clover pendant embedded in the fused, silver vines that wrapped around the book. These Grimoires were flawless and new, and unlike hers, they had no rips or tears in them.

"There are a hundred Grimoires on that bookshelf," the Vagabond said in her ear.

He stood suddenly beside her, his body once again nothing but white and gray wisps of light.

She stepped back. "I don't—I—is this the unfinished project you were talking about, Vagabond?"

"One of them. Each of these Grimoires is as powerful as yours, with a few exceptions. This is what you came for, Kara. I wanted to give my vagabonds the same power I carried, but I was too late. If you're to succeed, you must spread the Grimoire's knowledge and its power, as I was about to."

"Are you kidding?" she demanded.

He didn't answer.

"Making other vagabonds is what made the Bloods fear you! It's the reason every vagabond was murdered! You didn't learn anything!"

"The night I watched my people die was the worst of my life, Kara," he said, obviously hurt. "Of course I learned from it. But everything worth doing comes with a risk. They knew that they might die, but chose to stay by me anyway.

"That is what your friends Twin and Braeden both lack: the freedom of choice. You can't trust a yakona with the blood loyalty. Whether or not they *want* to help you, they can be controlled. They can betray you. You will fail if you don't have free yakona whom you can trust."

"I won't," she said, shaking her head. "Maybe you can't see it, but creating vagabonds is what made you a threat. The drenowith admitted it. Your own memory proved it. So yeah, if I create more vagabonds, I'll definitely be killed."

"But you *must* create free vagabonds. You're already a threat! If your allies aren't free, the Bloods will find a way to control you."

"I don't *have* to do anything. Obeying you even though I think it's wrong will make me no better than a yakona with a blood loyalty!"

The Vagabond snapped his head back, and for several minutes, the room was silent.

"I've seen far more than you have," he finally said. "I should hope that you would employ the lessons I've gathered from my failures. You'll take your own road, Kara, but please know that I only want you to succeed."

"I know. But even for all the pages in the Grimoire, you haven't seen everything. I think you're wrong about this."

"Then I'll wait to see where this takes you," he said with a sigh. "I know you rely on Braeden, but he is just as susceptible to his blood loyalty as any other yakona. You've already seen that. He will not always protect you, even when he wants to. If you don't get him killed, he will likely kill you."

"That won't happen." She shook her head, as if doing so hard enough would make it true.

"Please trust me," he said. "Yes, I failed, but not because I created vagabonds. It was because I didn't offer them the same power which I possessed. I kept it for myself, afraid that they would misuse it. I didn't trust them and I should have. *That* was my mistake."

"I'm sorry, but you're wrong. I trust Braeden and I trust Twin. Twin defied an order from her Blood to protect me."

"Are you certain?"

Kara paused, Twin's scared face flashing across her mind. A familiar, flickering doubt came with it: that the tiara was all a ploy to learn where the village was. If Twin learned its location without becoming a vagabond, Gavin could force her to tell him the next time he was close.

"Yes," Kara finally said. "Yakona are stronger than you think."

A cloud parted, and light shoved its way into the room. The library shifted and brightened, animating the Vagabond's face with its sunbeams. His lips were twisted in a smirk, but his face was tensed and wrinkled with worry.

"I hope you're right, then," he said.

"Me, too."

"We will find out soon enough."

The flickering wisps that made up his outline began to fade, each twisting out of its proper shape as it dissolved into the air until he was gone.

Kara looked again around the library before she walked into the hall and closed the great, wooden double doors. An ornate brass key sat in the lock, now, new and glimmering. It was definitely not there when she walked in. She turned it, locking the library doors, and slid the key into her satchel before trotting down the stairs and out onto the porch.

She took a deep breath of the valley's crisp air and glanced out over the courtyard. The rocking chair creaked beside her, moving slowly back and forth in a lazy way. She watched it for a moment before she sat in the seat and leaned back. The rocking stopped. She set her feet on the railing and crossed her arms, unsure of what else to do.

"I have a question," Braeden said, appearing in the doorway.

"That's nice," she muttered, closing her eyes.

He leaned against the railing across from her and nudged her toes to get her attention. She cocked an eyebrow and peeked through just one eye.

"Why did you rush over here alone when I told you that I'd come with you? All you had to do was wait a while longer."

She sighed and examined her fingernails. "Gavin tried to trick me into wearing a tiara that was tainted with Hillsidian blood so that he could control me. I didn't want to stay in Hillside after that."

Braeden bit his cheek and glared at her with unfocused eyes. The sun shifted so that half his face was hidden in a shadow. Whatever he was thinking, wherever his mind had gone, it was dark. He snapped awake with a sharp breath and rapped the railing with his knuckle.

"He isn't ready to rule," he said, shaking his head. "It would be understandable if you didn't attend the Gala next week. I hope you know that."

"So you know when the Gala is? And where?"

"You would be surprised how much the muses know. They told me where to find you, even."

"Hmm," she muttered, unsurprised. Her thoughts drifted back to the Gala. "I actually really want to go."

"Why?" Braeden asked.

"The Vagabond showed me his most important memory. Kirelms killed the love of his life, but he still wants to help the yakona unite. He really wants peace. He forgave them, and I want to forgive Gavin. Ourea is all I have left anymore. I want to make it safe. If I'm not at the Gala, we'll lose the momentum we've built thus far."

"You've done more than enough as the Vagabond," he said. "But if you want to go, then we will go."

She smiled and her grin spread to his face as well. His eyes lit up, the darkness in them dissolving.

"So what do we do next?" he asked.

"Relax."

"Just relax? Sit and do nothing? How boring."

"My, how the tides have turned," she said, grinning. "But yes, I think we should enjoy this quiet time while we have it."

"You look exhausted." His voice softened. "Did you find something up there on the second floor?"

She chewed her lip and watched a robin—at least, she thought it was a robin—duck through a line of trees by one of the cottages lining the courtyard.

"The Vagabond made more Grimoires. He wants me to create vagabonds to go with them."

"But making vagabonds was what upset the Bloods in the first place. What is he thinking?" Braeden rubbed his neck, apparently just as confused as she was.

"He doesn't believe that's why the Bloods really feared him, I guess." She sighed. "But he's wrong. I won't do it."

"How did he take that?"

"I don't really care."

Kara sat and listened to the summer day. Birds chirped, and the wind rolled off the mountain, carrying a sweet, biting chill and the smell of snow from the distant summits.

"I've never been so content to stay in one spot before," Braeden said. "If we get too comfortable, we might miss the Gala and let the world fend for itself."

Kara wanted to reply with something sarcastic, but the weight of what was ahead distracted her. The Gala was a great start, but it was just the first step on a long road. Gavin wanted a war with the Stele, and if the treaty with the other kingdoms was signed, he would have it.

She thought of Twin and Adele and Garrett and Braeden and wondered how many of the people she still had in the world would survive. After all, she didn't quite have the best track record with that sort of thing.

The warm summer took over. A war was coming. There was no stopping that, so she might as well enjoy herself until it found her.

❦EPILOGUE
THE ISEN

Deidre knelt behind a tree and looked out over a sparse meadow lit by what pale light the moon could offer. The field's tall grasses reflected moonlight and bent in a quiet wind she couldn't feel. She was very early.

A tall man dragged a young Ayavelian woman into the meadow and glanced around. Deidre ducked behind a tree and listened. She didn't have to watch to know who it was, since she could recognize the man's thin blond beard and sharp glare anywhere: it was Niccoli, master of the most powerful isen guild in Ourea. Deidre had no idea who the young woman was, so she held her breath and listened.

The girl whimpered. "Please, let me go!"

"Do be quiet," Niccoli said, his baritone threaded with the Russian accent he'd never tried to shake. His syllables rolled together.

"I'll never tell anyone so long as I live!" She sobbed.

"No, you will not," he agreed. "However, I must know how you came to discover such a thing." His voice echoed, louder now that he thought that he was alone with the girl.

Deidre smirked. *Yes, Niccoli. Let me hear what she knows.*

"I—I—" The Ayavelian sniveled and lost her voice. A bone cracked. The girl screamed.

"Tell me!" Niccoli said with a snarl.

The girl gasped through her tears. She cried so hard that her words were almost inaudible when she did finally manage to answer him.

"A guard followed Blood Aislynn the last time she came to visit you. He was worried that you would kill her, that you had tricked her into coming to you, but then she kissed you. He ran away and told me, unsure of what else to do."

Deidre's stomach churned with betrayal and revulsion. Niccoli was the master of the most feared isen guild in any world—*her* master—and he'd snuck away in the night to woo a yakona Blood! He'd had the power of an entire nation in the palm of his hand and let it walk away more than once from the sound of it.

"I see," he said.

Deidre peered around the tree, taking care to press herself as close to it as possible. Niccoli knelt over the girl, who lay curled around herself on the ground, her arm bent backward from his torture.

"Is there more?" he asked, his voice gentle now.

Deidre rolled her eyes. He was just playing with his food at this point. He wanted the girl as confused and frightened as possible when he stole her soul. The high was more powerful that way. She did it all the time.

"It has been an exciting summer for the kingdoms," he said over the girl's sobbing. "I've heard many rumors."

No, you heard news from me! Deidre seethed, and her teeth clinched in annoyance. He didn't listen to rumors.

"I heard the Vagabond has returned," he continued, brushing the hair out of the girl's eye. "A human by the name of Magari."

The girl nodded. "Yes, but she's safe and strong. You leave her alone. She'll give you hell if you go near her. We all will."

Deidre slipped back behind the tree, reminded of her failed attempt to steal the Magari girl's soul.

"Well, you won't give me trouble, little one," he said, laughing. "But I suspect the rest will. I ask only because her name is familiar. Now, I have just one more question for you. Who is this guard that discovered me?"

"No! He is my brother! Please leave him be, please—" Something else snapped. The girl shrieked.

"Tell me his name."

"Never!"

"Then you're useless."

There was a plopping sound, like a knife slicing wet skin. The girl gagged, and Deidre heard the thump of a body hitting the grass. She peered around the tree again. Niccoli stood over the young woman's corpse and sighed with relief and pleasure. The barb in his hand retracted as he conquered the girl's already weakened soul. He looked up and caught Deidre's eye. She swallowed hard, caught in her eavesdropping.

"You're early, my friend. Come," he said with a frown.

The weight of her master's command pulled on the space between her ribs. Her body obeyed while her mind fumed. She stood and crossed to him, stepping over the already dissolving corpse of the Ayavelian girl as the wind rustled deeper in the trees. Branches and leaves clapped against each other in the breeze.

"Find this Magari girl and bring her to me, whole," he said.

"Why?"

He glowered down at her. She shifted her gaze away in reflex. A master was not to be questioned.

"I will," she said, clenching her fist.

"And you're forbidden to speak of Aislynn to anyone, living or dead."

"With all respect"—she paused, trying to word her thoughts carefully—"She's a yakona. There's little to love there."

"If you believe that, then you have never known love, my friend."

"I did once," she snapped before she could stop herself.

Her chest panged with regret as his eyes narrowed. His muscles tensed. This would hurt.

He grabbed her arm and pulled her closer, ripping away the fabric covering her wrist to show a blue scar shaped like an eight-pointed star. She twisted in his grip and pulled away, but he would not release her.

"I know you blame me for your lover's death all those centuries ago," he said. "But I must remind you of your last attempt at revenge. That didn't bode well for you, and it was your only warning. Don't try to kill me again."

He dropped her arm, and the weight of his power over her forced her eyes to the ground. She heard him leave as her torn sleeve twisted in the wind and listened for his breath to disappear into the woods.

Deidre had known love; she'd worshipped it. It had been the demon darkness that stole it from her, and she would have her revenge. She couldn't destroy the darkness itself, but she already had a plan to destroy the master that forced her into it.

She would not *try*. She would succeed.

A NOTE TO READERS

I hope you enjoyed *Lichgates.* If you have a moment, please leave a review on Amazon, Goodreads, Barnes & Noble, your blog, or any combination thereof. If not, that's cool. You're still amazing.

I love hearing back from my readers. If you want to reach out and say hi, feel free to tweet me (@thesmboyce) or send me an email by heading over to my contact page (smboyce.com/contact-boyce).

Like free stuff? Me, too. Well, I like giving it away. For chances to win prizes four times a year, join my Street Team (check out the footer on smboyce.com for the link). It's really a lot of fun, so head over when you can.

You can also get signed eBooks and sign up to get ARCs of my future novels. To learn more, check out the "Awesome Extras" section of the footer on smboyce.com.

If you want more Grimoire goodies, take a look at The Grimoire Online (GrimoireSaga.com). It's your lichgate into Ourea and has a host of bonus material—including free chapters and free access to an online encyclopedia of the world.

The biggest Grimoire geeks can also check out my store (store.smboyce.com), which has tons of fun extras that bring the magic of the Grimoire Saga to life. You can even find real-life Grimoire pendants and blank journals that let you write a Grimoire of your own.

Thanks again, and stay awesome.

—S. M. Boyce

ABOUT THE AUTHOR

S. M. Boyce is a lifelong writer with a knack for finding adventure and magic.

If you would like to receive an email alert when Boyce's next book is released, sign up at:

www.smboyce.com/newsletter/

Your email address will never be shared, and you can unsubscribe at any time.

Word-of-mouth is crucial for any author to succeed. If you enjoyed this novel, please consider leaving a review at Amazon, even if it's only a line or two. Your review will make all the difference and is hugely appreciated.

To learn more about Boyce, visit her website.
smboyce.com
